CLOSER TO THE HEART

THE HERALD SPY
BOOK TWO

MERCEDES LACKEY

DAW BOOKS, INC.
DONALD A. WOLLHEIM, FOUNDER
375 Hudson Street, New York, NY 10014
ELIZABETH R. WOLLHEIM
SHEILA E. GILBERT
PUBLISHERS
www.dawbooks.com

First Printing, October 2015

1 2 3 4 5 6 7 8 9

DAW TRADEMARK REGISTERED
U.S. PAT. AND TM. OFF. AND FOREIGN COUNTRIES
—MARCA REGISTRADA
HECHO EN U.S.A.

PRINTED IN THE U.S.A.

To the memory of Sir Christopher Lee

Technically, this was spring, but it certainly didn't feel like it. There was a definite bite to the air, and although there was no snow on the ground, the clouds looked as if they were contemplating dropping flakes any moment now. There was no scent of growing things in the air at all, only a vague dampness.

Herald Mags trudged along the street with his arms wrapped around his chest under his tattered cloak—tattered, because he was in disguise, coming to visit his little tribe of spies-in-training, in one of the poorer neighborhoods of Haven. The street was surprisingly smooth, but people did a lot of walking in this part of Haven, and this was also one of the older neighborhoods. There had been a couple hundred years' worth of patient, ill-shod feet wearing down the cobbles.

It was not, by any means, a *bad* neighborhood. For the most part, folks here were working poor, with honest jobs; the neighborhood itself might have fallen on hard times over the decades, but it hadn't turned into an absolute den of filth and thieves.

That was why the house full of orphans and cast-offs fit right in and caused no curiosity. The only real difference between "Aunty" Minda's houseful of discarded children and every other congregation of cast-offs around here was that Aunty Minda had the financial backing of the Heralds, so that they were guaranteed not to starve, go half-naked, or freeze.

Well, that, and the fact that they were right next to the "Weasel's" pawn-shop, and at the first sight or sound of trouble, one to three very large and heavily armed men would come rushing over from the shop to beat the living daylights out of anyone stupid enough to try and cause the little household grief.

The few people on the street were in just as much of a hurry as he was to get where they were going and into the shelter of four walls. Like him, they strode briskly, heads down, worn and faded clothing bundled tightly around themselves. Unlike him, they'd be fortunate when they got to their destinations to find any sort of a fire going. In this part of town, people generally couldn't afford a lot of fuel; they lit their fires only when they returned from work, and banked them as soon as they were ready to get under the covers in bed.

The street was relatively narrow, and the houses and shops were crowded closely together and on the dilapidated side. Most of them hadn't been repainted in decades, and although they were in repair, you couldn't exactly call it *good* repair; priority here was on keeping the building standing and the roof sound. After that, the landlords often left it up to the tenants to patch holes and repair shutters. The two- and three-story buildings crowded close together, sometimes leaning a little toward each other like whispering gossips. About half of them had a shop of some sort on the first floor, though many people, especially women, worked out of their homes—doing things like sewing, mending, and laundry. The wind that whipped down the street at him carried some of the scents of that business: cookshop aromas (redolent with the two staples of the poor, cabbage and onions), wet laundry, and beer. It was too late in the day for bread-baking, at least around here. The couple of bakers on this street baked their wares in the very early morning, so it would be ready to buy as people came out of their houses. The common breakfast around here was a hot roll, with a smear of fat, or jam, or for the most prosperous, butter or butter *and* jam. By this time of the day, the bakeshops were closed, except to serve people who had left their dinners to be cooked for a fee as the ovens slowly cooled. If your hearth was tiny, or you didn't *have* a hearth, or you lived alone but couldn't afford to eat out of a cookshop every day, that is what you did for dinner. You made up a pot of something and brought it to the baker as you left for work, and picked up your cooked dinner when you returned home. This was *not* the poorest part of Haven, poor though it was—those streets had the dubious distinction of being around the tanneries; where extremely cheap rents made up for the stinks associated with tanning leather. It was poor enough that quite often entire families crowded into a single room, or two and even three families shared a flat meant for one. The landlords didn't care how many people you squeezed in, as long as the rent got paid regularly.

Almost no one here owned the flats where they lived, unless they were the shop-owners, living above their shops. Shops in this street tended to stay open for as long as the owner could manage, or find someone to man the counter for him, since people here worked long and irregular hours. It wasn't uncommon to find a young child at the counter of many of these places, the offspring of the owner, learning the work of the business he or she would be inheriting by doing it.

It was only after dark—and in the summertime, *well* after dark—that these streets became dubious, even dangerous.

Once the folks who worked for a living shut themselves behind their doors, the ones that lived in the shadows came out. After dark, when you heard shouts or noises, it didn't pay to be curious, unless you recognized the voice as that of one of the neighbors.

He was glad to reach the converted shop where his little horde of helpers lived, and even gladder to get the door open and pull it tightly shut behind him as a wave of welcome warmth struck him.

He turned and took in the room. He'd had the building gutted when he bought it; since then, he and Minda had taken on so many littles that he'd had a sleeping loft built around all four walls and a staircase to reach it. There were a couple of lamps up there, but nothing else but bedrolls and chests for clothing and trinkets. On the ground floor there were more bedrolls and chests, neatly stowed against the walls. There was only one real bed here, and that was the one reserved for "Aunty" Minda, who tended the children. There was a fireplace at the back of the room, nicely kitted out for cooking, and on either side of it, a row of buckets and basins for washing-up.

Two big kettles hung on hooks over the fire, both of them full of soup. Loaves of bread were waiting, stacked on a table beside the fire. Minda had the fires going briskly and the kettles pulled away from them so the soup didn't burn, as well she should, given the weather. She was virtually alone here at this hour, since her charges were all either at lessons or at work. Most of them were at work; most of them were messengers and delivery runners, installed at various taverns and inns around the city.

Minda was seated on a stool at the side of the hearth, stirring one of the kettles of soup. She rose to greet him; he was pleased to note that regular meals, reliable heat in the winter, rest, and the (relatively) easy work of mothering a brood of youngsters had vastly improved her health. She walked easily now, only slightly favoring knees that had been swollen from years of scrubbing floors. She looked like every other respectable lady around here; maybe cleaner than most, since she was fanatical about cleanliness now that she had the means to enforce it. Her woolen gown and heavy linen undergown were much mended, patched and faded, but not in tatters. Her kindly face was older than her years, but that was the case with just about everyone down here. "All the littles are out, Master Harkon," Minda told him—calling him by the name he used down here, Harkon, nephew of "Willy the Weasel," who owned the pawn shop next door. She knew his real name of course, but no one here used it. Minda called all the youngsters "littles," despite the fact that food and proper care had caused a few of them to sprout so fast they were as tall or taller than she was. And it was about three of those few he had come.

"I got it set up, Aunty," he told her. "Berk, Ray, an' yer li'l Sally'r set up t' go inter service up on th' Hill. I'll come get 'em termorrow, an' next week it'll be Starlin', Kip an' Jo."

Minda sighed, and looked both sad and relieved. "Well, th' bigger lads ain't gettin' th' work as runners so much," she admitted, "now thet they's tall as me. An' we're getting a wee mite crowded here. An' Sally'll be more'n a girl soon, an' ain't no place fer a girly wench here, 'mongst all these boys."

Mags nodded. Having a girl who'd begun to bud womanbits in a ramshackle "household" full of boys was just asking for trouble. Younglings *would* go experimenting when urges started, after all. And more likely to go experimenting among friends. "Sally's t'be i' Palace itself. Gonna put her in trainin' as lady's maid, all the airs and suchlike. She'll be mighty handy t'me in a year or so, an put up in a room full'f other liddle gels in the meantime, so safe as houses. She'll be gittin' a day off ev' fortnight t'run down here an' see ye."

Now Minda sighed with more than relief; she beamed to hear her "daughter" was going to be placed so well—though

Mags never had learned if Sally was really Minda's offspring, or someone the woman had just swept up the way a motherly cat will sweep up any kittens left orphaned. Minda would never have been able to *dream* of the girl going into service in the Palace before Mags had come along. The most she would have hoped for would have been that Sally could find a place in the kitchen of a tavern, or as a serving girl in an inn. And that would have been if she'd been lucky.

"Th' lads 're all gonna be placed as hall-boys 'round the highborn houses. I'll be keepin' good track of 'em, an' I'll get 'em out if they're treated bad. They'll be damn useful, you bet. Hall-boys hear 'bout ever'thin'." Mags was particularly pleased about that. The job of the hall-boy was quite literally to stay in a little cubicle shrouded by a curtain just off the front hall and answer the door so that visitors were never kept waiting more than a few moments. For the extremely wealthy families where he was getting his boys placed, it was a matter of pride to have a hall-boy that did *nothing but that*, day or night. He answered the door, got names and rank, and ran to get the steward so the visitors could be properly attended to. The hall-boy would know the names, rank, and business of every single person that came visiting, and would certainly be able to pick up pretty much everything in the way of gossip that he cared to.

"Well, nobody could'a ast better nor that," Minda agreed, bobbing her head. "And t'ain't gonna be no harder work than runnin' messages all day." She took his elbow and drew him over to a second stool on the hearth. "Now. Let's hev us a bit uv gossip."

———

Minda didn't have a lot of information for him, but Mags hadn't expected too much. Spring was the quiet season, at least until the Spring Fair. The highborn who only came to Court in the Winter were already on their way back to their estates, taking advantage of snow-free roads that were not yet axle-deep in mud due to spring rains. Merchants were busy planning their sales or purchases for the moment the weather turned warm. Farmers were hardest at work; it was already well into lambing season, and soon enough cattle and horses would start dropping babies. Anything that hadn't gotten mended over the winter would have to be put in shape to use once the ground softened enough to plow. Common folk were too busy at this season to get up to much mischief, and it was unlikely that his ears all over the city were going to hear anything. So what he got was a rough litany of minor affairs— what prosperous fellow was sending presents and messages to a lady who was not his wife, what major robberies had taken place and who the likely perpetrator was, who had been seen in places he ought not to be.

He waited until the younglings began trickling in, and gave his chosen half-dozen the good news as they stood in line to wash hands and faces. And they took it as such.

"Oh!" Sally cried, her cheeks turning pink with pleasure. "I *am* going to be trained for a lady's maid, then! I am *so* glad!"

Mags grinned; Sally was not only a bright little thing, she'd been making concerted efforts at "bettering" her speech and her manners, drilling herself as well as studying with the Sisters of Nenya, ever since he'd suggested he might be able to get her such a placing.

As for the boys, if their speech was a bit rougher than hers, that wouldn't matter at first; all that was asked of a hall-boy was that he be quick to answer the door, self-effacing, and able to pronounce names and say "yes, milord" or "no, milord," properly. They'd learn.

And all five of them had had occasion to see hall-boys at work, when Mags had sent them to various wealthy houses ostensibly delivering flowers or sweets at Midwinter. It was hard and often long work, since a hall-boy rarely had time off except to eat—but it certainly was easier than spending all day running messages or parcels all over town.

He gave the first three their letters of introduction and the directions to the Palace Gate and the Great Houses where they would present themselves, and drilled them in exactly what they were to say when they turned up at the servant's entrance as near to sunrise as they could manage. When he was satisfied they would make a creditable impression, he patted each of them on the shoulder. "Now, Sally, you're gonna be i' the Palace. I'll be findin' a way t' talk to you about once a week, but if you hear somethin' that's important, you find a way t' get to the kitchen of Herald's Collegium and talk t' the cook. 'E'll get me." As she nodded, he turned to the two boys. "You'll have a harder time gettin' away, so if *you* hear anythin' I should know, take this—" he handed each of them a ball of red string "—an' tie a piece t' a tree near the servants' door. I'll figger a reason t' come callin' as Herald Mags, and ye kin tell me what you've got then."

"You 'spect us to hear anything, Master Harkon?" Berk asked curiously.

"Honestly? Not really, no," Mags told them. "At least not 'til yer well settled inter your jobs, and they'll give you leave t' take an hour or two for yourselves now an' again, an' a regular day off. But I druther have a plan in place where you kin let me know we need t' talk, than have you learn somethin' then ruin all thet hard work I went to in order t' git you in place by having t' run off straight to me." He clapped both boys on the shoulders. "So concentrate on settlin' in, keepin' yer minds on yer jobs an' not on pretty chambermaids and handsome footmen, an' not getting sacked!"

All three of the youngsters grinned at him, but promised that they would do just that. For his part, Mags felt perfect confidence in them; they'd already shown they were sharp and clever. They were ready for this . . . and Minda was right. The little refuge was beginning to get a bit crowded. It was time for the first of the lot to move on.

And he already had some ideas in mind for the next batch, after these six were safely in place.

He took his leave of all of them, since it was about time for Minda to gather them for supper, and he didn't want to cut into their last hours with their friends. Wrapping his cloak tightly about himself, he left the converted shop and headed back to the inn where he had left Dallen. With the wind at his back, he wasn't quite so cold, and it gave him an excuse to walk briskly rather than sauntering as Harkon would have done in better weather.

Anyone with any sense was inside. This was no weather to linger on the street. Even if you didn't have much fuel and your walls whistled like a flock of birds with leaks, you were still better being inside than out. *:Think they'll do all right?:* he asked his Companion, as he let the wind push him back up the way he had come.

:Barring accident, they'll do splendidly,: Dallen replied. *:And all three of them are quick; even if there is some sort of mishap, they're clever enough to think their way out of it again.:*

———

Council meetings, Amily had decided, must have been specifically designed to occupy as much time as possible for people who had a great deal of free time to spend. The participants seemed to delight in arguing over minutiae. Maybe things would change once better weather started, but right now the members of the King's Greater Council seemed disinclined to leave their comfortable chairs and the warm Council chamber.

On the other hand, the fact that they *could* spend entire candlemarks arguing over tiny things like whether the wool from *chirras* should be taxed at the same rate as wool from sheep or from lambs meant that things were . . . safe. Or relatively so. *So. Small blessings.* There was no war, not even rumors of war. Banditry was at a level where the local Guard garrisons could handle it.

After the near-riots at Midwinter, caused by the feud between the noble Houses of Raeylen and Chendlar, even perpetually disputing highborn families were keeping their quarrels confined to vicious gossip and cutting remarks. Street-brawls and threats of exile by the King had made their due impression on other feuding families, but what had *really* sent shock rippling through the Court was that the son of Lord Kaltar of House Raeylen had very nearly carried out a plot to murder all but one of the members of *both* Houses, marry the Chendlar girl, and inherit the lot. With all that to occupy them, most people were still chewing over the gossip-fodder.

And there were no more mysterious assassins sent by Karse scattered about the city. *Large blessings.*

"Perhaps," she said gently, although she got their immediate attention when she spoke, "We should be looking at how rare this wool is, compared with mature sheep's wool or lambswool, and tax it accordingly."

She looked around at the circular table—circular, so that every member of the Greater Council could easily look into the faces of every other member, and no one could claim he or she had anything but an equal seat. All the faces that met hers wore relatively contented expressions, cementing her notion that the Councilors were mostly "arguing" for the sake of argument, and being in not-unpleasant company while being served the King's best wine and manchet breads flavored with rose water. Not a bad way to spend a bitter afternoon.

"But what if the market becomes depressed by an excessive tax?" someone demanded, and they were off and running again, but this time at least the argument was getting somewhere instead of being an endless circle.

She was more than a bit gratified—who wouldn't be—that now she was taken seriously in the Council meetings. Or seriously enough that when she spoke up, what she said was given due consideration. She'd been afraid that it would take years before she got even a fraction of the respect the Council had given her father.

Maybe the office of King's Own Herald by itself brought along a basic level of respect.

:Or perhaps,: Rolan said gently into her mind, *:They've been paying attention on the rare occasions when you speak up, and have learned that when you do say something, it's worth listening to.:*

:Or both,: she replied, successfully keeping herself from blushing. She wondered if her father had gotten this sort of encouragement from Rolan when *he* first became King's Own.

It had been a long day, and she was just as glad that there was not an official Court dinner tonight. Kyril had made it quite plain that he intended to dine in his quarters with his family, which meant that only about half the members of the Court who were in residence would take dinner in the Great Hall. Those would be the members of the Court who had no residences of their own. The rest would return to their own fine town-houses here on the Hill for dinner, and possibly to entertain or be entertained. There could be music, informal dancing, and gaming. That meant she was free to have dinner with Mags, and they would probably do so with the instructors at the Collegium. The King only had Court dinners about once a week, although the Crown Prince and Princess, Sedric and Lydia, presided at Court dinners roughly three times as often. Lydia had told Amily that they did so in order to take the burden off Kyril, who frankly loathed the long dinners even more than he disliked tedious Council sessions. She couldn't blame him. The Great Hall was huge, people had to talk so loudly in order to be heard that everything was a babble, and even with the best will in the world, not every dish arrived at the tables better than lukewarm. It had occurred to her, more than once lately, that Kyril was looking . . . older. Not *old,* but older. The office was wearing on him.

While Father is actually looking younger. No longer having to juggle the dual duties of King's Spy and King's Own, now that he had completely recovered from what could only be described as "returning from the dead," Amily's father Herald Nikolas seemed to her to be reveling in the chance to get away from the Court and *do* things.

I certainly can't blame him.

On the other hand, these Council sessions were a unique opportunity for her to learn a great deal about the individual members of the Council. As long as she remained quiet, they tended to treat her as part of the furniture. It wasn't that they *ignored* her, it was more that they were used to her father, who had a very powerful Gift of Mindspeech, and could tender his advice to Kyril silently. They probably assumed she was doing the same, and it suited both her and the King to allow them to continue with that impression. Thus far she hadn't uttered so much as a single word during Council sessions that would make any of the members think she was challenging them, or even observing them with any attitude other than respect for their age and experience.

Which, of course, she *was* . . . but she was also weighing everything they said against what she knew were their own personal agendas and interests. Cynical perhaps, but Amily was a realist, and she had been observing these selfsame personages for years at the behest of her father, back when she was nothing more than quiet, unremarkable Amily, Herald Nikolas's crippled daughter, of no consequence whatsoever.

Yes, they were all experienced. But they were also seasoned politicians and courtiers, and all of them had left defeated rivals in their wake. Now, they wouldn't be on the Council if the King and the Heralds didn't think they would keep the welfare of the Kingdom foremost in their minds. But there was no doubt that the continued accumulation of wealth and power lurked in the background whenever they came to a decision. As long as there was no conflict between these two motivations, Amily held her tongue. But she was always on the watch for a moment when the latter edged out the former.

Today had been one of those days. They all had commercial interests, whether it be mercantile or agricultural, or a combination of both, and edging the taxes one way or another could shift the balance of wealth and power around this table and around the Kingdom. It had been like watching people playing a card game for very high stakes.

The Crown Prince and Princess had sat in on this meeting as well, although they had not contributed anything to the discussion. She could tell from their expressions, however, that neither of them missed a thing—and it was very likely that tonight, at dinner in the Royal Suite, this entire meeting would be hashed out again between the soup and the dessert.

She was just as glad not to be a part of that. Going through it once was enough. Prince Sedric seemed to take a great deal of pleasure in this game of politics, though, and for that she was grateful. When—as she fully expected—the King stepped aside to allow his son to become the reigning Monarch, she was not going to have to educate him in a thing.

Nor Lydia, either. Like Amily, Lydia had been playing the quiet, unassuming observer at the behest of her elders—in this case, her Uncle—for many years. If Sedric knew the highborn players in this game intimately, then it was Lydia who knew the merchant "princes." Together they were going to make a formidable team.

And thank the gods for the greater favors. That barring a tragedy, we're going to get a pair like Lydia and Sedric as our monarchs when the time comes, and not a child.

That was the current situation in Menmellith, a Kingdom near Valdemar's southern border. The situation had been *so* precarious, in fact, that Menmellith had not sent an ambassador to Sedric and Lydia's wedding.

This, among other reasons, was why Kyril was pressing Amily and Mags to have *their* wedding soon. He wanted to make a state occasion of it, so that those foreign lands who had not sent a representative to the Crown Prince's wedding would have a second chance with a lot less international political pressure attached to the ceremony.

Politics. We can't even escape them when it comes to our personal lives. She sighed internally. *Evidently, once one is King's Own, one doesn't actually have a personal life. No wonder father seems younger. I think I'm taking on all the years he shed.*

———————

Mags and Amily both ended up at the Collegium dining hall late—so late that they missed all their friends and the instructors, and there weren't more than a handful of Trainees still there. He glanced over at her, thinking how serene and simply pretty she looked in her Formal Whites, and how deceptively unthreatening. She could have been any highborn girl; brown hair neatly braided and pinned around her head, big, soft brown eyes, delicate face—

—and he had seen her kill men, taking carefully placed, precise arrow shots. Not that he hadn't killed his share, and more, but he didn't *look* harmless, the way she did. He wondered if any of the Councilors ever thought of that, when they faced her across the table.

"Well, at least there ain't a crowd," he said, watching the few Trainees desperately trying to combine eating and studying, and the Trainees on kitchen duty bustling about cleaning up. "We can always beg at the kitchen hatch for some crumbs."

But they hadn't even picked a spot to sit before the Cook sent someone out with loaded trays for both of them.

Mags grinned and thanked the Trainee who handed them their dinners. "Bless you and Cook, and tell him I said so," Amily added, and they took their food and found an out-of-the-way spot to enjoy their dinner in peace. One near the fireplace, and away from the windows. The ruddy light of sunset was *not* improving the bleak lawns and gardens outside.

"This weren't—wasn't—ever Collegium dinner," Mags remarked, looking at the succulent roast pork, baked apples, and fancy-cut mixed vegetables. Not to mention the little pastries shaped like swans and filled with whipped cream with dollops of jam on top. The food looked and smelled heavenly.

"No, tonight was supposed to be stew," Amily told him. *"This* is what went on the plates over at the Great Hall." Then she considered the plates. *"Part* of what went on plates at the Great Hall," she amended, and shook her head. "I should be used to it by now, but I still find it difficult to contemplate dinners that consist of a dozen courses or more. Our people make sure that nothing goes to waste, but the sort of excess that the highborn expect to see as a meal still bothers me."

"I spent most've my life half-starved," Mags reminded her. "I try not t'think on it too much or it'll make me mad. What goes back t'the kitchen after one Court meal'd feed all the mine-kids fer a month." He shook his head, and dug in. "I expect the Cook sent over for a couple of plates and kept them warm for us."

"Sometimes I suspect Cook of having a Foresight Gift." The two of them ate silently for a bit; it had been a long day for both of them, Mags suspected, although his had at least been spent in doing constructive things rather than sitting around a table and listening to Councilors argue.

Speaking of which. . . .

"I had me an idea," he said, contemplating his pastry swan. It really did look too pretty to eat.

"Oh?" Amily clearly had no such reservations about *her* swan. She lifted it carefully to her lips and bit the head off. *She looks so sweet, like a little brown coney, all big eyes and soft hair. And then she bites the heads off things . . .*

Which, of course, made them perfect for each other. Just like his cousin Bey and his little assassin-trained wife.

:Dallen . . . sometimes I think I might be more like Bey than I'd like to think.:

:And this is bad, how?: Dallen replied archly.

:Point.:

"Well . . . you know how they're tryin' t'make a big thing over the weddin'. An' you know how *our* lives go. An' the chance fer a whole lotta things t'go wrong on the way is pretty high . . ." He raised an eyebrow at her; she sighed and nodded, and nibbled pastry.

"So, it occurs t'me . . . why not just run off some afternoon, an get married? You, me an' yer pa so's he don't feel left out. We just won't tell anyone else. That way, if ev'thing *does* go sideways, we'll be married already anyway." He looked at her expectantly. "Whatcha think?"

She stared at him for a moment. "I think it's very clever!" she replied, much to his relief. "And I am all in favor of this plan!" She finished her swan thoughtfully. "The best thing is if we just wait until we both have several candlemarks free at the same time, rather than planning, because you *know* if we try to plan this, something will go wrong."

"That's a fact," Mags agreed. "I'm mighty glad you think this's a good idea."

She smiled, which quite transformed her face from "quiet"

to "lovely." "I don't think it's a good idea. I think it is a great idea. Maybe I will stop having nightmares about things going wrong." Then she made a little face. "Mind you, thinking of second-chance plans is much more entertaining than most Council meetings."

He laughed. "Well, don't let *them* know that. Oh, I got my young'uns coming up in the mornin'."

She gave him a little sideways smile. "So, you insinuate your little spies in amongst the unwary then?"

"Better'n tryin' to be twenty places at once, like your Pa did," he observed. "Now, I know why he done things that way, but the way I figure it, when I start out with the young'uns, I know they're gonna be loyal to me once they've growed up. So I don' need to go huntin' about for servants I can trust."

She nodded. "And he never could devote more than half of his time to either job."

"Too right."

The Trainee who'd served them took away their empty plates while they sat together and discussed the business of the day—or at least as much of it as either of them was willing to talk about in such a public place. Finally it dawned on both of them that they could do this *much* more comfortably and privately back in the quarters Amily occupied that had once been Bear's.

The walk to Healers' Collegium was more than a bit chilly, and the warmth of the hothouse that Amily was responsible for came as a relief. And it just seemed silly not to take the conversation to the most comfortable spot in the suite of rooms and then one thing led to another, and there wasn't much talking getting done for a goodly while.

"So . . . anythin' I really need t'know 'bout?" Mags asked into the soft dark.

Amily settled her head on his shoulder, and he pulled the blankets up closer around both of them. There was a very little light from the glowing coals of their fire, their featherbed felt very good after a day of walking all over Haven, having Amily cuddled in his arms was all he could have wished for and he would have been quite happy to never move again. Which, of course, was impossible, but it was a very nice thought.

"Kyril wants the wedding to be just after the Spring Fair." She sighed. He understood. She hadn't wanted their wedding to be turned into a spectacle in the first place, and having it right after the Spring Fair made him suspect the King planned to make use of some of the entertainers that would arrive for it. Then he sensed her smile. "But it won't be *our* wedding, will it? Just a kind of pageant where we are the chief actors. Meaningless, really."

He chuckled. "Ayup. An' we'll get all dressed up an' say our lines, an' if th' thing falls apart 'cause my cousin decides t'pay a visit, it won't matter a bit."

She laughed. "That's the spirit!" Then she stiffened. "You don't think Bey is—"

"No. Besides I ain't invitin' him." He mulled the situation over. "So, walk me through th' reasons."

"Kyril wants to make this another reason for gathering in important people in the Kingdom and ambassadors. Of course, Sedric's wedding was an occasion for that, but they were all rather preoccupied with it, and not with politics and negotiation and maneuvering. Plus, I wasn't King's Own then. That's the next reason, Kyril wants outsiders to think of me as innocuous. With attention fixed on me as a *bride,* people are more likely to dismiss me as not as sharp as my father. They'll underestimate me. The only people who need to understand just how sharp I am are the ones on the Council, but for anyone else, it could be very advantageous for me to be overlooked."

The fire popped a little, as Mags mulled all that over. He nodded thoughtfully. "That's all good reasons. Gotta agree with 'em. Even if I don' much like bein' trotted out an' put on show."

"Kyril had reasons for that, too. This is a good time for *you* to continue to create the impression you're good-hearted, solid, dependable, and a bit thick," she pointed out, and he had to laugh, because that was *exactly* what Nikolas had told him to do, back when he began learning the same craft that had made Nikolas the King's Spy.

"So I'm a bit thick, an' you're just a pretty thing at the King's side. Well, don' we make a likely pair!" He laughed harder as she gave a most unladylike snort.

"The more I think about running off and making the vows before a priest, the better I like the idea," she said after a while, just as he was drifting off to sleep. "The sooner, the better."

"Aight," he agreed, and drifted away.

In the morning, Amily was already gone when Mags finally crawled up out of sleep. His dreams had been full of wedding nonsense—not nightmares, and not of things going wrong, but of nonsensical stuff. Like the King insisting that he and Amily get married on a platform built in a tree, or of Amily's dress somehow being made entirely of bees. He couldn't quite make out what had triggered *that* image.

Or Bey and roughly a hundred assassins turning up at the last minute to outline them in thrown knives as they kissed.

As he dressed, then made his way to the Collegium and ate, it occurred to him that he was not entirely happy with the King's plan. The Spring Fair was not all that far away, and if the King intended to make some sort of enormous political and diplomatic event out of it, there wasn't a great deal of time to get everything ready. . . .

He spooned up oatmeal loaded with chopped nuts and drizzled with honey, and considered all his options. Now, granted,

Spring wasn't a bad choice for this thing. After all, no one ever went to war in the Spring, or almost never. Spring warfare meant pulling your people away from their fields and flocks at the worst possible time. It meant that the area where you were fighting would be utterly ruined; fields trampled before seeds even had a chance to sprout, calving, foaling and lambing disrupted—and you'd have the devil's own time trying to move herds with pregnant females and young animals out of harm's way quickly. You went to war in the Spring and you insured that part of the country would starve, so unless that was actually your goal . . . it was a monumentally stupid idea, one that gained you nothing. If you lost, the local populace would descend on your country in an orgy of desperate looting in order to make up for *their* lands being ruined. If you won, you'd have to support a starving population.

And that didn't even touch on trying to march and move and fight in mud, because the combination of Spring rains and newly plowed fields meant you *would* be up to your knees in mud. And so would your supply trains.

But Prince Sedric's wedding had taken nearly a *year* to prepare, and even if this wasn't going to be as elaborate, how would they ever have the time to get it all ready?

:You won't,: Dallen admonished him. *:The King wants this; the King will do the arranging, or rather, delegate people to make the arrangements for him. Remember what you and Amily agreed on last night; neither of you are under any obligation to concoct a "perfect wedding" for each other. It's a show; just do your parts and let other people worry about doing theirs.:*

:And if it all falls apart?: Mags could not help asking, although with a wry cast to his thoughts.

:Then as players ever and always do, we all blame the director. Who will probably be Lady Dia.:

Mags thought of that, as he got a plate of bacon and eggs

and bolted it down. *:I'd rather not. Lady Dia can be very . . . fierce.:*

He had an appointment to meet Nikolas down at the shop, in their guises of Harkon and Willy the Weasel. The Weasel rarely put his head in at the shop anymore; it was understood that he was leaving the bulk of the work to his nephew and his nephew's hired toughs, but it would have been altogether out of character for him to stay away entirely. Although the shop did the bulk of its business after dark, it was the Weasel's way to open it for a few hours in the morning, so that men who'd pawned their tools and had the money to redeem them could do so before hurrying off to a job.

This meant subterfuge, of course. Mags went down into Haven as a Herald, and left Dallen at the stables at a Guard post. Then he left the post by means of a tunnel under the street, and emerged in a back room at a tavern, where he became Harkon. Harkon staggered out, giving a convincing imitation of a man who had been drinking all night and needed to sober himself up before facing his uncle—stopping at a cookshop for a mug of tea so strong the spoon should have melted, at another for a second, not quite as strong, and at an apothecary for a dose of his "Sovereign Remedy." By the time he got to the pawn shop, he was apparently sober enough to evade the Weasel's wrath.

The shop was already open, and as Mags entered, a fellow in a carpenter's apron was just finishing redeeming his tools. The man hurried out with a nod to the "nephew," as Nikolas—aka "Willy the Weasel"—grunted and unlocked the door into the protected part of the shop.

Even if you had known that "Willy the Weasel" was the same person as Herald Nikolas, it would have taken a trained eye to see the Herald in the pawnshop owner. The Weasel's greasy, graying hair straggled down his back in a most untidy manner, he had an unattractive squint, and his mouth was always primmed up tightly, as if he was afraid to give away so much as a word. If anything, the Weasel was *very* memorable, as opposed to Herald Nikolas, who was so very ordinary that if it had not been for his Heraldic Whites, he would have faded into the background of any crowd.

The shop was really two rooms; the front part held the bulkier, heavier, or more inexpensive items on shelves all around it; the back part, behind a wall so sturdy it could have been a jail cell, had a locked door and a barred window, through which the pawnbrokers conducted their business. That part of the shop held all the valuable stuff, and, of course, the cashbox.

"See, Stef turned up like 'e promised, nuncle," Mags said, locking the door behind him and taking Nikolas's place on the stool so that the "Weasel" could drop into a far more comfortable chair that stood behind it. *:Have you been told about the circus we're to put on?:*

"Le's 'ope 'is work's more reliable this time," Nikolas growled. " 'E's got 'alf 'is 'ousehold on our shelves. I'd be best pleased t'clear 'is trash out." *:I had breakfast with Kyril, so yes.:* Nikolas shook his head imperceptibly. *:I can't make up my mind if it's the idea of a genius or a disaster in the making.:*

"Could use th' space," Mags agreed, carefully counting out the money in the drawer under the counter. This was routine. Every time someone new took over the window, he was supposed to count the money. *:Amily and I decided last night that we aren't taking any chances. We're going to pop off quietly to a priest when we both have a free morning or an afternoon and just do the thing. We know half a dozen holy folk who'd tie the knot for us without a second thought, and neither of us care much who is the deity in charge. That way, when the disaster looms, at least we'll already be shackled and it won't matter to us if the thing falls apart, or gets stormed out of* *existence, or gets raided by bandits . . . or any of a thousand other things goes wrong.:*

Nikolas blinked at him blankly for a moment, then covered it by half-lidding his eyes and tucking his chin down as if he was about to take a nap. *:I take back everything I ever said about you being an idiot,:* he replied, with a mental chuckle. *:Am I invited?:*

:How could I dare say no? I'm not anxious to be knifed in the dark by my father-in-law.:

A very faint chuckle emerged from the "drowsing" Nikolas. It sounded enough like a hint of a snore to pass for one. *:Definitely not an idiot. I approve. And I take it we keep this a little secret amongst the six of us?:* Nikolas had included the three Companions, of course. It wouldn't exactly be possible to keep something like this a secret from *them.*

:It wouldn't do to disappoint Lady Dia and Princess Lydia,: Mags agreed. *:Better to let them bask in the illusion that they're creating a perfect wedding for us. They'll probably wallow in it, actually.:*

Nikolas chuckled again. *:Considering that Amily's mother and I essentially did the same thing as you plan to—running off to a priest to avoid the hash that our two mothers were making, arguing over every detail, you are upholding a fine tradition.:*

:Good to know. And speaking of "knowing," what is it I need to hear?:

Mags spent the rest of his candlemarks, right up until mid-morning (when the Weasel declared that keeping the shop open until "the lads" turned up to take it over after dark was a waste of time), trading information with his mentor. None of it was terribly important, but any part of it could *become* important. One thing Mags had learned above all else; when it came to being the King's Spy, the most unexpected things could turn out to be relevant.

As he and Nikolas locked up the shop, he saw Nikolas's head cock in that odd way that let him know that Evory was speaking to him. And at nearly that same moment, Dallen chuckled.

:Be careful what you ask for,: Dallen said. :You might get it. The King cut short the Lesser Court in order to see to some detail of the Treasury. Amily is free. You are free. Nikolas is free. And Brother Elban just down the street is tending his garden and is essentially free and of all the people you know who would do this thing, Brother Elban is your favorite. So. Would you like to get married?:

It was with a feeling of profound relief that Mags kissed his bride under the combined (beaming) gazes of his new father-in-law, Brother Elban, Healer and tender of the little Shrine of Alia of the Birds, and three Companions.

He actually could not have planned this better. Everything had conspired to be perfect.

Elban was a lone cleric at his little Shrine; he didn't need much, just a room to live in and his garden. Alia of the Birds was a very minor Goddess, as such things went, with a tiny congregation and no real rituals of Her own. Her clerics were solitary, but not hermits; they dedicated their lives to healing and teaching the poorest of the poor. Several of Mags' youngsters took lessons with him. The Shrine occupied the same footprint as any of the houses or shops in this area; it consisted of a walled garden mostly planted with healing herbs, with Elban's little living quarters at the back. The walls of the garden and the dwelling were pleasantly weathered stone, a soft, pinkish granite. The statue of Alia, a motherly looking lady of middle age, with a round, smiling face and carved and real birds perched all over her, was made of a similar stone.

Within the shelter of the Shrine's walls, true spring had come early to Brother Elban's garden, lilies bloomed at the foot of Alia's statue, and the birds perched in the vines on the wall provided all the music they needed. He and Nikolas had detoured just enough to resume their identities as Heralds before meeting Amily here.

And the deed was done. They'd managed to get married without *anything* going wrong or interfering. Mags had never heard the wedding ceremony as performed by Alia's clergy before, but it had been lovely.

*Now you will feel no rain, for each of you will be
   shelter for the other.
Now you will feel no cold, for each of you will be
   warmth to the other.
Now there will be no loneliness, for each of you will be
   companion to the other.
Now you are two persons, but there is only one life
   before you.*

*Treat yourselves and each other with respect, and re-
mind yourselves often of what brought you together.
Give the highest priority to the tenderness, gentleness
and kindness that your connection deserves. When
frustration, difficulties and fear assail your relation-
ship, as they threaten all relationships at one time or
another, remember to focus on what is right between
you, not only the part which seems wrong. In this
way, you can ride out the storms when clouds hide the
face of the sun in your lives—remembering that even if
you lose sight of it for a moment, the sun is still there.
And if each of you takes responsibility for the quality
of your life together, it will be marked by abundance
and delight.*

"Now, remember," Nikolas reminded the beaming cleric. "Unless it is vital, no one is to know they are already wed."

"Oh no, it would disappoint all those people who are likely planning a spectacle," the thin little fellow replied, bobbing his head with understanding. He had no special robes; Alia's clergy wore nothing more ostentatious than a long, brown tunic and trews, with a leather bird sewn over the heart. "No, we cannot possibly have that. It is not every day that the King's Own gets married. People have expectations and we shouldn't deny them their holiday, now, should we?" Then he beamed at them. "It will be our little secret."

He let them out the garden gate, and Amily immediately swung herself up onto Rolan's back. "I—"

"—have t' get up the Hill, I know," Mags finished for her. "Go. I'll see ye at dinner if not afore. I got law-court this afternoon."

"Don't starve yourself," was all she said, and then she and Rolan were trotting up the street and rounded the corner.

Mags looked to his mentor. Nikolas nodded in the general direction of a cookshop they both favored, and Mags grinned in agreement. He felt positively euphoric, actually, now that everything was settled. A weight had very much fallen from his shoulders, and it looked as if Nikolas felt exactly the same.

The explanation for that came only when they had finished their meal and were about to part company, with Mags going on to the law-court, and Nikolas to whatever mysterious errand would occupy him this afternoon. "Now if something takes me out of Haven, it won't matter," Nikolas sighed.

Mags nodded. "That be true," he replied. "If somethin' had called ye away afore the circus, Amily'd've been . . ." He groped for words.

"Very sad. Absolutely understanding, but very sad." Nikolas's normally inexpressive face took on a melancholy cast for a moment. "I have had to miss too many of the important moments of her life. I am glad I did not have to miss this one."

Nikolas did not say where he was going, and Mags didn't ask. This was *not* because they were ignoring the one cardinal rule of their occupation, which was *always make sure someone knows where you will be.* It was because Dallen had already spoken to Evory, and Dallen knew where Nikolas was headed. So that made two other creatures that knew exactly where Nikolas was going and what he intended to do, and that was enough.

Mags had quite enough on his plate with attending the Law Court; he didn't need to start fretting about whatever possibly dangerous place Nikolas was going to go.

Any Herald who was not already teaching at the Collegium— and truly, what was Mags actually qualified to *teach?*—was assigned to the Law Courts in various parts of the city. Prince Sedric was assigned to the Court Royal, which tried all cases that the lesser Courts passed to the higher, or those cases that were appealed. Not that many cases were appealed, because before one could appeal a case, all parties involved had to agree to re-testifying under Truth Spell in the Lesser Court. And was where Mags and the others came in, because in order to set the Truth Spell, you needed a Herald.

Mostly the Heralds of the Law Courts merely had to be present; a constant reminder that if the parties on either side or the judge demanded it, the Herald in attendance could set Truth Spell on any witness. Not the coercive version—although Mags could do that. Generally the coercive version of the Truth Spell was not needed in these simple trials.

This particular Court was in the same district as Willy the Weasel's pawn shop; the Guard and the City Watch here all knew Mags both in his guise of Harkon and as Herald Mags. That was useful, since they could arrange for trials where Harkon might be called in to identify someone who had pawned something to take place when Herald Mags was off-duty and some other Herald was taking his place.

Like most of the district, the courtroom and the building it was in had seen better days. Meticulously repaired and scrupulously cleaned, nevertheless, everything was old, worn, and a bit shabby. There were six benches for onlookers and witnesses, a table and bench each for the accuser and the accused, and at the front facing the rest, the judge's bench and the witness box. Then there was Mags' seat, at the back of the courtroom, off with the bailiff and a couple of Guards and a couple of members of the Watch who made sure things didn't get out of hand. The walls were whitewashed plaster . . . just a bit dingy. The furnishings were all dark wood that had long ago lost any semblance of polish.

Mostly, to tell the truth, Mags was just there for show, to remind the witnesses that they *could* lie under oath, but if they were challenged, they'd be caught at it, and might be in as much trouble, if not more, than the accused.

The courtroom was empty when he entered it, except for the bailiff, who greeted him like the old friend that he was by now, and offered him a mug of hot cider. Mags accepted it gratefully. The courtroom was cold and damp, and he kept his cloak on, as did the bailiff. There were fireplaces in the building, but none in this room.

"Seems like Spring ain't never gonna come," Bailiff Creed said, blowing on his cider before taking a sip.

"Seems like it's comin' too soon, iff'n ye ast me," Mags replied. "King wants me an' Amily leg-shackled after Spring Fair." He said this with a sigh, though inwardly he was chuckling. There was no time like the present to get the rumor-mill going. The less the general public knew about how things really stood between him and Amily, the better.

"Criminy! No more tom-cattin' 'bout fer *you,* me lad!" said the bailiff (who was, of course, married; the King encouraged marriage among the Watch and those of the Guard who were posted within the city as he felt it encouraged stability). Creed laughed, not unkindly. "Not thet I ever heerd all that much 'bout you kickin' up yer heels."

Because I am very careful that my visits to my eyes and ears at the brothels are done by Harkon or some other rakehell. "Nah, an' truth is, it ain't the bein' married, it's the mort've fuss an' feather of *gettin'* married I ain't lookin' forrard to," Mags replied mournfully. "On'y good thing 'bout it is, I'm orphant, an' Amily's on'y got her Pa, so at least we ain't got two Mamas fightin' over weddin' thins."

"But she'll have a mort've friends makin' hay over this, you mark my words," Creed replied. "You're in for it, m'lad. Just smile an' nod an' say ever'thin' looks bootiful. An' if it's costly, make sure th' King's a-payin' for it." And at that moment, the Court began to fill up, which meant they both had to be on best behavior.

The first several cases were either quite clear-cut (the Watch having caught someone in the act of theft or mayhem)—or boring (quarrels between neighbors that had gotten to the point of being brought before the Court).

Then something came up that made both Mags and Creed sit up and start paying attention.

The first hint that matters were out of the ordinary was that a parade of five people trudged into the courtroom and took seats on the witness bench.

Then an enormous man was brought into the dock in irons that looked like dainty bracelets on his massive wrists. He was incredibly muscular, with muscles like a stonecutter or a blacksmith, taller than both the Watch that were with him, coarse features and a bald pate. And yet, the man's expression and body language were that of a terrified child.

The man's accuser came into the Court, and Mags took an instant dislike to him. Mags could read both his body language and his surface thoughts, and what he read proclaimed this "Cobber Pellen" to be a bully and a liar. He looked as if he was someone who was accustomed to take what he wanted from those who were weaker than he was. Once he had been muscular, but now he was going to fat, with a round head and features that could have been considered handsome, except for the petulance of the mouth and the ugly glitter of his eyes. Both accuser and accused were positioned in front of the judge, and the accuser was the first to speak, according to the rules.

"This *animal* attacked me without no reason yer Honor!" Pellen proclaimed. "It shoulda never been 'llowed on the streets! It shoulda been locked up years agone! It's *dangerous!* It nearly broke my arm!"

All the while Pellen was proclaiming how "dangerous" the huge fellow was, all the man did was cower—which was a strange thing to see from someone who looked as if he earned his living by throwing rowdies out of taverns. But all that Mags could sense was fear . . . fear, and confusion.

"And have you any witnesses?" the judge began, when he was interrupted by a shout from a ragged young woman who pushed her way into the court. Mags didn't get more than an impression of a wild mop of curly brown hair, a whirlwind of ragged skirts and shawls, and clenched fists, before she was already at the front of the courtroom.

"Cobber Pellen's a damn liar!" the woman shouted, and launched herself at him as if she was going to tear him to pieces with her bare hands. And the court erupted into chaos, with the Watch intervening between them, Cobber Pellen shouting one thing, the young woman shouting another, the five on the witness bench making a hasty exit from the room, and the bailiff trying to subdue Cobber as one of the Watch tried to subdue the woman.

Mags considered wading in himself, but decided instead to keep an eye on the accused.

Who was huddling in the corner, looking as if he was going to cry at any moment. There was something very odd going on here. The surface thoughts of the poor fellow were in chaos, and it was as if every single thought had to fight its way through treacle to come to the surface. It took Mags a moment to figure what was going on, and by then the bailiff and the Watch had separated the combatants and put them on opposite sides of the courtroom.

The judge looked on with a neutral expression, but then, he was used to eruptions in the courtroom. This was *not* a neighborhood where people came meekly into the court and calmly dealt with their side of an issue. It was only the first time this week that a brawl had interrupted things here, and there were still four days to go before the week was over.

By that point, Mags had gone from confusion to pity, because it was clear that the accused man was not at all right in the head. Whether he was born that way, or had been injured, he was, frankly, not fit to stand trial. But before he could intervene, the judge had leveled his gaze on Pellen.

"Cobber Pellen," the judge said. "Where are your witnesses to this so-called attack?" The judge raised an eyebrow. "Because frankly, right now the man you say tried to harm you is acting more like the one who's been beaten rather than the one doing the beating."

Pellen looked frantically around the courtroom, but the people he had been counting on to back up his story had fled. *:He probably didn't pay them enough,:* Dallen observed cynically. Mags was inclined to agree. He wasn't sure what Cobber Pellen's scheme was, but he rather doubted that matters were as Pellen had stated.

"I had witnesses!" Pellen blurted.

"Who don't seem to be in my courtroom," the judge pointed out. "But this wouldn't be the first time you've been in my courtroom, now, would it, Cobber Pellen?" The judge leaned over his desk and fixed Pellen with a stare. "This time, how-ever, I've got a way to get to the bottom of things." He raised his voice. "Herald Mags!"

Mags got up and marched to the front of the courtroom, and bowed his head slightly. "Yer Honor?" he said.

"This *gentleman* claims this other fellow attacked him. This young lady claims he's a liar. And the alleged attacker looks to be in no condition to be questioned. Can you clear things up?"

Mags chuckled and cracked his knuckles. "I'd be happy to, yer Honor." He nodded to the bailiff. "Master Creed, would ye care to escort th' gennelmun t'the witness box?"

Cobber Pellen went red, then white. "That ain't how it's s'posed t'go!" he protested.

The judge sat back in his chair, and Mags got the distinct impression that he was very much amused indeed. "In fact, Cobber, once a Herald takes over the proceedings, they go however the Herald wishes them to go. I suggest you get into the witness box. I wouldn't want the bailiff to have to exert himself."

Pellen was quick to take the hint, and got into the witness box, grumbling under his breath. The judge let him stew for a moment, then waved a hand at Mags. "Herald Mags, if you would be so kind as to set the Truth Spell on Cobber Pellen, I would be much obliged."

Mags bowed a little, and did as he had been requested. Setting the Truth Spell in a courtroom, where things were under control and there were plenty of armed helpers around was nowhere near as fraught with hazard as was setting it in an uncontrolled situation. It didn't take him long at all before there was a bright blue glow about Pellen, visible to everyone in the courtroom. Except Pellen. And every time he lied, that glow would vanish.

"All right, Cobber," said the judge. "Let's hear your story."

That was when something Mags had never seen before in his life happened. "It's like this, yer Honor," Pellen said . . . and the glow vanished.

Mags was so startled he quickly double-checked himself— but the spell was still in effect. It was just that *every word coming out of the man's mouth was a lie.* This was astonishing. When faced with the prospect of being under the Truth Spell, most people at least *tried* to weasel their way around the truth. Not Cobber Pellen. Mags could scarcely believe such audacity, and from the look of things, the bailiff, the Watch and the Guards present were all equally flummoxed.

The judge, however, did not turn a hair. In fact, he managed to keep his face completely expressionless. "That will do, Cobber," he said, and the bailiff took that as his cue to escort Pellen back to the benches. The judge turned his attention to the young woman, who had only gotten more furious with every word Cobber spoke. "Now, young lady, who would you be?"

"Linden Pardorry, yer Honor," she got out from between clenched teeth. "An'—"

The judge held up his hand. "It is clear that you have a great deal you want to tell the Court about this story. Herald Mags, are you inclined to let her speak her piece?"

"So long's she does it under Truth Spell, jist like Pellen, yer Honor," said Mags agreeably. The judge nodded and gestured to the young woman to take her place in the witness box.

As she turned to face him and the rest of the courtroom, Mags finally got a good look at her.

The first thing that anyone would notice was her dark brown hair. There was . . . quite a lot of it, unbelievably wild and curly, and down to her waist. It appeared she had tried to confine it with a scarf and a threadbare ribbon or two, but it was not to be tamed. Like most people in this neighborhood, in weather this cold she had on many layers of clothing, which muffled her up somewhat. She had probably put on every stitch she owned. Nevertheless, her figure was anything but bulky under the layers of skirts and shawls. Her face was narrow and her features angular, and right now her green eyes were ablaze with fury. So were her surface thoughts. Mags figured he had better get things in motion immediately; she looked ready to burst with the need to speak, and Mags rushed through the Truth Spell, setting it to glow in a blue aura all around her.

"All right, young woman," the judge said, calmly. "Let's hear what you have to say about this case."

"Tuck may not be right i' th' head, but he been my frien' all m'life, an he niver hurt a soul!" she burst out. "It ain't in 'im! But that Cobber, ever since 'e moved t' Cabbage Row, all 'e done was torment Tuck! All th' live-long day, 'tis one mean trick arter another! An' Tuck niver said nor done a thin' 'bout it, niver raised so much as a finner t'defend hisself!!"

The blue glow remained strong and steady with every word she spoke. The surface thoughts Mags skimmed from her matched her words, under a wash of fiery anger. Mags was actually quite impressed with her self-control; most people who were as angry as Linden was would be sitting on Pellen's chest with a knife to his throat by now.

And Cobber Pellen was beginning to look very uneasy. Clearly matters were *not* going as he had planned, and he had finally figured that out. Evidently he was not terribly bright.

She stuck out an accusing thumb at Pellen. "That Cobber, 'e wanted Tuck's liddle shed what he got from his Ma, an' 'e wanted Tuck gone. 'E's been plaguing the life outa 'im; not jist yellin' an name-callin', but dirty tricks an' *'urtin'* 'im! Bin goin' on since afore Midwinter, it 'as! An' Tuck, 'e just took it. 'Til Cobber come arter me, t'day."

She peeled up her shawls and sleeves, and showed black and blue marks all over her arm. "'E figgered on makin' me whoore fer 'im," she spat. " 'E ambuscaded me an' grabbed me an' I fought 'im an' 'ollered, an' thet's when Tuck come a-runnin'. Tuck mighta put up with bein' bullied, but he ain't *never* let anyone bully 'is friends."

The girl was *ablaze* with anger now, and it was a good thing she had no Gifts, or Cobber Pellen would surely have been dead by now. She'd have killed him with the force of her mind alone. The rest of the people in the courtroom were absolutely riveted by the performance—the story itself was ordinary enough in this part of Haven, but Linden . . . Linden was utterly astonishing.

"An' even *then,* Tuck bare touched 'im! Tuck jist pulls Cobber offa me, 'olds 'im up by th' arm, an' gives 'im a shake till 'is teeth rattle, and throws 'im inter th' wall, then comes t'make sure I be all right. Next thin' I know, Cobber's hollerin' fer the Watch an' actin' like 'e's 'bout beat t'death, the friggin *coward.*" She shook her clenched fist at Cobber, who was looking frantically all about himself for a means of escape.

But there was no escape; he was surrounded by two men of the Watch and one of the Guard, all of them eyeing him with extreme disfavor. It was clear that Linden had won all of them over.

Even the judge.

:Nonsense, it was the Truth Spell,: Dallen pointed out.

And in all that time, Linden's Truth Spell aura had kept blazing a bright blue for everyone in the courtroom to see.

"Bailiff," the judge said, lazily. "The Truth Spell has told the tale. Cobber Pellen did not utter a single word of truth and we are all witnesses to that.

"I'd like you to place Cobber Pellen under arrest. If that suits you, Herald Mags?"

"Suits me jest fine, yer Honor," Mags replied. "I kin think of 'bout a handful of laws he's broke, startin' with makin' false accusations an' lyin' t'the Court an' yer Honor."

Bailiff Creed had happily taken the irons off the big man called "Tuck," and now just as happily was slapping them on Cobber Pellen.

"Oh I can think of a great many more, Herald Mags. For instance, there is nothing illegal about a lady deciding to *peddle her wares,* as it were. And there is nothing illegal about her doing so under the auspices of someone else. But it is *highly* illegal to attempt to force a lady into such a life against her will. And there is the assault charge on her as well—" the judge turned from Mags to Linden. "May I assume you wish to press as many charges against Cobber Pellen as you are entitled to, Linden Pardorry?"

She had shaken her sleeve and her shawls back down over her bruised arm, and looked up at the judge. "Yessir," she said forthrightly. "Thenkee kindly sir. I ain't gonna look down on some'un thet whoores, it's a 'onest livin' fer them as is 'onest 'bout it, but I ain't no whoore m'self. I pick up stuff, belike, an' take it t'Tuck, an' 'e makes likely trinkets an' I sells 'em." As Mags removed the Truth Spell from her, and Cobber was "escorted" out of the courtroom to the gaol, she lost some of her anger. "'E's a dab worker wi' 'is 'ands, milord. 'e ain't stupid. 'e ain't right i' head, but 'e ain't stupid, 'e knows right from wrong, an' 'e's a magician at makin'. Ye'd marvel t'see what 'e kin make outa a liddle bit've nothin'."

Tuck was still shivering in the corner, and Linden made an abortive move to go to him. The judge stopped her with a word. "I should like you to come with me, Linden Pardorry, and we'll find as many things to charge Cobber Pellen with as the two of us can prize up from your memory. And meanwhile—"

"I'll take charge've Tuck, yer Honor," Mags said immediately.

"And so, since there is nothing but driblets of civil suits to hear, I adjourn the court." Bailiff Creed returned at just that moment, and the judge turned to him. "In the interest of making sure no one has to wait until tomorrow for justice, would you kindly get Judge Madows from his chamber and ask him to hear the rest of the cases?"

"Right away, yer Honor," Creed replied, and took his truncheon and knocked it three times on the nearest bench. "All rise fer the honorable Judge Bryon!"

Everyone in the courtroom rose, and the judge offered Linden his arm quite as if she was a highborn lady. She took it with great dignity and the two of them left the courtroom, leaving Creed to fetch the second judge—and Mags to handle the terrified giant.

It actually didn't take Mags very long to calm Tuck down, once the poor fellow understood he was not in any trouble, and that Linden would be back to fetch him as soon as she was able. Mags sent a runner—one of his own boys from Aunty Minda's place—out after some cheap sweets, figuring that someone as childlike as Tuck appeared to be would be both pacified and comforted by the unexpected treat. The ploy worked as well as Mags could have hoped. By the time the judge was through with Linden and she came looking for them in the hallway, Tuck was full of spicebread with nuts, and licking the last crumbs from his fingers. He looked up expectantly at the sound of Linden's footsteps, and beamed at her when he saw her.

"'as 'e been any trouble, Herald, Milord?" Linden asked anxiously.

Mags chuckled. "Ain't bin none at all," he assured her. "But ye got me curiosity a-goin'. I fancy goin' alongside've ye, an' seein' the bits an' bobs Tuck kin make."

To his slight surprise, Linden frowned a little. " 'Tain't jist bits an' bobs, Herald," she corrected. "Ye tell 'im whatcher want, though it may take some long 'splainin' to 'im; once 'e gits it, an' ye give 'im what 'e needs, he kin make it. I tol' ye, 'a bain't stupid. 'is 'ead jest don' work like ourn."

Mags kept his skepticism to himself. It would be more than enough if the addle-witted fellow could make some pretty trinkets with the right supplies; he could see to it that Tuck never ran short of what he needed, and make sure the results went somewhere they would fetch what they were worth. "Then you an' 'im could be some use t'me," was all he said. "I'd admire t'see what Tuck kin do."

Within half a candlemark, he had to completely revise his assumptions.

The "shed" that Tuck owned turned out to be a building that had once been a small stable, built to hold four animals. It served Tuck as living and working quarters, and what he had done inside those four plain walls was astonishing. This was clearly the work of years.

To begin with, every bit of it had been carefully, meticulously, even artistically reinforced. Tiny bits of wood and handmade brackets had been put in place to make the building as solid as any on the Hill. Then, it had been weatherproofed. Mags actually went outside to have a look at one of the walls when he realized just how much work Tuck had gone to, and there was no sign on the outside of the building that this was anything other than what Linden had called it, a "shed."

But on the inside, Tuck had carefully pieced together an entire floor made of mismatched cobblestones and bits of wood. He'd weatherproofed using horsehair and plaster on the interior walls, exactly as was done in the best houses on the hill. From the look of things, he had waited until he had somehow gathered enough materials to fill in a section, done that section, and waited until he had gathered enough for another section. Then he'd whitewashed the lot. The old hayloft had been devoted to a sleeping place; the four stalls were gone, although the posts supporting the loft that had anchored the stall walls were still in place. There was a workbench all along one wall, under windows just under the eaves that Mags marveled at—windows pieced painstakingly together from mere fragments of glass.

The place was heated by a remarkable stove; Mags couldn't make out exactly how it worked, but it was bolted and hammered together from scrap metal, and produced heat all out of proportion to its small size. The windows were fitted with louvered shutters clearly made of scrap wood; they were above head-height so it was unlikely anyone would ever see in here to discover just how well Tuck had fitted the place out.

In fact, those shutters were closed when they arrived, and the first thing Tuck did was open them to let in the light, using a long stick with a metal hook on one end. It was pretty clear he knew the dangers of letting anyone see what he had.

There was a little kitchen next to the stove, with beautifully mended pots and pans on the wall. Everything was so clean Mags would have been willing to eat off any surface, and so neat he reckoned Tuck could put his hand on whatever he wanted in the dark.

On the workbench, it was clear that Tuck had made nearly every single one of his own tools, all from scavenged materials, including a wire-straightener of amazing design, dozens of jigs, a saw-sharpener. . . .

On one part of the bench was a brooch, made of a pebble that was polished until it reflected light, held in a frame of wire, with the wire twisted around to the back—clearly it only needed to be finished into a pin for the brooch to be complete.

And Mags now knew where so many of the trinkets that had come into the pawn shop had come from. Here.

He could scarcely believe his eyes as Tuck proudly showed off his little kingdom.

"Linden," he asked urgently. " 'Ow many folks know Tuck kin do all this?"

"Nobody but me, an' 'is ma what's gone," she replied. "If they know'd . . . people like Cobber, they'd 'aul 'im away and chain 'im to a bench an' make 'im slave fer 'em. It wuz bad 'nough with Cobber wantin' this shed, wi'out Cobber knowin' it were this nice inside. If 'e'd knowed . . ." She shook her head. "Reckon 'e might not've stopped at bullyin'. Reckon 'e might've gone t'murder."

Mags nodded. Cobber might not have stooped to doing the murder himself, but it would have been easy enough to take poor Tuck off to some cheap tavern in the tanning district on the river, then arrange for the fellow to "fall in." Most poor people couldn't swim. When could they take the time to learn? And teaching Tuck, Mags suspected, would have required immense patience and the ability to somehow keep him calm.

"This's flat 'mazin'," he said. "You was right, Linden. Tuck's got real smarts where some thins are concerned."

Linden nodded. "Ain't *nothin'* 'e ain't been able t'make, iffin 'e unnerstands whatcher need. Jist takes time gettin' 'im ter un'erstan'."

"Tuck good?" rumbled the giant anxiously, looking from Mags to Linden and back again. For some reason known only to him, he had made up his mind that Mags was as much to be trusted as Linden. And from what Mags could read, dimly, his lost mother had driven it deep into his soul that *only* she and Linden were to be trusted.

Maybe it was the Heralds' Whites. Maybe Tuck's mother had given him that much, as well. Perhaps she had a notion it would be a good idea to give Tuck someone he was willing to run to for help in case she or Linden weren't around.

"Tuck very good," Mags replied, and took a deep breath.

"Look, Linden . . . yer got any quarrel w' Tuck workin' fer th' Heralds?"

She shook her head, but looked puzzled. "No. But—"

He interrupted her. "Lissen. Th' more Tuck keeps makin' thins an' you go out an' sell 'em, the more like it's gonna be that somebody like Cobber figgers out what 'e kin do." He held up a hand to stop the words she had opened her mouth to say. "I *know* yer careful. But it on'y takes one slip. It on'y takes some'un breakin' in here whilst yer gone. Kin ye keep 'im safe forever? Lookit whut jest 'appened! What'f there wasn't no Herald on duty when Cobber 'auled Tuck in?"

She closed her mouth, and looked thoughtful. He pursued his advantage. "So here's what I got ter offer. Herald's'll keep you an' 'im. We'll send down stuff on the quiet like, so's ye kin fix this place up all snug an' *locked* tight, an' make it comfy. We'll make sure ye git whatever ye want. An' Tuck on'y makes two kinds've stuff. 'e makes trinkets and shinies ye take t' Willy the Weasel t'sell, 'cause Willy don't ast no questions, an' we kin pay 'im t'keep 'is mouth 'bout you an' Tuck. An' Tuck makes special stuff just fer us."

She blinked at him in confusion for a moment, then, before he could explain further, enlightenment dawned over her face. "Oh! Like lockpicks!" She sucked in her lip. "I thought 'bout hevin' Tuck make 'em, 'cause they sells good . . . but it didn' seem smart 'cause then people'd wanter know 'oo made 'em."

Mags nodded. "Thet was smart, 'cause some'un would'a figgered it out. We need 'em, on account've sometimes we gotta get inter locked places and boxes. An' we'll want 'im t'make other things, like thet there stove, thet we kin take apart, see how she works, an' set up some'un t'make by big lots. Stuff that'll make thins better fer lotsa folk. On'y thing is, Tuck ain't gonna ever get credit fer all 'e kin do."

She actually gave him a withering look. "Thin' 'e cares?

Thin' *I* care? You Heralds, you jest keep us cozy an' fat, an' thet's all we need."

"D'ye live wi' Tuck?" he asked.

"Like sibs," she replied without hesitation. " 'is Ma arst me t'look out fer 'im, on account'a 'e looked out fer me when we was liddle. Once 'e started makin' thins, she 'ad no notion where t'sell 'em. Me, I been pickin' through trash an' ever'thin all me life, so I knows where t'sell about anythin', an' . . ." She let out her breath in a long *whoosh*. "Too much t'tell. It ain't no kinda story," she said. "Jest folks gettin' by."

For a moment, he wished he'd started his gang of street-orphans long enough ago that he'd picked up Linden. She could have been so much more. . . .

:And if you had, where would Tuck be now?: Dallen pointed out.

"Ye know Aunty Minda's boys?" he asked, and she nodded. "Good. I'll be sendin' stuff t' you an' Tuck an' I'll use them t'fetch it. If anythin' turns up that one've them ain't bringin', it ain't comin' from me."

"An' I'll send it away." She nodded sharply. "Cobber might look fer a way to get hisself outa trouble by getting hot goods inter this place, then sendin' th'Watch."

"Linden, yer a sharp gel. I like ye." He grinned. She grinned back.

"An' I like ye back, Herald Mags, an' that's somethin' I niver 'spected t'say 'bout no Whitecoat."

———

"And now what do you expect to do with your inventing fellow and his keeper?" Amily asked, amused, as they snuggled together in front of their fire that night.

"Introduce you to 'em, for one thing," Mags replied. "And your Pa."

"Why on earth?" she asked, sounding surprised, as the fire popped and crackled.

He kissed the top of her head. "Because, m'love, yer supposed t'be the King's bodyguard, an' I think it'd be a good notion if ye had a couple'a sneaky weapons like Bey had around about yer person. Yer Pa, too. An' me, that goes 'thout sayin'. Mostly, we gotta figger out how t'tell Tuck what we want."

"I'd say firstly we need to figure out what we need," she said, in a slightly admonishing tone. "Because if we don't know, how are we supposed to tell this poor fellow?"

"Oh, I already know the first thin'," he said immediately. "I want me some climbin' gear I kin hide on me. Then I want knives. Lotsa knives. Differen' kinds, an' all stuff that's hid."

She craned her head around to look at him. "You've been rummaging through the Sleepgiver memories again, haven't you?"

"Got a reason why I shouldn't?" he countered. "Just 'cause they're killers fer hire, that don't mean they ain't got some good notions." He grinned at her dumbfounded expression. "Well? Am I right?"

She shook her head. "You're impossible," she replied, and kissed him.

In the back of his mind a voice chuckled, that was not Dallen's for once. It was his own, chuckling over the fact that back where that internal voice lived, there had been a fear that once he and Amily were "properly" married, things would get . . . dull. And they wouldn't find each other as exciting anymore. And that certainly wasn't the case.

. . . not in the least.

In fact, there was a sort of blessed relaxation, partly because he *wasn't* having to think about all the ways that wretched wedding could go wrong, but mostly because there had always been the lurking fear that something would *always* prevent it.

He firmly shoved into the dark depths of his mind the certainty that sooner or later he'd find a brand new fear, and enjoyed the moment, which shortly turned into something more than just a moment.

———————

Mags got up earlier than Amily, and she waved him off drowsily. For once she was going to lie abed a little while longer. This was the only thing she missed about her "old life," when she had been of no consequence—that she could no longer sleep late when she chose, nor stay up as late as she chose to finish a book!

When was the last time I read a book for pleasure? she thought, a little mournfully, as she fluffed the pillow to make it more comfortable. It seemed forever.

But this morning the King was not taking his usual working breakfast with her, he was taking a working breakfast with her father. *She* had taken the chance to stockpile something suitable for breakfast yesterday afternoon—pocket pies made a lovely breakfast—so she didn't even have to go over to the Collegium to eat. She could just drowse until a guilty conscience or Rolan woke her up.

Her thoughts drifted, as they were inclined to do when she was trying to get back to sleep. *I wonder what sort of thing I could ask this odd genius Mags discovered to make for me.* Perhaps a necklace that could be turned into restraints? And perhaps some clever tools to take the place of corset stays? Certainly a pair of stilettos in place of the front busks. Amily didn't *need* to wear a corset, but she found that it helped with back fatigue when she had to stand for long periods of time. Substituting something useful in place of the stays seemed like a good idea. *I'll bet Mags will have useful things secreted in seams and hidden pockets all over himself before long.*

Bear had warned her that after so many years of being a cripple, it was going to take a body a long time to adjust to the other extreme, and he was right. Yesterday had been one of those days; formal and informal Court and she'd been standing behind the throne for all of it.

On the other hand, yesterday the King had finally gotten around to formally requesting that Lady Dia "help" with the wedding . . . and Lady Dia had basically said, in lovely, courtly phrases, that anyone that got between her and the wedding planning was going to find him- or herself cut off at the knees. Having Lady Dia doing the planning meant that Violetta was going to find herself doing a *lot* of work, and the sort of thing she seemed to be very good at. If the wedding came off well, Violetta's reputation as a clever planner of festivities might even eclipse her reputation as the featherbrained wench whose romantic foolishness had nearly got two entire noble Houses murdered. *And hopefully she won't make any further mistakes; even trivial ones are always going to eclipse your successes,* she reflected ruefully. *Though . . . in the end, what could have been a complete disaster turned into the end of a bloody feud. I cannot say that I will miss Lord Kaltar, and I suspect neither does his Lady. Anyone that bloodthirsty was probably terrifying to be around. There's probably a good reason why he and Lady Kaltar only ever had a single child.*

Well, between standing all day, and Mags' brilliant idea to just *run off and get married* . . . well, maybe another reason why she was aching all over was that she was finally relaxing muscles she hadn't even known were tense.

Today there were no Council meetings, and no Court sessions, which meant that Amily was basically free. And she knew exactly what she was going to do.

This would be a good day to do a little snooping in the households of some of the Council members by way of the working cats and pets they had in their homes. A good many of them had one or more of Lady Dia's little spaniels; they all had cats kept specifically for mousing. No well-regulated household could do without at least one cat in the kitchen, pantry and cellars, and at least one to patrol the upstairs. Most had more. And thanks to Amily's peculiar Gift, every single one of those animals could serve as eyes and ears for her.

So today would be a day when she could laze by the fire and see what she could learn.

Sometimes it bothered her, all this spying on people she should have been able to trust. But that was the thing, really, she *should* have been able to trust them, but they were still people, and people got their judgment swayed by personal considerations or ambitions, or things she couldn't even predict. *And if Father had this as a resource, he'd have used it without a second thought.*

The apple had not fallen far from the tree after all. She might be King's Own, but like her father, she was also the King's Spy. *I wish I had a troupe of spies of my own, the way that Father and Mags do,* she thought, turning over and punching the pillow again. *Someone who could make sure I had little dogs I could listen through in every household where I might need one. Someone who was trusted, but invisible. Someone who. . . .*

And that was when she had what *possibly* was a brilliant idea all her very own. So brilliant, that she sat straight up in bed, all thoughts of sleep vanishing.

There was one thing that Amily had been able to do very, very, well, back in the days when she could not move about without help. She could *observe.* And one of the things she had observed, forgotten until now, was the plight of young, highborn women with a title and no money.

Mostly, they were hangers-on in the entourages of wealthier relatives—hoping for a crumb of a dower in some cases, in others hoping to prove they had some form of talent so they could get the Crown to sponsor them to the Collegia. Often they served as unpaid governesses or companions. She had heard whispered stories of exceptionally pretty ones who had blatantly become kept mistresses—or had even become the star attractions of a brothel.

But mostly, they languished in the households of those who were wealthier than they were, grateful for a bed and regular meals, trained in all the skills a highborn girl was supposed to have, but not in anything that made her fit to *work*.

Amily had seen over a dozen girls like that, either exploited or ignored by their well-off relations, and that had been before she was actually looking for them. How many more were out there? For the most part, so far as the *truly* wealthy and highborn were concerned, they were so invisible they might not even exist. The sort of highborn that frequented the Court left such girls to their seneschals to deal with.

Now, what if Amily was to actively start recruiting some of them? Some would probably object, but there should be some who would be willing to help.

:If you are waiting for me to voice an objection, you will be waiting until your hair turns gray,: Rolan observed. *:We should give them incentives in the form of . . . hmm. Perhaps the incentives should vary.:*

The urge to drowse forgotten, Amily squirmed out of bed and grabbed a fresh uniform.

After fortifying herself with breakfast, she called on Dia. Unlike most of her peers, Dia was an early riser, and invited her old friend to have a tour of the kennels and inspect the new litters of puppies. There were two litters of the tiny muff-dogs, sweet-tempered spaniels that Dia had bred to keep bored ladies company. The puppies were adorable, and so small two of them would fit in Amily's hand. But muff-dogs were not all Dia bred; she supplied the Guard with hounds they could train to search for hidden enemies or search for people who were lost, she bred enormous, patient dogs that were first-class nursemaids for adventuresome littles, courageous rat-terriers who never hesitated in taking on the vermin even cats feared to attack, and she bred enormous mastiffs as protection dogs. Amily always enjoyed taking the tours of Dia's kennels, and secretly got a lot of amusement at seeing the elegant Lady Dia with her lush, brown hair tied in a knot on the top of her head, bits straggling out, in an old moleskin tunic, trews, and tarred boots, getting down on the floor and being covered in giant herds of dog.

When they were done, both of them were ready for a second breakfast—and in Lady Dia's case, a good wash and a change of clothing.

"Now, what is it that you need to talk about that you'd endure getting dragged through my kennels in order to get to talk to me?" Dia asked, as she settled herself on a comfortable seat, her sensuous body wrapped in a gorgeous robe. Her handmaid put her hair in order while she hungrily devoured miniature egg pies. Dia's handmaid was exactly the sort of young woman Amily wanted to recruit for her informants— not Miana herself, because if Dia became untrustworthy, the next thing that would occur would be for the sun to rise in the west—but the sort of beautifully bred and absolutely impoverished highborn girl that had *no* prospects in front of her without someone like Lady Dia. Miana, aside from knowing the ins and outs of everything needed to keep Dia looking stunning, knew every detail of the voluminous genealogies of the highborn families of Valdemar. Dia called that, "deep knowledge of the studbook." And Miana was as plain as plain could be. With her mousy brown hair, flat, uninteresting face, and equally flat figure, the only way many women would take her as a handmaiden was as someone to feel superior to.

Which was ridiculous, because Miana had a mind as sharp as any scholar's. There were so many things she helped Dia with that were *not* involved in making Dia look gorgeous that it sometimes made Amily's head spin.

"Actually, this is a perfect time to talk to you, because Miana is here," Amily replied, helping herself to some as well. She explained her idea as both Dia and her handmaid listened intently. When she was done, Miana was the first to speak up.

"If Lady Dia hadn't asked me to be her companion, I'd have given something like that serious consideration, Herald," she said soberly. "Especially if there was some sort of reward at the end of it." Lady Dia reached up and patted her hand as the young woman continued. "Milady has assured me of a pension and a pretty little apartment of my own, but not every lady's handmaiden is so lucky." She patted the last strand of Dia's hair into perfection, and handed Dia a mirror for her approval. "Given the consideration that a girl might uncover something to the undoing of the family she is in, Herald—"

"I think such an assurance goes without saying," Amily replied, sensing Rolan's immediate assent. "Basically, what I wanted to know was, did you two think this was a good idea, and did you have any way of reaching out to such girls?"

Dia handed the mirror back to her handmaiden and the two exchanged a long glance. "I can reach some," Dia said. "Probably the ones Miana can't."

"And I can reach a great many," Miana replied. "There is a sort of . . . unofficial network of us. We are always looking out for a good place for those who don't have one." She handed Lady Dia a lambswool puff and a little pot of pink powder, and Dia lightly dusted her cheeks. "I suspect those of us who are in less than comfortable positions would be happy to join your ranks, on the assurance that they would be taken care of if the position became unendurable." She took the lambswool and pot away, and handed Dia the exotic stuff from Kata'shin'a'in that Dia used to darken the eyelids over her melting brown eyes, turning them from lovely to seductive. "That's our worst fear, you know, that we have no choice but to starve or continue to endure places where we are treated worse than servants, because we can't leave."

Dia finished and handed the implements back to Miana, then spread her hands. "Well, there you have it. I think it is a good idea, and so does Miana. We can also ask these girls to insert one or more of my dogs into their households so you'll have a second set of eyes and ears there."

"At the very least they can tell you where the cats are," Miana pointed out. "But we are practically invisible, unless our Lady is like Lady Dia. People say horrid things right in front of us, and pay us no heed, as if we were furniture. Of course, that's if we're plain. . . ."

Amily seized that. "We wouldn't ever ask anyone to do anything she wasn't comfortable with. I would *never* ask someone to go into a man's bed just to get information."

"But there are some that wouldn't object to doing just that," Miana pointed out firmly. "For a pretty one, it's very hard to say *no* and be heeded. Almost impossible, in fact. So if being used is going to happen anyway, knowing you'll be protected and can get away afterward—"

"I would much rather get a girl out of such a position *before* anything happens," Amily said firmly, then wavered, when both Dia and Miana looked at her steadily. "But . . ."

"Let's not create nightmares and work ourselves up over them yet," Dia said firmly. "And let's not make decisions for girls we have not yet recruited." She nodded and got up, so that Miana could help her into one of her gorgeous, and terribly complicated gowns. "And it is time for you to take this idea, first to your father, and then to the King. Come back to me when you have his approval, and we three will put our heads together."

Mags had given a careful report about Tuck and Linden last night to both Nikolas and the Seneschal and his Herald. All three of them had agreed whole-heartedly with his plan, and the Seneschal had given him leave to draw whatever funds he needed out of the Treasury. So the morning was spent, first in going by Aunty Minda's and rounding up four of the bigger boys, then in buying things all over Haven, and having them taken to Tuck's shed. Discreetly. Quietly. Stealthily. It would not do to have the neighbors wonder why Tuck and Linden were suddenly so prosperous.

The only thing he couldn't have delivered was a full load of wood, but he reckoned Linden would find a way to explain that away.

At around lunchtime, he turned up himself, with a stout purse full of coppers and some silver. He hadn't had much chance to look over the immediate neighborhood of Tuck's shed yesterday, but today, when he did, he finally deduced *why* there was a shed in the yard of a larger building in the first place. The main building was a large structure now divided up into rooms people could rent. But it had been a brewery, and the stable had held the delivery-van horses.

He slipped past the larger building, through a wooden gate, and into what had been the stableyard, and now served mostly for littles to play in and women to hang laundry, although there was a sty for a single pig, a couple of henhouses and four pigeon-coops. It was the gate that made all that possible of course. It was probably locked at night, so no one would steal the livestock.

He had come in his Herald Whites, so that Tuck would not be afraid; he had every right as a Herald to be here, of course, especially after yesterday. It would not seem at all out of the ordinary for him to see how Linden and Tuck were doing.

Us Heralds is nosy like that.

:It's our job to be nosy like that,: Dallen reminded him.

Dallen was with him this time, pacing along beside him, and the moment the two of them entered the former stable-yard, Dallen was the center of attention. The children swarmed him, as children always did. What child could resist a snow-white, silver-hooved, blue-eyed horse? And even their mothers, busy hanging laundry on lines that crisscrossed the yard, with barely enough space to move between them, paused in their work to cast looks of wonder and admiration.

"Afternoon, ladies," Mags said, affably. "Jest checkin' in on that feller Tuck. I mean t'make sure he didn' take no hurt from thet bully, Cobber Pellen."

Well, he'd intended to find out just what the neighborhood thought of Pellen, and those simple words unleashed a torrent. Evidently it wasn't only Tuck's stable he'd wanted; he'd intended to take over the whole building. At least half of these women had a story of how Cobber had "come calling," intending to find out what they were paying in rent and what the terms of their leases were. As Mags had surmised, this neighborhood was one of hardworking poor folk. It had immediately been clear to these folks that Cobber intended to acquire the place and evict them all. "Startin' wi' Daisy's shed," said the most talkative of the lot, whose empty laundry basket showed why she was willing to stand and chat after the others had unloaded their complaints and tales of woe into his willing ears. "I guess 'e found out poor Tuck owned it outright and reckoned t'set up some sorta tavern an' make as much trouble as 'e could fer us."

Mags thought that over. "Aye, I kin see thet," he agreed. "Keeps th' place open all hours, drunks i' th' yard, thievery—mos' of ye are laundry-women, aye?"

"Aye. Well an' wash-house inside, where th' brew-kettles useter be," his informant told him. "Well with good, sweet water was used fer the brewin'. 'Bout twenny years agone, we all clubbed t'gether, made a wash-house outen it. Landlord was all fer it. Made sure there was niver a room wi'out a tenant."

Mags nodded. Taking in wash was a good, stable job, and although it was a hard one, it was one that ensured that the woman in question could always pay her rent. But that begged the question—if this landlord owned the former brewery, how had Tuck's mother gotten hold of the shed?

:That's a question for another day,: Dallen advised. *:Start asking too much, and you'll raise suspicions.:*

"So, Cobber sets up a tavern, an' pretty soon there goes yer business. All of ye lose yer rooms, landlord's got no choice but t'take what 'e kin get, an' that'd be Cobber." He tilted his head to the side, inviting comment, and the woman grimaced and nodded.

"But not this time," she said firmly, and patted him on the shoulder. "Now git, do yer duty an' be off tendin' t'more 'portant things than th' likes of us."

"Nothin's more 'portant than th' likes of ye," he countered, and skirted the edge of the yard to stay out of the way of the flapping laundry, and got to the door of the shed and knocked. The door cracked, and Linden peered out of it.

"Herald Mags!" she said, opening the door for him in the sight of the others. "Thenkee fer comin' t'see 'bout Tuck." She reached out and tugged on his arm and he let her draw him inside.

She shut the door, and looked up at him, her face pink with excitement. Tuck was bent over his workbench, deep in creation, humming tunelessly to himself. "When ye said ye was gonna send us ev'thin' we needed, I didn' think twould be—" Words failed her, and instead, she flung herself at him and hugged him tightly. "Yer a angel, Herald! Yer a right angel!"

He patted her shoulder. "Nah, nah, Tuck'll be earnin' it, an' right quick. I got a mort'a things already I wanter get him t'make up fer me. But I cain't keep sendin' boys with parcels.

So here—" He detached her and put the heavy purse in her hands. Her eyes widened. "This'll keep ye awhile. I want yer t'meet me at Weasel's shop arter dark in three days. We'll work out there how I kin send ye stuff 'thout anybody the wiser. Meanwhile, I want a set'a lockpicks. Thet'll be the fust job fer Tuck, an' I want him t'take 'is time over 'em."

Linden nodded. "Iffen 'e says 'e's done wit' 'em, an' there's time t'spare, want 'nother set?"

Since a set of really good lockpicks would probably make Nikolas's eyes light up like candles, Mags nodded. "Thet'll do fer now. I figger yer better at 'splainin' thins to 'im than I'd be, so I'll 'splain to ye the next thin' I need at Weasels." He cast a glance over at Tuck's hunched back. There was no sign of fear or tension now. " 'Ow's 'e doin'?"

"I tol' 'im you was gonna make sure Cobber couldn' be mean t'im no more. I ain't niver lied t'im, an' 'e b'lieves me."

"Well, Cobber *ain't,* " Mags said firmly. "Them was some purt' serious charges, an' once word got aroun' 'e was in gaol, other folk started comin' in an' layin' charges. So 'e's a-gonna go be workin' a prison-farm for a good piece, an' when 'e gets out, I 'spect 'e'll hev other worries than Tuck."

Linden chuckled and rubbed her hands together with glee. He looked her over with approval. Some of what he had sent over was a bundle of used clothing. Gone were the ragged skirts, worn in layers so that the holes could be compensated for. She had a nicely darned, thick woolen tunic that came down past her knees, a pair of faded moleskin trews, and the sort of knitted "boots" with leather soles that would fit many sizes of feet. The wild mop of hair had not *quite* been tamed, but it also didn't look as if it had a life and a mind of its own anymore. She noted his glance, and grinned, held out her arms and turned in place. "Lookit me! I'm respect'ble!"

"No such bad thin' t'be," he replied. "Now, come say 'lo

t'my Companion, or the ladies out there'll thin' there's somethin' wrong wi'ye, an' then I'll be on m'way."

She scampered off and hid the pouch of coins under a floorboard, then followed him out of the shed. Tuck took no more heed of them than if they'd been a couple of moths.

Dallen was accepting the adoration of the children with his usual aplomb, but Mags caught his chuckle when Linden stopped dead, staring at him with her mouth falling open. Mags nudged her gently with an elbow to wake her up.

"I—ain't niver seen one on 'em, close up," she admitted, and took a couple of steps nearer. "Kin I touch 'im?"

"All ye want," Mags assured her.

And as she joined the children, looking into Dallen's blue eyes and stroking his silken mane with an expression of bliss, Mags was very aware that while *he* might be Linden's benefactor and hero, it was Dallen whom she had given her wholehearted worship to.

:As it should be,: noted Dallen. *:This is the proper order of things.:*

:Quiet, horse.:

4

Three nights later, the three of them—Mags, Amily, and her father—shared a quiet meal together in his rooms. They didn't do that nearly often enough to suit all three of them, but in this case, it was part wedding feast, and part planning session. Nikolas was very interested to hear about Tuck and Tuck's genius in crafting things, and his eyes did, indeed, light up at the sight of Mags' gift, the better of the two excellent sets of lockpicks. Tuck had taken less than two days to make both sets; Mags had tried them both and he was extremely impressed.

"If I have to run off, and actually have a place you can send things to, I'll let you know through Dallen," Nikolas said, as they feasted on food straight from the King's table. "As long as I am still here, I'd like to put in another request. I would really like a set of that climbing gear you're having him make you. Especially if the two of you can make a grappling-hook-arrow actually work."

Nikolas was looking very good these days; fully recovered from the ordeal that had nearly killed him. Nikolas was—purposefully—very difficult to describe, so ordinary as to blend into any crowd. It had taken years for him to get his appearance that way. Even in Herald Whites he was utterly forgettable. In any ordinary clothing, from rags to velvets, it was unlikely anyone would remember him long enough to describe him. Mags actually suspected some sort of minor Gift at work; Nikolas *was* a very strong Mindspeaker, and that would be a Gift that could easily go hand-in-hand with Mindspeaking.

At any rate, Nikolas was looking good. Healthy and a little impatient for something to go wrong so he could investigate it.

I just hope whatever it is has nothing to do with me and Amily.

:From your mind to the ears of the gods,: Dallen replied fervently.

"I have no notion, no more does Linden," Mags admitted. "But if *she* can figger out how to explain it to him, like as not, if it can be made, he can do it. And I borrowed one of Amily's corsets, Linden's gonna get him t'make thin knives t'fit where the busks'd be."

Nikolas's sitting room served as their dining room; he had pressed the table he used for a desk into service as their dining table, and three of his mismatched sitting room chairs were arranged around it. There was just enough room. It was still too cold to seem like spring, so a fine fire burned in the fireplace.

Nikolas nodded in approval, then chuckled, as he passed Mags the salt. "What a strange lot we are. Any other father would be reacting in horror to the notion of such a thing, and here I am, trying to think of something *else* lethal that could get fitted into a corset!"

"Well, I like to have my lethality hidden, thank you, and where better than in my underthings?" Amily countered, snatching the last roll from the basket in the center of the table. Mags passed her the butter dish.

"I'd like you just's lethal *out* of your underthings, wife," Mags retorted. "An' I like you lethal in whatever ye choose to be wearin', or not. The more lethal you be, the better I like it!"

"Just as long as you look like the most harmless thing on earth," Nikolas reminded them. "Both of you. It's always better, not just for us, but for the entire Kingdom, if those like you and me and Mags are not what we seem."

"Speaking of not what we seem. . . ." Amily bit her lip, and Mags knew why. She was still very conflicted over this idea of hers, this little army of female informants. It was not the problem of placing them where they would be expected to tattle on their hosts—because obviously, the placement would only be with those that Nikolas and the King deemed . . . problematic. The problem was that potentially she was putting them in danger. She didn't think twice about putting herself in danger—but she was balking at the notion of doing so to someone else.

"The King, the Seneschal, and I all spent all of last night discussing your idea," Nikolas told her. "I do understand why you feel some misgivings over it. But it seems to me that as long as each of these young ladies is very carefully briefed on *every* possible repercussion, and is given a route of escape if the situation becomes unpleasant or intolerable or even dangerous, don't *they* deserve the right to decide whether or not they wish to serve the King, and just how far they are prepared to go in order to do so?" He caught her hand in his and looked deeply into her eyes. "Are we to assume these young ladies are less brave, and less intelligent, than those who join the Guard? Are we to assume they can't *be* that brave and intelligent? Remember, they can always decline, which is more than fighters in the Guard can do." He shrugged. "Mind, the comparison with the Guard isn't exact. Things are quite clear-cut when the Guard is sent in, and the opposite will be true of your young ladies. But still . . . it's a valid comparison so far as bravery is concerned."

Amily gave her father a long, measuring look. Mags held his peace; he agreed with Nikolas. Why, every single one of Amily's friends before she had been Chosen had been spies—of a sort. Granted they reported straight to their parents, who in their turn went to the King, but how was that different from this? Finally she let out her breath in a long sigh. "Of course not," she replied. "You're right. And since you seem to be in agreement on this, I'll talk to Dia in the morning and we'll get things in motion." She sat back in her chair. "I get the feeling that Miana already has some acquaintances in mind. If you have any families in which you think my ladies should be placed, I'd like a list at your earliest convenience."

Mags noted with approval that, once she had made up her mind, Amily was quite prepared to follow through. He took a few bites of baked apple, and then cleared his throat. "I got me an ideer," he said, as Amily and her father looked over at him. "I dunno if this'd suit ye, but it seems t'me that Dia might could have an open hand in this. An' that'd take any suspicion that th' King was behind it right off, on account of Dia does things like this all th' time."

Amily turned toward him and smiled. "I am all ears."

He put down his fork, and noted that the wind had picked up outside. He sighed mentally. It was going to be a long, cold walk to their quarters. But then, getting warmed up afterward would be worth it. "Dia kin set up a kinda school fer hand-maidens. What *she* gets outa it is she gets a buncha ladies she kin hand out some of her work to—like weddin' an' festival stuff. What *they* gets outa it, is they get a nice place t'live an' access t'all the best families an' gatherin's an' all. An' any-body Dia'd trained, well, the people we wanta get 'em placed with, they'd think first of all—Lady Dia!—that'd be a status thin', t'get yer handmaid trained by her. They'll prolly compete with each other to get them girls. And second, they'd all git t'know each other, an' they'd know how t'get in touch with each other in case'a trouble. Whaddya think?"

"Great good gods, Mags, I like it!" Nikolas exclaimed, his brown eyes lighting up with unabashed enthusiasm. "No one would ever suspect Dia of spycraft. The Crown can fund it all, and no one will ever know."

"Dia's got the room," Amily mused. "She's always complaining that her husband's manor house is *a great mausoleum we have to keep three-fourths closed up, lest the echoes from the empty rooms drown out our actual conversation.* I'll ask her about it! And with the Crown footing any additional expense of taking on a dozen young ladies, not even her husband will object." She smiled a little. "Not that he would. He complains about the place being too quiet himself, and I think he would enjoy a lot of feminine company around him."

"Then you two should see him tomorrow afternoon at the latest," Nikolas decreed. "I'll go with you."

Something about the way Nikolas said that, made Mags take sudden notice. There was something going on here. . . .

Mags gave his mentor a look that said, *And just what is it you aren't telling us?* But Nikolas was keeping his mouth firmly closed, though there was a faint gleam in his eye. . . .

Well, Nikolas didn't usually keep secrets from Mags, and those he did, generally were not his to tell.

:You got any notions?: he asked Dallen.

:I expect you'll find out tomorrow afternoon,: came the bland response, which only cemented Mags' suspicions into certainty. Nikolas was keeping a secret. And not just from him, but from Amily.

And tomorrow afternoon they were going to find out what it was.

They had ridden in through a pair of beautiful wrought-iron gates and had been met by three grooms in Lord Jorthun's special crimson livery. The grooms escorted—not led—them and the Companions through a lovely little paved courtyard, past the main entrance, and to Lord Jorthun's magnificent stone stables. There, they displayed the accommodations that the Companions were to enjoy, and Mags was impressed. There were special stalls just for Companions in Lord Steveral Jorthun's stables. Stalls with mangers full of sweet hay and water-buckets that looked freshly scrubbed until they shone. And grooms—plural—that knew exactly how to treat Companions.

:*With the admiration and deference due to us, of course,*: Dallen said smugly as he, Rolan, and Evory were escorted—once again, not *led*—away. It was clear the Companions were about to be treated better than many humans.

:*Naturally, horse,*: Mags replied, following the footman who had come to greet them at the stable door. He looked up at the manor house. A *real* stone-built manor house, not one of the "town-houses" the highborn usually had, even up here on the Hill. It wasn't the size of the Palace, but it was certainly big enough, and it was small wonder that Dia joked about it being a mausoleum. It was four stories tall, plus an attic, and probably cellar-rooms as well, within its own grounds and gardens, and it must have taken a staff of at least eighty to a hundred just to keep it all going, whether it was full of visitors or not. He knew Dia held a great many gatherings, and Lord Jorthun often played host to several contingents of relatives during Court season—and you couldn't exactly put staff members in a closet and take them out again when they were needed. Lord Jorthun never left Haven anymore, and so perforce his manor house was fully staffed, all year around.

Mags had never been here before. Lord Jorthun was an old friend of the King, and the King's father before him, and there had never been any need for Mags to pay the highborn a visit in any official—or other—capacity. In fact, until now, he hadn't realized there actually *were* any manors this size on the Hill. Most of the highborn contented themselves with a town-house, for the very good reason that a manor this big required so much staff, and even a skeleton staff, with most of the house closed up, would be a minimum of twenty servants.

This place looked as if it might even date all the way back to the Founding. If that was the case, then it had probably been meant to serve more than one highborn family—or one really enormous extended family.

They were almost at the front portico when another foot-man opened the door, and a very tall, very erect, very fit man with silvery hair, dressed in Court finery of black and gray velvet with silver ornaments, stepped out into the sunlight.

"Ah, you have arrived!" It was Lord Jorthun himself who intercepted them at the front door, his distinctive and powerful voice carrying out into the courtyard. He took a half dozen strong steps toward them. "Thank you, Jem, that will be all," he said, as he took Amily's hand and bowed over it.

Mags had only ever seen this powerful member of the high-born at a distance, on the rare occasions he came to a gathering at Court himself, rather than sending his wife as his delegate. He was even more impressive near at hand. He was one of the tallest men Mags had ever seen—he towered over Nikolas by a good head. His dark eyes suggested that the mane of silver hair he boasted had once been jet black. Beneath a silver beard and moustache, his features were those of an heroic statue. And the way he carried himself told Mags his excuses for stay-ing away from Court events because he was "fatigued" were a fabrication; this was a fit man, and despite his years, still per-fectly capable of anything he put his mind to.

"So this is our King's Own, my little Dia's childhood friend. Well met at last, my dear," he said, in a voice that was rich and deep. "I have known your father for many, many years, of course. In fact, I knew him before he was King's Own." A genuine smile crossed his face. "You are a credit to your family." Amily blushed, but kept her composure.

"I am very pleased to meet you at last too, sir," she said. She was about to say more, but he released her hand and waved them in ahead of him, through a pair of doors of ornately carved, light-colored wood. These led straight into an entrance hall; the walls and support pillars were of a pale stone, but the staircase rising from it was of the same intricately carved wood as the doors, as was the padded bench where the footman and the hallboys—two of them—waited patiently to be needed. Lord Jorthun led them through an open doorway to the left, into what looked like a version of a Great Hall, with a massive fireplace, a great deal of seating, and a gallery running around all four walls. Clear light came from skylights in the roof above; Mags guessed that the rooms off the gallery were probably guest rooms, but he was only guessing. Whoever had planned and built this building had intended to showcase the pale beige stone it was made of; the only places where the stone of the walls was covered was where the magnificent decorative tapestries had been hung. Mags didn't get much chance to look at this room, however, as their host whisked them through it and into a much smaller room beyond.

He hurried them through the entrance and closed two massive wooden sliding doors behind them. Mags stared a little; those doors were definitely an impressive feat of building. He couldn't for the life of him imagine how they worked; they seemed to have been literally built into the walls on either side of the doorway.

This was a library, with floor-to-ceiling bookshelves taking up every bit of wall that wasn't occupied by a window or the fireplace. Above them was a paneled wooden ceiling. The fire-place was just as big as the one in the Great Hall, and had a fine blaze going in it. There was enough comfortable seating in this room for at least thirty.

They weren't going to need that much seating, obviously, but that particular point made Mags think that Lord Jorthun must use this room fairly often for entertaining. Near the fire, Dia rose from beside a table loaded with food and drink, and waved them merrily to seats around it. In a nice nod to the company, the seats were each two-person sofas, comfortably upholstered in plush.

They all took their places, Mags and Amily taking the seat nearest Dia, Nikolas taking the one opposite her, Lord Jorthun settling beside Dia and taking her hand as she dimpled at him. "Help yourselves," she said, "Steveral says I needn't play the hostess with old friends."

Nothing loathe, Mags poured wine for himself and Amily; Lord Jorthun's wines were second to none by reputation. The cups were of silver, the plates were as well. There was a small fortune here on the table, without even counting the out-of-season fruits heaped on one of the plates. There was probably a hothouse here. And it was a good thing that what he had poured was a white wine, because he nearly ruined his Whites at Steveral Jorthun's next words.

"So, how is my best pupil in the Great Ungentlemanly Game fairing now that he doesn't have to juggle his clandestine as-signments and the position of King's Own?" If the last words of that sentence hadn't given away who the question was di-rected at, the arched brow in Nikolas's direction certainly would have. "I trust your life is less complicated now?"

Mags spluttered and choked and quickly put down his gob-let. Amily simply looked stunned. Dia giggled. Nikolas . . . shrugged.

"It's infinitely easier now," was all he said, while Mags

struggled for breath. "And very much less complicated, thank you."

But if Mags couldn't speak yet, he could most certainly think, and he directed those thoughts straight at his mentor, with no little outrage. *:Why didn't you ever tell me Lord Jorthun was your teacher?:* he Mindspoke accusingly. *:It would have saved me a great deal of trouble if I had known who I could come to during the times you went temporarily missing!:*

:It wasn't my secret to reveal,: came the laconic answer. *:If Jorthun had thought you needed to be informed, he would have sent for you himself.:*

Amily must have had much the same question on her mind, although hers was directed at Dia and not her father. "*Why* didn't you ever tell me that your husband was Papa's spymaster?" she sputtered. "Even if you weren't married to him back in the days when Papa would vanish with no notice, it would have been very helpful if you had told me once you knew!"

"It wasn't my secret to give," came the similar reply. Dia's expression gave no hint that she was being anything but honest, and perhaps a bit regretful. But not regretful that she hadn't told—regretful that she had not been free to tell.

Lord Jorthun smiled at Nikolas; it was the smile of a man who is very proud of and pleased with his boon-companion. "Never let it be said that I can't pick those who will keep a secret. Right, my dear?"

Dia squeezed his hand and chuckled. "*You* didn't lay any prohibitions on me, so I told Steveral about your Handmaiden Army this morning before you arrived," she said to Amily. "I presumed this meeting was what that was about, so I thought I would save you the explanation." She chose a small bunch of grapes and ate them thoughtfully while waiting for Amily's response.

The library was exceedingly quiet, and Mags thought he knew why Lord Jorthun had chosen it. They were far enough from the doors that anyone who had his ear pressed to them would probably not be able to make out anything of their quiet talk. The books absorbed a great deal of sound, and damped any echoes off what little exposed stone there was. The plush brown curtains at the windows were fully pulled aside, so no one would be able to hide and listen at the glass. And anyone watching would only see five people having an informal luncheon together.

"Yes it is, and last night Mags had a very good idea about it, but we need your agreement and help if we are going to make use of the notion," Amily told her friend. "Mags can probably explain it best." Mags picked up his goblet and took a sip to refresh his abused throat. *Right. Your best proper speech, lad. This is Lord Steveral Jorthun you're talking to, not some rat-catcher.*

He settled himself, and concentrated on forming each word, and each sentence, as skillfully as he could.

"Something that troubled me was how we were to keep this group organized, and how we were to keep the purpose secret. The Crown is going to have to fund this, of course—aside from the question of rewarding these young ladies for their work, there will have to be measures taken for women who have to abandon their positions because of incipient exposure or some other danger, and the cost of feeding, housing and clothing a dozen young ladies in appropriate style is nothing to be sneezed at. But I quickly realized that if we were not to tip our hand simply by virtue of the fact of Crown funds, we would somehow have to make that funding look like an absent-minded but generous gesture—perhaps from the Princess Royal—and make the actual person *doing* the organizing someone with no direct ties to the Crown except, perhaps, those of friendship. . . ."

Dia caught on immediately, and her face lit up. "You mean me! Oh, what a *good* idea! You want me to do this! Create a—a kind of handmaiden's school, here, in the manor? Turn out exquisitely trained women of *many* talents? Oh, Steveral, may I?"

"Now, when it makes your eyes sparkle like that, how can I possibly say no?" Jorthun chuckled, patting her hand. "Not to mention that having a dozen or so young ladies here will be good company and help for you, and give *me* something pleasant to look at as well as another lot of eager students to impart my particular wisdom to. And if the Crown will be funding this Handmaiden Army, well, that would remove the last possible objection—"

"Oh *wonderful!*" Dia looked as if she was about to clap her hands with glee, forgetting that one of them was clasped in her husband's. Her beautiful brown eyes shone with happiness. And it occurred to Mags that Dia *missed* those days when she had been one of several youngsters who had been informants for the Crown via the auspices of their parents. Could it be that Dia actually envied her friends Mags and Amily? That despite being cradled in the lap of luxury, she longed for something more productive than breeding dogs and planning festivities?

"*But—*" Lord Jorthun said, warningly.

Dia blinked and faltered. "But?"

"As I said, *I* must be in charge of teaching them proper spycraft. *And* the means by which they can defend themselves. I will not take any other answer but 'Yes, of course, Steveral.'" He smiled, but his eyes were deadly serious. "They will be my pupils as much, if not more, than yours. I will not allow these young ladies to go into a potentially dangerous situation without doing everything I can to ensure that they emerge from it intact."

"You would do that?" Mags said, before Dia could respond.

"I insist on it. I agree with Dia, this is a very good idea, and it is something I wish I had thought of and had the resources to put together." Lord Jorthun nodded at Mags. "Then again, perhaps it's just as well I didn't. Having that many young ladies about when I was younger and not nearly as self-controlled as I am now might have been too great a temptation to resist." He arched an eyebrow at Dia.

"I rather doubt you would have been able to create the fiction that you were doing a work of charity, my love," Dia said dryly. "People would have assumed you were gathering young ladies for some form of pleasure palace."

He shrugged. "I did that, too. I still do. Who do you think is the silent owner of three of the most honest brothels in the city?"

Mags was glad he wasn't drinking this time. As it was, he nearly choked. *"You* own the Doll Market?" he asked, naming one of the places where *he* had informants, bequeathed to him—he had thought—by Nikolas. This was a house of pleasure not far from Willy the Weasel's pawn shop, which catered to those whose pockets ran to coppers rather than silver.

Jorthun nodded. "And Flora's and the Lunar Lady," he added, naming the house that Mags had taken young high-born friends to in yet another persona, and a house he had not *dared* go to as he simply did not have the wardrobe or the years to be let anywhere near the door. Nikolas was the one who went to the Lunar Lady. When Nikolas wasn't around, and information needed to be gotten to them, the Mistress of the Lunar Lady passed it in carefully sealed packets on to Flora's by special messenger. "I haven't troubled to get any intelligence from them myself for years, however. You and Nikolas are doing that for me. The further I can distance myself, the more effective my ownership is."

Mags felt very much as if someone had stolen all the breath from his lungs. He sat back in his chair, grateful for the cushioning. "I am now terrified to hear what other pies you have your fingers in."

Jorthun laughed. "Not so many. I am mostly retired; I keep my ownership of the brothels mostly because it would be awkward for either of you to attend to. You and Nikolas are doing very well without me."

"Don't lie, my love. You've been very sweet about it, but you've been wanting something productive to do for several months now." Dia patted his hand admonishingly. "This will be an excellent opportunity for you to create something exceedingly useful. *And* free some worthy ladies from very dreary lives."

"I'll speak to the King about funding, and Lydia about making it 'her idea,'" Amily told them. "Then you can come to Lydia in public and suggest the school for handmaidens."

"And I can complain that my wife is now filling my house with her 'good works,'" Lord Jorthun laughed. "Then she and Miana can recruit."

"Huh . . ." said Mags, something else occurring to him.

"I know that look," Amily said. "I think I know what you're thinking. Tuck?"

"Aye," Mags agreed, and briefly outlined his discovery of Tuck and the poor fellow's amazing ability at constructing and crafting objects. "And now here I am thinking two things. One, that you, sir, might be even better than me and Nikolas at thinking what sort of things he might make for us that'd be useful. And two, that I reckon Tuck can make all manner of useful things for your handmaidens. A wench has got a lot more places she can hide things than a man does, just cause she has all those skirts and petticoats and shifts and things."

"And hair ornaments, and jewelry," added Dia, pursing her lips thoughtfully. Mags dug into his beltpouch and pulled out his new set of lockpicks, passing them over to Lord Jorthun, who looked them over with a knowledgeable eye.

"These are better than my set," he told Mags, passing them

back. "I am extremely tempted now to see if I can transplant the fellow and his keeper to my own workshops."

"It'd be safer for them both," Mags admitted, "But the poor man's not right in the head. He might not take to the transplanting. I can ask, though."

"In the meantime, just for the sake of caution, I'll have my man see about buying out the current owner of the building his 'shed' adjoins, so there is no chance anyone else gets the idea of taking it over." Jorthun smiled thinly. "I would imagine making some repairs, and offering any vacant rooms or apartments to members of the Watch at a greatly reduced rate will put paid to the notion of this Cobber Pellen or any of his crew coming around and making further trouble."

"That it should, my Lord," Nikolas replied, with a wry smile.

"So, now that we have disposed of business—how goes the planning of the wedding?" Jorthun said, obviously expecting *one* of them, at least, to have some sort of spluttering reaction.

But if that was his intention, in this, he was disappointed.

"That's all in Dia's hands now, my Lord," Amily said smoothly. "And Lydia's. We're nothing more than actors in whatever play they come up with."

"It just seems more sensible to think of it that way," Mags added. "Amily and I have got enough to worry about—and no relatives other than Nikolas to please. So we don't *care* what sort of pageant is ultimately decided on."

"Hmm. A sensible attitude, if a rare one," Jorthun observed. "So many young ladies seem to create hysterics trying to have a *perfect day.*"

"Possibly because it is the only day in their entire lives where they are the center of attention," Amily pointed out. "Most of the time, they are pawns to be moved about on the game-board. At least on their wedding day, while they might still be pawns, they are treated as queens."

"Whereas you have rather more power than you are sometimes comfortable with, I suspect," Jorthun replied. At Amily's startled look, he smiled. "No, don't suspect me of Mindspeech. Your father was the same. The King's Own should *never* be comfortable with the amount of power he or she can potentially wield."

"Well, to get back to the subject you *asked* about, my love, I do have some ideas," said Dia, and began relating them. Despite Mags' relative disinterest in such things, he had to admit that Dia's ideas were interesting, surprisingly practical, and would not require all that much of the two purported principals.

After a pleasant candlemark or so, Lord Jorthun excused himself—after first giving Mags carte blanche to contact him at any time—giving the three Heralds a graceful way of taking their leave. As if by magic, they found the three Companions, saddled and bridled and with three escorts attentively waiting beside them, at the front door. The three of them rode out of the front gate with Mags still feeling somewhat bemused.

"Did Lor' Jorthun mean thet?" Mags asked, falling back into somewhat less formal speech with a feeling of relief at not having to think over every single word he said. " 'Bout callin' on 'im at any time, I mean."

"Oh, definitely. And with Dia in charge of your alleged wedding, you'll have all the excuses you need to do so." Nikolas patted Evory's neck, as they rode alongside the wall around the Palace complex, heading for a side entrance. "Plus, some evening when you're free, I'll show you the *special* way to get into his place. It's one method you are very familiar with, and much better at than I am."

"Ah. Roof-runnin'. Thet makes sense." Mags nodded.

"There's a tree that grows very near the walls, an entire grove of truly ancient goldenoaks at the rear of the house that come right up to the back and provide shade for the east-facing bedrooms, and an access to Jorthun's private study attached to his bedroom," Nikolas told him. "I'll give you the key."

:How long have you known about this?: Mags asked Dallen.

:Always. It was not my secret to share,: Dallen replied. And then, the Companion relented a little. *:If there had ever come a time when you desperately needed help and could not get it from the Heralds, I would have told you.:*

Well . . . Mags couldn't fault his Companion for that. What was the old saying? *Two can keep a secret if one of them is dead.* He wondered how Jorthun had managed to be the Royal spymaster for what must have been *decades* without anyone catching on to his dual identity.

Money and rank had certainly made it possible.

"Jorthun was very much a rakehell in his youth," Nikolas said, in a lazy tone that told Mags that he was speaking not only to satisfy Mags' curiosity, but in case there was anyone within listening distance. "The only thing he was not reckless with was his father's money. That, he had a magic touch with. Anything he invested in prospered. Which, of course, caused his father to overlook his other failings."

"Wasn't there a wife before Dia?" Amily asked. "And children?"

"Yes, and they were none too happy about Jorthun marrying her, even though she came with a substantial dower of her own," Nikolas told them. "They still aren't happy, but there is nothing they can do about it. From time to time one of them will make a complaint to the Crown that Dia is spending his money recklessly, and Jorthun's steward will show up with the documentation that proves that the money she is spending is her own, and that is that. Jorthun has guided her to some excellent investments. By the time she is a widow, she'll be ridiculously wealthy." He snorted a little. "And if his own children would stop throwing temper tantrums and come to their father for advice, they will be more than ridiculously wealthy."

"Sense flies out th' winder when greed flies in," Mags said, philosophically.

:I must admit I am glad Jorthun chose to reveal himself before I have to hare off on the King's business again.: Nikolas told him, as they all entered one of the side gates to the Palace complex. The Guardsman at the gate just nodded and let them through without comment; their Companions were identification enough—and no Guardsman here at the Palace was ever likely to mistake an ordinary white horse for a Companion.

:Me too,: Mags replied.

"**I**deally," Amily said, her brown head close to Dia's raven tresses as the two of them bent over a list of names and attributes, "we want orphans." It was too bad that she, Dia, and Miana had to work today. Dia's study was perhaps one of the most comfortable rooms Amily had ever been in. It was so tightly built that not even a hint of draft from the bitter, damp wind outside got in to make the candle flames waver, and the fire in the fireplace not only kept the room wonderfully warm, but also scented it.

Dia nodded. "The fewer ties, the better." She made a little tick against another name on their list.

This morning, Dia had made her "request" of Lydia, during one of Lydia's personal open Court sessions. As the fourth in rank in the Royal hierarchy, Lydia was viewed as "important" by those who were power-seekers only insofar as she had unlimited access to Sedric, and through Sedric, to the King. And she was well known as someone who never tried to persuade Sedric to hear a petitioner due to flattery or presents, so the people who were "political" seldom or never attended more than three or four of these gatherings every season. Lydia's Courts served two purposes; for those who were there for social attention, and those who hoped their petitions would attract her sympathy. These were often people who had causes to espouse, for Lydia was very well known for her charitable works. There were none of the charitable sort in attendance that morning. Instead, the gathering had been as light-hearted and light-minded as a Royal Court session of any sort could get. So when Dia had made her carefully crafted speech about how unfortunate it was that there were so many highborn, yet disadvantaged ladies who were left languishing for lack of anything they were fit for, and that she proposed to train them, and as *what* she proposed to train them, the eager whispers started immediately. The more Dia spoke, describing loyal, skilled companions, more trustworthy than a servant, someone that could be confided in, like "my own Miana," the more the whispers strengthened. Everyone knew Miana. Every woman of rank *wanted* someone like Miana. A lady's personal maidservant was all well and good, and many of them were highly skilled in grooming and assisting their mistresses with their hair and wardrobe. But . . . one didn't give confidences to one's maid. Not unless one wanted those confidences spoken of down in the servant's hall.

And if one wished a conspirator in the matter of an extramarital affair, one *certainly* didn't look for such a conspirator among the maidservants.

Oh, of course, a great many ladies did have handmaidens already, picked out from amongst their own poor relations, but often these were . . . unsatisfactory. And they often came with divided loyalties.

But this idea proposed by Lady Dia meant that one could *apply* for someone who came with few or no family ties at all, and there were many ways, not all of them monetary, by which one could buy that precious loyalty.

Lydia, who knew exactly what was going on, of course, became quite enthusiastic, proposed that she fund it out of her household monies, and that it be called "The Queen's Hand-maidens" in honor of her mother-in-law. And that she herself would see to placing the young ladies when they were deemed skilled enough to look for appointments.

That only increased the buzz of excitement. What lady with any Court ambitions at all *wouldn't* want one of her attendants to be from this elite, prestigious, and exquisitely skillful, group? Why settle for taking on some needy, untrained, bumpkin from your cousins in the country, when you could have a poised, cultured, amusing, infinitely resourceful and always helpful creature like Lady Dia's factotum? Having a Miana of one's own meant different things to every lady in the Court that morning, but every one of those purposes was one that currently was going unfulfilled, or only partly met, for most of them.

Miana made the third of the party bent over papers; in Miana's case, she was perusing what Dia rudely called the "stud-book"; the painstakingly created and updated book documenting every highborn family in the country. Amusingly enough, in other countries, it was the duty of "heralds," in the sense of that corps of glorified secretaries in charge of the arms and genealogies of noble families, who were responsible for such documents. Not here, of course. Here, that was the duty of the Chroniclers—who themselves were a combination of historian and glorified secretary. Additions were made to the book by the Royal Chroniclers every year in the form of new pages sent out right after Midwinter, which was why it was more of a loose-leaf folio rather than a book. It was the job of one's secretary or Chronicler—if you had one—to keep the thing under control. If you didn't have one, well, it was generally the job of whatever hanger-on or family member was of a scholarly and detail-oriented bent.

Dia *and* her husband each had a personal secretary, and the household had a Chronicler as well. Though Jorthun often joked that he did so little that he could have shared his Chronicler with three or four other Houses and not had anything go amiss.

Every so often, Miana would nod, and add another name to the list that Dia and Amily were going over.

Their interesting task was interrupted by one of the footmen, who tapped politely on the doorframe of the open door, and waited.

"What is it, Liam?" Dia asked immediately, looking up. She knew most of her servants by name, and never kept her servants waiting. *It's rude,* she'd told Amily once. *And aside from the fact that it's stupid to be rude, there is the fact that if you are rude to them to their faces, they are going to be rude to you behind your back. And how can you have a happy and disciplined staff if everyone holds their master and mistress in contempt?*

"My lady, a young person wishes to speak with you. Keira Tremainet, daughter of the late Sir Halcon Tremainet and his late wife Maonie. Her parents were remote cousins of House Holberk." Liam paused. "I would not have ventured to interrupt you and the King's Own, but she seemed somewhat urgent and a trifle agitated. I asked her to wait in the lesser antechamber." Liam bowed a trifle as he finished speaking.

"Quite right Liam," said Dia. "Wait just a moment will you? Hopefully a moment or two will allow our visitor to compose herself, rather than increasing her agitation." She turned to Amily and Miana. "I could swear that name is familiar. . . ."

"It is," Miana said instantly. "She's right here, under *Possible, but questions.* I believe there was some sort of rumor?

Nothing approaching a scandal, but . . . the faint suggestion there might have been one?"

"Well." Amily replied. "If she's here, I can't think of any reason for her to *be* here except to petition you for a place in the Handmaidens."

Dia blinked thoughtfully. "If so, and there was some sort of scandal, that alone makes me interested." She paused. "Given what I know about Brendan Keteline, I can easily guess what may have happened, and . . . it's possible that the lady might be exactly what we are looking for. Let's just see what she's made of, shall we?" She looked over at the footman, still waiting patiently. "What do you make of her, Liam?"

"A very forthright young woman, my lady. The sort to seize a scandal by the throat and deal with it, in my reckoning." He coughed. "If you don't mind my saying so."

"Not at all. I find your observations of visitors to be universally cogent, Liam. That is why I asked you. Please bring her up." Dia shuffled the papers into a neat pile, and the three of them turned in their seats to await the young woman's arrival.

Lady Dia's personal study was a bright, well-lit room that was as organized as the King's Seneschal's—and probably contained quite as much information. Dia could put her hand on every bit of information on any member of her household in an instant, from the little boys who were the gardener's assistants to Miana. She could also put her hand on every bit of commonly known information about every highborn member of Court as well as those wealthy enough to be seen at Court on a regular basis.

It could be said, Amily thought, *that knowing all these things about the people of the Court is her job. Just like it is Lydia's.* And, just as it would be hers. . . .

The study contained relatively little furniture; like the library downstairs, every possible scrap of wall was lined with bookshelves or beautifully made document boxes. What wasn't wood, was upholstered in lambskin suede in a dark buff, which matched heavy curtains that could be pulled over the windows at need. There were six comfortable chairs, Lady Dia's desk, plenty of lighting—although the sun streaming in the windows meant there was no need for that—and a species of reclining couch Lady Dia confessed to using when she had a lot to read.

But the entrance of the young lady in question put an end to idle thoughts.

Keira Tremainet was *beautiful.*

I can see why there was scandal. . . .

Sky-blue eyes, blond hair the color of wildflower honey, a perfect heart-shaped face, full lips, flawless complexion, and a figure to match the face. The rest of her, however, clearly reflected her fortune—which clearly wasn't much. Only a very practiced eye would have discerned that she was anything other than a shopkeeper or a superior servant. Her gown was several years out of fashion, plain, the natural color of brown wool, unrelieved by any trimming except some hand-embroidery at the neck, and to Amily's practiced eye, had been turned twice, at least. She had no jewels except the sort of garnet pendant in the shape of a flower that the average daughter of a prosperous craftsman might own. Her chemise was equally plain, linen with no lace or ribbon trimming; her shoes were sturdy things of the sort people wore in the country, that would last for years and years, and then could be resoled, not the sort of dainty embroidered slippers Dia was wearing. Her cloak was plain black wool, also untrimmed, and lined with more wool rather than even rabbit fur.

Daughter of a poor knight with no lands of his own. In the normal course of things, if she had shown no Bardic or Healer talent, no academic brilliance, and did not find the gumption to join the Guard on her own, she would probably have married. And married someone very like her father, or perhaps a moderately well off farmer with the sort of large house he styled a "manor." But without parents to arrange this sort of thing for her, she'd been thrown on the hands of her nearest relatives, who had, without a doubt, taken her in only because leaving her in the lurch to fend for herself would have reflected badly on them.

"Lady Dia," the young woman said—in a voice that was low and sweet, and very pleasant to listen to. "I was hoping you would consider me for a position in the Queen's Handmaidens. What little obligations I have can be instantly discharged, and no one in the household I am in at present would begrudge me this opportunity, should you grant it."

Dia steepled her fingers and looked bland. "Lady Keira, I will be frank with you. There are some . . . awkward difficulties, regarding that."

They all waited, with Amily holding her breath, to see what Keira would make of that.

Keira visibly straightened her back. "Ah, so you heard the rumors. Then I will be frank with you, Lady Dia," Keira replied. "I believe that I know precisely why this group is being put together. The King would like eyes and ears in dubious households, and who better than young women? If they are plain, they are regarded with about as much consideration as the kitchen cat, and if they are handsome, they are boasted to . . . or hear much across a pillow."

All three of the ladies exchanged a startled look. Dia cleared her throat slightly. "Even if that were true, Lady Keira . . . that does not negate the rumors concerning you, which might make placing you problematic."

"I think that you can turn that to your advantage," the young woman replied immediately, taking several steps nearer, until she stood within arm's length of them. At this distance, although she appeared calm, Amily could tell that she had clasped her hands together to keep them from shaking.

"Firstly, there are not many who know me by sight, and I am related to all of them. Secondly, sooner or later, you are going to want someone who is willing to climb into someone's bed. I have nothing to lose."

"My goodness," Lady Dia said mildly. "You certainly do not believe in beating around the bush."

"My lady, I cannot afford to," Keira said, and to Amily's surprise, there was very little bitterness in her tone. "I have very little time to make use of my looks. Before my cousin seduced me, there was a chance I could use them to make a decent marriage. Now? I am certain that my dear cousins would make certain that rumors followed me so that any hope of *that* would be ruined. No one will take me as her companion except perhaps a bitter old woman who will use my foolishness to bully me at every turn. And what else am I fit for? I can't farm, I can't cook, and I loathe children—and that's if anyone would take me for any of those things that didn't also plan on using me for his pleasure. We both know how unlikely that is."

Amily was forcibly reminded of the lecture that Lady Dia had given Violetta. Here was someone without means to hide the fact that she had been romantic and foolish, and had been through everything Dia had threatened Violetta with, and worse.

"All I know is how to look beautiful, how to make someone else look beautiful, and the usual useless things highborn girls are taught. I can sing, dance, and play a lute passably. I can embroider and alter a garment. . . ." She shrugged. "You know what we are raised to do as well as I. Nothing of use. So I have one opportunity to make the most of my current skills, whatever other skills you can teach me, and my beauty, and that's as an informant for the King. And I know that the *King* will not desert me and cast me aside as others have, when I have outlived my usefulness."

Her knuckles were absolutely white, and so was her face. Coming here, admitting what had happened to her, and essentially begging them to take her in had cost her a great deal, and Amily could only wonder if Violetta would have had the fortitude to admit what an idiot she had been and do the same.

:I don't think Violetta is a good candidate for the Hand-maidens,: Rolan advised.

:Honestly, neither do I.:

"Sit down, Keira," Lady Dia told her quietly. "It clearly took much strength for you to come here and speak so frankly to us. And you were quite clever to see through our illusions and understand what we intended to accomplish. Even if the Handmaidens were not precisely what you think they are, I would have found a place for you in my household anyway. Courage is always a useful characteristic. Being able to look your own mistakes in the eye and deal with the consequences without whining about it is another." She dimpled. "Besides, my husband likes having pretty women about."

Keira's knees gave out, but Miana had been watching her closely and got a chair under her so that she collapsed into it rather than on the floor. "I—cannot begin to thank you for this," she said, breathlessly. "Lady Emaline—"

"Used your folly to throw you out when her son ruined you, claiming you had seduced him rather than him being the aggressor, then spread rumors herself to make sure if you told anyone a different story, hers would have reached their ears first," Dia replied, pouring a cup of water and pressing it into her hand. "This is not the first time I have heard that tale, and it will not be the last, I am sure. But I thought some other cousins took you in?"

"Not willingly," said Keira. "And only when I threatened Lady Emaline Keteline that I would go to the Heralds and demand a Truth Spell on myself and her son Brendan to prove that he was the one who lied to me and then discarded me."

Now she looked . . . exhausted. "I leave it to your imagination how these cousins treat me. At least the scullery maids are paid wages and get time off and two suits of clothing a year."

For the first time in this conversation, Lady Dia's expression hardened. And there was a flicker of anger in her eyes. "In that case, I expect you won't be unhappy if I ask you not to return there, even to collect your things."

Keira looked up with an expression of incredulous joy on her face. But Lady Dia held up a cautionary hand. "As I said, I'll find a position in my household. But before I admit you into the Handmaidens, I need to know if you were *absolutely serious* when you made that offer to climb into someone's bed, if that was what was required. I won't ask you to do that unless it is absolutely necessary—but you are right, I suspect that at some point I *may* need someone to do that, and I don't want to count on someone who will back out at the last minute."

Keira's chin came up, and she looked Lady Dia straight in the eyes. "It will serve Valdemar. I'm tired of being a nothing, doing nothing, and helping no one, not even myself." She shrugged. "I enjoyed being in a man's bed when I thought Brendan loved me. I expect I can use that as a tool. I've been called a whore . . . and I am not so sure anymore that being a whore is a shameful thing. A whore is honest, which is more than I can say for a man who tells you he loves you just to bed you, and throws you out with the fruit skins when his mother objects." Her jaw tightened a little. "I considered actually turning to whoring rather than endure how my cousins are treating me, but then I realized they'd probably declare me insane and lock me up in a little room rather than be shamed in public that way."

"Very likely," Miana agreed. "They'd probably hire some street tough to hit you on the head and abduct you. Assuming they didn't hire some street tough to quietly murder you instead before word got around what you were doing, which I think would be far more likely."

Keira sucked in her breath in alarm. "That . . . hadn't occurred to me."

"Actually, Miana," Amily said, "Declaring her insane would
be easier. There would be nothing to explain; dead bodies tend
to require explanations."

Keira looked a bit more relieved.

Dia's expression softened. "My dear Lady Keira, it is not
often I find someone with the ability to look at herself and her
situation as directly and honestly as you have." She patted the
hand that was still holding the goblet of water. "Consider
yourself the first of my pupils."

"I approve as well, my lady," Miana said, with a firm nod.

They both looked at Amily, who shrugged. "I could put her
under coercive Truth Spell in order to make sure everything
she said was in order, but we all know she'd pass it," Amily
said dryly. "I just have one question. Why *didn't* you just go
straight to the King and demand the Truth Spell on you and
that little slimy bastard?"

Keira let out her breath in a long sigh. "As long as it was
within the family, it was nothing but rumors, and I thought
that with Cousin Jerrold I could live it down and perhaps . . . I
don't know, I wasn't thinking that far ahead. But if I brought
it out in the public, no matter *what* the Truth Spell revealed,
there would always be people who would say I tempted him,
or I teased him, or I had it coming, and it wouldn't be rumors
anymore. I'd be in a worse situation than I am now, because
the family would completely disown me, and I would still have
no way to support myself. Other than whoring, and all I have
to recommend myself *there* is that I'm pretty."

Miana stood up. "Lady Dia, if you don't mind, I'll get Keira
settled into a room, and arrange for wardrobe and other needful things. Am I correct in thinking that we are going to see
about changing her appearance somewhat, and giving her a
new identity if we can?"

Dia sucked on her lower lip, then slowly nodded. "First we need to know how many people in the Court know her by sight. Not many, I don't think. . . ."

"No one outside House Holberk," said Keira. "They never allowed me to go to any Court functions, and never allowed me to show my face when there were visitors. My entire function was to wait on Lady Emaline, and when I was sent to Cousin Jerrold, it was to stay out of sight and do whatever they told me to. Originally I think, perhaps, that eventually they planned on marrying me to Cousin Nathan. He's the only one outside the immediate family they let me be around."

"Nathan? Nathan Delmat?" Lady Dia snorted. "That would be to throw him a sweet so he'd will all his possessions to Emaline, I suppose. Dear gods. I'd rather bed a boar." She waved her hand at the young woman and Miana. "Off with you. Miana, I think there are gowns of mine stored in the wardrobe in the Red Suite that just need some taking in at the bust to fit her. The shifts and under-things should do well enough as they are. I'll send a note to Jorthun to let him know we have a guest and the first recruit, and I'll see you at dinner, Keira."

Miana led the young woman off, and Lady Dia sat back in her chair and looked at Amily with astonishment. "Well!" she said, finally.

"That . . . wasn't how I expected our recruitment to go," Amily replied. "Do you think that anyone else has guessed what we intend to do?"

Dia chewed on her lower lip for a moment, then shook her head. "No . . . no, I don't think so. That is an uncommonly sharp young woman, and she must have been searching for some way to escape her situation for some time. I'm not entirely sure *she* was certain until she came here and gauged our reactions. Nevertheless, we should be very careful whom we approach from now on. We should go to *no one* that we are not already certain we want."

"Agreed," Amily replied, with a nod. "Good gods. I wonder how Jorthun is going to take this?"

"He'll laugh," said Dia, wryly. "That's the problem with having a charming husband who treats me as an equal. It means when I find myself in a situation where I deserve to be laughed at . . . I am. He doesn't coddle my feelings at all."

"Would you want him to?" Amily asked teasingly.

"Are you serious? Of course not," Dia chuckled. "It means I get to laugh at *him,* too."

———————

Mags found himself at Lord Jorthun's dinner table, a position that was unexpected to say the least. He hadn't really known what to expect when Amily contacted him via Rolan to suggest it. He'd *seen* the enormous formal dining room, rather like a Great Hall, but with the installation of permanent tables. There had been a dais, just like the one at the Palace, with a High Table on it, and three long tables at right angles to the dais where guests presumably ate. Would the Lord and Lady dine alone on the dais with the rest of them sitting at one of the lower tables? Would the servants dine with them, or would they all sit uncomfortably in that echoing room, trying to make some sort of conversation?

But when he arrived, he was directed to a smaller room at the side of the dining hall. To his relief, there was a much smaller table there, and Amily, Dia, Lord Jorthun, Miana and a stunningly beautiful young woman he did not know were there. The footman directed him to an empty seat beside Amily, and quickly brought him a filled plate from the sideboard. It appeared that when he was not hosting vast parties, Lord Jorthun much preferred a far less formal sort of dining, where everything was brought at once and set out on the sideboard, and you asked the footman for whatever you wanted.

". . . walnut should do a very good permanent stain to your hair," Amily observed, "And your skin, too, if you'd like to pose as the hearty type who is fresh from the country and used to being outside in all weathers." She turned to Mags. "This is Keira, she is the first of the Queen's Handmaidens. Keira, this is Herald Mags."

Keira showed no recognition of his name, which was something of a relief. Normally young ladies knew him as the Kirball champion, and he didn't much feel like playing that particular card tonight.

It had been a very long and hard day, in fact; it had begun with him literally running down a professional poisoner-for-hire he and Nikolas had been trying to catch for months, and ended in Law Court in which he had used coercive Truth Spell in three cases in a row. Right now he was very happy to be sitting here in this handsome room, eating some of the finest roast beef he'd ever touched in his life, with people whose minds didn't make him want to crawl into a hole.

"Very pleasant to meet you, Lady Keira," he said politely, and went back to eating.

"*Mags!*" Amily laughed. "Don't you even want to know why we want to change her appearance? Don't you even have an opinion?"

"I figgered you had a good reason for it, but I wouldn't use walnut," he said. "It's too inconsistent. You can get dark patches on the skin that look like a disease. Unless you *want* her to look like she's diseased . . . which I'd think would make her not very attractive as a handmaiden."

Miana and Amily exchanged a look of *why didn't we think of that* and Lady Dia just laughed out loud.

"I had a couple thoughts," Mags continued. "You know how highborn that don't have their own manors end up getting put up in suites in the Palace? And you know how there's not much room for servants? Well, seems to me that *right* off, there's a use for the Handmaidens whiles they're gettin' trained."

"Ah! I see where this is going!" Lord Jorthun exclaimed. "We have the King request that the ladies in question send their handmaidens and personal maids away, and make use of the Queen's Handmaidens. Sharing them, as it were."

"The Seneschal might vote to give you a medal," Amily said. "All those personal maids are forever getting into trouble, what with the Guard barracks right on the Palace grounds, and the handmaidens are forever fighting and jockeying with each other." She made a face. "Not that the highborn ladies are any better, but at least they don't resort to clothing-sabotage and hair-pulling contests."

Mags gave her a startled look. "Serious?" he asked incredulously.

"They cut a rival's skirts to ribbons or dump ink or wine all over it just before a High Feast," Amily told him. "And since they have to use the same back stairs as the servants, they'll ambush each other out of sight of their masters and get into catfights. If you thought all the jockeying for husbands was vicious among the girls of Violetta's rank, you should see what happens among the handmaidens."

"I can't personally vouch for that," said the stranger, with a little frown. "I was never allowed near Court. But I have heard stories."

"Well, *I* can vouch for it," said Miana. "Since I live here with my Lord and Lady, I never was on the receiving end of any nastiness, but I've certainly come upon girls in a tussle over some fellow who probably didn't even know either of them existed, and my Lady can vouch for the fact that we've had to find clothing on short notice for someone whose gown was destroyed."

"As I said, the Seneschal will want to kiss you," Amily told him.

"And this will give our girls a chance to show their paces," mused Lady Dia, in between sips of wine. "It's not as if the ladies who come to Court *need* their handmaidens in the way they do at home. There's entertainment nearly everywhere you look, the Palace is full of pages and footmen and other servants."

"Most of the time, they sit idle," Miana confirmed. "Which is how they manage to get into so much mischief. Herald Mags, this was an excellent idea."

"I've been known to have one or two," Mags chuckled. "But why are you wantin' to make Keira look different?"

"Because she's essentially run away," Amily told him. "There probably aren't many people who know her on sight, but it would be just our luck for one of them to turn up—"

Mags held up a hand. "Whoa. When you want someone kept away from folks that'll recognize her, the thing you do is just that. Keep her away. So I reckon for right now, Keira's stayin' here? Any chance at all of those folks as know her'll come here?"

Now everyone looked at Dia, who pursed her lips. "Keira, did you drop any hints that you were coming here?"

She shook her head. "The only reason *I* knew about the Queen's Handmaidens is because Cousin Jerrold's daughter came *flying* back after the Princess's Court full of how she wanted Cousin Jerrold to get her a place in them. She and her mother and father got into a full-scale fight over it, with Cousin Jerrold absolutely incensed over the very idea. He doesn't want Tiayada catching the eye of any man, period. He fully intends for her to go into a temple so he can save the money he'd otherwise spend on a dower. I doubt any of them knew I was listening to them. I just grabbed my cloak and began walking up to the top of the Hill, hoping Lady Dia would give me an audience and hear me out."

"We didn't let her go back, and we haven't sent for her things yet," Dia put in.

"Don't," Mags advised. "For all they know, she went for a walk an' didn't come back. Hasn't been a hue and cry raised, neither. My guess is, there ain't—isn't—gonna be." He raised an eyebrow at Keira. "Likely you know best the reason for that."

"They'd be completely relieved if I fell off the face of the world," Keira replied. "I certainly got told as much three and four times a day."

Mags paused, and thought a little more. "Best let sleeping dogs lie," he said finally. "If they *do* decide to let the Watch an' the Guard know you're missing, I'll see about plantin' some stories of you bein' seen ridin' out of town with a good-looking fellow. I guess that wouldn't grieve them any?"

Keira shook her head. "Not in the least. I'm of no consequence and nothing but a burden. The gods know they've all, at one time or another, said I'd be better off dead."

"There you go. Forget the disguises," Mags said. "Lord Jorthun, *you* know."

"Indeed I do," his lordship said, much amused. "Disguises are three parts acting to one part appearance, and you, my dear, are no actress. You *will* be when we are done training you, but you are not, yet."

"Oh aye," Mags said with a grin. "You will be."

Keira looked from Mags, to Lord Jorthun and back again. "Is that a promise?" she asked, a little apprehensively. "Or a threat?"

"Both," they answered in chorus, causing Amily, Dia and Miana to break out into laughter.

Keira only shook her head. "Bring on your lessons," she said, bravely. "As many as you like. I already told Lady Dia; I'll do whatever is needed, and master it."

Mags smiled. Because he had no doubt she would.

$\mathbf{M}$ags awoke to find Amily curled up in his arms; he thought he must have turned over in his sleep and was holding her for his own comfort. He couldn't remember his dreams, but they had been uneasy, full of vague premonitions and unsettling visions.

"What's wrong?" Amily murmured. It was quite dark, so he knew it was far too early to be up. The bed, and Amily, would have felt delicious, warm and comforting, and it should have soothed him back to sleep immediately. But it didn't. This was going to be one of those nights.

At least I ain't waking up screaming, dreaming of the mine falling in on me, or faceless spirit-things in the mine hunting me.

But he knew he had to explain himself to Amily so at least she could go back to sleep. "Thins are goin' too well," he said without thinking. "Ever'thin's just tickin' over too nice. Some-thin's gonna go wrong."

"Thank you, my Lord Optimist," she replied, touched his cheek, and was back to sleep within a few moments. Which was entirely sensible of her, since she already knew that when this sort of mood came on him, there was nothing to do but wait it out and see if his pessimism bore fruit. The first few times this had happened, she'd stayed awake with him, but he had finally persuaded her that the best thing she could do for both of them was to go back to sleep herself.

Dallen could usually talk him out of this mood, but Dallen was asleep, and he didn't want to disturb his Companion in the middle of the night when he already knew there were things he could do for himself. So he gently disengaged himself from Amily when he was sure she was *quite* asleep again, and went to make himself some warm honey-milk. Sitting down in front of the fire in their common room, he set to work breaking the hold of his anxiety over his mind.

You're not a Foreseer, he reminded himself, as he sat staring into the coals of their fire, watching the colors come and go. *And as you know good and well, even they can be mistaken. They always see things that are going to happen, all right, but sometimes their interpretation is miles off.*

He himself was proof of that. The Foreseers had thought *he* was going to kill the King. In fact, what happened was that he had prevented the Companions from being burned to death in their stable, had nearly died at the hands of the hired killer doing the arson. It was the King had saved his life, which is why the Foreseers had Seen him, the King, and a great deal of blood. What they remembered from their visions was often fragmentary, and subject to interpretation.

Still : . . he shook his head as he sipped his drink, because his instincts were that this anxiety of his was not faulty. His own experience was that you could never trust it when matters were going too well. Bad luck tended to average out. It was always better to have lots of little things go wrong, so you weren't blindsided by one big thing.

And things were going too well. He and Amily had managed to sideslip problems by getting married quietly. The Queen's Handmaidens had two more recruits, young ladies Miana knew, plus Keira, who was working just as hard as she had promised. No one had reported Keira missing, which meant her relations were just as glad she was gone. Tuck was hard at work, making some truly ingenious gadgets for climbing, suggested by Mags' memories of similar instruments the Sleepgivers used. No one was harassing him. Lord Jorthun's man of business had acquired the building where Tuck's "shed" was—but for Lady Dia, rather than Lord Jorthun, and using her money. There were six of Mags' orphans installed as hallboys in various homes. The Seneschal absolutely *loved* the idea of sending personal handmaidens packing, and was planning how to rearrange the Palace to allow for a Queen's Handmaidens dormitory.

Even the arrangements for the now-unnecessary wedding were going swimmingly. Everyone involved was quietly excited about it and enjoying the work they were doing on it. Now that Lady Dia had three sets of hands to help her with the planning, she was down to planning details rather than painting the broad strokes.

Yes, things were going entirely too well. He sat and stared at the coals, wondering when Fate or the Universe was going to drop a mountain on him. And what it could possibly be. He stared, and stared until he noticed his hands were aching where they were clenched around the mug.

He looked down at his mug, and realized he had finished the milk. At least now he felt worn out, and his brain was tired, tired enough to let go of the problem for now. Time to go to bed again. Maybe his dreams would turn pleasant.

He still wasn't going to stop looking over his shoulder, however. Not when things were going this well.

———————

This was a full Formal Court day; a day when the King took only the most urgent petitioners, and received important visitors. Amily was at her usual position, behind the King's throne and to his right. The Greater Audience Chamber was not the most comfortable room in the Palace, except for ideal days in spring, fall, and a bit in summer, when the windows could be thrown open and a good breeze came through. In winter, the size made it almost impossible to heat properly, and the people farthest from the fireplace behind the throne had better be wearing their cloaks. This was one reason why Lady Dia's little muff-spaniels were so popular; at least a lady who had one would have warm hands during the long Court sessions. In summer, when there wasn't a breeze, the air was close and faintly stifling, and the various perfumes the courtiers wore mingled in a way that was not quite pleasant.

Today it was cold, although there were some hardy bulb-flowers out in the gardens that were making a brave attempt to bloom. The snowdrops were particularly thick, and some of the ladies were wearing some in their hair. The attendance was thin today; those who had estates to oversee had packed up and taken their families back to them, not to return until after the Harvest was over. By the time the pleasant days of Spring arrived, there would only be the people attending who never left Haven. There were those like Lord Jorthun, who left their estates to the management of trusted others, and only rode out to them once or twice a year to inspect them. There were those whose fortunes were linked to things other than crops and land. And there were those whose duty was to represent their vast, noble families while other members of the family spent their time happily far away from the Court.

For those who resided here year-round, Formal Courts were a must; with the attendance lower, it was easier to maneuver for status or power, and much easier to get the ear of someone in the Royal Family. Amily looked out over the courtiers and noted that the braver—or hardier—of them had put away their winter things and were displaying new spring outfits. Or trying, at least. The effect was rather spoiled by wintery shawls and capes. . . .

Still, it was, like the first bold songbirds to appear after the winter snows, the harbinger of better days to come, this timid display of fluttery sleeves, trailing ribbons, light colors, and lace replacing velvets in jewel tones, wools in more somber colors, and fur.

The King, well aware of how cold the Greater Audience Hall was, wore the winter version of his Royal Herald's Whites—which differed from Formal Whites in that all the trim and decoration was in gold and blue, not silver and blue. Like the King, Amily was in winter Whites and she was very glad for the extra lining to the tunic and sleeves.

The King was a handsome man, square-faced, brown hair faintly showing a bit of silver, with a ready smile and kind eyes. Prince Sedric was the image of his father; though Sedric's face was longer and his hair was a bit lighter, there was absolutely no doubt whose son he was.

As she was musing over this, there was a stir at the door to the Greater Audience Chamber. The heavy wooden doors opened, and a Court Crier stepped in and took two steps to the side. "My Lord Aurebic Lemanthiel, Ambassador of His Most Royal Majesty, King Klerence of Menmellith, and his delegation!"

What?

Well, *that* caused a stir. Even Amily was startled. So far as she was aware, the Ambassador was not expected. The invitation to Menmellith to send a delegation to the wedding was not due to be sent out until next week at the earliest. As the group entered the Audience Chamber and strode down toward the King, she was further startled to note they were all still in sober traveling gear, and had barely paused to brush the worst of the road-dirt from themselves before coming here.

That . . . was not good.

Maybe Mags' fretting last night wasn't just over-thinking.

:Rolan, we didn't hear anything from Heralds between the Border and here about them coming, did we?: she asked her Companion urgently.

Rolan was baffled. *:No. Nothing. And they must have traveled fast enough to nearly ruin their horses. The grooms in the stable are having to administer emergency aid to the poor things—and these are animals that were otherwise carefully cared for.:*

All that Amily could think was what Mags had said last night. *Things are going too well. . . .*

The Ambassador and his entourage reached the throne. Kyril stood up to greet them. "I see you have come in haste, my friends," the King said, quietly, before they could even greet him, keeping his voice pitched low enough that it reached only the Ambassador and perhaps the two men nearest him. "Is your business urgent enough that I need close the Court?"

A flicker of gratitude passed over the Ambassador's weary face. "Yes, your Majesty," he said, in a voice that sounded a bit rough, probably from fatigue. "It is."

That was Amily's cue. She stepped forward a pace or two, and nodded at one of the Guardsmen, who rapped the butt of his spear on the floor of the dais three times, loud enough to silence the murmurs going all through the Court.

"His Majesty, King Kyril of Valdemar, declares that this Formal Court is closed!" Amily cried, making sure her voice carried to the back of the room. "Should any have business to be brought before the King, let it be known to the Seneschal and it will be addressed."

Not that it looked as if there had been much business left anyway, today. *And what there had been was probably driven into the farthest corners of their minds.* Ambassadors from other kingdoms didn't just show up, fresh from the road and fatigued to death, unless there was something seriously wrong. Right now, *what's gone wrong* was in the mind of everyone here. Some would linger to try and find out. Some would seek other sources of information. There would even be some who would pack up and flee to presumably "safe" or at least "safer" places in the country. No one had forgotten that assassins had penetrated right onto the grounds of the Palace not that long ago, and no one wanted to be the "unintended victim" if they managed again.

Within moments, the Guard had ushered the uneasy and wildly curious courtiers out, canceled all further business, and shut the doors on everyone but the King, his Guards, and Amily. The Ambassador began to speak, but the King held up his hand.

"Wait a moment. You are clearly exhausted, and surely nothing you must say is so terrible that it cannot wait a quarter candlemark while I have seats and wine fetched," the King said, and this time it was more than a flicker of gratitude that passed over the Ambassador's face. "You would not have come here to speak with me directly if whatever brought you here cannot be mended, either. So wait a moment."

The King sent servants running, and when they returned with a chair for the Ambassador and stools for everyone else, the Ambassador saved himself from collapsing into the chair by an act of pure will, though he did sit down heavily into it. The rest of his entourage hesitated before taking a seat, however. The Ambassador had been given specific leave, but . . .

except when eating, or attending some festivity or performance, protocol dictated that one did not *sit* in the presence of a reigning monarch.

"Sit!" ordered Kyril. "You are all exhausted. We will not stand on ceremony with you in such condition."

Now Amily wished she had Mags' Gift of Mindspeech. She would have given a great deal to be able to pick up their surface thoughts. The best she could do was employ the skill she had acquired over the years of reading hints of expression and body language.

As the rest of the entourage sorted themselves out and gratefully sank down onto the stools, servants with wine and food arrived, and the Ambassador wearily accepted a cup poured for him. As he drank, Amily got a chance to study him further.

If he and his men were anything to judge by, the people of Menmellith were as mixed as those of Valdemar. The Ambassador was swarthy, with black hair shot through with silver; his face was round, but in no way soft. His eyes were a dark gray, and at the moment, stormy with suppressed emotion under heavy brows. But he had among his entourage men who were fair-haired and dark, and even one who was so blond his hair looked like fine gold thread. He and his men wore clothing that looked exotic to Amily's eyes; heavy lambswool robes, divided for riding, with baggy trews beneath. The robes fastened up along one shoulder, and were trimmed with bands woven in colorful patterns; the Ambassador's had a background of gold threads. Amily was not a judge of fabric the way Princess Lydia was, but the garments looked very costly. They all had what she assumed were familial badges on the left breasts of their robes, embroidered in colors that matched the trim.

"Now," the King said, when they had somewhat caught their breaths and looked as if they were beginning to recover.

"What in the names of all the gods brought you posthaste to us?"

The Ambassador took a deep breath, and looked up at the King, soberly.

"War, your Majesty," he said.

It was a good thing that the Court had been cleared, because that would almost certainly have caused a panic, and sent rumor flying out the door with some of the courtiers. The King merely furrowed his brows. "Explain, please."

"You know that our King is only ten years of age, Majesty," the Ambassador said. "There are those who are taking advantage of this, raising rebellion in the north of our land." He nodded at one of his men, who brought up a bundle. It looked heavy. The man laid it down on the floor before the King, untied it and opened it, showing that it was a bundle of weapons; bows, arrows, two or three swords. "These weapons were captured from the rebels, Majesty," the Ambassador said heavily. "They were supplied by persons unknown from outside of our Kingdom. But as you can see for yourself if you examine them . . ." He paused. ". . . they were made in Valdemar. They all bear makers' marks, and all those marks are from well known armories within the borders of your land. And this is no fluke. There are thousands more like them, not just arms, but armor. If Valdemar does not put a stop to this . . . it will mean war."

———

The Ambassador had been escorted to his quarters, and now, presumably was sleeping as well as a man in his current situation could. The King had called together an emergency Council. It consisted only of his Inner Council, his most trusted advisors—about half the size of the full Council.

Unlike the full Council, the only merchant or Guild Master

here was Lydia's uncle, Master Soren. Amily was not certain why Soren would be useful in a session where the discussion was imminent war and perhaps how to prevent it, but the King wanted him here, so here he sat. Prince Sedric and Princess Lydia were at the King's right, as was Amily. As the rest of the Council members took their seats, the King leaned over to Amily. "I know you don't have that sort of Gift," he whispered, "But what do you *think* is the Ambassador's state of mind?"

"I don't think that he personally believes that the Valdemaran Throne is behind funneling the weapons to the rebels," Amily whispered back. "But the Menmellith Council, or at least enough of it to make up a majority, does."

The King's expression didn't change by much, just a slight tightening of the lips. "If he'll come talk to me alone, I'd like you to arrange that."

Amily only had time to nod before all the rest were seated. The King rapped on the table to get their attention. "I am fairly certain no rumors have escaped about the purpose of the Menmellith Ambassador turning up, but I am sure you all know he did, that he clearly came in haste, and that therefore what brought him must have been urgent. And by the mere fact that I called an emergency Council session, you deduced that it must be extremely urgent. This is true. It appears we are on the brink of war with Menmellith." While they were still speechless, he continued. "Their King is a child of ten, and the Council rules until he comes of age. Unsurprisingly, given such circumstances, a rebellion has broken out, led by one of the King's cousins. *Someone* has smuggled arms in apparently significant numbers to the rebels; those arms all have makers' marks of armories in the south of Valdemar. The Menmellith Council has jumped to the reasonable conclusion that Valdemar is supporting the rebellion, and evidently are debating war with us."

Ebon Aleric, the Lord Martial, who attained his position entirely on merit and experience rather than wealth and connections, cleared his throat.

"Yes Lord Aleric?" the King prompted.

"They are scarcely in a position to prosecute such a war, your Highness," Ebon pointed out. " 'Tis folly to fight a war on two fronts."

"Ordinarily I would agree with you," the King replied. "But they must have some strategy in mind even to contemplate it. The Council of Menmellith is not composed of dotards, or armchair fighters. I think we should assume they must have some idea of how they could manage such a feat in mind, and make our plans from there."

"Obviously, we *aren't* supplying weapons," put in Master Soren. Who then paused, and added doubtfully, "Are we?"

"If anyone is, it is without the knowledge of anyone here in this room," the Seneschal said firmly, before the King could speak. "What's more, I have seen no expenditure out of the Treasury sufficient to account for enough weaponry to cause the Menmellith Council to assume we are."

"You couldn't sneak enough out of the Treasury to buy a good hunting dog without Lord Barethias noticing," Prince Sedric observed, making a couple of the Council members laugh nervously.

The King tapped on the table to get their attention. "So, what we need to do, and quickly, is to find out *who* is supplying these weapons, *why* they are doing so, and *how* they are getting them over the Border."

"And how they are buying them in the first place without anyone making note of it," Amily pointed out.

"And *quietly,*" the King added. "Whoever is doing this does not want attention, and probably is unaware that Menmellith has discovered what is going on. I'm exceedingly disturbed by all of this, because I can think of many possible sources and reasons for someone to be funneling weapons into another Kingdom, and I am not happy about any of them." He looked around the table. "You are all here because I know you can be trusted. Assume no one outside of this room can be."

Into the silence, Amily said the one thing everyone was thinking, but no one dared say. "Does that include the Heralds?"

"Yes," said the King, the Prince, and her father, all at the same time. All three looked at each other, and the King gestured to Nikolas to explain.

"While I am completely certain that no Herald would countenance such a thing, we can't know who every Herald trusts, and if the rest of the Heraldic Circle knows what is going on, someone might innocently alert the guilty party." Nikolas shrugged. "We're only human. Our Gifts are many and varied and not all of them are useful in alerting us to people we shouldn't trust. Some of us trust the wrong people."

"So this stays in this room," the King continued, "Because what goes for the Heralds goes doubly for the rest of the people in *your* lives. No talking to spouse, best friend, trusted counselor, priest, or second-in-command. *No one.* I am going to get more details, if I can, out of the Ambassador. We will reconvene here after dinner. In the meantime, I would like you to think of ways in which we might be able to discover the *who, how,* and *why* of this." He nodded at them all. "We need to get to the bottom of this, and we need to do so quickly."

Amily tapped on the door of the Crown Princess's suite. Lydia herself cautiously cracked the door.

"Would he come?" she whispered.

"He's right here," Amily whispered back, moving aside a little so Lydia could see the exhausted face of the Ambassador.

He had gotten food, more wine, and a good hot bath and change of clothing, but no real rest. Still, he had been willing to come with Amily for a private meeting with the King. That spoke volumes for him, so far as Amily was concerned. He couldn't have assassinated a pocket pie in his current state of exhaustion, and he very well knew it. So his only reason for agreeing to a private meeting must be exactly what King Kyril hoped; he did not believe that Valdemar was supplying the rebellion, and he was going to tell everything he knew.

"Come in, quickly." Lydia opened the door and the two of them slipped inside. They had gotten this far without anyone noticing only because Amily had taken all the servants' corridors. Growing up in the Palace as she had, Amily knew every inch of the servants' corridors. Most of the Heralds here in residence generally did too; it was the best way to get around if you didn't want anyone highborn to know where you were going.

The solar of Lydia's suite was quite empty—except for the King, who waited for the Ambassador before the fire. In fact, the entire suite was empty; Lydia had sent away all her servants and her ladies, pleading a headache. The solar was a corner room that got light most of the day during the winter and was shaded during the summer. Lydia encouraged her ladies to be productive, so aside from the usual embroidery frames and fancywork projects there were many books that had been laid aside, and a musical instrument or two. There were window seats in all the windows, but at the moment the only seats occupied were the ones at the hearth, heavily padded and comfortable.

"Thank you for coming, Ambassador," the King said. "And please sit down immediately. You and I have known each other for a very long time. Let's not have any ceremony; there is a problem here we must get to the bottom of."

All of the tension drained away from the Ambassador's

body, and he took a seat across from the King, easing himself down into the cushions as if he ached. He probably did. Riding as long and hard as he had was no joke, even for a young and seasoned rider. "We grew up together in a sense, my lord King," he said reaching for the goblet of wine the King handed him. "I was esquire to my father, the former Ambassador, when you were serving in the train of your own Father as Crown Prince, and I recall many weeks of the two of us amusing each other while we waited out meetings on the Border. And of course, we have had many dealings since you became King. I had hoped you had not suddenly changed into a man I no longer recognized. I am unspeakably relieved to discover I was correct."

The King spread his hands. "Tell me what you know. The people I trust are completely in the dark, and my Seneschal tells me there is no discrepancy in the Treasury to account for the mass purchase of weapons."

The Ambassador sipped his wine, carefully choosing his words. A good habit in a diplomat, Amily thought. "The King's cousin, Astanifandal, made no secret of the fact that he felt he should have been named Regent, or at least Lord Protector, when the little King's parents died of that fever that swept the country last summer. When winter arrived, he decided to act on that discontent and raise an army." The Ambassador paused, and then drank half the wine, and the King poured him more, as it was obvious he needed it. "Winter is not as bad a season for making war as it is in Valdemar," he continued. "The roads are firm, the weather generally is—I'm maundering."

"You're exhausted," the King pointed out. "I'm surprised you can still string words together in any coherent fashion. I'm very certain I couldn't, after a flat-out ride from Menmellith to here."

The Ambassador shrugged, as if his own exhaustion didn't

matter. "The point is, he formed an army from his stronghold; the northwest corner of the country, where his lands are and where the nearest landed men loyal to him dwell. He put together quite an alliance, and managed to raise enough money for a mercenary army as well as his own sworn fighters. And he's been fighting a shrewd campaign. He doesn't pillage the countryside, he moves slowly, but surely, and he leaves behind him people who are convinced that a strong, adult man is a better King than a boy with a Council."

King Kyril frowned. "Given that . . . if I were faced with such a persuasive argument, and the fellow that was in charge of the armies had kept his men from looting my property, I'd find it hard to disagree with him," he replied.

The Ambassador groaned a little. "Honestly, I feel the same. I wish that the old King had named a Regent, just in case something happened, rather than leaving things in chaos. I think that the boy will make a very good King one day, but having a child on the throne is like setting out a feast in front of the starving and expecting them not to touch it." He shook his head sadly. "Rethwellan has a sword that chooses the proper King. At least, I think it's a sword. You lot have your horses. I wish we had something, something that gave a definitive answer so ambitious cousins would just have to swallow their bile and deal with it. But wishes buy nothing; the boy *is* my King and I swore my fealty to him. And the Council thinks they can make a bargain with Rethwellan to crush his forces between ours and theirs—then move north with their help and take some of Valdemar to teach you a lesson."

A less temperate man than Kyril would probably have shouted, or burst into a bout of swearing, or flung the wine in the Ambassador's face. Kyril just tapped the rim of his goblet against his lower lip. "They could do that," he said, finally. "We have treaties with Rethwellan, certainly, but if we really *were* supplying the rebels with weapons, I believe they could reasonably say they assume we'd violate the treaties we have with them as well. We have no other ties binding us than those treaties, not even marriages with highborn across our borders. I have not got the faintest idea *why* Rethwellan would want stony hills fit only for pasturing sheep and goats and hill ponies. . . ." Then he shook his head. "Forgive me, I am trying to be humorous in the light of a serious situation. How *likely* is the Council to decide this, and how long do you think it will take them?"

"I left on my own recognizance when I realized how near to it they were." The Ambassador turned the goblet around and around in his hands. "I left others whom I trust to try and persuade them into some sense, while I came north to warn you. But all it will take is one or two more significant victories to tilt the balance against you. As for how long?" He shrugged. "It's Spring. That is in your favor. Astanifandal cannot start riding his men roughshod over newly planted fields and through herds with lambs and calves without losing everything he has gained by treating the common folk well. Moreover, *his* men who are not mercenaries must return to their own lands if he is to be able to feed and support his forces. That means the best that the mercenaries can do is hold what he has already taken. So . . . you have a moon, perhaps two."

"Majesty—" Amily interrupted, tentatively.

Both of them turned to look at her as if they had forgotten she was there. "Speak," Kyril ordered her.

"The Seneschal has said that the money for these weapons did not come from the Treasury. Although he did not say so, I think he also means it did not come from taxes being held back; he knows to the half-copper-bit how much can be expected in a given year." She took a steadying breath. This was where her intensive study of old records for all those years was proving its worth. "Money does not spring into being on its own. But there is one place where it *does* come out of the ground. The mines."

Kyril's gaze riveted her, and the Ambassador's eyes widened. "Go on," Kyril urged.

"I am not going to speculate on motive," she continued. "We can worry about motive later. But the gem mines would be the easiest place for money to come from that simply seems to appear out of nowhere, buying Valdemaran weapons. Not the gold and silver mines; I am certain that the assessors generally have a very good idea of what can be expected out of the mines producing precious metal. But Mags told me that the gem mines are . . . capricious. One can expect a steady output of average gems, but the unusually valuable ones cannot be predicted. It's not usually possible for the workers to tell if a large gem is an insanely valuable one, or so flawed it is only worth breaking into smaller ones. And all it would take would be for the mine owner to hide away gems of unusual value, smuggle them off to a third party, and have that third party sell them over the Border. The mines would be producing at the 'normal' rate as far as the assessors were concerned. Gems are much more valuable than gold, impossible to trace, and easy to conceal."

"Where did you find this paragon of a young woman, Kyril?" the Ambassador asked, startled into using the King's given name.

The King didn't rebuke him even with a look; he merely answered. "The same place we always do; the Companions find them. I take it you agree with her?"

"It is by far the most logical thing I have heard yet in this situation. But have you any way of proving it?" the Ambassador asked.

Instead of answering him directly, Kyril turned to Amily. "I am very, very, sorry, Herald. I am afraid you are going to have to postpone your wedding."

"Because you are sending Mags back to the mining country," she replied, thinking with relief how glad she was that Mags had foreseen this particular "disaster." "Our duty is to Valdemar, and anything else comes second. We wouldn't have it any other way."

"**W**ell," said Lord Jorthun, rubbing his hands together in glee. *"This* is something I didn't anticipate!"

Lord Jorthun and Lady Dia had been let in on the secret at the orders of the King. With the King's permission, Mags himself had brought the information to them, because he had a plan, but it was going to involve one of the new Queen's Handmaidens. Keira, to be precise.

Mags' dismay must have shown on his face, because Lady Dia turned to her husband with a slight frown. "My love, that is not at all kind. This is a serious situation."

"It is not *yet* a serious situation; when it becomes one, believe me, I shall react with all due gravity," Lord Jorthun replied. "For now, however, I am going to regard this as an opportunity. So, you say that Nikolas is going to trace the origin of the weapons themselves, and dear young Amily is going to pursue what faint leads there may be here in the city by means of your young rapscallion tribe and the new Handmaidens and her own odd but useful Gift. And *you* are going to investigate the gem mines and take Keira with you as a distraction. She is to be a wealthy young widow, and you are her manservant. That allows her to tease any secrets that might be had out of young men, and you to go snooping about."

"That was our plans, m'lord, aye," Mags agreed.

Once again they were seated in the library; it seemed to be the room of choice for conferences that Lord Jorthun did not wish anyone to overhear.

"Excellent." Once again he rubbed his hands in glee. "I shall go along as her doddering old father. That will give us three points of attack."

Mags was, frankly, stunned by the—well he couldn't exactly call it an *offer*, since it was phrased as a *fait accompli*. But he could not deny that having Jorthun, *who had taught Nikolas all he knew*, and who was teaching Mags plenty of new tricks, would be invaluable on this trip. "I—don't know what to say," he managed.

"Pish, don't say anything," Lord Jorthun replied airily. "I can supply the coach and horses, the livery, Keira's wardrobe— well, that is mostly taken care of already—the traveling kit that no highborn lord or lady would *ever* travel without. And you are not going to procure those on short notice. I've been wanting to get out and do something again, and this will be perfect."

"I hope you aren't running away from me," Dia pouted, then dimpled and leaned over the arm of her chair to kiss her husband. "You've been itching to get back to the Game ever since I married you, and I can only thank the gods that at least you've chosen something that isn't likely to get you shot at or chased."

"No, if anyone is going to get shot at or chased, it will be young Mags," Jorthun said complacently. "I assume that your Companion will do what Rolan used to when Nikolas was incognito?"

:I'm going to ghost along with you, staying out of sight, while you ride a regular horse,: Dallen said, helpfully.

"If you mean he'll come along but stay out of sight, then aye, sir," Mags replied.

"Then we'll concoct some means of getting him fed. Fortunately things are beginning to green up nicely, so he'll have that." Jorthun went to a table and got a stylus and palimpsest paper. He returned to his seat and began making notes. "For once, young Mags, you may leave the planning to someone else. We'll be ready to leave in two days."

Mags left feeling a bit stunned. Lady Dia escorted him as far as the front door. "Jorthun has been craving action for . . . well, far too long. There was not a great deal he could do about those foreign assassins the Karsites had hired—it was obvious they were something outside of his expertise, and they were certainly beyond what he is physically capable of handling now." She smiled as he gave her a quizzical glance. "Trust me, Mags, my husband knows exactly what he can do and how far he can trust his body. He won't undertake anything he can't finish."

"So—this is like exactly the sort of thing he's been lookin' for?" Mags hazarded.

She nodded. "He wouldn't wish ill fortune on the Kingdom, but men who are used to being needed get in the habit of it, and it frets them when they feel they are sitting about uselessly."

They paused at the door. Mags looked back in the direction of the library. "He's anythin' but useless, Dia. I didn't figure to get away before a sennight."

"Well, make use of the time wisely," she advised him. "We'll send you a message when all is ready."

Dallen was waiting for him just outside; Jorthun's stable-hands could read Companions almost as well as if *they* had Mindspeech. *:Amily wants to meet you down at Willy the*

Weasel's so you can properly introduce her to your mob.: Dallen tossed his head in amusement at his start. *:Don't worry, she's properly dressed for the area.:*

Well, he had to wonder just what she thought was "properly dressed for the area . . ." It was after dark. And although any pack of thugs trying to rob or harm her was likely to end up a pack of thugs with broken heads, the point was not to draw attention to herself. But then again, she was Nikolas's daughter.

He left Dallen in the usual spot, and transformed himself into Harkon. He chose to travel conventionally rather than over rooftops, just in case he'd run into Amily on the way.

But it took him a few moments to recognize the young tough loitering under Willy the Weasel's street lamp. She looked *nothing* like a girl. And there were plenty of beardless boys in this part of Haven who could gut you before you could blink, so the fact that she wasn't sprouting chin-hair was no indication of whether or not she was dangerous. The rapier and dagger in well-worn sheaths at her side, however, were.

She tugged on her hat brim. "Harkon," she said, pitching her voice low enough it could have passed for a young man's tenor.

"Yer early," he said, deciding to err on the side of caution by not giving her a name, in case she'd dropped one out here already. "C'mon then. Let's get yer innerduced."

He unlocked the next door, and the two of them walked into Aunty Minda's warm and welcoming space.

"That went better than I expected it to," Amily commented in a voice just above a whisper, as the two of them made their way back to where their Companions were—for Amily had used the same inn stabling that Mags had used; he just hadn't noticed Rolan since he had been in something of a hurry to get to Amily before—if—trouble did.

"They're good lads," said Mags. "An' it ain't like they don' take orders from a woman now."

They were walking quickly, but so was nearly everyone else on the street. *Finally* there was a sense that Spring was in the air. Mags hated leaving Amily . . . but on the other hand, he wanted to get into gem country as quickly as he could before the Spring rains started. It was going to take a week to get where they wanted to go by coach, even in good conditions on firm roads. It could take half a moon to get there if they got bogged down.

"Well, I expected some resistance. I'm glad there wasn't any." She trudged on. "I have the sinking feeling this is going to be difficult."

"Gotta be," Mags agreed. "Some'un's runnin' a tricksy deal here. Wouldn' surprise me none iffin there's layers and layers. We gotter unravel 'em somehow. Rolan tell ye what Jorthun tol' me?"

She didn't get a chance to answer him. They had reached the stable. Carefully checking to make sure no one was watching, they slipped inside, then into the hidden storage room where Mags kept his disguises.

"Yes," she said, as they quickly changed, though it was a tight fit for two in the little room. "And I'm not happy, but what can we do? Not happy about how short a time we have left, that is," she amended as they took turns pulling each others' tunics down into place. "I'm actually rather relieved Jorthun is going."

"Ye thin' I need a chaperone," he teased, and opened the door just enough for her to squeeze through it.

"I think he has an awful lot to teach you," she corrected, then left him long enough to get Rolan and saddle him.

"No argument fr'm me on thet score," he said, as they both

mounted up and headed up the Hill. "Wish't ye was comin' wi' me."

"Wish you were staying here," she replied. "But neither of us is going to get our wishes. So let's get up the Hill as fast as we can, so we can make the most of the time we have."

The livery was unexpectedly comfortable. Mags had anticipated something stiff, perhaps scratchy, too warm or too light for comfort. Instead, what he'd gotten was a variation on the Palace livery, made with an eye to the fact that people were going to be working long, hard hours wearing it. Dark brown, heavy canvas trews that had been softened somehow so they were as easy on the skin as good linen. A white linen shirt with a high collar. And a selection of tunics in either brown wool or brown canvas with the design of a lozenge divided in four quarters, two white, two green, embroidered on the breast. He had no idea whose device this was, but Jorthun assured him that no one was going to either recognize it, nor contest Keira's right to it, where they were going.

The same device was on both sides of the coach. Now that was a bit of outright cleverness; Jorthun had shown him how any device at all could be bolted to it and taken off at will. It made him wonder just how many times in Jorthun's past he'd been on missions for the King that had required a change of identity. *Has to be pretty often if he's still got something like this coach about.*

They set off before dawn, in part so that no one of any consequence would see the strange device bolted onto Jorthun's coach, rolling out of Jorthun's gates. It was Mags' first time in a coach. He wasn't entirely sure he liked it. The interior *looked* comfortable enough, all padded plush and fitted out with all sorts of little luxuries. But it rocked and rolled from side to side and bounced up and down in a way that didn't give him any chance to appreciate those luxuries. And in addition, he and Coot were sitting with their backs to the horses—the least comfortable of the two bench-seats in the thing—since they were the servants here.

It had been bad enough as they'd gone slowly through the streets of Haven—but as soon as they made the open road, the driver had picked up speed, and Mags began to regret breakfast.

"Here," Jorthun said, leaning forward and handing him a little metal box. He took it, and opened it carefully. His nose was hit with the scent of fresh mint, and he immediately felt a little better. He took one of the hard, square lozenges, and stuck it under his tongue.

"Thenkee, sir," he said, handing the box back. Jorthun tucked it into one of the many pockets crafted into the sides of the coach.

He hadn't been able to get a good look around the object that would essentially be their home for the next week or so, because it had been so dark. But now the sun had crested the horizon, and he gave the interior a thorough inspection.

The exterior of the coach was dark brown trimmed in lighter brown. The interior matched. The entire interior of the coach had been upholstered and padded; the covering was a soft wool plush, and from the way they were being bounced around, it was obvious *why* every inch but the floor and ceiling was padded. They were sitting so closely together their knees touched. There was a single window in the door of the coach; there were lanterns on either side of the interior of the coach but Mags could not imagine anyone being foolhardy enough to *light* them while the coach was moving. There were a great many of the aforementioned storage pockets in the walls.

He glanced at Coot, who had scooted himself to the edge of

the seat and was watching the countryside scroll by with huge eyes. It took him a moment to realize why.

Coot had never been out of the city.

Coot was wearing the same livery Mags was; Jorthun had advised him to pick out one of his "lads" to bring along as an all-purpose errand boy—and lookout, in case he needed to do anything that required breaking and entering. That seemed an entirely sensible idea to Mags, and Coot had been eager to go.

"Be—be there bears, sor?" Coot wavered, seeing Jorthun's eyes on him.

"Not so near the city," Jorthun replied, soothingly. "Nor wolves. In fact, you are far more likely to be bitten by a farm dog than by a wolf." Coot relaxed a little, and turned his attention back to the window. Jorthun amused himself by answering all of the boy's questions about the things that they passed. Keira dozed; she'd been up quite late, making the last minute adjustments to her new wardrobe. Though how she could sleep in this rocking, rolling coach Mags had no idea.

When they stopped for luncheon, Mags was more than glad to get out and was not at all happy about the fact that he was going to have to get back in again. Coot was now full of all manner of useful information about life in the country, which he was clearly storing in his mind with the alacrity of a squirrel hoarding nuts for the winter. He knew his role and snapped to it, however, as the coach came to a stop. He was the first out the door, got the stepstool in place, and was waiting at one side to assist "Mi'lor' an' Mi'lady" down as Mags did the same on the other. Jorthun and Keira went inside the inn; a servant was sent out with hot ale and pocket pies for Coot, Mags, and the coachman—who was as stolid as a statue of wood, and just about as talkative.

In due course, Jorthun and Keira emerged, Mags and Coot sprang into action again, and they were on their way.

Keira was awake now, and the four of them discussed every

aspect of the coming job that they could think of as the coach bounced and rolled over the rutted road. Jorthun was particularly concerned with making certain that Coot was prepared for what would essentially be—to him—living in the country.

But poor Coot was only getting more confused by the moment. Finally Keira sat up a bit straighter as the coach lurched over another rut, and said, "This is ridiculous. Instead of trying to make poor Coot into what he *isn't,* why don't we simply work with what he is?"

Jorthun furrowed his brows, and offered Mags a flask of water. Mags took it gratefully. "I'm not sure I follow, Keira. . . ."

But Mags understood exactly what she meant. "But how's a lady with money supposed to have come across a street waif an' taken him up? An' *why* would she?"

Keira laughed. "Because I am eccentric, of course. As to how, let's work out a story with enough truth in it that it will be easy to remember. Coot, did you get any education at all?"

Coot nodded enthusiastically. Nothing pleased him better than to be able to show off his reading skills. "Aye, m'lady. Harkon sent me t' Brother Elban at Alia of the Birds, on account of I was hevin'—*having*—problems an' 'e recked Brother Elban could sort 'em out."

"Well then, there you are." Keira nodded. "I like to do little acts of immediate charity. I went to Brother Elban after my husband died and asked if he had a boy he could recommend as a hallboy. He offered me Coot. Coot did so well and was so very good at keeping pickpockets and thieves from me that I promoted him within the month to my personal page."

Coot took up the tale eagerly. "An I'm good at thet, on account'a my old master was a thief an' tried t'make me thieve, too. But I wouldn' hev none'a thet, an runned away t'Aunty Minda."

Jorthun's mouth curved up in a broad smile. "I believe, young man, that Mags should promote you further in his ranks. You have a natural ability at weaving truth into an entirely different sort of cloth than it actually is."

"Not t' mention 'e's a fine breaking-and-entering an' upper-story man," Mags added. "It's already in th' plan, Lord Jorthun. Once this job is over, I figger t' place 'im temporary-like in a page or footman's position so 'e can learn all that 'e needs to know t' fit in with household servants, and then we'll see what other skills 'e can acquire." Mags was not keeping as tight a level of control over his speech as he usually did when speaking with the highborn; he needed to have a certain touch of the common about him in order to fit in with "fellow servants."

Coot beamed. Mags was very happy with the young miscreant. In Aunty Minda's hands, and under Mags' eye, he had blossomed. He'd been extremely good at thievery, so much so that his former master *had* set him to do more difficult jobs—like the theft of a spurious silver vase that had been the bait in a trap Mags had laid for one of those boys. But his heart hadn't been in it. Once given the chance to "go honest" Coot had never looked back.

Good food and a comfortable, warm place to sleep, regular baths, and clothing that wasn't made of rags, had all turned him from a skinny, snot-nosed, filthy urchin no one would trust with a bent pin, to one of Mags' best runners, and someone who had been consistently chosen over the others to carry valuable messages and parcels. But he'd put on a growth spurt, and was being chosen less often these days—people in need of runner-boys generally picked small, nimble ones, under the impression they could dart their way through traffic faster than the taller, lankier ones. So Mags had been about to place Coot as a hall-boy to continue his education in becoming an all-around informant, but it had been obvious Coot's addition to their party would be of tremendous aid, so he'd added Coot at the last minute, and promoted one of the others into the place Coot would have taken.

"I like this," said Lord Jorthun. "There is no reason why Keira should not have done something of the sort. It makes her look soft-hearted, which is not a bad thing, considering we want the gentlemen of this district to underestimate how shrewd she is."

"Ye'll have t' fight some," Mags observed. "On account'a yer a city-lad. But I don' think we coulda drilled ye t'show country in the little time we got."

Coot sniffed disdainfully. "I ain't feared of no fight," he said. "Less'n it's 'gainst some giant. Then I ain't feared t'run."

"If you have to run, come straight to me," said Jorthun. "Or Mags. Make sure your foe follows, so don't run too swiftly."

"Ah!" Coot brightened up. "An' let 'm cotch me an' mebbe get in a lick'r three. Then ye kin get 'im thrashed, an ev'body knows ye ain't takin' no truck wit' people messin' wit' yer sarvants."

"Precisely." Jorthun beamed. "Mags, I am more and more impressed with this boy of yours by the moment. May I take him in hand when this is done with?"

Coot's eyes went as big and round as dinner plates, and Mags felt his own eyes widening. "I'd be more'n happy t'turn 'im over to the Master," Mags said. "This is uncommon kind of ye!"

"Nonsense. It's been far too long since I had a sharp lad to train in the Game. I can't take on more than one at a time—but once we decide Coot is polished, then send me a half dozen more and I'll pick out another." He turned to Coot. "And because I am a master that likes his man to know what direction this is going, boy, I have in mind to train you up as Mags' spymaster. You'll be in charge of others, and take on the riskiest and most dangerous of tasks. Does that suit you?"

"*Does* it!" Coot looked fit to burst with excitement and pride.

Because at his age, he doesn't even think about death . . . Mags thought, with a sudden burst of misgiving.

:But by the time he'll be risking death, he'll be well aware of the hazards, Chosen,: Dallen reminded him. *:And he'll have been taught by the best. You rescued him; he wants to pay you back. He'll never be a Herald, but let the boy be a hero in his own way. He has the right.:*

Dallen was right. And Mags ruthlessly pulled his mind back to the present. There was very little risk even of bodily harm in this venture, at least for Coot. And even that was no worse than every city-bred servant faced when coming out to the country.

"Very good. We'll speak of this when our task is over." Jorthun settled back against the cushions of the coach. "Now, since we are concentrating on you, young man, we need to give you a thorough drilling in your duties as Keira's page. When you are the page in a small household like hers, you generally have the combined tasks of the page, the hall-boy, and the general errand boy. So let's speak about shoe-cleaning. I understand you have never done it. . . ."

———

Over his lifetime, Mags had made his bed in many places and in varying levels of comfort. The worst, of course, had been in the mines; bedded down with a heap of other children on whatever straw, leaves and dried weeds they could scavenge, covered with the tattered remains of blankets too ruined for the mine-ponies to use. The best, well, that had to be snuggled in that lovely bed next to Amily. This was somewhere in the middle.

They arrived at their first inn after dark, but before the horses had any chance of stumbling. Keira and Lord Jorthun were whisked off to a private room to be fed the best the inn had to offer. Mags brought in their traveling bags; with ears about, Lord Jorthun merely told him to get himself and "the boy" seen to.

So Mags brought Coot in to the common room, where the serving girl seized on them at once. They both were given tall mugs of ale, two rough plates full of stew with bread piled on top, and told to take a seat in the common room where they fancied. Fair treatment so far as Mags was concerned; Coot was thrilled. This was a different sort of food than Aunty Minda served the gang; different herbs, and it was thicker than Minda's soups. Aunty Minda was careful with bread, since she had no real oven and it had to be bought. The serving girl had heaped three thick slices on top of his bowl, and told him "There's more iffin ye wants it. An' drippins."

"We'll be havin' more bread an' drippins, iffen ye please," Mags said for him. "The lad's still a-growin'."

The serving "girl"—who was older than Mags by at least a decade—grinned and winked. Mags led Coot over to a table that was only half full. He nodded affably at the fellows already there, who looked to be locals enjoying their pint. They nodded cautiously back. Mags sat Coot across from him and started in on his food. A moment later the serving girl brought about half a loaf and a little crock of dripping from the roasts for Coot to dip the bread in. Since Aunty Minda never served roast *anything*—she did serve good healthy food and lots of it, but roasts were for people better off than they were—this was Coot's first taste of dripping. He ate until he nearly popped; the girl kept coming by to see that he was eating well and nodded at Mags in satisfaction. "Yer master sez not to stint," she told him with approval. "Must be a good man."

When Coot had eaten until he could not swallow another crumb, the girl took a moment and led them to the chamber they would share with other servants. There was one big bed; two fellows were already in there, and thankfully were not snoring. Mags carefully took off his trews and tunic, folded them, and put them at the head of the bed to use as a pillow. Coot watched him and did the same. "Outside or inside?"

Mags whispered. Coot surveyed the strangers in the moonlight coming in through the window. "Outside?" he said, making a question of it. Mags nodded and took the inside. Both of them rolled up in their cloaks, then pulled the blanket on their side over the top of everything.

He'd had worse beds. This one was vermin-free, not too lumpy; the blanket was warm enough when you added the cloak, and the other two men were like a couple of hibernating bears and didn't stir. The rest, well, neither he nor Coot were carrying anything to be robbed of, so he calmly went to sleep.

He woke when his bedmates rose before dawn. One of them touched his shoulder. "Best get a-movin' iffen yer want fust brekker, mate," said the fellow when he turned over.

"Well, thenkee kindly fer the warnin'," he replied, and shook Coot awake. All four of them pulled on their outer clothing, and trooped out into the common room.

It was much less full this morning, what with the locals gone. The serving girl—a real girl this time, not much older than Coot—put bread trenchers down in front of them beside wooden bowls. The coachman joined them in time to get a bowl and a trencher. Moments later she came back and spooned pease-porridge into the bowls and slid bacon and fried onions onto the trenchers. She came back a third time with mugs full of hot ale, and then returned to the kitchen, not to be seen again.

Everyone dug in. The bread was left over from last night, a bit stale now which was why it was being used as trenchers, but with the bacon grease and onion juice soaked in, it was tasty enough. Coot certainly didn't look as though he intended to complain.

Then the coachman went out to ready the horses, and they waited. And while they waited, Mags sensed Dallen prodding tentatively at his mind.

:How was your night?: Mags asked.

:Tolerable. There's a Waystation, so I had a nice sheltered sleeping spot, and it's not that hard to get into the feedbin even without hands.:

Mags considered that. *:Lord Jorthun says we're taking a lodging of some kind in Attlebury; the local Waystation can't be that far, and I can take Coot out and we'll get you set up comfortably. After that, he'll know what to do, and if I can't get out there to make sure everything's to your liking, he can.:*

:I knew you'd figure something out. How's your backside?:

:Wishing it was planted in your saddle. Why in the name of all the gods do the highborn travel like this? It's torture!:

:Because riding in the rain or snow on a common horse is worse torture. At least when it starts raining today, you'll be dry and reasonably warm.:

Mags did not ask Dallen how he knew it was going to rain. If Dallen said so, it probably would. He just hoped that the rain wouldn't turn the road to mire. The last thing they needed was delay on this trip. He would have said something else, but he caught sight of Lord Jorthun in the doorway to the better rooms in the inn. He leapt to his feet.

"Coot, go an' tell Coachy his Lor'ship's ready," he ordered, then went to collect the traveling bags. He and Coot stowed them while Lord Jorthun and Keira lingered over a last cup of something.

"Coach," he said, when the bags were stowed. The coachman looked down from his perch on the box above the carriage. "Me bones say it's gonna rain."

The coachman nodded, and cracked a smile. "Ta fer th' warnin', lad," he replied, and extracted a waxed and oiled rain-cape from a storage place on the roof of the carriage, strapping it into the seat next to him to have at hand when the weather started. "If it be fine, an yon youngun'd fancy time up wi' me, say th' word. Iffen th' road's good, I'll gi' 'im a turn at the reins, belike."

Coot's eyes went huge again. *"You would?"* he gasped. "Oh *thenkee* sor!"

"Hark—m'lor' an m'lady's comin'," the coachman warned, as Jorthun and Keira appeared in the doorway. Mags and Coot hurried to put down the footstool, help them both in, then stow the stool and hop in themselves. Then they were off.

"Sleep all right, sir?" Mags asked conversationally. Jorthun and Keira looked at each other and burst out laughing.

"I can only hope your neighbors were nothing like ours," Keira said, when they stopped. "There is *nothing* on the face of the world I can compare to the chorus of snores we heard once dinner was over."

"First came the usual sort of thing," Jorthun elaborated. "Except it was quite literally loud enough to rattle the walls. But then our neighbor began this high-pitched variation that came in fits and starts. Then it stopped, and we sighed in relief, and it started again."

"Then it stopped and we thought it was over for good, when the most hideous chorus of *moaning* began," said Keira. "And when that finally ended and we thought that he was either soundly asleep or dead—and we didn't care which at that point!—it all began again with that loud, low snoring!"

"Keira finally made us earplugs of wax, and between those and putting pillows over our heads, we managed to get to sleep." Jorthun chuckled. "I must say, this is a new experience for me. I've never encountered anyone with a repertoire like that."

"Our neighbors was quiet, an' neighborly," Mags replied. "Soun's like you'd'a been just as pleased bein' in servants' quarters."

"Better pleased," came the reply. "If that should happen again, I am sending Harras to my room and sleeping in the coach. Harras can sleep through anything."

"Does he know—" Mags said tentatively.

"Everything. He's been with me for dog's years. We'll rely on him for information from the other drivers and drovers."

"Good." Actually, it was more than good, it was perfect. That meant Mags wasn't going to have to try and get information out of a class of folks he knew absolutely nothing about—but who might be the ones who'd be able to guess if gems were being smuggled out.

"Well, we have many leagues to go, and the best way to employ them is to fit ourselves for the parts we intend to play—and you, youngling, are the weakest at the moment." Jorthun fixed Coot with a measuring gaze. "We created your story yesterday. Now let's fill it out and get it so firmly in your head you cannot be surprised into a mistake."

And Coot stood right up to it. "Yessir," he said, straightening in his seat. "Le's get drillin', sir."

Mags gave him an approving nod. Then they got to work, as a light rain began pattering the outside of the coach.

The rooms at Healer's Collegium seemed echoingly empty without Mags. She missed waking up to see his head on the pillow next to her, his unruly brown hair making him look like a sleepy mongrel puppy when he turned over to face her. She missed having to sort clean uniforms for two people. She missed his silly half-grin, and the sparkle in his brown eyes when she made a joke. She missed him reading over her shoulder, then asking incredulously, "An' ye read thet fer *fun*?"

And he'd only been gone two days.

Amily actually had thought about moving back to her little room in her father's suite at the Palace, when she realized that being there would be just as bad. When Mags left, Nikolas had headed south to the Border to find the armories that had produced the fateful weapons and learn what he could, which meant that he was gone for who knew how long. She was lonely and no matter how many friends she had here—and she did have many—all of them were busy, and none of them made up for the fact that Mags was gone.

It was true that if she wanted she could have almost hourly reports on him by way of Rolan, whose limits on Mindspeech didn't seem to have been discovered yet, at least when it came to Mindspeaking another Companion. But that just wasn't the same. He was the one person besides Rolan who could Mindspeak with her, because he was the only Herald she knew of who could Mindspeak with anyone, whether or not they had Mindspeech of their own. And hearing Rolan tell her what Mags had "said" just wasn't the same as hearing his voice in her ear, or her head.

Just before she went to bed, Rolan would tell her what had gone on that day. The first day, the coach had nearly rattled their bones apart, the second, they slogged through rain, but at least the roads weren't terribly muddy, and nobody had needed to get out and push. And he missed her, but wouldn't wish the coach ride on her no matter how lonely he got.

At least now if something goes wrong, I'll know. *And as long as I don't hear anything, it means things are boring and safe.* That might have been the worst part of being the daughter of a Herald, with no Gifts of her own, especially a Herald like her father, who was prone to vanishing without warning. She'd never known what he was doing back before Rolan had Chosen her, and generally he did not tell her when he was leaving, where he was going, or when he would return. He could be gone hours . . . or days . . . or even a sennight or more, and she would have *no* idea what was going on for him. She could only have faith that as King's Own, and partnered with Rolan, he would come back home safe.

This was better. That didn't mean she liked it, but there was a great deal about being a Herald that was just . . . hard. This made it a little less difficult.

So she did *her* job, because she might be King's Own, but

that didn't make her some special, privileged and protected hot-house bloom. She was a Herald, she had a job to do, and she did it, regardless of circumstances, just as every other Herald did.

And that was how she spent the first two days without Mags. Much of her day, but not all, was taken up with the duties of the King's Own . . . which in her case were not as "full" as she would have liked. The King's Own was the King's confidant and sounding board . . . but this King had not only her, but his Queen, his eldest son and his son's wife, and his Inner Council. Kyril had had a long, long time to set up his support system, and do so in such a way that any one, or even several of them could be preoccupied for sennights or moons at a time, and the King would still have people he could trust around him. That was how her father had managed to go absent for so long, so often.

This was the morning of the third day. Rolan told her that the rain had passed and Mags and company were already well down the road, having started at dawn. She paused in the hall outside the Council chamber. The King had just told her she could consider herself free for the rest of the day. It might be time to check on Mag's crop of orphans.

The thought was father to the deed, although she stopped to get something to eat before she ventured down into the city. Shortly after the noon bells rang, she and Rolan were nearly at the inn where the disguises were kept—*after* letting Kyril and Sedric know where she was going. If there was one thing that reading many, many books had taught her, it was that when someone like a Herald decided to go off somewhere by herself, it was sheer stupidity to do so without telling *someone* where you were going and what you were doing. Granted, Heralds had Companions, who presumably could relay the need for help if something went badly wrong—but that was only true if the Companions themselves were not incapacitated or extremely busy staying alive.

Don't divide your party, no matter how much more efficient it might seem, always check to make sure your equipment is working, and never go off on your own without making sure someone else knows where you are going. It was all very well to hinge a story on mistakes like those, but she had no intention of ever becoming a "bad example."

Spring was finally on the way. Bulbs were blooming in gardens and window-boxes, and the trees definitely had buds on them. Which meant there would be Spring rains soon. That wouldn't matter to her, but she only hoped that Mags and Keira and Lord Jorthun got to their destination before the roads became mired messes. Streets here in Haven were paved by cobblestones or some process only the old Mages understood, so it wasn't so bad here, and even the four main Trade Roads were paved. But once you got off the main Trade Roads . . . and they *would* be off them almost as soon as they left Haven . . . you were dealing with plain old dirt. Which would be rutted after the thaws, and in a rain, could turn into something that was not unlike a swamp. She did not envy them. He had had no idea what he was in for when he'd set off on this journey; she had, for she had traveled by coach and carriage quite a bit before being Chosen. *I'll bet he thought it would be like the caravan trip we took when he was making his first circuit to get his Whites.* A coach traveling as quickly as the horses could pull it was nothing like as comfortable a ride as a caravan traveling at an amble over those roads.

And if it turned really mucky . . . they could find themselves having to get out and push. Mags wouldn't mind that, but Keira would be of little use, and she didn't like to think of Jorthun putting his back into it.

You'd think someone would notice all the Heralds coming in and not coming out here, she thought, trying to muster up a little amusement, as she left Rolan in his special box in the stable and headed for the secret room where her father, Mags, and now she kept their disguises.

:With all the people that come through here?: Rolan pointed out *:That's why Nikolas chose this place. Hundreds of people come and go from this inn over the course of a day. Lots of Heralds come here to watch the players or hear the musicians, no one will notice one more or less. And I am watching out to make certain no one notices; that's my job.:*

Well, that was certainly true. This was the largest inn in Haven, fully big enough to have its own small acting company that performed short comedies every night. *And* another room where a rotating group of musicians played all day and night. *:You're right, of course.:*

She changed quickly, and became the young street tough that she and her father had concocted. It wasn't that hard; she was slender, and the right underpinnings took care of any betraying curves. Once she'd redressed, tied her hair back, and smudged up her face she made her way out into the open again. The character was surprisingly effective, actually; her swagger and the way she rested her hand on the hilt of her dagger—not her sword—convinced people that she knew how to use the weapons she carried. She rather liked the effect, actually. The way people glanced at her uneasily, tried not to catch her eye, or even moved across the street to avoid her was amusing.

Once down in the poorer parts of Haven, the signs of Spring were not as decorative; people used window boxes to grow practical things like beans and peas. But there were tender shoots starting there. Windows were open just a cautious bit, and people were beginning to shed some of the layers of clothing they had worn all winter.

She got to Aunty Minda's and used her key. Those orphans who were not currently at their new jobs as maid and hall-boys, or at their jobs as runners at inns, would be here getting luncheon. And some of those who were runners might be here too; if business was slow it was better to dash back here for some food than spend a precious coin on something at the inn.

A dozen pairs of eyes riveted her as she turned after shutting the door behind her.

"Ah!" Aunty Minda said, perking up as Amily took off her battered hat. "Herald Amy! How's Harkon a-doin' on his journey?"

Amily did not correct her; she just smiled. "Hello Aunty Minda, I heard this morning he was doing well. Now, how are you all getting along? Do you need anything?"

"The lads i' Weasel's takes care'a us nicely, thenkee," Minda said. "But, act'lly, one'a th' young'uns 'ere 'as a notion fer ye."

One of the boys stood up. "Aye. We 'as a notion. Iffen yer a-gonna do wut Harkon do, yer oughter be able t'be wut Harkon be."

She blinked at him, confused as to what he meant. There was no way she could judge gemstones as Mags could, and she rather doubted anyone wanted her minding the counter at Willy the Weasel's. "Which is?"

"Roof-runner," the boy said, and grinned. "We reckon we kin teach yer."

Her initial reaction was to tell him such a thing was impossible—that she could not possibly, with her leg. . . .

But she didn't say that, and in the next moment she realized there was no reason why she couldn't . . . because hadn't she already managed to learn to fight with multiple weapons? This would be harder than that, yes, but why not at least *try?*

"I'd like to try," she agreed. "But I do have a leg that used to be lame. . . ."

The boy shrugged. "We try, aye? No 'arm in tryin'."

"I agree." She nodded decisively. "But can we find some-where we can use in daylight? I am certainly not capable of trying any climbing in the dark."

The boy grinned even broader. "Oh, aye. Thet we kin."

Well, this is . . . going to be interesting.

Amily's first lessons were to take place right here, in the back yards and on the rooftops of the orphans' home and the pawn shop. "We be startin' ye slow, m'lady," the boy—Renn—told her. "Fust thing's t'get ye jumpin' about, like." They had actually set up a sort of course, like the Collegium course, composed of what would otherwise have been obstacles, but different. She thought that Renn would start her on jumping on and off some of the objects out here, the bench, the broken bits of column, and so forth. But he surprised her.

"I wantcher ter galumph 'long this-a-way," he said, and proceeded to scamper about the yard on all fours at an as-tounding pace. He stood up after a few moments of this, and regarded her with a slight smile. "It be 'arder nor it looks."

"I can already believe that," she said . . . but still. . . .

I might not be as unsuited to this as I think. I used to have to crawl everywhere. . . .

Well, it *wasn't* easy, and it used all manner of muscles she wasn't used to using, but she could certainly see how this would be crackingly useful for scampering about on steep rooftops. She couldn't get to Renn's speed, but she did man-age a lot better than a crawl, although after a while her mus-cles began complaining bitterly and cramping, and she got a hideous stitch in her side.

"I've got to stop," she said, panting and looking up at the boy.

"Ye done better nor I recked," said Renn. "Yer wanter stretch oot. Then we'll get ter next thin'."

She nodded, and slowly stood up, groaning a little. This muscle pain was not something that came as a surprise to her; the moment that Renn had told her to run on all fours, she had known she was in for a genuine workout. The only thing that *had* come as a surprise to her was that Renn seemed to be as serious and dedicated an instructor as the Weaponsmaster and any of his assistants up at the Collegia. It was impressive to see someone that young who was as focused and disciplined as an adult.

Then again, his livelihood depended on this. The boys were in great demand as message runners and package deliverers because they could be counted on to let nothing stop them. They would cut through yards, go over walls, and even run on the rooftops. And most of the younglings here had been rescued from a gang of thieves by Mags, and running the rooftops at night had been part of their business.

These children were really not "children" as she knew them at all. At a far too early age, they'd been forced into adult responsibilities. *And I should begin treating them that way,* she realized. *And thinking of them in that way as well.*

So she took care with stretching out the muscles that felt strained and sore, and only when she thought they were ready did she turn back to him and say, obediently, "And now what, Renn?"

"Thet, there," he said, pointing to a piece of wood no wider than the width of her thumb, and about the width of two fingers tall, running from one side of the yard to the other. "Yer balance an' walk it. No fallin' off! Then yer turn in place, an' come back."

This was actually not so bad; a lot of learning to use her mended leg had involved balancing along boards like this one.

She felt a great deal better about her performance balancing on the narrow bit of wood than she had with running about on all fours. When she had performed this action to Renn's satisfaction, making nice, quick, tight turns at the end, he agreed she was ready for the third exercise.

"Now yer gonna learn 'ow t'jump, proper," he decreed. But he did not have her jump onto and off of *anything.* Instead, he had her making precision jumps at ground level, jumping to and from a series of cobbles in the yard that were lighter colored than the rest. Slowly she began to notice that there was a *proper* way to jump. And that she certainly had not mastered it.

He noticed her chagrin, coached her on her form and how to set her feet and bend her knees, and when she stopped to rest, patted her arm gently. "No worries, m'lady. Yer doin' better nor I thought ye might."

She was soaking wet at this point, and needed to at least go inside and dry off a bit before she walked back up to the inn. And she was *exhausted,* so if she went traipsing about in damp clothing, she'd be likely to catch something.

:*And you are going to ache in the morning,:* Rolan observed. :*I suggest a hot bath as soon as we return to the Collegium:*

"Yer go in, yer don 'nuff fer t'day, m'lady," Renn decreed. "Want yer t'practice thet stuff up on Hill fer three days. Iffen yer figger yer ready fer next part, ye come down agin. I be 'ere. I be trainin' the wee 'uns, the new 'uns we got, t'be new runners. They's three on 'em now, but I reck there be six soon."

"Thank you, Renn, I will," she promised, determined she would *master* such seemingly simple movements by the time she saw him next. "You are uncommonly kind to take on such a clumsy wench as I."

He patted her again. "Yer no worse'n some, an better'n some," he reassured her. "Yer in good shape. It'll come faster.

Le's go in, ye git dry, so's ye don' ketch nothing; an' ye kin git 'ome again."

At least he isn't throwing his hands in the air and proclaiming me useless, she thought later, as she headed back the way she had come, toward the stable where Rolan was. *There's comfort in that.*

She felt Rolan snort in the back of her mind. *:You are in good physical condition as all Heralds should be,:* he reminded her. *:A Herald that can scamper about on rooftops like a stray cat is a rare one. But I do agree with the boy; you should become one of those rare ones. You never know when such a skill will be needed.:*

:True, oh wise one,: she thought back at him. *:No learning is ever wasted. Especially when it comes to us.:*

Three days later she returned to Renn, and he proclaimed himself satisfied with her progress. Now he added more variations on jumps to the previous exercises.

Using the same colored cobblestones as her targets, he had her leaping off on one or two feet, landing on one or two feet, jumping from the start of or at the end of a run across the yard, jumping from a standing start, across a gap, or at an odd angle. He also added jumping off and on relatively low objects, and jumping from object to object.

Last of all he tested her ability to fall, or fall and roll. Fortunately that was one of the *first* skills she had ever mastered, back before her lame leg had been mended. After all, back when she'd been unable to walk, she could not always count on someone being around to help her if something happened and she fell. He was very impressed with her falling skills, which soothed her somewhat wounded pride.

Once again, he sent her away with the direction to return

in three days. "Yer doin' dem good, m'lady." Then he hesitated a moment. "Ye heerd aught'a Harkon?"

She smiled as he looked up at her anxiously. "Every morning and every night. He's fine. Well, other than having his bones rattled for days in a coach. They arrived at their destination today. I understand your friend Coot is having quite the adventure. It seems he has seen many things he never saw before. This morning he saw a fox, for instance. And last night he heard a wolf pack howl."

Renn's eyes grew big. "Wuz they gonna eat 'im?"

She smiled. "I think they were busy hunting rabbits. Unless they are starving wolves will generally leave you alone if you leave them alone."

Renn looked dubious. "Take yer word fer it, m'lady. I be seein' ye i' three days agin. Keep practicin'."

––––––––––

Attlebury was a country market town, in the middle of country full of gem mines. That made things a bit different than any other country market town in Valdemar.

To begin with, there was the quality of the buildings, which was high. For another, there was a Guild Hall in the middle of it that was the equal of any in Haven. Most country market towns would probably boast a market square, which might or might not be paved in some manner. This one boasted, not only a paved market square, but a large central livestock structure which was roofed. This was where the *finest* livestock went to be looked over and eventually sold; the best horses, the prize sheep and cattle. Animals that were intended for breeding. Real money was the norm here, not barter. There was a goldsmith, a silversmith *and* a coppersmith. There was more than one butcher. Several houses of worship were here, devoted to different deities, most of them having to do with either mining or farming; most market towns were lucky to have one. And they all seemed to be prospering.

Another thing that was different; most market towns had one public pump or fountain; this one had several, four in the market square alone. And cobblestone paving on all the main streets. And the fact that the best inn in the town had an entire floor that could be taken that would not have been out of place in one of the highborn's town-houses. Mags and Jorthun knew all this of course; Mags had seen a lot in his year or so on circuit, and Lord Jorthun was, Mags suspected, *vastly* experienced in wanderings over the face of Valdemar.

Needless to say, that inn was where they were now; it was huge, easily as big as the one in Haven that played host to the theater company from which some of Nikolas's pawn-shop crew had been drawn. It was four full stories tall, and L-shaped, with a yard for horses and carriages in the crook of the L and an enormous stable and bathhouse. The bottom floor was the common room and taproom, the kitchen and the living quarters of the innkeeper and his family. The attic was for storage and cramped little garrets right under the thatch where the staff slept. The top floor was common rooms, where people slept several to a bed, the third individual rooms. The second floor was actually made up of suites. The two largest were four rooms each, the two smallest were two rooms each.

The large suites were sumptuous indeed. Mags suspected that the furniture had been acquired over time, as the wealthy mine-owners divested themselves of "old things." The two small ones were quite as comfortable as any set of rooms in the Collegium. After sharing beds with herdsmen, traveling tradesmen, bards on their Journeyman circuit, and assorted other folk whose occupations were not immediately obvious, it was a relief to have not just one, but two rooms to himself. He installed his traveling trunk, took out and hung up clean livery to air out, and disposed some of his personal things around the room, then went to check on Coot.

Coot scarcely knew what to do with himself. He had *never* had a room to himself, much less two.

It was fairly obvious to Mags that the suites he and Coot had been given were intended for people higher in rank than mere servants. In fact, it wouldn't surprise him if they were normally used by Heralds. And the innkeeper clearly thought the same, as he had delicately hinted that "the help" could "find accommodations elsewhere." "Elsewhere," of course, would be those little garret rooms. Obviously.

But Lord Jorthun had stared down his nose at the poor man, and asserted that he was "not accustomed to having to do without" his *own* servitors, and wanted them to be near at hand "so they could respond with no inconvenience." The innkeeper reflected on this, then named a price, tentatively. Jorthun agreed to it with impatience. Keira solidified the innkeeper's opinion of them as easy marks by exclaiming that she had *much* preferred that there were no strangers about during the hours of repose.

Mags could almost see the speculative thoughts running behind the innkeeper's eyes as he regarded Mags, then Keira, then Mags again. He didn't make any attempt even to skim the man's surface thoughts, but they were easy enough to divine.

Let him assume whatever he likes.

So Coot and Mags had gotten their own suites, each consisting of a small bedroom with a very nice bed and a bit of a sitting room with a fireplace. Coot sat on his bed and stared at his surroundings with wide eyes, once he and Mags got the luggage upstairs and stowed in the proper suites.

"I ain't nivver seen th' like, Harkon," Coot managed. They had all agreed to use Mags' street-name from Haven. Harkon was common enough as a name, and Mags . . . was not.

Someone might remember the slavey that Master Cole Pieters lost to the Heralds—shortly before he lost his mines for mistreating and murdering his mine workers. "What'm I s'pposed t'do wi' all this room?"

"Well, this's pretty out'a th' ordinary fer the likes of us, lad," Mags told him. "Mostly ye an' me'd be sharin' a bed, or I'd git a bed and ye'd get a truckle 'neath it. An' one room. Or like 'keeper said, we'd be tucked up like afore, w' some'uv th' inn folks. Ye gonna be all right alone?"

He knew from personal experience that someone who was used to sleeping in a pack often had difficulty getting to sleep and staying asleep the first few nights in their own bed.

Coot scratched his head. "Reckon so." He looked at his nails and made a face. Mags smiled to himself. Aunty Minda was very strict about cleanliness, and Coot had gone from a boy who had been an entirely different color under all his dirt and grease, to one who thought the highest form of luxury was a good hot bath and felt abused if he didn't get one on a regular basis.

"Inn this big, there'll be a bathhouse," he told the lad. "Lemme go find out."

Actually, he went to discover, not only if there was a bathhouse, but if it had one big common room or several small rooms—or both.

There was a bathhouse, and it had both. He bespoke two of the private rooms, one each for Lord Jorthun and Keira, because after a week on the road, that would be expected of him. He tentatively arranged for bath attendants as well, and went back up to inform them that their baths would be ready momentarily.

Lord Jorthun looked up as Mags tapped the side of the doorframe. "I've bespoke a bath for you, m'lord," he said politely. "Would ye prefer us t'be assistin' ye? M'lady'll have to make do with the inn-girls."

"I'd prefer for you and the boy to get the grime off of you," said Lord Jorthun, in a lofty tone of voice—but with a wink. "Tell the innkeeper we require attendants while you do so."

"Aye m'lord. An' I'll hev dinner sent up an' waitin' for ye, when ye get out."

"Excellent."

Mags informed Keira, who dimpled at him, and waved him off, then went back downstairs as ordered, and made sure that Lord Jorthun's wishes were carried out. Only then did he fetch Coot, get fresh, clean livery for both of them, and take him down to the common bathhouse.

At this hour, right at the dinner hour for most folk, it was empty. Like most such bathhouses, both sexes used it without any pretense at modesty. You scrubbed off to one side of the big tub, above a grate in the floor, using soap that could range from just a bare grade above that used on floors to something that would not be out of place in a lady's bathing room, depending on the quality of the house. You rinsed off there, and the dirty water drained away through that grate in the floor. And then you went and soaked in the common tub until you were good and relaxed. There would be a similar arrangement in the private bathing rooms—with better soap and towels of course, and attendants to help you.

Getting really clean was a godsend. Getting into the hot tub was heaven. Mags sighed as his bruises encountered the hot water and felt his muscles finally relaxing. Coot looked utterly blissful; Mags reflected that as bony as the poor lad was, the coach rides must have been harder on the boy than they were on him.

He was just getting comfortable when five more people came in, two women and three men. All of them were dressed in what looked like the general costume of the inn servants, so he assumed that was what they were, and their conversation confirmed it.

". . . took the whole floor, they did!" said the older of the two women, evidently resuming a conversation. "And they got a coach and all! I have never seen the like!"

"But what brings 'em here, I'd like t'know?" asked one of the men, sounding genuinely puzzled. "They're takin' the rooms for a moon at least, Master says, an' what's there to see here?"

Mags pondered for a moment, and decided that this was the time to ingratiate himself with the locals.

"M'lady Keira," he said, and they all started, because he and Coot were deep in the steam and they probably hadn't been noticed. "is widowed and jest out'a mournin'. M'lord Jorthun's 'er father. They took a notion to travel away from th' sad 'ouse of death fer a while an' away from far too many so-called frien's that ain't nothin'a' th' sort, an' jest go where fancy took 'em. They like this 'ere town. They partic'larly like this inn. So here we be." He waved to the dumbfounded and silent people on the other side of the tub. "I be Harkon. The lad'll be Coot. At yer service."

He was hoping that his overtures would be accepted. They might not have been in a smaller, more insular town. Here, well, it was obvious that by all rights he and Coot could have put on airs, being the servants of highborns who were wealthy enough to just take a fancy to hail off into nowhere on a whim. Technically, he and Coot outranked every servant in this inn. But he wasn't putting on airs. He was meeting them halfway, as equals. *And* he gave them a great deal of information they could now use in gossiping with the others. That disposed them to like him.

"Good e'en to ye, Harkon," said one of the men, finally. "I be Darvy. This's Klem, an' this's Jon. The ladies be Jone an' Bet."

"I reck we should all be friendly-like, since M'lord recks t'stay here about a moon, mebbe longer," Mags replied, nodding to each of them in turn. " 'E's a good man, is M'lord, and

M'lady was leg-shackled to a bedridden invalid an' weren't nothin' but a nurse an' never got no chance to go outside the four walls'a Hartcliff Manor for year'n. Reckon she wants t'kick up 'er 'eels a bit, an no blame to 'er for it. 'Ardly outa leadin' strings when she got 'itched to m'lord."

"No blame atall, atall," chuckled Jone. "Though it'll be tame for heel kickin' 'ere."

"Mebbe not." Klem finished his wash and eased himself down into the hot water, and the others followed. "We got all them mine owners, 'ereabouts, an' plenty sons. Plenty money 'round 'ere. Reckon a purdy widder might could do worse'n one of 'em. Get yer sparklies direct, eh? An' no frettin' 'bout iffen 'e's marryin' fer money."

"Well, thet ain't none'a my business, Klem, but, if it were, I'd agree wi' ye'." Mags nodded sagely. "'Tis a good thin' when a lad an' a lass come t' terms an' ain't too much money overweightin' either side. She's a good an' kindly heart, has m'lady. She tookit this lad in from the wicket streets a'Haven, an' made 'im 'er page, an' she 'as a good eyen, 'cause 'e's a good lad." He allowed just a hint of menace to come into his voice. "Like a liddle brother 'e is t'me, an' any'un thinks t'bully 'im'll be answerin' t' the back'a me 'and."

The inn servants seemed to judge at that point that they had probably probed Mags for as much information as he was likely to impart for now, and they turned their conversation to details about the inn's inhabitants, and some of the townsfolk. Mags listened. There was a lot he could learn just by sitting here and saying nothing. Sometimes it seemed as if that was more than half of his job.

Lord Jorthun was perusing the stock of books at one of the local temples, with Coot in tow. Of course no temple would loan out something as precious as a book to just *anyone,* but Jorthun's very generous deposits in the offer-bowls pretty much guaranteed him favors granted that had nothing to do with the state of his soul. Lady Keira and Harras, the coachman, were in search of riding horses to hire; the coach horses obviously would not do for that, and the only time they would take the coach out would be if they intended to be out after darkness fell.

That left Mags plenty of time to see to Dallen. The Companion's directions were quite clear, and the Waystation was not all that far out of town. It was a pleasant walk, and he could easily make the case that he was exploring the environs for his master and mistress.

His road led out of town to where the cobbles ended, across a little stone bridge, down a road with commons on either side, goats and milk-cows and geese grazing under the eyes of watchful children. Then it plunged into forest, but from the general state of things, he judged this, too, was common land. There were next to no fallen branches, and the underbrush had that semi-pruned look that suggested people were running pigs here in summer and fall, gathering deadfall for burning, and generally making as liberal use of the woods as they were of the common meadows.

He passed two side-paths, and at the third, heard in his mind, *:Yes, that is the one,:* and turned aside to follow it. It brought him to a snug little hut with a very nice stabling arrangement big enough for two beasts. The hut was shut up tight, but Dallen was waiting for him right beside it.

"How'd you pass the night?" Mags asked.

Dallen switched his tail and bobbed his head. *:Tolerably well. I'll be better when you can get the grain out of the Station and spread some of the straw for a bed.:*

Mags grinned, and flipped the latch on the Waystation. It was obvious from the good condition it was in that these people took care of their Heralds. He found a barrel of oats in a storage area, and rolled it out to the stable. "You want me to do anything special with this?" he asked.

:Just get the top off, and rig some kind of handle so I can put it on and pull it off myself. I don't fancy sharing my meal with mice.: Dallen watched over his shoulder with interest as he pried the top off the barrel, bored a couple of holes in it, and affixed a loop of rope to it.

"Think that'll do?" he said, putting the top back on. Dallen tried it for himself, taking the top off and putting it back on again, and nodded with approval.

:Excellent. Now, that bed. . . .:

That was a matter of a few moments of pulling one of the bales of straw out of shelter, breaking it open and spreading it until Dallen was satisfied.

"I assume there's a stream? 'Cause there don't seem t' be a water bucket for ye."

:A very nice one. I think it's spring-fed. This will be quite the little vacation for me.: Dallen ambled into the bit of meadow in front of the Waystation, and dropped down for a roll in the grass—in the area where it was *much* shorter; obviously where he had grazed his fill last night.

Mags chuckled. "Don't put a curse on it, horse. Let's hope it stays that way. I'll leave the Station open, that way anyone that comes by will just think your Herald's off doing something. And if ye want to, ye can help yerself to those dried apples in the pantry cupboard."

:They're not pocket pies,: Dallen said wistfully, rolling to his feet again, with a daisy somehow stuck in his mane so it peeked over one ear.

"Play yer cards right, and ye might get some of them too," Mags replied, then gave him a long and affectionate hug and turned to make the pleasant walk back to the inn.

Amily stood uncertainly in the courtyard of the former brewery where Tuck and Linden's "shack" was. Before he had left, Mags had introduced her to Linden, but she had never yet encountered Tuck. She'd met Linden at the pawn shop; Mags had made certain that she and all three of Nikolas's former-actors-turned-agents knew *who* Linden was, what she and Tuck did, and that she could come to Amily or the pawn shop for help. He'd had Amily take off her hat and let down her hair so Linden would know her as a Herald. There hadn't been time for him to take her to meet Tuck.

She reckoned it was about time she did so. But now that she was here, she wondered—just how was she supposed to do this? Linden wasn't expecting her, and there had been no way to send a message. What should she do? Go straight up to the door of the shed and knock? Find someone to get Linden for her and explain she had come to see how the girl and her charge were doing? Mags had emphasized that Tuck was timid and easily startled, and the last thing she wanted to do was disturb him. First, she didn't want to make him upset, and second, she had the notion that doing so would definitely make an enemy out of Linden.

The courtyard was full of laundry lines, and for the most part all she could see of the laundresses was feet moving among the flapping linens. The air was also full of the very pleasant aroma of extremely clean linens drying in the sun. One of the ladies hanging laundry came around to Amily's side of the lines, turned, and spotted her. Amily noted her strong arms and shoulders with respect. Evidently being a laundress was not for the weak. "Oi, Milady Herald!" she called, tucking stray bits of hair back under her cap. "Here t'see Linden?"

"Yes I am," Amily replied. "If that's—"

Taking no notice of what she was trying to get out, the laundress marched across the courtyard, avoiding flapping shirts and shifts and other manner of garments, and pounded on the door of the shed with her fist. The door looked as if a single knock would break it apart, but it *sounded* as solid as bronze. "Linden!" she called cheerfully. "Lady Herald t'see yer!"

Linden's head—instantly recognizable by the tangle of curls that didn't look as if it was *ever* going to submit to taming—popped out of the shed door. Spying Amily, she beckoned, and Amily trotted across the courtyard, avoiding laundresses and baskets and ducking under line after line of clothing.

"Mags told me to make sure you and Tuck were all right while he's gone," Amily said, as Linden pulled her into the "shed" and shut the door. "I thought it was time I came to see if you needed anything." She looked around, impressed with the cleanliness of the place as well as the general look of it. It might have been a stable once, but it was certainly the equal of plenty of homes she'd been in, and virtually every Waystation she and Mags had used. Whatever was on the outside was mere "decoration." The real, load-bearing walls were the ones on the inside. They might have been pieced together out of scrap wood, but every piece was carefully fitted together and reinforced until the building could probably take having half a dozen cattle on the roof.

Tools were hung on the walls in a precise order; she couldn't tell what the rules for what went where *were,* but it was clear that Tuck knew. There was a loft above; that was probably where Linden and Tuck slept. Down below was the kitchen of sorts, and a lot of workbenches; one for each separate project, it seemed. The poor fellow himself was hunched over a workbench, humming to himself, evidently so deep in a project that nothing was going to disturb him except, perhaps, an earthquake.

"That's mightily thoughty'a 'im, Milady," Linden replied. "We're doin' right well, what wi' thet man'a Lord Jorthun's makin' sure we got ever'thin' we needs. I do mean ever'thin'. He even ast us iffen we wanted ter move up ter 'is fine place, but no. Tuck, he don' like strange places. Makes 'im skeerd. So all I gots ter do is ast, an' we gots it." She chuckled. "Who'd'a thunk it? Moons ago, we wuz jest makin' 'nough t'live on. Now?" she spread her hands wide. "We're in cream!"

"Cream?" Tuck turned around, attracted by the word. "Tuck likes cream."

"An' Tuck'll hev cream," Linden said fondly, going over to the big fellow and patting him on the arm. "Ye bin slavin' at thet there whassit all mornin', an' ye shell hev cream an' strawberries too, aye."

Tuck's poor, perpetually puzzled face lit up. He got up from his stool and went to a chair at a little bit of a table, pieced together like a puzzle from all sorts and kinds of wood. Linden sliced a thick piece of bread into a bowl that had been broken and mended so successfully that the cracks in it were now a kind of beautiful pattern of their own. She covered the bread with sliced strawberries, then took down a little jar from a shelf above a stone sink that must have weighed as much as she did, and was probably a relic from when this was a stable, and carefully poured cream over it all. She handed the bowl and a spoon to Tuck, who began eating the treat carefully, taking tiny, tiny bites and savoring them.

And that was when Amily nearly jumped out of her skin. Because she *heard* him. She actually heard Tuck! Not with her ears, but her *mind.*

Tuck's thoughts felt . . . nearly exactly like those of a highly intelligent creature like a dog, or a *chirra*; not because he was dull, but because they were wordless. Right now, those thoughts were concentrated on the pleasure of eating, the overall taste of the unaccustomed sweet (which was something he had never tasted until a few days ago), the richness of the cream, and the comforting substantial texture of the bread. But there was more to it than the thoughts of an animal, even though his thoughts were experiential rather than in words. Tuck was perfectly intelligent . . . in his own, peculiar way.

She sat down next to him. "The strawberries are so good, aren't they, Tuck?" she said quietly. "The seeds on them crunch, and the meat is tender and sharp and sweet at the same time. The cream is smooth and feels in your mouth the way soft leather feels on your hand, and it makes you feel full and warm, too, doesn't it? And the bread soaks up the sweet from the strawberries, and the smooth from the cream, and holds everything together . . ."

Tuck stopped eating, his spoon halfway to his mouth. He looked straight at her, mouth open a little in surprise, eyes big and round. "You—" was all he could manage. "You!"

Linden stared at them both in confusion. She put her hand over one of Tuck's huge ones. "Yes, Tuck," she said, smiling.

"I can *understand* you. I can hear you. Not your words. I can hear what's in here—" She tapped him lightly on the forehead, between his eyes.

And Tuck put down his spoon and burst into joyful tears. Amily could tell they were joyful, not fearful, or sad, because Tuck's thoughts were veritable thunderclaps of happiness.

Linden nearly upset the table trying to get to him and clasped his head to her chest. "It's all right, baby!" She crooned. "Milady Herald didn' mean—"

"No!" Tuck said, pushing her gently away. "Tuck no hurt! Tuck *happy!*" And he burst into tears again, but seized Amily's hand, mouthing the word "happy" over and over again.

"It's my Gift," she said to the poor bewildered Linden. "I have a peculiar sort of Animal Mindspeech. I can't talk to them, but I can hear them, and somehow, Tuck thinks the same way animals do. He's as smart in his way as you or I, but he can't make that come out in words. Mostly he thinks in feelings and experiences rather than in words, like you and I do. I think it would be interesting to watch his thoughts while he's working on something. I heard him thinking about his treat, and I just said the same things in words that he was feeling."

"So when 'e's too upset'r too flibberted t'tell me wut's goin' on, ye kin 'ear 'im an' tell me?" Linden asked, excitement clear in her face—a relief to Amily, since she had been a bit afraid that Linden would be jealous that someone other than her could understand her charge.

"I should be able to, yes," she replied. "And . . . I should be able to explain to him what other people want from him, when he can't understand it."

"Bloody 'ell!" Now *Linden* burst into happy tears, and Amily had to explain to the startled Tuck that Linden was all right, she was just happy that Amily could hear Tuck.

And when the waterfalls of tears were finally dried up, all

three of them were exhausted. Tuck and Linden from crying so hard from happiness, and Amily from being in the middle of it all. And all three felt the need of the simple comfort of more strawberries, bread and cream.

Amily left them, then, promising to be back at least once every two days, feeling drained but more satisfied by the morning's work than by anything she had accomplished earlier as King's Own.

Because she and everyone else seemed to be going in circles when it came to figuring out who was about to tip Menmellith and Valdemar into war. At least this morning there had been a straight line, and an accomplishment at the end of it.

Too many mysteries, she thought, as Rolan came down the street to meet her half way.

:And probably politics as the cause of it all,: he agreed, as she mounted. *:It's always politics, in the end.:*

———————

This was probably the best spring day to come along this season. It was too bad that Amily was halfway across the Tanner and Dyer's District. There was nothing "nice" about the air here, and the warmer it got, the more it stank.

Renn had been giving her instructions; today would be her first real test of her new skills. "Don' take too long 'bout it, but don' rush it neither," Renn instructed. He and Amily were walking to some destination where he assured her she would be able to undertake her first attempt at "roof-running" unhindered and uninterrupted. "Ye watch me go fust, an' ye foller, doin' wut I'll be doin'."

She nodded. Unlike Renn, she had some tools to assist her, things that the clever-handed Tuck had made for her. A little grappling hook on a slender but astonishingly strong rope, a thick, heavy belt with iron rings attached with rivets, and fingerless gloves with abrasive palms. Now that she knew how to "talk" to Tuck, and more importantly, how to listen, it was a simple matter to explain what she needed and why, and let him come up with the solution for her needs.

Mags would be amazed to discover just how many effective little weapons she had hidden about her person, now that Tuck understood that *she* was supposed to protect people, that she had to do it while looking "pretty," and she might have to kill someone in order to protect the good people. Tuck understood the concept of bad people and good people very well. Possibly better than many people up on the Hill. His instincts were incredibly good when it came to detecting those who hid evil intentions behind a smiling mask, at least in her experience so far. Tuck also readily understood the concept of death, although he understood it in the form of "and now this person or creature is done, and gone forever" and his grief at finding a favorite pigeon dead had nearly broken her heart.

On the other hand, that meant that when she had told him, solemnly, that "sometimes I have to make bad people go away forever," he had known that she needed something lethal. And he had delivered it.

Right now, though, her weapons were the least of her concerns.

"Where are we going?" she asked Renn, for what must have been the tenth time. He finally relented.

"Temple, outside 'Aven. Burned down whiles ago, nobut ever bothered rebuildin' it. Folks sez it's 'aunted." He chuckled. "That's cuz we 'aunts it an' keeps folks away so's we kin learn t' roof-run there."

When he said that, she knew *exactly* what he was talking about, since practically everyone in the city knew about the "Haunted Temple."

"But—" she began hesitantly, thinking of how dangerous it must be. Weakened roof-timbers, places where there was no support on the roof and you could fall through, walls that could give way and collapse—there was a good reason why even if a fire got put out, most people just pulled down houses that had burned and started over.

"No worries," Renn chuckled, as if he was reading her mind. "We knocked down anythin' that wuz gonna fall down or git knocked down long time gone. Ev'thin' there now's solider'n rocks. Alls ye haveta look out fer's the starlin's an' rooks."

She finally was able to stop holding her breath once they got a street or two past Tanner's. She could certainly see why the rents were lower here than anywhere else in Haven, but she could not imagine how anyone could live here, even with the rents that low.

:I am told you get used to it,: Rolan observed. She shuddered. She could not imagine how.

In the near distance, the last of the city walls rose above the roofs of the houses. The walls were a legacy of crueler times; there were several concentric circles of them, representing times when the city outgrew its environs and had to expand past the last walls—and then more walls had to be built to protect the extended city. She couldn't imagine an attacking force getting as far as Haven now . . .

:Unless the attacking force came from within Haven,: Rolan reminded her. *:Remember what is happening in Menmellith at this very moment. If something happened to wipe out the Royal Family and there were no Heralds in the bloodline, inevitably, near relations of other Heralds would propose their own as monarch, and there could be fighting over it, whether the Heralds themselves participated or not.:*

She bit her lip, feeling a little sick at the very thought. *:But how? What Herald would ever go along with civil war?:*

:Lock him away from his Companion, and go to war in his name,: Rolan replied bluntly. *:Or lock up his Companion and threaten to hurt the Companion if he didn't go along with it.:*

That made her even sicker. She realized at that moment she had been laboring under a delusion that nothing could harm the Kingdom as long as there were Heralds and Companions, and that nothing could make a Herald do anything against his will. But that wasn't true. She knew she would do anything rather than have a moment of harm come to Rolan. And without their Companions, Heralds were just . . . people. People with Gifts, but still, just people.

"Ye all right?" She turned her head and saw that Renn was looking at her oddly. "Iffen yer skeert 'bout all the climbin'—"

She shook her head. "No, I was talking to my Companion and he reminded me of something unpleasant. I'm looking forward to the climbing."

"Well, good, 'cause we're gettin' there inna bit." Renn thrust his chin at the open city gates. The walls were high— three stories high at least. There used to be patrols of Guards on them, but not so much anymore. The Watch used them for looking down into the city streets and the alleys behind, not for their original purpose.

Renn was looking up at the walls wistfully. "Gi' a lot t'be able t' take a free run up there."

"Maybe someday it can be arranged," she replied, with a little smile. "Maybe even a race."

His eyes lit up. "A race! Cor, aye, that'd do 'er!" Renn, unlike some of the lads, was not a chatterer. She could see he was thinking about such a race, but he wouldn't say anything about it until the idea was well formed in his mind.

They passed under the walls through the gates standing open, and came out into common lands. They hadn't been common lands before; they'd belonged to the temple that had burned.

:I remember when it burned,: Rolan said, as they looked across the overgrown meadows where cityfolk who could afford such things had their goats, cattle, and geese grazing.

Horses, too. Each little group was watched over by a young caretaker. Each young caretaker was armed, with a sling at the least. And anyone trying to walk off with so much as a goose-egg was going to be set upon by six or eight or ten of them.

:You do?:

:It was your father's second year as King's Own. It—the Temple—was all but abandoned. It was one of those religions that died out for being too rigid, too many rules, too exclusive. Too judgmental. I think this was one of the offshoots of whatever religion the Holderkin practice. They began by having charismatic priests, got themselves quite a lot of money and built this monstrosity out here outside Haven to show how very much more superior they were to every other religion and sect. That was, oh, about a hundred years ago. They had a lot of influence in some circles during their heyday, and in another land, might have had a lot of power. But not here.:

Rolan tossed his head and uttered something that sounded like a chuckle.

:With every succeeding generation, more and more youngsters questioned, were put down ruthlessly, and left—left the Temple, left their families, everything. By the time lightning finally hit that ugly pile and set it ablaze, they were down to one half-crazed old priest and a handful of adherents who were almost as old. Needless to say, there were plenty of people who said the strike was an act of their own God, passing judgment on them. They scavenged what they could out of the ruins, and went South. I really have no idea what became of them.:

She regarded the ruined Temple in the distance. *:And you don't care?:*

:Someday they might be relevant. Right now, they are not. So I will not lend them so much as a single moment of my time.:

"Come on," said Renn, and led off at a trot. "Runnin' a bit'll warm ye up."

Amily was winded, and there was the start of a stitch in her side, but as she looked out across the meadows from her perch astride the rooftree, she felt exalted. Renn sat in what she would have considered to be a much less stable position, and grinned at her.

"Not bad," he conceded. "Ye ain't gonna be a messenger wi' thet gimp leg, but ye'll be able t'climb yer way outa 'bout any trouble. An' thet's the point, I reck."

"You're right, it is the point." She surveyed the rest of the ruins with a now-experienced eye. She could see Renn had only taken her over the easiest part. There was more here, a lot more. "Think I can learn to run the rest of this?"

He nodded, slowly. "It'll take time."

"However long it takes." She was just ecstatic that she'd been able to get *this* far. A few months ago she never would have dreamed it.

"Then keep on practicin' where ye kin, an' meet me 'ere ever' three days," he said, as if he had figured on doing that all along.

Maybe he had.

"Thanks Renn," she said, with feeling. "This is . . ."

He held up his hand to stop her from saying anything else. "Ye jest do wut Harkon tells *us*. Cain't pay back, so help th' next."

"I will," she pledged. And he grinned at her.

"Now we got th' *hard* part," he told her. "Gettin' down!"

She was glad she'd had that moment of triumph, because when she got back to her real work, it was all . . . frustrating.

So far, the King had managed to keep the reason for the

Menmellith Ambassador's presence quiet, and the Ambassador himself had kept himself and his men mostly in the suite of rooms in the Palace that had been provided for him. But everyone in on the secret was fully aware that the candle was burning down, and eventually. . . .

She knew she shouldn't be feeling so frantic about trying to *find* something. Mags had only just gotten to Attlebury, and they'd settled in. Her father couldn't have gotten to the first armory yet. And as for her. . . .

She spent most of every evening eavesdropping on the people the Inner Council considered the most likely culprits for supplying the rebels in Menmellith with arms—those who themselves were arms-dealers, or had near friends or relatives who were, those who had what the Seneschal considered to be "close" contacts on the other side of the Border and who might have some stake in who became King. Mostly she eavesdropped through lap-dogs, or some hunting hounds, and in addition there were quite a few cats—not pets, for the most part, but mousers. Amily's odd form of Animal Mindspeech allowed her to see and hear through the eyes and ears of any animal and most birds. She could also sense their thoughts, but so far, had not been able to actually communicate with them. This was unfortunate, because if she *had* been able to do so, she'd be able to get them to move to places where *she* wanted them to be, rather than hoping there would be a suitable spy in place by happenstance. Still, she had been able to overhear a lot of conversations. The problem was, none of them had been pertinent to the revolution in Menmellith. She'd learned a great deal more than she really wanted to know about who was going to bed with whom, quite a lot about interfamily marriage negotiations, and more than she had imagined there was to know about estate management. But there had been nothing even remotely related to the situation in Menmellith.

Tonight the King was sharing dinner with the Ambassador. They were on an informal, first name basis now, "Aurebic" and "Kyril." She was with him, of course, as was Prince Sedric.

Aurebic picked without appetite at the roasted chicken. "I wish I could help you more, Kyril," he said at last. "I've told you everything I know, which is not a great deal. Unfortunately, I know very little about that side of our King's family. Without resorting to a herald or genealogical records, both of which are in Menmellith, I don't know who in Valdemar he might be related to. If anyone. And as for his adherents—" Aurebic shrugged eloquently.

Sedric sighed. "And of course, you have no way of getting swift answers—"

"I have no idea if anyone would *give* them to me," Aurebic pointed out. "I don't know if I've been missed as yet—I don't often have duties involving Valdemar, as you have been a very good neighbor, and my post up until now has been largely an honorific. If someone notices I am gone, the Regent and the Council may think I merely went back to my own estate to find more men for the army. I hope that is the case."

"But if not?" asked the King.

Aurebic shrugged. "As I told you, there will be a limited amount of time before the negotiations that they have opened with Rethwellan bear fruit—or not. In any case, I must return within a moon or two, and sooner if Menmellith and Rethwellan come to an accord and declare open war on you."

"What if Rethwellan declines to enter the quarrel?" Sedric asked, and glanced at his father. "We sent our ambassador down there at the same time Herald Nikolas left. We might be able to work some persuasion there."

Aurebic put his plate aside, and reached for his wine cup. "That might buy you more time," he admitted.

They continued talking, speculating, making half-plans that depended on information they simply didn't have—and they knew it. And all the while Amily sat there, silently listening. And she knew that they *wanted* her there—they weren't ignoring her, they needed her there in case she came up with some tidbit her father or Rolan might pass her. Because she was King's Own, and she needed to know everything that was going on.

But Rolan said nothing, although she sensed him listening through her, and she felt . . . helpless. Definitely out of her depth. But she also knew her own father would have been feeling the same, because, after all, what could he do, either, except what he was doing now?

Now she understood, as she had not before, what it was that had driven him into the streets of Haven and beyond, hunting for that most precious of things, information. Now she knew why he was the King's Spy. Because pursuing *anything* that might help was better than sitting here feeling helpless.

When they had chewed over the last, ragged bit of ideas they had, Prince Sedric took his leave, and Aurebic and Kyril began pouring wine and reminiscing. "If you don't need me, your Highness . . ." she said then, tentatively, the first thing she had said all night.

"You're welcome to stay, Herald Amily, but I suspect it is shortly going to get boring, maudlin, or both," the King said with a smile. "You probably have better things to do than listen to a couple of old men lie about what handsome, charming, and utterly irresistible fellows they were when they were Sedric's age."

Amily stood up, murmured something about how she would never be bored, but they would probably prefer privacy, then bowed and left. The King was perfectly safe with Aurebic; she was sure of that, Rolan was sure of that, and the King's Companion was right outside the window. And there were two Guardsmen in the hall right outside the door.

The night air smelled clean and green with all the new things pushing their way up in the gardens. *:Mags is climbing about on a roof,:* Rolan said, as if anticipating her next thoughts. *:He misses you as much as you miss him.:*

:And Father?: she thought.

:Is getting someone very drunk. I believe he is quite hopeful about getting something useful out of this man.:

:Thank you,: she thought, as she reached the door of the greenhouse, opened it, and stepped through.

If anything the air smelled even greener in here; it had come to be a scent of comfort to her. So many good things had happened to her here!

She knew her way without setting a light and walked with steady, sure feet into the sitting room. She thought about going straight to bed but—

—but there were still a few candlemarks until her usual bedtime. And she might just learn something herself tonight.

There was no harm in trying.

She settled herself into her favorite chair, and sought for the mind of a particular cat who was welcome on the hearth of her master every evening about this time. . . .

———————

I do love Guild Halls, Mags thought to himself, with a chuckle. The thing about Guild Halls was that if it was a Guild that wanted to, well, show itself off, they did that on the outside of the Guild Hall with all manner of carved decorations, pillars and posts and unnecessary little toy turrets and things. All these bits and pieces made for ridiculously easy climbing. He had managed to find a place completely hidden by a false parapet, right at the chimney that led down into one of the upper rooms where the Guild Masters liked to gather and drink and gossip.

Gossip? They'd put a gaggle of old women to shame.

And since this was the Jewelers' and Gem Cutters' Guild . . . and since these were the men who were charged with assessing every gem, if there was anything amiss about what was coming into the assessment houses, this would be the place to find out.

It was that rarest of things in his line of work—a perfect night, a perfect place to listen, and the perfect perch to listen from. The night air was mild enough that he didn't need to hug the chimney for warmth. In fact, the men hadn't even bothered to light a fire, so their voices came up clear and easy to hear. It was an utterly cloudless night, and he could lie on his back with his legs tucked up and his feet comfortably braced against the false parapet and look at the stars while he listened.

:Wish Amily was here,: he said to Dallen.

:She does, too,: Dallen replied.

He was here for two reasons, mainly. One was to see if there was any gossip about one mine or another having bad luck of late—which could signal the fact that they were skimming the cream of their gems off and sending them elsewhere. The other was just to learn how these fellows did their business. He knew the mining end from the inside, of course, and he knew in general how to evaluate gems. But he didn't know it as these men did, who could tell you the worth of a particular rock down to the copper.

So he listened, simply absorbing the information, and watching the stars.

He did make a few notes about particular mine owners to concentrate on, as their fellows commiserated for a bad run or a shaft gone dry. This was mostly the first probe; he also needed to find out *so* much more about this town. It wouldn't be as hard as it was in Haven. For all that the buildings here reflected a high level of prosperity, this was little more than a large, wealthy village.

:That would be because the poor are concentrated at the mines,: Dallen said, picking that thought right out of his mind.

:Course they are. Those're the only jobs here, 'cept the ones at this inn, an' the skilled ones. An' if ye got a skill, ye ain't gonna be dirt-poor.: At least things were better for the miners now after the sweep through here when Cole Pieters' wicked ways had been uncovered. Cole was by no means the only mine owner who had kept his workers as virtual slaves, just the worst. Now, at least, the miners had decent homes to live in, enough to eat, and clothing that wasn't rags. That didn't make their jobs less dangerous, and it certainly didn't keep the mine owners from paying them as little as they could possibly get away with—but compared with how Mags had lived, this was paradise.

And likely it won't be hard to get 'em to talk. He just had to figure out how to get onto the mine property, how not to get caught doing so, and how to talk to the miners without anyone seeing him.

Have to find out if they allow peddlers and the like into them mining villages.

Not for the first time, he missed Bear and Lena. Having a couple of Bards about had been very useful for getting eyes and ears into places where a Herald wasn't welcome. But then again . . . he wasn't a Herald at the moment, was he?

Wonder if we could get Keira flat invited out to visit these places? I'd have'ta go along as her escort an' all. When she was bein' entertained, I could go snoopin'. . . .

It was certainly an idea.

:How'd you fare today?: he asked Dallen.

:Now that you ask . . . I've been doing some snooping myself.: Mags did not ask how it was that something the size of a horse, and stark white, could go "snooping." He already knew that Dallen had ways of not being seen that he could not use when he was with his Herald.

:*Do tell!*: Mags replied, still keeping half of his attention on the increasingly inebriated conversation floating from the chimney. :*And what did you learn?*:

:*To begin with, there is an astonishing number of young heirs to these mines that have no marriage prospects . . .*:

In the sitting room of Lord Jorthun's suite, Keira was holding court.

This was a sumptuous room by Mags' standards, although, of course, it didn't measure up to Lord Jorthun's manor. The furnishings were all antique, very heavy, unornamented, dark wood, softened with goose feather cushions in equally dark colors. Lord Jorthun would normally have been the one "presiding," but he had taken a throne-like chair off to the side, by one of the windows that had a small, square table next to it. Keira sat in a similar chair, placed with its back to the fireplace. One of the young men stood leaning on the mantelpiece. Two were in window-seats. The rest were on various ordinary (though still heavy) chairs and stools, and one occupied a sofa on his own. Coot served as page-boy, which meant he was *right* there to hear everything, but so was Lord Jorthun. That meant that Mags was perfectly free to bugger off and do investigations on his own, but right now, things were interesting enough that he was staying right here at the inn, acting as the second servant.

Lord Jorthun looked elegant, with just the right touch of dishevelment that suggested he was relaxed and enjoying himself. Keira was . . . splendid. She was wearing a gorgeous dark green gown that had been Lady Dia's, and suited Keira as it had never quite suited Dia. Dia had remarked without a hint of jealousy or rancor, that the color she had picked for herself made her look yellow, while it made Keira glow like an exotic jewel. Mags didn't know much about ladies' gowns, but he knew this much; the cut suited Keira as well as the color did, and it was modest enough and dark enough that it could pass for mourning. Lydia had tutored him through the ability to judge fabrics to the last copper, because knowing about the content of clothing told you a lot about the person wearing it. A gown of the latest style but made of cheap fabric would tell you that this was someone who was "reaching"—possibly far past her grasp. But a gown in an older style, but made of rich fabric meant this was someone who knew what she was getting and was willing to pay for it. He had no doubt that the gown Keira wore today was good enough to have been worn by Princess Lydia. And given that Lady Dia and Lord Jorthun were probably the wealthiest couple at the Court . . . likely Lydia had its twin somewhere in her closet.

Coot kept passing among the guests, offering top-ups to their wine-cups, and Mags followed him with hulled strawberries and single grapes heaped in a silver basket. You more or less had to offer something to eat, he supposed, but Lord Jorthun's plan was that the young bucks gathered here should get enough wine in them that they might start being loose-tongued. Strawberries would do next to nothing about soaking up the wine, of course. And offering them just underlined how wealthy Keira was supposed to be.

Jorthun was sitting back, playing his part to the hilt—that

of an indulgent father who might be enjoying the wine a little too much himself. Not so much that he was getting tipsy, nor so much that he was too talkative. On the contrary, he was mostly silent, merely sitting back in his chair and appearing to be a bit inattentive. Inattentive enough that he was completely missing all the flirtation going on.

He wasn't, of course. On the contrary. He was probably taking more mental notes than Mags was, and when this soiree was over, they'd all sit down and consolidate those notes.

Meanwhile Keira was playing her part to the hilt, being charming to everyone, and flirting with every young man equally.

There were seven of them. None of them were outstandingly handsome, which really didn't matter. Keira had already *had* a poor experience with an outstandingly handsome young man, and Mags had had a bit of concern before they arrived that she wouldn't be able to play her part as well if any of her targets had been good-looking. So that was one worry taken care of.

All of them were very alike in coloring, and it was apparent there had been a lot of cross-marrying in this part of the world, which was hardly surprising. The local mine-owning families had probably been intermarrying for as long as the mines had been here.

Their hair ranged in color from chestnut brown to a somewhat washed-out variation on the same color. They were all very tan. In this, they differed strongly from the wealthy young men of the Court. In this part of the world, being tanned meant you were well-to-do enough to be out-of-doors a great deal, and enjoying yourself in the sunlight doing things like hunting and fishing, rather than spending all your time underground or inside, sorting, grading, and cutting gems, or making them into jewelry. Of course, farmers and herdsmen were tan, too, but they'd never be mistaken for one of these fellows.

Mags was taking a particular fancy to one of them, who was *not* treating him like an invisible lackey, *was* trying to amuse Keira rather than impress her, and seemed to have a great many interesting things to talk about. His name was Tiercel, and his father was Mendeth Rolmer. Rolmer was not one of the gentlemen who had needed commiseration on a bad run of luck the other night, and he owned, not just one, but several mines. Mags hadn't yet been out to the Rolmer lands, but from the way Tiercel treated *him*, Mags fancied that Rolmer treated his mine workers fairly.

Tiercel had the typical local face—nose a bit too much like a hawk's beak to be handsome, cheekbones and chin both square, so that he looked as if he had been carved from a block of stone by an artist who either hadn't quite grasped that human faces have curves, or who was trying to make a point about the family connection to rocks and gems. His medium-brown hair was untidy—not the purposeful untidiness that some of the Court dandies sported, but as if his hair had a definite mind of its own and was determined to counter any effort to tame it. He smiled a lot, but not too much. He was drinking moderately compared to some of the others. Each time Coot and Mags came around with their burdens, he always thanked them, and looked into their eyes while doing so.

Mags actually felt sorry for him. He had come here, with intent, no doubt, to court a fine marriage prospect. He was very much taken with Keira. And this was all a sham. Poor lad, here he was, thinking he might have found someone he actually *liked* that his father would approve of, with no idea that his hopes were entirely in vain. It hardly seemed fair.

On the other hand, he was competing with several other young men who were just as much in the running—if this had been real—as he was. So his chances had never been outstanding in the first place. One out of seven, at best.

Mind on the job, lad, he reminded himself. Tiercel could be *anything* other than what he appeared to be. Just because someone was young, it didn't follow that he was callow. And if his family was slipping gemstones out of their mines to finance the Menmellith rebellion, there was no telling what was really in his mind at this moment. He could even be eyeing Keira with the idea of siphoning some of *her* income to the rebels. In that case, it was literally his job to be accommodating and pleasant to everyone here in order to leave the best possible impression with Keira.

"... oh, no," Keira was saying, in answer to someone's flattering statement that she must sing like a bird and play like a bard. "Father never wasted time on music lessons for me." She laughed. "And I do mean the time would have been *wasted.* I can't tell one note from another. Fortunately, this saves me from having to suffer through many, many mediocre performances of other girls. Not that I leave, of course, but it's no worse than listening to them read. It doesn't matter to *me* if they sing like a mule and play like a chicken pecking out notes! I can't tell the difference anyway!"

They all laughed, as they were intended to.

"Quite right," said Jorthun benevolently from his corner. "Gets it from me. Can't tell a Master Bard from a street-singer. Useful lessons, now, that's a different story. I made sure Keira had everything she wanted on that score."

"And what do you consider 'useful,' my Lord?" Tiercel was bold enough to ask, looking interested.

"History!" said Lord Jorthun. "Lots of useful things in history. If you know history, you're seldom unpleasantly surprised by what people do around you. And mathematics. Girl should know how to be able to check on her stewards and make sure they aren't cheating her. And shopping!"

The young men smothered laughter but a snicker or two snuck out. Jorthun merely smiled. "Oh, you laugh, but you won't laugh if you discover your wife spent a small fortune on some shoddy stuff for gowns that won't last a year! Or gets cheated in other ways! *My* girl knows how to find the best of everything and get it bargained down to a good price, and she doesn't send some steward to do it for her, she does it herself!"

Now, if this had been a Court circle, the assembled young men would have had far different reactions to this statement. They'd have ranged from astonished to appalled. Highborn women just did not *do* that sort of thing . . . or if they did (like Lady Dia), they took care to keep quiet about it.

But this was not Haven, and most, if not all, of these young men had been raised in extremely practical households where at least the *men* were overjoyed to hear this sort of thing about a prospective object of courting.

Keira smiled, and not at all coyly. "I was a young woman who was wedded to a kind, but very old man, who bought me anything I fancied. The household accounts were entirely in my hands, and I could lay those hands on as much of the income of his estate as I cared to. Merchants who assumed I would squander my husband's fortune on trash and trifles turned up at the door every day. My husband wanted me to have pretty things. *Father* made sure I was able to keep from being cheated over those pretty things. Father had experts in all manner of things teach me how to tell the good from the bad, and how to price it all." She reached across the distance between them and squeezed his hand. "He was a fine man, and so are you, Father."

Jorthun chuckled. "And no one taught you how to flatter, my girl, you had that from birth."

"Well, if I got a silver tongue it had to be from you," she countered.

They bantered playfully like that for some time, and Mags finally realized that they weren't doing this to kill time, they were doing it to create a particular impression—the impression that Lord Jorthun would approve of *any* young man who managed to capture Keira's fancy—and that Keira would not be easy to win, so they had best exert themselves in that department. But at least they were not going to have to fight their way past a protective guardian. All they had to do was win Keira herself.

You clever beggars.

He'd had no idea just what Lady Dia had been teaching Keira, and it was possible that some of this had come from Keira watching her own relatives. But Keira was putting on a masterful performance, and like every masterful performance, it appeared to be utterly unplanned and unstructured.

For that, she had his full admiration.

They brought the banter to an end on a natural note, as Jorthun asked Coot for a refill, and Keira turned her attention and bright smile to the company. And Mags could only watch with admiration as she manipulated them.

"Where'd ye ever learn t'lead fellers around like that, Keira?" Mags asked, after the last of the company had gone, leaving him and Coot to clean up the empty goblets and set the room to rights.

There wasn't much to clean up. The guests had been mannerly. Most of the work was setting the chairs back in their usual configuration facing the fireplace. The goblets had all been borrowed from the inn, which kept them for "gentry." Coot was picking them up and placing them carefully in the basket that had held the strawberries to take back down to the kitchen.

"Dia," Keira said, simply. "She pointed out that it was just *acting,* and I was always rather good at that as a child. I used to put on plays for mother and father, since we hadn't any money to spare on entertainment, and only got to see things like that when father's liege-lord invited us to his manor. The part I am playing is one she outlined for me, I merely have to make up the right words for it." Keira helped Coot with the goblets; poured the last of the wine into a carafe and added the wine pitchers to his burden.

"Dia is a good teacher, but *you,* my dear, are an apt pupil. I think you are going to make a capital agent for the Crown," Jorthun applauded, no trace of inebriation anywhere to be seen on him now. "I, for one, am grateful to the impulse that led you to apply as one of the Queen's Handmaidens." Jorthun remained where he had been the entire time; comfortably ensconced in his chair at the window. Then again, there wasn't much he could do; they were handling what little needed to be done. The last of the tidying up, Keira had said to save for the inn servants to do while she got her bath.

"And I am grateful that you accepted me," she replied, "And the only regret I have is that I am inevitably going to have to disappoint these nice young men." She turned and shrugged helplessly. "What am I to do? This is the job I am here for. I just feel rather sorry for them."

"You can certainly feel sorry for them, my dear," Jorthun said. "Just don't allow your sympathies to get in the way of doing that job."

Her expression hardened just a little. "No fear there. Really, I am seeing their best faces, and I know it. For all that I can tell, in private, they are beasts, and I keep reminding myself of that."

"As well you should, my dear," Jorthun replied, finally getting up from his seat. "Now, if you would all care to join me in *my* rooms, I'm having dinner sent up for all of us there. I think we have earned it, one and all."

"Coot, you jest go on over with m'lord and m'lady," Mags said, taking the basket from him. "Ye done right good fer your first try at playin' page-boy." He thought a moment. "Iffen ye ain't gonna starve, might could be a good time t'learn how t'wait on gentry at a meal."

"I ain't gonna starve!" Coot said with more enthusiasm than Mags had expected. "Iffen m'lord an' m'lady don' mind doin' the teachin'."

"Mind?" Lord Jorthun laughed. "I never mind teaching. To teach is both a privilege and a pleasure. Come, my lad, and together we shall explore the graceful art of meal service—an art that is seldom appreciated, and invisible when done well."

"Oh!" said Coot, as Mags went out the door carrying the basket. "Then it's 'xactly like pickin' pockets!"

Mags rode the appropriate number of paces behind Lady Keira; she had scandalized most of the town by appearing in a riding outfit with a divided skirt, much to his amusement. He couldn't imagine why all the pointing and whispering. It wasn't as if these people didn't see women in trews, after all. Female Heralds only wore dresses and skirts on formal occasions, and women who had physical jobs to do often wore breeches or trews, though some of them wore such garments under a knee-length skirt. But evidently the idea of a *lady* in a divided skirt was unheard of. He didn't blame her, though; the very few women he'd seen in that bizarre contraption called a *sidesaddle* had looked terribly uncomfortable.

:The only "ladies" they see in a very prosperous village like Attlebury are the wives and daughters of the well-to-do, who have their own rather stilted notions of propriety,: Dallen told him. *:Women like that seldom ride. When they do, it's on a pillion, behind a manservant or a relative. They don't ride to hunt, for instance, and they don't have property to oversee.:*

Well, that made sense, then. When he'd been on circuit,

they hadn't stayed long enough in any of the truly well-off places for him to get a notion of village manners. *:Seems I have plenty t'learn.:*

Dallen chuckled. *:Everyone does.:*

Once they were out of sight of Attlebury, Mags responded to Keira's gesture, motioning him to ride beside her, by urging his horse up those two lengths. When he got there, he could see she was smiling. "I shocked them, didn't I?" she said.

"Reckon so, Keira." He chuckled. "Dallen tells me that there's the difference 'tween Haven an' a village like thet. Odd little thins shock folks that don't see bigger towns much, and don't got much call t'leave their own streets." He gazed out over the fields on either side of them. "Country folk, not much shocks 'em. It's th' ones in towns thet git stuffy."

"Hmm," she agreed. "Well, they'll have to get used to me."

"Prolly you'll set a new fashion," he pointed out. "Been doin' my due snoopin' 'mongst th' servants. Maybe the mamas're shocked, but the gels'll be cuttin' up their skirts in no time."

She just chuckled.

They remained side by side until the walls of the estate Tiercel had invited them to shone as a gray line in the distance, marking the boundary between open fields and the estate and mine proper. He dropped back then; it wouldn't do to appear presumptuous, not if he wanted to remain invisible.

The last time Mags had seen a mine, his circumstances had been . . . rather different. Then again, it was evident from the moment that he and Keira rode in through the gates of Master Rolmer's property that this was nothing like the mines he had been forced to slave in.

Instead of the untidy sprawl of nearly wild forest that had been behind Cole Pieters' gates, the land on the other side of the walls here stretched out in neat fields alternating grazing and cultivation. Master Rolmer evidently didn't see any reason to waste good land in ornamental plantings, but he also didn't see any reason to put people off who were riding the lane up to his Great House, either.

Cole Pieters' Great House had been situated right at the mouth of his mine, and it had been the first thing you saw when you passed through his gates and got on the other side of his forest. Imposing, and more than a bit grim, there had been nothing ornamental about it.

Rolmer's Great House was something of a cheerful sprawl; it had several additions in different styles, probably added as the family had grown from the original Rolmer who had discovered the mine. But more to the point, unlike Pieters' unfriendly place, this Great House was surrounded, at least on this side, by a very tidy little village of well-constructed and well-maintained cottages. Mags had a very good idea of how many people it took to run a mine, and it looked to him as if this village was perfectly large enough to support two, and possibly even three shifts of workers with their families, *and* the folk it would take to tend those fields.

:I can't hardly believe my eyes,: he told Dallen, wishing that the Companion was underneath him and not a league or more away. Not because he was in the least fearful; more because he wanted someone who had been with him and seen the conditions at the Pieters' mine to see this.

:I really wanta believe this, an' I'm feared to,: he said, after a few more paces of his rather stolid horse. *:I wanta believe there's people that treat folks proper—:*

At about that moment, Tiercel appeared at their end of the road that led through the village, mounted on a good strong hunter. He waved at Keira enthusiastically, and sent his horse trotting toward them with a huge smile on his face. "Lady Keira!" he called as he neared them. "Welcome! We've been expecting you this past candlemark. Thank you for accepting our invitation!"

"Well, how could I fail to, when it was presented so hopefully?" she asked, with a smile. She waved her hand at the village. "What is this charming little village?"

"It's called Rolmer's Roost. We helped build it for our miners, and the folks that work the Home Farm." He wheeled his horse and brought it in beside Keira's. "My family has always been of the opinion that when you treat your workers well, they not only work well for you, but their children and children's children will *want* to work for you."

They were into the village now; Mags kept looking around himself to verify that he was seeing what he thought he was. The cottages were set pretty close together, but they were all two stories tall with plenty of room for a family. Each one had a bit of garden in the front, more garden in back, and they were all constructed sturdily of stone with thatched roofs. It looked positively idyllic.

Tiercel waved a hand to the right just ahead of them, where men were laying the stone walls of a new one. "I say *we* helped build it, because Father supplies the stone from the mine, and everything needed to finish each cottage, but the villagers themselves do the building. When a couple wants to wed, if there isn't a cottage vacant because of a death, we give those who want to work on it a day off every sennight besides their regular day off to build it. That way *everyone* has some stake in the building, and the families will make sure it's done properly. After all, who wants to have to dig your son and daughter out of the ruins of their home if you did it wrong?"

"Most enlightened," said Keira, with admiration.

Mags couldn't see their faces, but it sounded as if Tiercel was pleased with her reaction. "Servants from the Great House are given cottages to live in when they're too old to work, too," he continued cheerfully, seeing that she appeared to be interested. "We give the miners the option of building those cottages for the same pay as they'd get without bonuses in the mine, and they almost always take us up on that. It's a whole, real working village. No one has ever left."

"It seems like a logical scheme to me," she agreed. "My father runs his estate the same way, more or less. We have our manor village as well. But I confess I never considered the same applying to mines."

No more had I, Mags agreed silently.

Even though he was *looking* for trouble, he wasn't finding it. No sign of hunger, no sign of mistreatment. The cottages were clean, young children were busy at chores; usually baby-watching as their mothers did laundry or worked in the garden, or cleaned or cooked. There was one fellow sitting out in front of his front door in a willow chair, dozing in the sun, lacking a leg—obviously a victim of a rockfall. But he was *here,* alive and well if not whole, and clearly was being cared for. Mags could not help thinking of all the victims of accidents in the Pieters' mine who had been left to lie until they died or freed themselves, or someone took pity on them. And *then* there was no medical attention for them, so they generally died anyway. If they didn't, they eked out a miserable existence, dragging themselves about with no help, and more often than not, wasted away and died later.

No one ever helped them, much less gave them a decent place to live in.

Then Mags did notice one thing. There was no child older than about ten to be seen—

"Children ten or older work the sluices," Tiercel was continuing, as if he had read Mags' mind. "Of course, they can be at school, and some families choose that if their child is especially intelligent or not suited for the work. But most prefer the extra income, in case of things like Jake Dawe's accident." He nodded at the drowsing man. "His two youngest are at the sluice, and his oldest is in the sorting house. He'll likely go back to work in the sorting house himself once we are sure he is thoroughly healed, but that doesn't pay as well as the mine, and in any case, he's not fit to go back to anything yet. So the extra money coming in from the littles is welcome."

"When do they go down in the mines?" Keira asked. "The children, I mean. You say they tend to follow in their fathers' footsteps after all."

"There's no set age. We've got a height test and a strength test. If they pass those, and their parents are willing, then they go down. One young giant in Father's time went down at eleven, if you can believe it! Most go down at fifteen or there-abouts." They were out of the village now, and the Great House and all the mine buildings spread out before them. "In general we prefer not to have girls down there, because most of them simply don't have the strength in their upper limbs that the job requires, but there are a few girls as well as young men working the shaft. Now, would you like to be entertained at the House, or would you care to see more of the mines?"

Keira dimpled. "I'm sure you'll think it most unladylike of me, but the mines, please. I have never seen a mine, and I am most intrigued to discover where the stones come from."

Tiercel laughed. "Well, my lady, you won't be seeing ex-actly that. It's far too dirty and dangerous for you to go under-ground, and in any event, you wouldn't see much. It's a dark hole, the only light comes from very small lanterns, and the lads work close to the rock face. But I can show you the rest, and the mine-head, at least." He guided his horse toward the mine-head going into the hill that rose behind the mine build-ings. Already it was clear this was to Cole Pieters' mine as a dove was to a snake, because rather than overworked mine-ponies coming out dragging overladen carts, men were going into the mine-head carrying shoring timbers. Pieters had scanted on those as he had scanted on everything else. It mat-tered to him not at all if the shaft collapsed, as long as he could get miners back in to clear the debris away—but installing supports took time away from the mining, and it took money to buy the timbers.

Tiercel gestured at the mine-head. "It's not shift change yet. We don't work a night shift, and we don't work the lads before dawn or after sundown. The lads just opened up a new area though, so mostly what we are doing on this shift is putting in supports so nothing comes down on them."

Mags was aching to ask why they didn't work a night shift—after all, night didn't make any difference to men who were working in the darkness of underground.

Keira asked the question for him, again, almost as if she could hear his thoughts.

"Well, we discovered something—or rather, Father did. It seems that when you ask people to sleep during the day, they don't do as well, and you get less work out of 'em. So we don't work the mine after dark." He shrugged. "Father says by his calculations, because the lads are working at their peak all the time, and come to work well-rested, they don't make as many mistakes, don't get injured as often, and don't get sick, so in the end, you make as much money out of them as you would if you had the mine going the full day and night."

"Your Father sounds intriguing, reducing such things to numbers. I didn't realize one *could* do that with people and their work so exactly." Keira raised an eyebrow as her horse shifted under her.

"You can when you have four generations of insanely detailed record-keeping, my lady," Tiercel told her with a smile. "My family seems to have the head for such things. But come along, let's go to the sorting rooms, and then the sluice-rooms."

Sorting rooms, Mags was prepared for. But . . . sluice *rooms?* In Pieters' mine, the sluices had been out in the open, and it had been bitter work in the winter. . . .

There was a long, low building they were heading straight

for, stone-built, like everything else here, but with enormous windows. *Glass* windows! Made up of many, many small panes yes, but still—more glass than wall!

"Good gracious. . . ." said Keira, staring at them.

"Yes, yes, I know, more glass than most have in their manors," Tiercel chuckled. "But this, my lady, is the heart of our operation. We obtain the best prices because we grade our stones ourselves. And for that, we must have light, and plenty of it. But if we left the walls open, without windows, our people would freeze in winter and make mistakes. It is better to pay once for improvements, than to pay many times for mistakes."

He tied his horse to a post outside the door, and Keira waited while Mags dismounted, tied his up, tied hers, then helped her down. He followed them at a discreet distance, and saw what he expected to see; long white tables at right angles to the windows, with people sitting at them, sorting the rough gemstones, sometimes carefully freeing them from their matrix with small pick-hammers. This was just like Cole Pieters' sorting room, except that here the people looked perfectly healthy, not at all work- or careworn or looking nervously over their shoulders. They looked well-fed too.

"This is an amethyst mine, my lady," said Tiercel, waving at the first table, which was covered in rough, purple stone. "But we bring *all* our stones from all our mines here to be sorted. Pol, is there a particularly nice piece on the table today?"

The man at the table full of amethyst looked up and smiled. "Oh, aye, Tiercel. Sorted this handsome bit out not moments afore you come in."

He handed Tiercel a beautiful, deep purple crystal as clear as water and dark as wine, about the size of the end of his little finger. Tiercel handed it to Keira, who took it and exclaimed over its beauty, then handed it back to him.

Tiercel beamed at her. "This is the finest quality of gemstone, my lady. Not a pennyweight in a hundredweight is of this quality. Most are like this." He fished a piece out of one of the sorted piles. Larger, paler, and cloudy. "These are beautiful in their way, to be sure, and will give someone a great deal of pleasure. But *this*—" he held up the flawless piece "—*this* is what our reputation is made on."

Keira took it from him again and held it up to the light, then once again handed it back. "Truly beautiful, even without anyone forming it into a stone for setting. I had no idea." She nodded at Pol. "You, sir, must be very talented."

The man blushed a little. "Well, my lady, it do take a good eye and a mort of experience, I like to think."

"Now, a rare piece like the one you showed me—that is obviously going to the cutters. But what of the rest? Like this one?" Keira asked, touching, but not picking up, a clear, pale lilac stone.

"Clear ones go to the cutters. Cloudy we cut into cabochons— those are the domed gems you see in inexpensive jewelry." Mags noticed that he had not said "cheap" or "common," and appreciated the nuance. "Generally, the deeper the color, even cloudy, the more it is worth."

He took Keira on to another table, where a woman was sorting citrines. Mags examined the room itself without bothering to hide his interest—Keira might be the one getting the tour, but there was no risk in looking about curiously himself. There were a lot of things he noted about this place. The fireplaces at either end that would keep it warm in the winter . . . the jugs of water and a tumbler to drink out of beside each sorter . . . the fact that several of the sorters were clearly victims of accidents in the mines. This was nothing like Cole Pieters' sorting sheds. This was a good job, in a good place. Perhaps it didn't pay as well as doing the mining itself, but it wasn't as dangerous and difficult either. The sorters all looked contented—and again, healthy when you ignored their miss-ing limbs or other healed injuries—and most of all, not in the least intimidated by the presence of their Master's son.

After Keira had seen several more sorts of stones being sorted, they left, and moved on to the next low, long building. Outwardly it was like the one they had just left—except for the waterwheel, being turned by a small donkey, lifting water up to a sluice at the top of the building.

And except for the fact that the building was narrower, much narrower.

They went in. And there were the fireplaces at each end, and rows of children on either side, sorting through the gravel washed down the sluice. Dozens of sharp eyes and clever little fingers at work in the water.

But these children had pink cheeks, and weren't showing bones through their skin. They were well clad in soft canvas smocks over their shirts, and canvas trews, and wooden clogs. Mags stared at those clogs for a moment, as he fought down a sudden surge of envy. What wouldn't he have given for a pair of clogs and the nice, thick, handknit woolen stockings these children were wearing! His feet ached with the memory of the painful chilblains he'd suffered in winter . . .

"These are the sluices!" Tiercel shouted over the splashing water. "We bring out the rough and the obvious gems to send to the sorters. Then, we bring out all the rest, break it into gravel, and take it here, and the children look for the smaller stones. Even the smallest piece can be valuable if it is clear and of good color. Say hello to Lady Keira, children!"

The children all looked up at once and smiled, or waved, or even called out a hello according to their natures. Mags was shocked to the bone. Cole Pieters would *never* have so much as acknowledged that the children who worked his sluices were *there,* much less that they were living beings, much less that they were children. As for asking them to say hello to a visitor?

:Mags, you cannot fake this sort of thing. You cannot force children to look happy. This is . . . a good place, and good people in it. Whatever else you discover, keep that in mind.:

Mags was still feeling dazed as he followed Keira and Tiercel to the Great House. They all paused at the front door, and it was only then that Mags found his voice and was able to think of the proper thing to say. "My lady," he managed. "Would you prefer me to serve you, or remain with the horses?"

"My good fellow, go and take your ease in the kitchen," Tiercel said, kindly. "The grooms will get the horses. If you wish, feel free to roam about the village. I'll send a boy to fetch you when your lady is ready to leave."

Mags bowed. "Very good, my lord," he said, and held the door for Keira. Then he pondered his next move.

The kitchen I think. That is where the gossip is. . . .

Even Cole Pieters had not been able to stop that.

The only kitchen that Mags had ever been in that was better run than this was the one serving the Palace. And this one was a tie with the Collegium's for second place. The Collegium was not quite as well organized, in no small part because it was partly staffed by Heraldic Trainees who often had no more idea of what to do with a strange vegetable, or how to clean and stuff a chicken, than Mags had of how to make lace.

There was one hard and fast rule in every kitchen run like this one: find a place to stand that was out of the way until the head cook acknowledges you. Because until then, and until he or she decides what to do with you, you are an obstacle and a nuisance getting in the way of the important business of preparing food.

The room itself was all of the same stone as all the other buildings here, although, as in the sorting and sluicing sheds, there had been no effort at making the walls and stone-faced floor "pretty," just smooth. Enormous pillars made of entire tree trunks spaced at intervals along the wall held up the huge beams supporting the second floor. Pots and pans and utensils hung from hammered iron racks suspended from those beams, a clever way of keeping them out of the way but always accessible. It was a good thing that the hooks holding those racks were half as thick as his wrist; if one fell, there would be carnage.

The Head Cook here was a man, a surprisingly small but very nimble man with a head like a sheared sheep, in a bleached canvas smock and trews, who danced about the preparation tables like someone in an acrobatic troupe, admonishing, directing, stirring, scolding, and always tasting.

The very first thing Mags had noticed, was, of course, the heat. It was always hot in a well-run kitchen, even in the dead of winter. Your choice was to leave windows open for air but get flies in enormous quantities, or close them and close in the heat. Most cooks closed them, only opening them again when the cooking was over for the day.

The only kitchen Mags had ever been in that wasn't hot had been Cole Pieters'. It went without saying that Pieters had skimped on wood for cooking the way he skimped on everything, so that things were often burned on the outside and raw on the inside—or burned on the bottom of the pot, and cold on top.

There was lots of light here, though. Like the sheds, there was good glass here in the windows. *Easy to see, easy to keep clean.* That was what Cook at the Collegium said, anyway.

He found a good place to stand just to the left of the door and took it all in; one of the things that Nikolas had told him was that no matter what, the kitchen was the real heart of the household, and if anything was amiss in that household, it would show in the kitchen.

So, once he got past the heat and the controlled chaos that seemed to be the norm in any good kitchen, the second thing that struck Mags was the *aromas.* In Pieters' kitchen, they had been "smells." Burning smells, stale smells, the smells of food that was past its prime or even starting to rot or mold. Nothing could rid that kitchen of those smells, and Mags suspected they lingered even to this day, when someone else was running the mine. But this . . . these wonderful, wonderful *aromas* were enough to waken the dead. He hadn't been hungry when he stepped in the door, but he certainly was now.

Baking bread, that was the first thing that struck his nose. The loaves for the staff would have been baked overnight, but the "better" loaves, or smaller trencher-rolls for those that still used such things, of sifted white flour for the family were always put in just in time to come out hot for the meal in question and were just about ready now. Then came the hint of spice and sweetness that meant that desserts were also being prepared—given that it was strawberry season, he suspected it would be a white, lightly spiced cake to be covered in sliced berries, then "frosted" with beaten cream. Over in what would be a "cooler" corner of the kitchen he could see someone working with some small red objects with a bowl and a trimmed white cake next to her, confirming his guess.

Then there was the savory scent of roast fowl of some kind with sage and thyme—he couldn't tell if it was game bird or chicken, duck or goose. There was roast onion in the air as well; there would likely be other vegetables cooking, but the seasoned bird would overpower their scents completely at this point.

But . . . there was another scent as well, the rich and mouthwatering scent of a good thick soup or stew. And that was when Mags noticed that this was really two kitchens in one. To one side, the kitchen where all the things that would feed the gentry were being prepared. To the other, a smaller kitchen—smaller, because what was being made was much, much simpler—where the food for the servants and possibly even some of the workers was being made. And the Head Cook was weaving his way back and forth between the two of them.

The Cook was concentrating most of his oversight on the corner of the kitchen where the sweets were being made. A few moments after Mags took up his position, the Cook summoned a couple of servants and loaded up their trays with sweets and wine, and shooed them off.

Aha. Time to entertain Lady Keira.

As soon as he had seen to that, the Cook took a huge breath, slowly turned around to survey the entire kitchen, and spotted Mags.

"You there! Here!" he gestured and pointed at a little table in another out of the way spot, between two of the pillars supporting the ceiling. Mags obeyed him immediately, knowing the legendary tempers of Master Cooks, and knowing that it was not wise to arouse such tempers.

"You're hungry. Young men are always hungry. Sit!" The Cook grasped his shoulders and pushed him down onto a stool. "Maree!" he called, and gestured at one of the cooks on the "staff" side of the kitchen.

A round, red-faced woman turned, spotted both of them, and quickly filled a bowl at one of the great pots on the hearth. A moment later she had not-quite-slammed a wooden bowl of that stew he'd been smelling, a wooden spoon, and a healthy chunk of bread down in front of him. She dashed away and came back with a pitcher of cold water and a wooden mug, dropped those in front of him as well, and sped back to her work.

Well, all right then. Mags picked up the spoon and took a taste. Then another, and another, and soon was eating the stew as fast as he could get it into his mouth. Before he was done with the bowl, he had definitely identified several different kinds of meat in it—rabbit, pork, some chicken, possibly some venison, perhaps some squirrel. At a guess, these were pots that were kept going all day long, and filled in the morning with whatever meat was left over from the day before, with lots of vegetables added. Probably any game brought in that the gentry didn't want got quick-cooked then thrown in the pot as well. Thrift, of a kind, but smartly done. And *kindly* done. There were households in which the same procedure was followed but only when the meat had gotten too aged to put before the masters in any form. This was *good* meat, no one had shirked on the herbs, and there was no stale taste to it, which would have told him the pots were allowed to remain with whatever was in them overnight, and new added in the morning. That was a common enough practice even in otherwise good kitchens, but that kind of thrift led to sickness.

The bread was good; nothing special, but well made, not burned and not doughy in the middle, and of the dark, heavy sort usually reserved for people who were not of the gentry. It soaked up the gravy well enough, so what more could you ask?

When he finished his food, he looked around, and spotted the sink where a couple of industrious scullery maids were hard at work. He brought them his dishes and eased his way out of the door, carefully avoiding all the people rushing around doing what needed to be done. It was plainly evident that the only talking going on in the kitchen at the moment was confined to the business of getting the next meal in front of the gentry. Gossip would happen after the gentry's dinner was served, when the kitchen staff was eating their own, not before. He wouldn't learn anything here he hadn't already gotten by pure observation.

And after all, Tiercel had invited him to take a look at the village. So that was exactly what he intended to do. He strolled down the lane to the village, casting a more careful eye over it than he had been able to on the way in. It was a very fine village, from all he could see. He saw nothing to find fault with in the buildings or in the people busy about them.

But *he* was not expecting to be ambushed as soon as he set foot within the village bounds.

It came as a complete surprise when he was spotted by a couple of boys, and they came running straight at him. Shouting. It took him a moment for him to make out what they were saying.

"Oi, meester! Meester! Ye coom fra Haven?"

By this time they were standing in front of him, and fairly dancing with impatience. They were not like any children he had ever seen on mine property before—the mine slaveys had worn nothing but rags, and Cole Pieters' children were simply not to be seen before they were adults and able to work on the property as well. These children were dressed like the ones at the sluices but without the smocks—soft canvas trews and linen shirts. They were also barefoot rather than wearing clogs, but Mags suspected that was their choice, for what boy would ever wear shoes on a bright spring day who didn't have to? "Oh aye," he replied. "I coom fra hereabouts as a wee lad, but I bin in Haven many a year now."

"I tol' ye!" one said to the other, jigging in place. "I tol' ye! Didn' I tell ye?"

"Oh aye, now shet yer pie-hole," said the second, who looked to be about ten to the other's nine. By now other children were gathering about him, all dressed like the first two, girls and boys alike, and their mothers were finding ways to leave their chores and drifting along behind. The mothers were all dressed more colorfully than their children, in skirts of soft tones of pale blue, pale green, or pale brown, with white, embroidered aprons over them, and embroidered smocks over their linen blouses. Most of them wore their hair up rather than loose, often under an embroidered cap.

:Mags, do you see what I am seeing?: Dallen interjected while the children whispered urgently to each other, probably deciding who got to ask the next question. They were crowded so closely together around him he couldn't possibly have gotten past them without rudely shoving them out of the way.

:Just tell me, I'm a bit busy.: He didn't mean to sound impatient, but having all these children about him when he wasn't in Herald's Whites and thus accorded a fair amount of deference was distracting. He'd never attracted this many children, ever, not even when his little horde of messengers was flocking around him, wanting to tell him things to earn their extra pennies.

:These folk are making enough money at the mine that they have perfectly ordinary families. Families, Mags. The only family at Pieters' mine was Pieters' own.:

But Mags didn't have a chance to think about that, because the littles had decided that rather than take turns, they were all going to pelt him with questions at once.

And of course, what they wanted to know about was Heralds, and Haven. . . .

And *Kirball.*

He'd expected the first two, but not the third. Where in the names of all the gods had they ever heard of *Kirball?* He'd thought that no one outside Haven knew about the game!

"Kirball?" he replied, "Oh aye, but 'ow d'ye know about *that?"*

As he questioned them, it turned out that there was a pair of Kirball teams headquartered at Attlebury—not the kind that the Collegium fielded of course, but the simplified sort that didn't need Heralds and Companions.

"Master Hara an' Master Laon, they went ter Haven, on account'a theys gots 'Eralds in ter fambly! An' they seen Kirball! An' they gots the rules fer Kirball an' brung 'em 'ome an' started playin'!" One of the girls babbled all that out in a single breath, and when she paused to gasp, the boy next to her took it up.

"We seen it! We seen it at Harvest Fair! Oi! Don't it be *grand,* does Kirball! Ain't noothin' like!"

"Tell us'n meester! Tell us'n! Whazzit like wi' 'Eralds an' all?"

One of the women extricated him from the mob of youngsters and sat him down in her front garden. There everyone in the village who could get free, it seemed, gathered around to hear him talk.

He talked himself dry answering questions, and another woman brought him a tall mug of home-brewed ale. Then he continued, with the questions haring off in every possible direction, but always coming back to Kirball, like a bird coming back to its nest.

Finally one of the women asked him, "And did ye e'er *play* yon game, Lady Keira's man?" She smiled at him coaxingly. *Likely I'm the most exciting thing to come here all year . . .*

"I be Harkon," he said, finally having an opening to supply them with his name. "And aye. I played horseman." *Well, it ain't* quite *a lie.*

At that, the littles around him jumped about like crickets. "There be twa teams i' 'Bury!" one of them finally got out. "Ye gonna play? Ye gonna play?"

He managed not to roll his eyes. "That be 'tirely up t' m'lady," he said untruthfully. "Or maybe mi'lor'," he added, with more truth, because if Jorthun thought that there was a good chance of getting some information that way, then by all the Gods, Mags would play. Even if he did have to trust his safety to a mere horse, and not Dallen.

"It do be fair rousin', they says," said one of the women wistfully, wiping her hands on her apron. "I ain't never seen, but them of us as has say it be grand. Like tournament, an' there ain't niver been one'a them here, ever. Master Rolmer, he do say might brin' thet Kirball here, mebbe. I'd bid fair t'see un."

Mags really didn't know what to say to that. It wasn't as if it was in *his* power to get their Master to arrange for a Kirball match for the inhabitants of his village to watch. And anyway, this wasn't his business in the first place! He was here to get information, not chase a Kirball around a field!

"Harkon, are you boasting about your Kirball prowess? Or merely recounting the tales of exciting games as if you hadn't been on the winning team? If I know you, I'd bet on the latter." Mags turned around abruptly to find Keira and Tiercel standing behind him, separated from him by that crowd of villagers. There was a devilish sparkle in Keira's eyes, and Tiercel looked both amused and bemused.

What in the name of the gods can she be thinking? he wondered. Of course, he *could* have gone snooping in her mind, or even her surface thoughts, to find out, but anything other than surface thoughts would have been unethical, and she was very good at keeping most of her thoughts to herself.

And she'd probably kill me if she found out I had . . .

"Aye, m'lady, jest bin answerin' the liddles . . ." he said, ducking his head a little as if shamefaced.

"You were really a Kirball player in Haven, Harkon?" Tiercel asked, sounding extremely impressed.

"Aye, sir. On Collegium team, sir. Lord Jorthun, 'e liked me to." *A truth, a truth and a half-truth.*

"A *Collegium* team!" Tiercel's eyebrows rose. "They play a rough game, those Heralds."

"Not s'much rough, sir, as 'tis 'ard. Badder field, belike, 'tisn't smooth, 'tis full'a obstaculars. 'Tis like huntin' a-horse, or steeplechase. Hummocks an' dropoffs, bushes an' bits'a hedge. Bit of a stream runs acrost. An' th' goals ain't fer the faint; liddle stone forts, they be, 'alf buried. Nobbut could do it but Companions, *blisterin'* good riders an' Guard. We be lucky we ain't had more 'urt." *All true, that.*

Now Tiercel was getting a wicked twinkle in his eye. "I'd

imagine that you'd find our flat field and canvas goal quite tame."

Mags shook his head. "Differ'nt kinda trouble, sir, when's jest riders an' plain 'orses, an' none'a thet there Mind stuff. Not tame, attall. More dangerous, even, mebbe."

"So you wouldn't be interested in playing a game here, then?" Well, that explained the wicked twinkle in Tiercel's eye. "That would be too bad. One of the riders on Master Hara's team broke a wrist, and there's not going to be any Kirball at all until it heals, it's said. I could never get the teams to play here so my all people could watch, and not just the ones that could get to Attlesbury, because I never had anyone to place on a team. . . ."

"That'd be milady and milord t'say, sir," Mags replied, not sure if he wanted to kiss Keira for a clever idea or box her ears for a stupid one. " 'Tis on'y me an' young Coot t'do fer 'em. Were I breakin' somethin' it'd be Coot tendin' 'em alone, an' mebbe tendin' me, too."

"I'll have a word with father, Tiercel," Keira said gaily. "I'm sure something can be worked out!"

"We'll have to weigh all the points for and against this little plan of yours, Keira."

Keira had, thankfully, kept quiet about the whole scheme once she'd said "something can be worked out." She'd had a tour of the sprawling Great House, then an early dinner with the Rolmer family—early by Court standards, anyway. Mags had eaten in the kitchen with the staff; shepherd's pie, and excellent it was, too. Unfortunately, he'd learned nothing of any import because everyone was talking about Kirball. . . .

Then they'd ridden back to the inn, arriving just before the last light of twilight faded from the sky.

Now they were all gathered in Lord Jorthun's section of the suite, with fruit and wine and a night of consolidating information ahead of them.

"Well, the first thing I can think of 'gainst the idea is me gettin' hurt," Mags pointed out. "What'll ye do iffen yer roof-runner's down? An' Coot ain't bad at hearin' stuff, but 'e ain't got my experience."

"That is absolutely true," Keira admitted, swirling the wine in her goblet as the sound of crickets singing came in through the open window. "How risky is that?"

"I'd need t'see th'teams," Mags admitted. "An' play wi' 'em, a bit. I mebbe have a edge, belike. I cain't ride Dallen, but . . . I mebbe can use m'Mindspeech."

"How ethical would that be?" asked Lord Jorthun, soberly.

"Well, thet's the thing, ain't it?" He sighed. "Surface thoughts, that's all right. Dallen might could do somethin' with whatever horse I'd ride. Enough, maybe, I could figger out what people are gonna do afore they do it, an' get outa the way. An' I'm a damn good Kirball player."

"So let's count that as tentatively addressed," said Jorthun, passing over a plate of sliced apples. "Your next objection?"

"Thet it'd be a waste'a my time," Mags said bluntly. "I ain't gonna jest jump inter a team an' say, all right, let's play. I'm gonna haveta practice. I'm gonna haveta train m'horse, ye cain't jest take any ol' horse an' go play Kirball. All thet's gonna take time I won't be usin' t'snoop 'round."

"But the only way you are going to be able to snoop around the other mines is to go there," Keira pointed out. "And that means you'll have to go there with me, which means I will need invitations. Mind you, I don't think they'll be difficult to get, but still . . . But *my* little discussion with Tiercel revealed that the riders are all sons or cousins of the mine owners. Which should not be a surprise to you, since as you know, a Kirball match requires four or five horses for each rider, and only the mine owners could afford that many horses for something so frivolous. So while you won't be able to snoop around the mines, while you are training and playing, Jorthun and I can snoop around the young men and the owners."

"Next objection . . . I don't know that investigating these men away from their properties is going to bear any fruit," Jorthun put in.

"We also don't know that investigating them *on* their properties is, either." Keira nodded to emphasize her point. "Let's say, just for the sake of argument, that one or more of them are taking the large gems, passing them off to a common party, and having them sold elsewhere, out of Valdemar perhaps, to make the money to buy the arms. There simply won't be any records that the gems even existed, except, perhaps, in the memories of some miner who brought it out, or a crusher who found it in a large rock. The only way you are going to find that out, is if you are talking to that particular miner or crusher, and can compare his memories with the records at the Assessment House."

"Wait, the what?" Mags and Jorthun both asked at once.

Keira dimpled. "My afternoon with Tiercel was very educational. Once I passed his test by not begging shamelessly for that Royal Purple amethyst he showed us, and I evidenced interest in learning all about the business, he and his father opened up to me like spring flowers." She sat back in her chair and sipped her wine. "Mags knows all about how the gems get from the mine to the owner. I know what happens next. First, they are gathered in bags, each bag a particular value range as established by the sorters. Then, they are taken under guard to the Guildhouse, where they come under the eye of the Assessor. The least valued go immediately to Apprentice Gemcutters who make them into beads or cabochons, either irregular or regular, according to the value of the gem. The cheapest become beads, the ones a bit above that become

irregular cabochons, the ones above that become regular cabochons. The intermediate grade get sorted in the same way,
except that the beads are likely to be faceted instead of merely
ground round, in order to make them more valuable, and the
most valuable of the intermediates are also faceted. The most
valuable are sent on to the Master Gemcutters, who give them
especially brilliant cuts. When they are out of the hands of the
Gemcutters, they are re-evaluated, and that is when they are
sent out for sale. The mine owners pay the Assessor and the
Gemcutters through the Guild, so everyone is treated fairly
and equally. And when the gems are sold, the King's tax is
taken from the sale."

"That's all very interestin'," Mags said, rather puzzled as
to where this was going. "But—"

"But you see! There are only a few places where a large and
valuable gem can slip right out of the knowledge of anyone!"
Keira exclaimed.

"Oh . . . when the bags is made up." Now it dawned on him.

"Or before that. A very large and clear gem is going to be
brought to the attention of the supervisor before the miner
puts it in with the sorters," Keira pointed out.

"And if the supervisor had orders to bring such gems
straight to the owner . . ." Jorthun's voice trailed off as his
eyebrow rose.

"Sorters might have the same sorta orders," put in Mags.

"And there you go. The owner says something like *I'll see
this goes straight to the Masters myself.* And then it van-
ishes." Keira put her winecup down, empty, and did not seem
inclined to refill it. "But the workers are not paid by how much
in gems they bring out of the mine, they are paid by how
much time they spend mining—or crushing or sorting or sluicing. So they would have no reason to know it had vanished."

"So there ain't no records t'look through." Mags nodded.
"Or rather, the records ain't gonna show the missin' gems."

"So the only way to know if such things existed and if one or more owners is passing them off is to find out from the supervisors, the sorters, or the mine owners themselves. Or, possibly, the sons." Keira nibbled a slice of apple. "So my idea is to see what Jorthun and I can get out of them when they are at the Kirball game, or watching practices—or in the case of the sons, after the practices. We'll have them all together in one place, which will be useful. And if we are the ones generously supplying the drink, we can make sure it is a bit stronger than they are used to."

"It ain't a bad plan." Mags' furrowed his brows. "But is't good 'nuff to make up fer me spendin' so much time playin' a game?"

"Everything is a gamble, Mags," Jorthun pointed out. "We ourselves are gambling on the odds that our source of the funds is *here,* and not somewhere else, peddling some other commodity."

Mags rubbed his head, which definitely was aching at this point.

"But the truth is, you are the one at risk for wasting time, and not me, or Jorthun," Keira admitted. "So really, what do *you* want to do?"

Mags thought it over. Thought about how he was going to win the gratitude of all those people in Rolmer's Roost if he did this. Thought about how the game would bring together a great many spectators at the Rolmer mines. Remembered what Nikolas had always told him—

Two people can keep a secret, if one of them is dead.

"Let's try it," he agreed.

———

Keira had sent out invitations to all the young men who had turned up before, and a few who hadn't—this time, rising young men in the Cutters and Assessors Guilds. And fathers. There was not space enough in the sitting room of her suite for them all, but she had anticipated that, and had taken over one of the bigger rooms downstairs. Jorthun had a cask of something "very special" as he said laid in. Not strong enough to get everyone tipsy—they were saving the distilled spirits and the fortified wine for the day of the game—but certainly something strong enough to loosen tongues. And this time, invitations had also gone out to ladies—mothers and sisters. There was sweet wine for them, and cakes, while for the men there was strong cheese and salty snacks.

Once everyone had come that had responded to the invitations, Jorthun, rather than Keira, stood up and gained the company's attention by rapping on his glass.

"We've asked you to visit us for two reasons," Jorthun said, when the murmur of conversation had ebbed to nothing. "The first is that it seems only polite to introduce ourselves—although, by the miracle of gossip, you already know who we are, and very likely everything about us!"

There was a moment of laughter.

"But the other is that we have a solution to a small but vexing problem you have. Keira and I came to understand recently that you have been enjoying the sport of Kirball. But that sadly, you can no longer, because one of you—that would be Landen Wallis, I believe, over there by the keg—has had the misfortune to break his wrist, and there is no substitute for him."

Most of the gathering turned to look at poor Landen, who had one arm bound up against his chest. He flushed deeply, and looked profoundly unhappy. The surface thoughts Mags picked up from him got him Mags' instant sympathy. He *loved* the game with a passion he had never felt for anything else, and worst of all, it hadn't been playing the game that had cost him the use of his arm for a while. It had been dealing with a terrified horse during a thunderstorm.

"Well, as it happens, we have the remedy for you, at least until Landen can play again in a moon or so," Jorthun continued. "If you have no objection, Keira and I would like to offer the services of our man Harkon, who has played fourth rider on the Collegium Green team at Haven for the last two years."

Seldom had Mags ever felt the surface thoughts of a group turn round about so quickly. The initial reaction to *services of our man Harkon* had been negative, a sort of *how dare he offer a servant!* feeling shared by the young men on the two teams and their families, alike. Evidently, while it was perfectly all right for a servant to play one of the foot positions . . . it was *not* acceptable for a servant to be in the mounted role.

But all that reversed when Jorthun said *played fourth rider on the Collegium Green team at Haven.* The thoughts of the family members were a bit vague, more along the lines of "if he's good enough for the Collegium, I suppose we can accept him." But the young players? *Far* more enthusiastic. In fact, several of them started toward him. The thoughts spilling out of their heads were of admiration and desire to find out *what he knew* and *what he could teach.*

That was especially true of Merdeth Hara and Malcon Laon, the two young men who had actually *seen* the Collegium teams play. Mags was extremely glad at that moment that he had not used the name of "Mags" here. Even if they had been concentrating on the Trainees who'd been playing, and not the foot or the horse, they *certainly* would have heard tales of "Herald Mags" who had been such a wicked good Kirball champion.

It was Keira's turn to speak, since now people were beginning to talk, and it took a woman's high voice to carry over the crowd noise. "Father and I mean to say, if this suits you, we will be happy to do without Harkon so he can help you bring back your beloved pastime until your real player can come back to his team! Take your time and think about it, and let us know. Now please, enjoy yourselves."

It was absolutely clear to Mags that no one was going to need to "think about it." Medoes Kiren, the captain of the team with the missing man, was already most of the way across the room, and when he reached Mags, he held out his hand in an entirely egalitarian manner.

"Harkon is it?" he said, as Mags clasped his hand. "Well met, my good man. This is no end delightful! We'll be very pleased to take your services—"

"Master Medoes, I want ye t'know, I do know m'place," Mags said, earnestly. "Off the field, I be just Harkon, Lord Jorthun's man."

"But on the field, I damned well hope you'll be a demon on horseback," replied Medoes Kiren, as the rest of the riders gathered around and nodded eagerly. "Thing is, Harkon, it's a damned dull life for us fellows, out here in the back of no-where. Then along came Kirball, and well! It was as good as a war without anyone dying!"

Mags allowed himself a little bit of a smile. "I kin see thet, Master Medoes. Well, I 'spect all ye young masters are right quick an' clever an' smart, 'cause ye don' last long on the field iffin ye ain't. So if I knows summat that ye don't, be sure I'll give ye the knack of it. When kin we start a-practicin'?"

"By the gods, Harkon, you are a fine fellow! A toast, lads!" Medoes exclaimed, holding up his glass, as his friends did the same "A toast to Harkon, who has saved us!"

Mags dropped his head and did his best to look bashful, which was what these young men would think proper in a servant being so singled out for attention by his "betters."

They all drank down their wine and Mags refilled their glasses. "As to when, why tomorrow!" said Medoes. His eyes shone with pleasure. "We'll all send over some horses, so you can take your pick, right, fellows? That way you'll have trained beasts, that will only need to get used to you and we can start really playing right away!"

A murmur of assent from the young men of both teams followed that.

"Make sure you get six. We don't want you handicapped by having to play with an exhausted mount," Medoes continued. "Do you prefer tall horses, or ponies?"

:*Ponies, Mags,*: Dallen said immediately. :*I can handle their tempers, and ponies are better in the scrum as you know.*:

"Ponies, sirs," Mags said, this time bringing his chin up and looking them all in the eyes. "I be a scrummer, sirs, an' I ain't never backed down from a good mash."

"I like you more and more by the moment," Medoes exclaimed, his color high and his eyes sparkling—and Mags sensed very little of that was due to the wine. This fellow was utterly *passionate* about the game. He almost lived for it.

:*They are all second, third, and fourth sons with very little to do except try and find good girls to marry, and wait for their fathers to find them some job or other in the family business,*: Dallen told him. :*You've seen the like at Court. Except there is a great deal of mischief the young men at Court can get up to as you found out. There's not a lot that these lads can do out here that wouldn't be found out before the day was over. That leaves them with hunting—and you can't hunt in the spring— and fishing—and you have to have the temperament to fish— cards and dice—and none of them dares lose much or their fathers would have their heads. Horse racing, well, that's possible, but they are too well bred to race the horses themselves, it isn't much fun to watch someone else ride your horse, and again, if they lost money, their fathers would be furious. They'd probably be happier if they were poorer. But now they have Kirball. Small wonder they live for it.*:

Mags could certainly see that. It made perfect sense.

He continued to serve the guests all evening, making certain that the young men did not monopolize his time asking about plays he had made and plays he had seen. This was a very careful dance on his part; one false move, one slip that made it appear that he was not the born servant he was pretending to be, and he risked their mission here. Harkon, of all of them, was the one who dared have no questions asked about him.

When the last of the guests finally cleared out—it was the Medoes lad, who urgently reminded him that he was going to get about a dozen ponies arriving in the morning to sort through—he felt as exhausted as if he'd done a roof-run across most of Haven.

"The advantage of hiring this room is that the inn servants will take care of the ruins, Harkon," Jorthun said, as Mags made an abortive move to pick up a goblet. "I feel strongly in need of a nightcap and my bed. These festive evenings wear me completely out."

"Aye, m'lord," said Mags and held the door open for him.

"I'll join you in that nightcap, Father," said Keira, and followed him out, leaving Mags and Coot (who was yawning and trying to hide it) to bring up the rear.

When the door was closed on the rest of the inn, Jorthun got himself a glass of spirits of wine—something he seldom indulged in—and poured one for each of them. Even Coot, although he gave Coot only about half a tiny glass.

"Well, that came off better than I could have hoped," said Jorthun, sitting himself down and sipping his glass. "It's always a tricky thing when you barge into an established order and propose to shake it up, even a trifle."

"Aye that," Mags agreed, and threw himself into a window seat, taking care not to spill the precious liquor in his glass. He savored a few drops. "I was mortal glad of my particular Mindgift. At leastwise, I could read th' crowd."

"Well, we took a chance on a roll of the dice, and they came out in our favor," Keira replied. "How do you reckon tomorrow will be?"

"Easy sailin'," Mags told them, feeling much more confident now that the worst was over. "Dallen had a few thins t'tell me 'bout this lot."

He explained in a few words what Dallen had imparted to *him*, and Lord Jorthun and Keira both nodded in agreement. "So now, Dallen reckons, long's I don' get uppity, I got 'em like puppies followin' the pack-leader."

"To you and Dallen and the morrow, then," said Jorthun, raising his glass high. "And may the odds continue to favor us."

"Amen to that," Mags said fervently, and downed his glass.

The stableyard of the inn was crowded, but not with the horses of incoming and outgoing patrons. There was a string of ponies, and about a dozen handlers, lined up on the hard-packed earth of the yard. There were also a lot of onlookers, enough that you could reasonably call them an audience. Mags could sense Dallen's presence somewhere nearby; hiding, although it never ceased to amaze him how something as *obvious* as a big, snow-white horse could manage to hide. That was good, he was going to need every bit of Dallen's help he could get. He really wished Amily was here now. Her Gift of reading animals would have helped tremendously.

:Just put one hand on each pony's shoulder, and let me see what I can see,: Dallen told him soothingly. *:I'm confident we can get six good mounts out of this lot. They sent you good ponies, Chosen. None of them are too old, nor too young, none have been injured, and none of them have vicious tempera-*

ments. I think they're all mine-pony stock, which is good for us. Mine-ponies need patience.:

Well, Dallen would know. During Kirball matches, while *he* communicated with the other members of the team, and read the surface thoughts of their opponents during a match, Dallen was the one who kept track of the horses. He was the one who always knew if the ball was under the hooves of the ordinary horses during a scrum, and whether a mount was getting nervy about being crowded up against the fence.

Eighteen ponies were lined up in the inn yard, with more people loitering about than Mags had cared to count, watching him make his selections. He walked out into the yard, ignoring the impromptu audience, and surveyed the ponies slowly. Physically, they were pretty much of a piece; their colors varied about as much as rocks did, their coats were coarse, and they were strongly muscled. None of them wasted energy fidgeting, which was a good sign; you didn't want your horse wearing himself out before the game even started. They all seemed patient. Without looking in their mouths, he couldn't tell how old they were, but if he'd been sent good prospects, and it looked as if he had, they were all somewhere between five and ten. It was going to be Dallen's job to pick out the ones that had the *feel* for the game.

Until he had come on this journey, he had ridden a horse—as opposed to a Companion—no more than two or three times in his entire life. He had never been allowed nearer the mine-ponies than sleeping under their barn. He had always assumed, based on the behavior of the poor abused mine-ponies that they were stolid, dull things, capable only of going where they were led. It had never occurred to him before he joined the Kirball team that mere horses could have likes and dislikes and the temperament for something, but it was true. Now he knew better. He'd watched his non-Trainee friends schooling,

training, and choosing their Kirball horses, and the outstanding ones had been utterly brilliant. There were horses that
played because they were well trained, and horses that actually enjoyed what they were doing out there.

He put his hand on the shoulder of the first, a dun-colored
gelding, who didn't startle or even twitch, just flicked his ears
in Mags' direction. Then the pony turned his head slightly,
and looked Mags in the eye, then snorted with what sounded
like satisfaction and went back to watching the others.

:Him,: Dallen said, almost instantly. *:He'll be perfect. That
snort was because I pictured you during the game. He doesn't
want to be hitched to a cart, he wants to compete. He's played
before, and the only reason he's been sent to you is because I
think his rider likes taller beasts.:*

"This one," Mags said, and the pony was led away, and
Mags passed on to the next. He got a piebald one next, then
another dun with black socks and a black mane, then a cream,
and a black.

For a moment, as he was choosing his final mount, he was
afraid he'd have to settle for five instead of six—but the very
last pony in the string, a cheerful little bay who nuzzled him
as soon as he set his hand on the pony's shoulder, proved to
be as satisfactory to Dallen as the first had been. There was a
murmur of satisfaction from the crowd, quite as if *they* had
been mentally picking the same beasts as Mags was, and then
they all dispersed. The innkeeper had graciously volunteered
stalls for the ponies without being asked, so once they were
put up, Mags went to pay them each a visit. He knew from
talking to the riders on the Collegium teams that it was important to actually get to know your mounts before you asked
them to engage in something as potentially violent and dangerous as Kirball.

Unlike his friends who had not been Trainees, Mags had an
edge.

He stepped into the stall of the first one he'd picked, the dusty dun. *:This is Jess,:* Dallen told him. *:He likes the spot where his bit of a blaze is to be rubbed, not scratched. Right now he is wondering if you know how to rub correctly, and if you might have a bit of sweet about you.:*

"Well, Jess," Mags said, rubbing the indicated spot. "You an' me are gonna be partners fer a bit. Dallen tells me yer keen on th' game. Thet kinda makes two of us." The pony sighed and leaned a little into the rubbing, but kept one eye on him. Not wary, just interested. What was coming next from this new human?

Of course, he knew very well that what Jess heard was *babble Jess babble babble babble.* That was fine, the important thing was that Jess be used to him, the sound of his voice, the feel of his hands, and that the pony associate all of these things with someone to be relied on and trusted, with comfort, with steadiness. Horses valued reliability and steadiness. Horses valued trust. When Jess's eyes started to half-close, Mags picked up a brush and began running it, and his hands, over every thumb length of the pony's body, pausing to carefully pick up and gently set down hooves, and get itchy spots with the brush as Dallen instructed him. Then, to finish—as Dallen also instructed him—he breathed softly into both of Jess's nostrils, then gave him a piece of carrot. *:You give him the most intimate part of your scent,:* said Dallen. *:Your breath. They breathe into each others' noses, when they trust each other. When you do the same, that speaks to their hearts.:*

He did the same for all six of the ponies, as the stablemaster watched him. The stablemaster was working around him, puttering in the stalls, checking bits of harness and tack, trying not to *look* as if he was watching, but he was. Mags sensed surface thoughts of skepticism first, then a little surprise, then great satisfaction, and when he was finished with all six ponies and had left the last one's stall, the stablemaster came straight up the aisle to him, with his hand stuck out. Mags took it, as the stablemaster coughed.

"Wouldna thought it, city man," he said, as he enthusiastically pumped Mags' hand. "Wouldna thought it. I figgered ye was jest like them rich boys, get some 'un t' find ye a good horse, an ride it 'thout knowin' it. Ye knows yer way 'round a horse, ye do. That there was well done, an' proper done. I be Jess, like yon pony."

"Harkon. Thenkee, Jess," Mags said, releasing the man's hand. He gave the stablemaster a slow, quiet smile. *Looks like I have an ally.* "I'm a-gonna trust m'limbs if not m'life on these liddle fellers. Allus did reckon thet if yer gonna do thet with horse *or* pony, best ye get t'know each other."

"Aye t'thet. But where'd ye larn thet gypsy trick'a breathin' on 'em?" Jess scratched his head in puzzlement. "Thought I was the only man round hereabouts that knowed thet."

"From gypsies. I ain't allus bin a city-feller." Mags grinned now, and offered Jess a long, slow wink. "Spent almost a year-turnin' in a caravan." *True. Just not with gypsies.*

The stablemaster sighed with what sounded like envy. Mags was just a little surprised. All the other times he had seen the stablemaster, the burly man had seemed as stolid and unimaginative as any of the cart horses he used for the heavy deliveries to the inn. "Times I wishet I'd gone an' run off with them gypsies thet made me th' offer when I was a lad."

"Oh, well now, the road's a hard-luck life, which's why I ain't on it now," Mags told him, leaning back against a support and crossing his arms over his chest. "Looks free an' easy, but there's them as'll run ye off afore ye kin ast fer a night in meadow, an' ridin' along the road's a nice thing when yer belly's full an' it's Spring, but it ain't so nice when yer belly's empty an' yer got snow up t'the horse's belly."

The stablemaster put his index finger to the side of his

nose, then pointed at Mags, a little gesture that Mags had only ever seen in this part of the world, and meant "You couldn't be more right." Mags had seen the stablemaster use a lot of those gestures with his stable-boys, possibly because he didn't like to speak loudly and startle his charges. One of the cats that made the stable their home came walking along a stall partition at that moment, and the man absently reached out and petted her. She purred so loudly Mags could hear her from where he stood.

"I'll come by around dusk, an' palaver with 'em a little again," Mags told him. "If thet ain't no trouble."

"No trouble 'tall. Make free," the stablemaster told him, gave the cat one last long scratch, and finally sauntered off to his work. Mags aimed his feet in the direction of the inn, stopping at the horse pump to clean up a bit, as he smelled decidedly "horsey." *Well, that makes life a little easier. If I have to go sneaking about, the stablemaster's now less likely to stop me or ask me questions.*

This morning he had been instructed to take Lord Jorthun's boots down to just outside the kitchen today, and clean and polish them. *All* the boots, which was three pair, and would take him a good long time to do properly. This, of course, was an excuse to let people approach him and talk to him while he cleaned boots. So he sat down on a borrowed stool next to the kitchen door, and went to work. Shortly, one of the kitchen girls brought him a mug of water. Then one of the stable-boys offered to get him cleaner rags. As he worked, they'd come to him on some excuse, by ones or twos so they wouldn't get accused of loitering, and talk.

They wanted to talk about Kirball, of course. *He* asked about life in Attlebury, about the guests here, about local gossip, about anything he could think of that would teach him more about this town. And in the course of it, he insinuated questions about how some of the mines were doing, concentrating on ones he thought had the potential to give up some really outstanding stones.

Dallen listened through Mags' ears as the afternoon wore on, and he worked on those boots until they were as soft and supple as gloves, with the soft shine of satin. *:I'm gettin' the distinct impression that pretty much every mine that's doin' well has a lad in the Kirball riders,:* he said, finally, as he packed up the boots and his polishing kit and headed back to Lord Jorthun's suite.

:Well, that only makes sense,: Dallen pointed out. *:Who else can afford to keep eight or ten horses for one young man? It would have to be families that were doing very well for themselves.:*

He tapped lightly on Lord Jorthun's door but got no answer, and left the boots outside, lined up, just as a proper servant would. *:At least that helps us. I'm thinking Keira was dead right here. We've got all our targets in one place, an' distracted. If I didn' know better, I'd say she had a Gift.:*

:She does. The Gift of being a shrewd observer,: Dallen replied, as Mags went to his own room to get a bit of a better wash-up at the basin there. *:I'm very glad she is on our side. She's nearly as sharp as Amily and Lady Dia.:*

And that made him feel more than a little melancholy . . . because if there was one single person he would have wanted here, it was Amily, who had the knack of seeing things he missed, just as he had the knack of seeing what she missed. Together they were four times the Heralds that they were separately.

And just at the moment, *he* didn't have any progress to report.

I hope she's seeing more of this puzzle than me right now.

Music played distantly while courtiers stood about the Great Hall in small knots and talked, or, more likely, gossiped. Amily, in Formal Whites, stood at ease a little away from where the King was deep in a discussion of his own.

Before her stood . . . an inconvenient and importunate young idiot, who thought very highly of himself.

"Thank you, Lord Dalten, but my place is at the King's side," Amily said firmly to the third of a succession of useless young highborn who seemed to take Mags' absence as the signal to come and pester her with invitations to . . . well, ostensibly to "listen to a Bard in the next room," "join the dancers," and "come for a walk in the gardens." Kyril was taking no notice of them. He left her to deal with these idiots who should have known better on her own, as it should be. He was not there to rescue her; if anything she was there to rescue him, whether from someone he didn't want to speak with or from an assassination attempt. Though mostly, she was there to provide him with information, should he need it. Right now he didn't need it, as he was engaged with Master Soren, and there were things carefully *not being said* that were allowing Master Soren to read between the lines, so to speak.

She was trying not to show her exasperation. It was one thing to appear to be harmless and even a little naïve in order to make others of the Court underestimate her; it was quite another when things like *this* happened. It made her long to pull the concealed poniard out of her bodice, stick it under the right young idiot's chin, and hiss *"This is the third time you've asked me. No means no!"* before slipping it back into concealment before anyone else noticed she'd threatened him.

But of course, she couldn't do that. That would be . . . probably disastrous. Someone would notice, because he'd probably shriek and wet himself. Heralds didn't do that sort of thing. Not even when provoked. And oh, how provoked she had been, tonight!

And these same young idiots weren't the least interested in me—in fact, they snubbed me entirely—back when I was just plain Amily, Nikolas's poor crippled daughter. That rankled, actually. Not that she would have taken them up on whatever offer they'd made back then, or whatever condescending notice they'd given her. But it rankled that *now* they were all over her like flies on a honeycake, when *then,* she'd been something they literally did not see.

:*And now, you are King's Own Amily and single, as far as they are aware, and the next best thing to marrying the King's daughter, if he had one, to get the ear of the King. Of course they're taking Mags' absence as the opportunity to try and work their wiles on you. When are they going to get another chance?:* Rolan said, sounding rather too amused for her liking right now. :*Like it or not, you are a honeycake. No one takes you seriously as a guard, and this looks like a good chance to draw you off and try and test the waters. You can't blame them for trying.:*

Well, there Rolan was wrong. She *could* blame them for trying. They should know better, all of them. They all knew what the duties of the King's Own were! And if they thought that a Herald of any stripe could be lured away from those duties, they were idiots!

:*And mind your temper,:* he added, which . . . even though he was right, made things worse for a moment, as her temper flared dangerously high, making her cheeks flush and her eyes narrow—which the damn fool took for *his* work, making her blush and simper. His self-satisfied little smirk nearly pushed her over the edge.

And then, finally, her wits woke up and she smiled sweetly at the young fool. "Besides," she said, in dulcet tones, "I'm not stupid, my lord. No one who knows all about your special little pet at Mistress Bellamy's Crescent Moon is going to have a scrap of illusion that you are interested in *her,* and not the potential access to the King that she represents." She fluttered her eyelashes as he blanched. "Best that you retire gracefully, and drown your sorrows in her arms tonight. Do give Rosemiel my best, will you? I will say that at least you have exquisite taste. She's flawless."

He got even whiter, if that was possible, bowed stiffly, and made a hasty retreat.

The satisfaction she felt was tempered . . . a very little . . . by a slight guilt that she had taken a lot of pleasure in humiliating a young man who had himself humiliated her more than once.

:An interesting ploy. If you are trying to seem harmless and naïve, why did you do that, may I ask?:

There didn't seem to be any hint of accusation in Rolan's Mindvoice, so she answered him quite as seriously and unemotionally as she could. *:Politically, he's a nonentity. His father, however, is quite a different kettle of fish. He's on the Greater Council. I killed two birds with one stone. I made it very clear to the young fool that I know far more than he dreams about his doings, and he'll make it clear to his father, without revealing his secret infatuation with a courtesan, that there's no point in dangling any sort of bait in my direction because I won't bite. He absolutely* cannot *tell his father about his kept woman, so only* he *will be aware that I am not as harmless or simple as I seem. The old man will be left wondering about me, but one thing he will be sure of, and that is I cannot be seduced either by his son's handsome face or the father's wealth. With the implication, of course, that I might be female, but I cannot be bribed any more than a male Herald can be.:*

:Nicely done,: said Rolan, and he went back to lurking in the back of her mind.

"Thank you, Soren," Kyril said, just loudly enough to let her know that his private conversation was over. "That was most entertaining." Soren chuckled, and bowed, and rejoined the rest of the crowd.

"I don't think we'll extract anything more of any use out of the Court tonight, Amily," the King said quietly. "Shall we retire?"

"Certainly, my lord King," Amily replied obediently, and followed him to the door in the Great Hall that led to the passage to the Royal Suite. As she opened the door for him, the passage stretching before them was completely empty. Meant for servants, but generally used as much by members of the Royal Family, it was relatively narrow and very plain; wooden floor, plastered walls and ceiling.

As soon as the door closed behind him, leaving them in blessed, blessed silence, the King laughed quietly, and looked back over his shoulder at her. "Well done, by the way. Soren and I prolonged our discussion just to see how you'd handle him. There was silent applause from us by the way."

Now she flushed, and not with anger. "Three times in one night is above enough, Highness. And that's not counting the last Court gathering. Or the one before that. Evidently . . . well I don't know what he thinks. Maybe that any young woman without a male attached to her in some way is fair game."

"Soren thought you were going to take a dagger to him," Kyril opined, as they reached the door to the King's Suite and waited for the Guard placed there to open it for him. She was awfully glad the King had decided to leave when he did. She was beginning to get a headache, and the next young fool who decided to try that game with her *might* have gotten a dagger.

"I was tempted," she muttered, waiting for the King to enter and following behind him. The King's Suite was surprisingly subdued, given that it belonged to a reigning monarch. Everything was of the finest quality, but nothing was ostentatious.

When the door was closed, Kyril gestured to one of the

chairs next to the fire, where a light wine and two goblets were waiting. There was a very small fire in the fireplace, which seemed to be more for the ambience than the warmth. One of the chairs was already occupied by the Queen, who was embroidering; her hobby was to create book covers for gifts. Amily gratefully dropped down into the one next to the Queen. Standing for candlemarks at a time still made her leg ache.

"Nothing from Mags, I presume?" Kyril asked, as she poured him wine and handed it to him, then poured a goblet and offered it to the Queen, who waved it off with a smile, so she kept it for herself.

"Only that he's going to be in a Kirball game. Or games, he's not sure how many there will be." She sighed a little, this time with exasperation. She knew she probably should not be exasperated, that there was probably a very good reason why he was getting embroiled in sport instead of . . . finding things out . . . but it seemed to *her* as if he was taking this mission as a sort of excursion, while she was here, *working.* Just because he was there with Lord Jorthun and Lady Keira, that did not mean he should be wasting his time on . . . a stupid game!

The King shook his head. "If he doesn't find a game, the game finds him, I swear. Well, I am sure that he has a very good reason for this. And I am sure that he's not doing this for any frivolous reason. After all, he can't possibly play on Dallen, and that will put him at real risk for being hurt. He wouldn't hazard that if there wasn't the possibility of exceptional reward. Despite the fact that people think the Collegium games are dangerous, I think being out there without Companions and Heralds is probably a lot more so."

"Oh . . ." she said, chagrined that she hadn't thought of that herself. "No, of course he wouldn't." *Idiot!* she scolded herself. *Of course he isn't doing this because he's a games-mad thistledown-brained bumbler who is doing this so he can relive his days as a Kirball champion. Especially since he didn't particularly* like *being a champion, he just enjoyed the game itself.*

"It's certainly a fine way to ingratiate himself with the locals, and make them want to come to him, after all," Kyril pointed out. "Well, I have some word for you. Your father sent a message that he has visited the first of the armories on the list, and they have accounted for every weapon they sent out in the last year. He's moving on to the next. He said they seemed genuinely surprised that he should ask." The King swirled the wine in his goblet and frowned.

An idea occurred to her. It might be a stupid idea, but it seemed to her that it was worth proposing. "Is it possible that the weapons are counterfeit?" Amily ventured. "How hard would that be to do? Would there be a reason anyone would want to?"

"Not especially difficult . . ." The King pursed his lips thoughtfully. "That is a good question. If I may think out loud for a moment . . . there might be several reasons why the weapons would have been counterfeited. The rebels themselves might have counterfeit them in order to embroil Menmellith with us and gain an advantage. There is always Karse, of course, who could have counterfeited the weapons *and* supplied them to the rebels in order to increase the chaos in Menmellith and cause *us* problems. I'll see about that right now."

He closed his eyes for a moment, and Amily knew that he was doing exactly that; having Mindspoken conversations with the Seneschal's Herald, the Lord Martial's Herald, and possibly some senior Heralds who were here at the Palace but had not yet been given field assignments. She bit her lip a little, wishing she could join in on those conversations. It was to her eternal regret that the only way she could, was secondhand, through Rolan. There were advantages, she supposed. If she ever lost control of her Gift, the only person who would be affected would be her. And no one could wake her up in the middle of the night without *physically* coming to her door and knocking. But still, the disadvantages far outweighed the advantages. As far as she could tell, she was the *only* Monarch's Own never to have had Mindspeaking as a Gift.

Rolan laughed. *:You aren't missing anything. They're just deciding who is to go where. And apologizing to each other that none of them thought of the counterfeiting possibility.:*

Amily glanced at the Queen, who kept on working on the goldwork embroidery she was doing, with a little smile on her face. It made Amily wish for something to do with her hands. But that probably wouldn't look proper, having a Herald fidgeting with something, as if she found the situation she was in dull and boring. *I guess she's used to this by now, watching her husband get a blank look on his face while he has a long conversation in his head. . . .*

Her father had never done that, gone off into a Mindspeech conversation while she was in the same room. Then again, her father was not the King. Her father got brief respites from being the King's Own, even from being a Herald, in a way. Her father had probably been able to tell people, "Don't bother me, I'm spending a couple of candlemarks with my daughter, and she deserves all my attention." The King was the King every candlemark of every day. There was no escaping the terrible burden of the crown.

The Queen, who obviously was more used to her husband's expressions than Amily was, spoke up into the quiet room. "Well, my love, who are we sending away, where, and will we need to recall anyone?" Amily guessed she must be able to tell when Kyril was done with his conversations better than she could.

"Herald Tarlin is already right on the Border with Karse, and his Gift is Farsight. He'll do some spying without having to put himself in danger of getting caught by Karsite demons. Herald Jacinth has relatives in Menmellith right on the border with us and Karse; she's going to go visit them incognito and see if she can learn anything that way, either Karsites supplying the weapons, or the rebels counterfeiting them. I'm sending Herald Alissa with her, just in case she needs extraction." Kyril picked up his wine and sipped it, looking as if he was relieved that all this had been sorted out so quickly. "All of them are either on or near the border now. We'll just need to send down replacements for Jacinth and Alissa. I left that to the others to work out."

"I thought of another reason why the weapons might be counterfeit, Majesty," she said, feeling as if she ought to be slapped for not thinking of it sooner. "What if they were poorly made weapons being passed off as good ones by an unscrupulous trader?"

"That is a very good point, but it is one we can settle immediately," Kyril said, and chuckled. "We have samples in our hands. All we need to do is have one of our armorers test them to see if they are up to the purported source's standards. If a sword shatters at the first blow, we'll know that this was the simple reason, and we'll be able to call the Heralds back. It's better to get them on the job now and have to call them back, than wait and make a delay."

When she knew the other Heralds and their capabilities better, Amily knew helping to decide who would be substituting for the Heralds pulled off their circuits would be her job, and the only way she would *learn* that would be to go speak with the others now. "I should go—" she said, standing. "Majesty—"

"Quite right. You should go consult with Ferrin, Lyle and Watsen. I'll let them know you're coming. Go to Ferrin's rooms, and they'll all meet you there." The King smiled at her. "You can tell me the rest of what you had to say in the morning. I'm looking forward to hearing about your training and that odd fellow, Tuck. I have some requests of him I'd like you to make for me."

"I shall, your Highness," she replied, with a sketch of a bow. Then she turned and walked as fast as she could, heading for the Heralds' Wing. Already she was behind on what the others were discussing . . . and it looked as if it was going to be a very long night, if she didn't get there soon.

:I'll catch you up,: Rolan promised. *:We'll start with Herald Tarlin.:*

———————————

Morning came far too soon, after a long night of being treated to a rapid education on the Heralds in the South and their pertinent Gifts and abilities. Amily woke to the sound of the first bells with a groan. After fighting free of the covers and clambering out of the bed, she gave herself a good dousing with cold water, and felt, if not better, at least more awake. The one benefit of being overtired was that once she finished with the King, if she could justify a nap, she'd have no trouble drifting off to sleep.

It wasn't her day to visit Linden and Tuck, nor was it her day to get lessons in roof-running from Renn, so once the morning's work was done, she opted to snatch a bite or two of food in her rooms as she flung herself down on the bed, instead of having a "proper" lunch at the Dining Hall. The little page who regularly brought fresh rolls, butter, and other things that would not spoil had brought some fresh mixed greens and watercress. That on a buttered roll with thin slices of ham was a perfectly good lunch for someone who was so tired that her stomach felt a bit upset.

The bed felt wonderful. Someone had come in and made it up for her with fresh sheets scented with lavender, and her head felt better as soon as it touched the pillow and she closed her eyes. As she normally did during the process of falling asleep, she let her mind drift around to some of the animals she knew were in targeted homes "of interest"—mostly because these highborn or wealthy folk had kin in the south near or even across the border with Menmellith.

But all she got, as her concentration flitted from cat, to lapdog, to guard dog, to cat again, was general worry and unease. Unease from those who had kin on the Valdemar side of the border, and worry from those who had kin on the other side. No one knew, yet, about the threat of war between Menmellith and Valdemar, but it was obvious to folk who were used to getting regular letters from their Menmellith kin that something was wrong. Letters weren't coming. And letters were *expected,* given the situation with the rebellion going on. At least three families were anticipating that they might have to find a place to put displaced relatives. They hadn't been pleased by that, but what could one do? Family was family, and blood was blood, and you had obligations that went far past a little inconvenience and perhaps some crowding.

But now that communication had completely stopped, that was even more worrisome than the threat of having relations to house.

It was not at all a productive session, and she rather regretted the time she had wasted trying it. But at least she knew that none of these folk had any information on the smuggled weapons. Not that those relatives across the border were innocent—there was no way of telling that—but the ones here in Haven had no inkling of any smuggling going on, past the normal sort that every merchant family seemed to engage in.

She finally drifted off to an uneasy sleep, wishing her Gift was something more useful than this.

———————

The sun beat down on what had been a nice stretch of pasture; pasture that had been carefully groomed of any "presents" left behind by the horses that had been here. The horses themselves had cropped the new grass nicely short, which was one reason why it had been chosen in the first place. It was a pretty stretch of field. It wasn't going to stay pretty for very long.

"Well, gemmun. Reckon we're ready?" Mags looked around at the members of his new Kirball team; although he was not nominally the team captain, that young man had surrendered the title within moments of the start of their first practice. Willingly, even eagerly.

Kirball for non-Heralds required a much abbreviated team; four riders, and eight footsmen, at least as this group played it. It was also played on a perfectly flat field, hemmed in on all four sides by fences of some sort. In this case, two of the sides were painstakingly erected wooden fences, and two were hedges, long in place, since hedges were far more forgiving for horses that ran into them than wooden fences could be. The hedge ends were where the goals were, in case the horsemen overran the goals. It was much more likely that any hits against the fence would be at an angle rather than straight on; these were all excellent horsemen, and they would do whatever they could to save their beasts any injury.

The goals were nothing like the miniature fortifications that the Collegium teams used. It was much, much too dangerous to have something like that in a version of the game where there was no team of Healers on the sidelines, and there were no Heralds who could carefully coordinate every move of the entire team. These goals were canvas stretched over a wooden frame; one hole had been cut about window-sized and window-height, and another cut next to it, down to the ground, to represent a door. The flag was behind the blank canvas of the goal, out of sight, the better to enable the footmen to sneak up and steal it. If these goals got overrun, the worst anyone would have to fear would be the splintered uprights. That could be dangerous, but the wood was willow, and unlikely to splinter into lethal shards the way a hardwood could.

The eleven young men (eight footsmen, and the other three riders) around Mags nodded solemnly. The three horses—and Mags' pony—stood easily, showing no sign of stress, reins slack in the riders' hands. The other team was all on horses, for all four quarters. Mags' team was divided half and half, although initially the other three riders were on the taller beasts, while he was sticking to ponies for the entire game.

"All right. Fer th' first quarter, I reckon the best plan is t'run 'em up an' down th' field, an' see what they learnt from me," Mags told them. Just to be fair, Mags had taken an afternoon and taught the other side all the drills that the Collegium teams used, until he thought they had the basic notions down solidly. But that didn't mean he wasn't savvy enough to do a good deal more than just drill his team. He and his ponies had demonstrated how to *really* scrum, and gotten their horses used to getting shoved against the fence or into the hedge. With Dallen's help soothing some of their panic, he'd gotten them conditioned over the course of a couple of days.

But he wasn't blind to the fact that the other side probably had people watching those practices, and bringing back the information on what he was doing. They'd probably conditioned their mounts in the same way. He couldn't use his Mindspeaking ability to coach and direct every member of the team the way he could if he was Herald Mags. The best he could do would be to skim off the intentions of their opponents from surface thoughts. So this was very likely going to be a real battle.

"All right then. Let's get ready for it. Mount up, gemmun. Lads, get into the field." Mags suited action to words as he swung into Jess's saddle and felt the pony gather himself under him. Jess snorted and tossed his head eagerly. He wanted to play. He'd enjoyed the practices, but he knew that they weren't games. Jess had wanted to play in a real *game,* every minute they were practicing, at least according to Dallen.

The eight footsmen distributed themselves across the field; the goalsman at the goal, the other seven spaced at strategic points on their half of the field. Around the fences and behind the hedges were those folk of the Hara and Laon workers that could get leave to come, all the members of the actual families of the seven riders that had any interest at all in seeing the game, and every single person at the Rolmer mine here, for the entire lot of them had been given an afternoon off to watch the play. The gentry were sitting in nicely constructed bleachers on either side of the field; the rest found space where they could, and the more enterprising had gotten bits of log to stand on to see above the heads of the rest. It was actually a far more enthusiastic crowd than Mags had seen at the Collegium. It wasn't as colorful, however. There was no Bardic Scarlet, Healer Green, or Guard Blue in the crowd. Most of the spectators were in the slightly fancier version of their workaday clothing, but the colors were muted, all things they could get from herbal dyes. But even the gentry had opted for light colors, being as they were sitting right in the full sun.

The excitement among the spectators was palpable.

The eight riders formed a rough circle in the very center of the field. One of the judges held the ball. The crowd fell into a silence so absolute that every note of birdsong, and every insect call, echoed into the quiet and filled it up. Mags breathed, slowly and steadily, to keep Jess from tensing up so much that he jumped into the circle too soon.

Then the judge tossed the ball into the middle of them, Jess leapt for it almost before Mags had realized the ball was in play, and the game was on.

As he had expected to, Mags and Jess nipped in under the noses of the taller horses and got away with the ball, heading toward the Laon goal. But he couldn't keep the ball, not with four larger horses thundering down on him in a virtual stampede. They were so close behind him he could almost feel the hot breath of the straining horses on the back of his neck, and the pounding hooves drowned out any other sound.

He sensed, rather than saw, that his teammate Retner was free. With a powerful *thwack* of his club, he sent the ball hurtling toward Retner, then wheeled Jess to force the pony's shoulder into the chest of the horse overtaking him. Jess responded with enthusiasm, happily charging into the taller horse and throwing him off-balance. He didn't so much *hit* the other horse, as knock him off his course and startle him, making him blunder sideways and lose his momentum—and as luck would have it, in his turn stumbling into the path of a second Laon rider. That tangled them both up as Jess scuttled away, and kept them from following the ball. Retner got it, and was down the field in a trice.

He knew there was no way Jess could outrun the taller horses, so he backed off a little until the other two Laon riders caught up with Retner, and they all came up in a knot against the fence. *:The ball is under the hocks of that scrawny bay,:* Dallen told him. *:I think it's going to stay there, they can't seem to figure out where it is.:*

:Unless the bay kicks it afore we get there,: he replied. Then he and Jess dove in, again got in under the noses of the taller horses, shouldered between two of them, and got the ball away.

Then he got a lucky break, a clear shot all the way to the goal, with only the goalkeeper standing in the way—while the rest of the Laon riders still thought the ball was in under their horses' feet, and the Hara riders were perfectly happy to let them keep that illusion. Off he and Jess scuttled, him thwacking the ball in short bursts, and heading straight for the goalkeeper while Jess kept his head down and his nose practically *on* the ball, chasing it like a hound. He'd gotten about halfway there when the Laon team figured out they'd been jiggered, and came tearing after him, the Hara riders mixed up with them. He looked back over his shoulder and saw that two of the Laon riders had pulled a little away to the sides, intending to intercept the ball if he got it too far ahead of himself. But Mags was too wise in the ways of the game to let that happen. He kept dribbling the ball and Jess kept his head down, and no one could catch them with the head start they had to physically shove him away from it. His head was pounding as hard as the hoofbeats behind him, and the crowd was screaming. And as he suspected, the goalkeeper, unnerved at the spectacle of six animals heading straight for him, with no sign whatsoever they were going to pull up, dove to the side to avoid getting trampled. At the next to the last moment, the Laon riders lost their nerve and pulled up. At the last moment, knowing that little Jess could make a short, tight turn *much* faster than a taller horse could, Mags pulled him around and at the same time, drove the ball through the goal.

The crowd went insane. Mags took off his helmet, ran a hand through hair already soaked with sweat, patted Jess on the neck, put his helmet back on, and turned back to the center of the field for the judges to send out the ball again.

The rest of the quarter was spent running the ball up and down the field, without anyone managing to get full control of either the ball or the field. The footsmen all made some abortive attempts at the flag, but each time they were spotted by the opposite side, and prevented from making a run for it.

The next quarter, half the Laon riders switched to ponies, as did one of the Hara riders. That put things on a more even footing. The game turned from a race into scrum after scrum, while the spectators screamed encouragement until they were hoarse. By this time Mags was sweating freely under his armor and helmet, feeling runnels of sweat pouring down his back. The field didn't have any grass left over the parts most contested,

and the horses were kicking up so much dirt and grass that
Mags had his mouth full of it and kept spitting out grit. The
footsmen were hard at work, fielding the ball back to the riders
whenever someone hit it long. Finally Mags, on the cream pony,
who seemed to have a supernatural ability to interfere with the
other team's stratagems, somehow shoved his way through the
scrum, kicking the ball as he went, and freeing it. It dribbled
down the field and one of the Laon footmen got hold of it and
hurled it toward the Hara goal. But the Hara goalkeeper fended
it off with a miraculous save, and sent it back toward the horsemen. Mags and the cream dove after it, but they were too late;
the captain of the Laon team got hold of it, and ran it all the way
to their goal despite the valiant efforts of their goalkeeper.

Mags wasn't going to let that stand. He and the cream
nipped in and got the ball back and sent it round their riders
and footsmen until the Laon team was dizzy, then Mags
passed it to Tem Hara, and guarded his back all the way to the
goal, the cream shoving and shouldering for all he was worth,
collecting some bruises for himself and a bruised hock for the
cream. Even as Tem was making the goal, Mags reined in the
cream, and gestured to the sidelines where stableboys were
minding the horses.

He didn't have a pick in mind, but the boy dashed onto the
field with the reins of the piebald in his hands, and that was
good enough for him. While the others were still collecting
themselves, he switched ponies and the piebald charged right
up to the fray, leaving the stableboy to lead the cream gently
back to the lines to have that hock tended to.

The rest of the quarter was a scrum, in which no one gained
any advantage, the footsmen again tried for the flag but got
blocked, and they all retreated to their sides at the whistle for
a switch of horses for everyone but Mags.

"You going to stay with Jumper?" asked Tem, as they all
huddled up.

Mags nodded.

"He's mine; watch him, when he loses his temper, he bites. He's also got a clever trick of stopping dead when you rein him hard, going right down on his bum. It's damned useful when you want to block someone, but they *can* come right over the top of you if they're on something taller. If that happens, I expect you know what to do. I never dared try it under someone's nose, but you—" He shook his head with admiration. "You're neck-or-nothing."

"Good to know." Mags nodded. "I kin use thet. They're 'spectin' me t' run in under their noses now—Tem, yer on that lightnin' bay'a yern, ye jest go fer it, an' we'll block fer ye."

Tem was only too happy to do just that. His bay was strong and wicked-fast, and had the stamina to keep running for the full quarter, being a former steeplechaser. Three times, they went up and down the field, Tem never once giving up control of the ball, as the rest scrambled in pursuit, and the footsmen ran for their lives. Then Mags saw his chance, he and Jumper dove into the middle of a tangle of horse, and Mags reined his pony in *hard*.

Just like that, Jumper sat, going right down on his haunches as Mags made himself as small as possible.

He felt at least two horses blunder right into him and go down, and protected his neck with his hands and Jumper's neck with his body, and when the dust cleared, there were two Laon horses pulling up lame, a Hara horse shaking his head dazedly as his rider dismounted, and Tem had made the goal. And he? Well, he felt as if someone had been beating on him with stout sticks for a few moments.

Jumper had not gotten off unscathed either and he was going to take it out on someone if he could; he snapped viciously at the horse nearest to him, which shied away violently, evidently being well acquainted with the piebald's temper. Mags dismounted and soothed the pony with his hands.

:Let me quiet him for you. He's bruised all over, just as you are. I need to let him know he's done well and he'll cool right down.:

Mags continued to soothe the pony with hands and voice while Dallen presumably told him what a little hero he'd been and the rage faded out of his eyes. Finally he snorted once, stood up stiffly, and started walking on his own to the sidelines. Mags caught up with him and picked up the reins, waved for a remount, just as the whistle blew for the end of the quarter.

Bloody hell, I am sore. Cain't imagine what poor Jumper feels like.

Mags walked the pony back himself this time, and surveyed the remaining mounts. Finally he decided on the second dun, a filly called Dust. She wasn't the fastest, but she was the steadiest, and he had the feeling that the third quarter was going to be grueling. His mouth was already so full of grit he wasn't bothering to spit it out anymore, and under his armor, his clothing was absolutely sodden.

And so it was; it was one long scrum from beginning to end, and the other team got a goal about three quarters into it, and a second goal right at the end, by pure amazing luck. That put them all even.

Mags switched again; they all did, taking the biggest, strongest mounts they had. This was it. The last quarter. A goal made now would probably be the winning one, and everyone on both teams knew it. Beneath helmets, faces were set in determination—not grim determination, but a sort of half-mad, half-elated determination. Once again it was three horses to his pony, with the team counting on him to be the one that would dash in and pull the ball out from under the noses of the opposing team.

It was a brawl from start to finish, with the spectators screaming until they were hoarse, drinking down whatever was at hand to restore their voices and screaming again, and the ball changing hands at least a dozen times. And at last, the footsmen finally got the chance at what they were supposed to do, and each side made moves on the opposing flags, and Mags and Reg Killian of the opposing team were the ones that cut the runners off and snatched back the flags while the rest wrestled over the ball, horse and foot alike.

All to no avail. The quarter ended without either team scoring, leaving the match ending in a tie.

When the whistle blew, everything on the field just . . . stopped. Mags slid off his pony and laid himself down on the churned up-earth, and he was not the only one. The rest slumped over their beasts' necks, or slid to the ground like Mags and sat down where they were. Poor Dust just hung her head, sides heaving, sweat making runnels in the dirt that covered her, nose to haunches.

And then the spectators poured onto the field, and so did the attendants, bringing buckets of water with them. Mags seized one and poured it right over his head, then another and drank directly from it, then offered it to his pony, who lipped at it wearily. She was too wise to drink fast, a paragon among ponies, clearly. *If I didn' have Dallen . . . Oh, these are good beasts.*

:No worries, Mags, they have good masters, and after seeing that you picked them for your string, they'll be made very much of as long as they live.:

Their attendants shoved their way through the mob of deliriously happy people—who, truth to tell, didn't seem to care which team had won because the match was so exciting. The beasts got led away to be attended to. And so did the humans. Mags was absolutely certain he was not the only one who was bruised within an inch of his life. But he was also certain he was not the only one who was completely contented with the outcome of the game. Really, he was happier with it being a tie than he would have been if his side had won.

He was, however, hoping past hope that the mob was taking him to a bathhouse . . . and so they were.

It was the communal bathhouse meant for the people of the village, but the young gentry didn't seem to care that this wasn't one of their plusher arrangements, nor that they were sharing them with farmers and miners. Once they had all gotten the dirt off—and Mags was fairly certain he had a garden's worth in his hair alone—they all piled into the hot soaking tub, both sides together, and sipped at the lovely beer that was brought to them.

Mags sighed in mingled pleasure and pain as the hot water hit his bruises.

"That . . . was epic," someone said out of the fog.

" 'Twas," Mags agreed. "Cain't think of a better match e'en at Collegium." The bathhouse got very quiet as he continued. "Lemme tell ye somethin' gents. This were a total epic match. I ain't never seen one played harder, an' that includes ever' match I played at Collegium."

The silence was as thick as the steam that rose off the hot water.

"Now lemme tell ye why. At Collegium, ye got Heralds on both sides. They kin use their magic t'talk to each other, and some'un on 'em kin use it t'talk t'us. Thet means no shoutin', an' no guessin', an them Companions is smarter nor most of us, *jest* like humans. Then atop that, there's a whole parcel of Healers off t'side. An' what'd we hev? We had jest our own eyes an' ears. Jest our own wits, and muscles, an' how we kin handle a pony'r horse. An' no Healers. An' *look* how we scrummed! Tellin' ye, lads, yer all as good or better'n any Kirball player at Collegium, an' I am here t' tell ye I am *proud* t'hev played with ye all!"

They were all too tired to "burst out" into anything, but the pleased laughter and mild "huzzahs" and compliments returned were more than enough to satisfy him that he had ingratiated himself into their midst more thoroughly than any other stranger possibly could.

Then there was tired silence for a while, as one by one, they contemplated their various bruises, and tried to decide if it was worth getting out of the hot water for anything.

"I could eat a pony," said someone else. "I shan't, though, because Cousin Rolmer has got a pig roast going, and I intend to eat my way from one end of one to the other. Well *done,* my lads. And thanks to you, Harkon. Now we know how the game's to be played!"

"Aye," Mags agreed. "Thet ye do."

"Majesty, there is a problem."

If there was ever a phrase to make Amily's hackles rise, it was that. And to have, not a just a messenger, but a *Herald* arrive in the middle of the meeting of the Inner Council and demand admittance, only to say *that*—

A Herald who looked as if he had just seen a Karsite demon or a ghost. He was a ginger-haired man, which meant that he was so white now he was almost transparent. Amily clutched the arms of her chair and did not even try to look calm. This was the Inner Council and there were no secrets here.

The Herald took a deep breath and continued. "Two days ago, a large and heavily armed party with the credentials of the Menmellith Regent arrived at the Border. They demanded that we return their Ambassador. And they demanded that we let them across to get him themselves. They would not tell us anything else."

There it is. The headsman has turned up with the axe. . . .

"And you let them across, of course," the King said, calmly, quite as if he had no idea at all that this meant war was imminent.

"Of course, Majesty, but, I must tell you, that Herald Asher, who met them there relayed to me that—" the Herald looked as if he was groping for words, because the only ones he had were too terrible to speak.

"—that they believe we are guilty of acting against them and that they are about to declare war on us," the King supplied for him, calmly. "The Ambassador has already warned us. I had hoped that he and I were making progress but evidently his own government no longer trusts the progress reports he has been sending to them. Was there anything else, Herald Sai?"

The poor man shook his head. "Nothing but that. Herald Asher Mindspoke to the limit of his ability, which was to reach Herald Marga, who Mindspoke to Herald Fenris, who Mindspoke to me. Have you any answer for him?"

That was when Amily had an idea that was just audacious enough to work. Because what they needed now was *time,* and this just might buy that time for them.

"Majesty," she said into the stark silence. "I believe you need to tell Asher, and every other Herald along the way here, that what we need is to create as many obstacles between here and the Border as we can. The more we delay their arrival here, the more time we will have to prove that although the weapons might have come from Valdemar, the Crown in no way supplied them."

"What sort of delay did you have in mind?" the King asked, as the rest of the Councilors turned their gazes on her.

"Everything. Anything. Washed out bridges. Find someone who can slip into their camp at night, or the stables of the inn they lodge at, and lame their horses. Give some of them an illness, if that is possible." Not even marginally *ethical,* but what else could they do? "I don't know how big the party is, so I don't know if it's feasible to dress some of our people up as bandits and pretend to take them hostage, but I would not put that out of bounds," she concluded, desperately.

"Let's start with laming their horses," the King replied. "Any halfway competent Healer can do that. Herald Sai, I would like you to relay that back to Asher, and any other Heralds that are along the way. I am perfectly comfortable with ordering something that is marginally wrong if it will prevent war."

Herald Sai bowed. "Yes, Sire," he said, and left the room as fast as he had come.

The King turned to his Council. "Ladies and sirs," he said, his expression still one of calm. "It is time that you thought back to your pasts, and all the evil tricks you ever wanted to play on someone, and drag them out into the light for me. When we have finally exhausted every form of mischief we can think of, I will have it passed down the road to the South."

Then he shook his head. "Whoever this poor fellow is, in charge of this group, I feel very sorry for him. He is about to have the worst sennight or two in his entire life."

"Loosen the wheels, if he has a carriage, or weaken the axle," suggested Master Soren.

"It's easy enough to give them all the flux. I know a few things that will do that without harming them in the least." Healer Danil scratched his head thoughtfully. "I doubt they've brought enough provisions to last them the trip. They probably intend to get Auberic and take him home without saying anything about declaring war. I can give you a list, and the chosen misery can be either slipped into what they buy to cook or what they eat at an inn."

"If they camp, we can run off their horses," pointed out the Lord Martial's Herald. And so it continued, as Amily made note of every suggestion, no matter how unlikely. Because the suggestions might seem unlikely to *her* but there was no telling whether or not the right set of circumstances would present itself to let them carry out that suggestion.

But oh, how she wished Mags or her father were here— because this was exactly the sort of thing they excelled at.

And no matter *how* much they managed to delay the inevitable, it was, in fact, just that. Inevitable, unless they found the culprit responsible for supplying the weapons, and proof that the people of Menmellith would accept.

:*Rolan,*: she said, as she wrote. :*We need to warn Mags and Father.*:

:*We certainly do. Leave that to me.*:

"This 'un is yours. I'm s'prised," Linden said, handing over the package containing the outfit that Amily had left with her and Tuck to be modified. "It ain't as heavy as I thunk 'twould be."

"That's because Tuck is a genius," Amily replied, with a warm smile for Tuck, who ducked his head, flushed, and smiled back. "Just because his head doesn't work with speaking out loud, that doesn't mean he isn't smart."

The new income from Lord Jorthun, Mags, and now the King had made an immense difference in the little "shed" that Tuck and Linden called home—although not on the outside. The last thing that Linden wanted to do was to draw attention to the fact that their living circumstances had improved, and Amily agreed with her. Outside it still looked like a shed. Inside, in between his other projects, Tuck had made vast improvements with the materials that had been brought in. Cleverly, too, since on Lady Dia's orders, the former brewery that the shed was attached to was getting a major overhaul, and the materials for Tuck and Linden had been brought in along with the much bigger loads meant for the laundry.

Rather than moving anyone completely out of her room or set of rooms while they were being renovated, Lady Dia had sent over some very nice tents to pitch in the yard. It was Spring, after all, the weather was good, and in the event it became *very* bad, there were plenty of neighbors that would let you sleep on the floor for a night or two. The first thing that had been upgraded was the installation of a communal bathhouse and jakes. Then the basement was properly finished, rather than leaving it as a dirt-floored cellar, and lines strung in it so it could be used as a drying room in wet weather, and a *much* cooler ironing room. This allowed the women living here to work together rather than pressing clothing in their own rooms. With that done, the tenants were now getting their rooms redone, two tenants at a time. It wouldn't be palatial, but doors and windows would be weather-tight, there would be no leaks in the newly plastered walls, and a clever invention of Tuck's, a bed you could pull down from the wall at night, meant that every bit of floor space could be used during the day.

Tuck didn't have one of those. He had something even more clever, a bed on pulleys you could pull down from the ceiling and lock to the floor. Also his own invention.

He had done every bit of the work on the "shed" himself. All the walls had been finished with horsehair and plaster. He'd reinforced the floor of the loft and the ceiling. He'd repaired the roof himself, with all the proper materials, so it was as weather-tight as any Great House on the Hill. There were all manner of clever storage places now, and a new stove made on the same model as the one he had patched together out of bits and pieces gave Linden more cooking space, and would make the place cozy as could be, come winter. Two men from a foundry owned by Lady Dia had come to examine every thumb length of that stove, had taken the design, made some slight improvements that allowed for cooking and baking as well as heating, and were now selling it as the "Jorthun Stove," with part of the profits coming to Tuck and Linden.

That . . . had left Linden in tears, although Tuck hadn't really understood what it meant. Tuck understood trading—you made something, you could trade it for something else—but money had no meaning for him. But Linden understood what this meant.

"I thunk th' day Tuck got nicked an' taken up t' Court wuz th' wust day of me life," Linden said out of nowhere, getting a second package out of a cupboard. "But it were th' best. If 'tweren't fer thet, we'd'a niver met up wi' Mags, an' he'd niver ha' coom 'ere. Then Mags'd niver known wut Tuck kin do. An' 'e'd niver ha' tol' Milord an' Milady. An' then *you'd* niver ha' coom 'ere, an' we'd all still be scritchin' 'eads o'er 'ow t'talk t'Tuck. An' 'e'd still be makin' trifles. An' we'd still be poor. An' if anythin' 'ad 'appened t'me. . . ." She brushed tears out of her eyes with the back of her hand. "Now I knows thet if anythin' 'appens t'me, Tuck's got people t'look out fer 'im, an' 'e's got *money* should 'e git too old or 'is 'ands go bad an' he cain't work no more. This 'un is Lady Dia's."

"You can count on that, Linden," Amily said firmly. "More than that, you can stop thinking about Tuck all the time, and start thinking about yourself. You never know. There might be a lad in your future. And if he wanted you to set up house with just him and you, Tuck could stay *here,* and maybe you could get some rooms in the big house here, and if you were busy there would still be people looking out for Tuck."

Linden was no longer looking like someone's much-abused rag-doll. Her hair was still wild, but it was no longer hiding a face that, while not conventionally pretty, was lively and now wore an expression of happiness rather than constant fretting. And she had clothing that might be second-hand, but was at least made of entire whole garments rather than pieces of a dozen other outfits worn one over the other in an attempt to cover all the tears and holes.

"I dunno," Linden said reluctantly, glancing over at Tuck, who, as usual, was bent over a workbench humming to himself. But Amily could tell that she had set wheels turning in Linden's brain, and a possibility had opened to her that had never been there before.

"For that matter, now you can pay someone you trust to keep an eye on him when you want to go somewhere that might take all day," Amily pointed out. Linden nodded thoughtfully.

"Well, ye gimme a lot t'mull over." Linden was still getting out packages. "This 'un is fer His Kingness. An' this 'un is fer Mags. An' this 'un is fer Her Princesship." It was easy enough to tell them apart, as she had tied them up with different colored string. Amily's was the biggest package of the lot. The ones for Kyril and Mags were quite small, and the ones for Dia and Lydia about a quarter the size of Amily's. "Tuck still 'as lots t'do fer Lor' Jorthun."

"We don't expect him to get all of it done at once, Linden," Amily reminded her. "Let him work at his own pace."

But Tuck must have come to a stopping place in his work, since he turned and beamed at her. "Tuck like work," he said, radiating satisfaction like the sun.

"Do you still remember the other things I asked you to think about?" she asked him.

He nodded. This time his reply was wordless, conveying that there were some objects he had worked out how to make, and some that he hadn't yet. But he was sure that eventually he could.

"Take as long as you need to, Tuck," she assured him. "You've already done much more than we ever expected!"

He beamed again, then lost interest in the conversation, as he was inclined to do, and went back to what he had been working on. A moment later, he was humming again, deep in concentration on whatever it was he was crafting.

After making certain there was nothing that Linden could possibly need or want for her and Tuck, Amily bundled all her packages into a string bag she had brought with her—just in case—and went out to join Rolan. Rolan was waiting patiently in the drying-yard, politely accepting bits of bread or wilted flowers or whatever scraps of greenery the children could find. Tuck had gotten over the novelty of having the "Pretty Horse" come visit, and came running out to make much of the Companion with the other children only when he wasn't deep in a project.

She thanked all the children, and sent them back to their play; they went, reluctantly, as she mounted her Companion. They joined the traffic in the street. :*I'm frustrated,*: she admitted to Rolan, as the crowds parted slightly to let them through. :*We are running out of time, and there is* nothing *I can do!*:

:*You can be the King's Own,*: Rolan told her. :*You can be steady and keep everyone else from panicking. And . . . there actually is one more thing you can do, now that I come to think of it. Something only the King's Own could get away with.*:

:*There is?*: she demanded. :*What?*: Just the *idea* there was something she could contribute had her excited.

:*After you give your packages to be delivered by pages, you can go talk to the Rethwellan Ambassador,*: Rolan said, with a . . . could there be such a thing as a mental smirk? :*He's planning to leave in a few days. He doesn't yet know that Menmellith is trying to recruit Rethwellan should they declare war on us. And as you are aware he is extremely susceptible to aiding pretty young women.*:

Her jaw nearly dropped. Was Rolan suggesting what she thought he was?

:Yes, I am saying to go behind Kyril's back. You and you alone could get away with this; it's the prerogative of the King's Own to do what the King would like done, and can't, for various reasons. It is better to beg forgiveness in this case than ask permission.:

She looked down at Rolan's ears. They were pointed back at her. *:Is this . . . ethical? We all pledged to tell no one.:*

:How is it not?: he demanded. *:Technically you pledged to tell no one in Valdemar; and all you are going to do is tell the Ambassador something he is going to find out in a fortnight anyway. You like him. You know he is an honorable man. You know he is prepared to help as long as it doesn't compromise his duty to Rethwellan in the least. Do you really want to let him walk into that situation with no preparation and no warning?:*

She chewed her lip, as Rolan eeled his way through the traffic, heading ever upward to the Hill. *:Well,:* she said. *:No. Not really. That's not really fair.:*

:It just so happens that all this information will be trusted *more if it comes from the King's Own, and more palatable if it comes from an attractive young woman.:* Rolan swiveled his ears for emphasis. *:When your opponent hands you a weapon, then use it. And yes, Maranthenius Vorthelian is not an opponent. And yet, he is. He is always going to work for Rethwellan's best interests. It is your* job *to make him understand that in this case, Valdemar's best interests are Rethwellan's as well. How you do that is your business.:*

Well . . . this was just politics again, and it was all very well to say that word as if it were a curse, but the job of King's Own was always going to be about politics. There was no other way around that. And it was not as if she was going to be trying to seduce Maranthenius. She was not even certain she *could* if she wanted to. The Ambassador was an old, old hand at this game. He'd certainly see a seduction attempt coming and deflect it.

But he deeply enjoyed the company of pretty women. He

enjoyed the company of intelligent, pretty women even more. She *thought* that he valued the kind of candor that came of being a fundamentally honest person, even though—or perhaps because—he was not one. This could work.

:*You're right. I'll just "drop in" on him with a farewell token. And we'll see what happens from there.*:

:*An excellent plan,*: said Rolan with great satisfaction, and he picked up his pace to a slow trot, finding holes in the traffic with such surety that she suspected Foresight.

Amily tapped on the door of the Rethwellan Ambassador's suite in the Palace, with a nod to the Guard at the door—also a native of Rethwellan, but wearing the sort of non-uniform of one of the mercenary companies that were often employed there, rather than something official. He nodded back at her but maintained his wary pose, as was only proper.

The Ambassador maintained a small entourage of a Secretary, a couple of personal servants, and his guards. It was the Secretary who answered her knock, a small, balding, deceptively mild-looking little man who always wore charcoal gray and black. He said it was to hide the ink blotches. Amily, who was well aware that he kept two poniards in arm sheathes on him every waking moment, rather thought it was because such colors hid other stains as well.

He blinked at her in confusion. "Herald Amily," he said cautiously. "the Ambassador was not expecting you so far as I am aware. Is there an appointment I was not made privy to?"

Amily smiled at him. "Not at all, Kleventhalaril. I just wanted to say goodbye to the Ambassador as Amily-the-person before I had to do so as Amily-the-King's-Own-Herald."

"Oh, well then!" The Secretary favored her with a smile that *did* reach his eyes—as his smiles often did not. He held open the door. "By all means, please come in, and have a seat. I'll see if he can pry himself away from the packing."

She entered the little reception room, and took a seat on the sofa near the fireplace. As small as the room was, it was organized into two very distinct sections—a desk with a chair facing it for official business, and a sofa and chairs at the fireside for informal meetings. She set the tone by taking a seat in the latter section. Like all of the guest suites in the Palace, this one was themed—in honor of Rethwellan, the theme was "prosperity." All the furnishings were in jewel-tones and rich woods, and the rugs and tapestries featured the Rethwellan symbol of wealth, an apple tree bearing apples of gold. The golden apples were everywhere, woven into the rugs, carved on the vases, made into lamp-bases. She wondered if he ever got tired of them.

While she waited, she turned the little carved goldenoak box in her hand over and over, smiling a little. It was Tuck's work, one of his "pretties." Interestingly enough, Tuck never tried to carve anything that resembled something living; he always carved geometric patterns, in the mode she was told was called "chip carving." Tuck had made clever little leather hinges, and a leather and bone "hasp" to hold it closed. This wasn't a box you would use to hold something that was exceptionally valuable. It was the sort of box you used to keep something of sentimental worth.

"Amily, my dear," said Maranthenius, both hands outstretched, as he entered the room from the private part of his suite. "How immensely kind of you to give an old man the pleasure of a personal visit from such a lovely young Herald!" Maranthenius was a short man, like his Secretary; his hair was likely white under the yellow he tinted it with, and curled, which probably was also not natural. Even though he had been overseeing his packing, he was dressed as if he was expecting important visitors, in a shirt of the finest ramie, under a sleeved tunic of twilled linen in a muted scarlet and matching breeches. His boots were brown, and polished to a high shine, and he wore the seal of his office on a heavy gold chain around his neck.

Amily put the box aside and rose, taking his hands in hers. "How kind of *you* to allow me to give you a proper farewell!" she said, smiling. "Of course, we will have you back again before the end of summer, but I was hoping to find out if you would be here for my wedding."

"How can I possibly know that, when that ever-so-energetic young man of yours keeps haring off when plans are half made?" Maranthenius asked, waiting for her to resume her seat before he took one. "Now, if you think you might have it done about Midsummer, that, I can promise." He made a little face. "Though if you people would just loan me one of your Companions, I could be home and back in no time at all."

She had to laugh at that. "Now Maranthenius, don't tell me that you would be willing to ride day and night, sleep in the saddle, and touch your feet to the ground no more than four or five times in the day!"

He shuddered theatrically. "No . . . no, that would be far too much for this old man. I do like the comfort of my carriage, and overnight stays in fine lodgings. And regular meals of something other than pocket pies. I believe that I will settle for slow and pleasant."

"Well, I can't loan you a Companion, but I thought you might like this," she said handing him the box. He took it, his shrewd green eyes brightening.

"This is very handsome work!" he said, with pleasure. "The intricacy and the detail are astonishing! Whoever made this must have both phenomenal control of his hands and phenomenal eyesight!"

She smiled. "He does, but the box is not the gift. Open it, please."

He did, and lifted out the two short white bits of leather with silver grommets and silver bells attached, and the braided lengths of white horsehair with complicated knots at one end and loops at the other that went with them. His eyes widened and his smile was completely unfeigned and without any calculation or guile whatsoever.

"My *dear* Amily! You could not have pleased me better! What a wonderful gift!" he said, fingers caressing the soft leather, and the silken horsehair. "Are these jesses what I think they are?"

She nodded. "Braided Companion hair, yes," she said. "Mags makes things like this for gifts; he's terribly clever at it. I know how much pleasure you get from flying your falcons, and I remembered how you admired our style of bracelets and jesses. I thought I would give you a set, both as a memento and so you could have them copied when you get home."

"These are wonderful," Maranthenius said fervently. "And you are a delight to have thought of such a gift. So clever of you Heralds to have thought of jesses and bracelets that a bird can free himself from, should he escape. And to have the jesses made of Companion hair! No one will be able to boast of that at home!"

"Oh, it wasn't Heralds that invented those jesses, it was the Hawkbrothers. We just adopted them." She patted his hand, and he freed one of his to place it over hers. "I know how tender you are with your birds, and what a good falconer you are. It gives me as much pleasure to give you these as it will for you to use them." She cleared her throat a little. "Now, that wasn't the only reason why I came to say goodbye to you . . . there's something you need to know that your friend Amily can tell you, that Herald Amily cannot."

He put the jesses away in the box and handed it to his Secretary, who took it with a slight bow. "My goodness gracious. That sounds serious."

"Well," she said. "It is . . ." and she proceeded to explain the situation to him, and how *they* had learned of it. He listened to her, his face still, his expression neutral, until she finished. "You are likely to be walking straight into a Court where the envoys of the Regency Council of Menmellith are already there, and have been demanding that Rethwellan join them against Valdemar, on the grounds that if we have fomented revolution on their soil, we are likely to do the same to you."

"And did you?" he asked, raising an eyebrow. "Send arms to their rebels, that is."

"I can't say that *someone* in Valdemar didn't, but it wasn't done at the behest of Kyril, nor anyone on the Privy Council," she said, as earnestly as she could manage. "We've gone over all the records carefully. There's no unexplained expenditures of money. Every coin in the Treasury is accounted for. There's no arms missing from the Guard outposts. The accusation came as a complete shock to the King and the Privy Council, and we have been working day and night to try and discover where the money to buy these weapons came from, what armory they originated from, and who bought them in the first place."

He sat back in his chair and pondered what she had told him. "Well," he said. "To begin with, I believe you. I honestly cannot see what Valdemar has to gain by encouraging a disgruntled fellow with pretensions to royalty in his quest for a throne. It is not as if the lands on the border with Menmellith are good for anything but grazing sheep and breeding hill ponies and goats. There's nothing *under* those hills worth digging up. If you want to expand your lands, you will do what you have always done; expand your western border, where there are nasty creatures and even nastier bandit-lords and petty warlords and the like and the people will welcome you and your Guard with open arms. Why trouble a civilized nation? Why interfere with a situation that is already unstable, in a dubious partnership with unreliable people?"

She sighed with relief. "Exactly so," she said. "Exactly so. As I said, we are trying to find out who did this, and when we do, the King intends to punish them somehow. We're not quite sure *how,* because there are no laws against sending weapons to people you like, but—"

"But the King's word is law, and I think that is sufficient here," Maranthenius waved off legal complications as if they were of no matter. Well, probably in Rethwellan they *were* of no matter. "Well, my darling girl, I already know what you want of me, and fortunately for both of us, it is powerfully *not* in our best interests to join with Menmellith in an ill-conceived attack on Valdemar. Think of the trade that would be destroyed! Think of the money lost! And that doesn't even get into the insanity of waging war in the summer, when there are crops and herds that will be destroyed! What are they *thinking?*"

"If you are asking about the Regency Council of Menmellith, I don't believe they are thinking at all; they are panicking and seeing monsters everywhere," Amily said sourly. "Perhaps they think if they convince their own people that danger *is* everywhere, they will somehow muster . . . more energy? I don't know. As for the rebels, well, rebels often tend to be of the sort that would rather poison the well should anyone else look likely to take it back."

"I can't speak to that. I believe the fear is that a country with a boy on the throne will be seen as a weak country, and a land ruled by a Regency Council is less prone to successfully defend itself than one with a man and a sword on top." He shrugged. "I can't speak to either. Weak men see monsters under the bed and enemies in every bush."

"That may be," Amily agreed. "But if you will tell your people that no, we of Valdemar are not behind this . . . unbelievably *stupid* ploy, that Valdemar holds as it always has, to the maxim that *There is no one true way,* and that applies to not meddling in other peoples' political battles, and that we are spending a great deal of time and energy on finding the culprits behind this, I will be eternally in your debt."

His eyes shone a little, and for a moment she felt a chill. *Oh no. What have I let myself in for? What is he going to ask me to do?*

But then his gaze softened and he smiled and patted her hand. "I won't hold you to that, my dear. In fact, I am in your debt. I would have walked into a dreadful situation without any warning whatsoever, and there are many parties who would have applied all manner of pressure to me to get me to say what *they* wanted. For profit, of course, everything in Rethwellan comes down to profit and loss. I must say, I find that a more reasonable way to run a country than depending on the vagaries of royal births. Still, it does leave the government open to . . . influence."

She nodded, waiting for him to finish.

"So, to be less brief than you would like, but more brief than is my wont, yes, I will argue against joining with these hotheaded fools and squandering resources when there is absolutely no profit to be gained and a very great deal to be lost. I assume since you have shared certain information with me, that I can share it with my fellows." She beamed at him with relief, and he smiled back at her. "Really, it is a pleasure to be able to help you in this, Amily. You have always been kind and courteous to me, when I am well aware that there are those in your Court—not the Royal Family, of course, but I suspect even some Heralds—who have dismissed me as a *trumped up merchant.* You never have, and for that friendship, I am grateful."

"Certain people in the Court live in glass houses and should refrain from throwing stones," she said, and leaned over and kissed his cheek. "But there are people with their noses in the air over something everywhere. Thank you, Maranthenius. I'll let you get back to your packing."

She stood up, and so did he. This time he leaned in to kiss *her* cheek. "And now I know where that athletic young man of yours must be, trying to get to the bottom of this mess. I shall be saying prayers for you all the way home that we are all back in Valdemar in time for a Midsummer wedding, and laughing about what a ridiculous situation this was."

"From your mouth, to your gods' ears," she said fervently, and left, feeling that *finally* she had accomplished something of value.

Now to go tell Kyril what I have done, she thought with a sigh. *Well, he should have gotten Tuck's toys by now. Hopefully that will have sweetened his temper enough that he'll be pleased rather than the opposite.*

Coot basked in the reflected glory of Mags, who was very much the hero of the moment so far as the town of Attlebury was concerned. It was probably a very heady experience for someone who had once been on the very bottom of the pecking order. Mags occasionally had to thump him on the head and remind him not to start putting on airs. "We ain't here t'show off," he had to remind the lad. "We're here on account of some'un here in this place might'a slipped out somethin' wuth a lot so's some'un else kin buy up a lotta trouble. Get me?"

Fortunately Coot was a sensible lad at bottom, and didn't need reminding very often. He was also a lad who remembered past misery and was not inclined to do *anything* that might cause Mags to throw him back on the streets, prey for older, stronger, and crueler people.

Not that Mags would ever do that. The worst he would be likely to do would be to have Coot sent to be a manual laborer on one of the Royal Home Farms, far from the street life he knew so well, and without the means to *get* back to an urban landscape. It would take a lot more than Coot boasting about being "Harkon's" best friend in all the world and giving play by play descriptions of Great Kirball Games of the Past. But Coot didn't know that. And he was not inclined to ever tell Coot that.

At the moment, Mags was conferring with Lady Keira and Lord Jorthun in Lord Jorthun's rooms, all the while keeping an eye on the young miscreant through the window. Coot was almost directly below the window, in the yard by the kitchen door. Mags could see and hear everything.

On the whole he was satisfied. Coot was doing a very good job today.

Coot had wanted details of Kirball games, details that Mags would *surely* know in character, and Mags, with his permission, had implanted some memories for him.

So now Coot was regaling an audience of mixed servants with tales of Mags' Kirball prowess—except that with Mags' careful tinkering, it was tales from the viewpoint of one of the four Riders on his team. The fact that Harkon had played on the same team as *the great Kirball player Herald Mags* made it all doubly thrilling for his audience.

It was positively surreal to hear people hanging on Coot's every word just because Mags was a "Great Kirball Player."

Coot was benefitting quite a bit from this. The inn's chief cook kept bringing him little bits of this or that, "just to taste," and made sure that his mug of cider never went empty. He'd gotten some harassment when they had first arrived as being a "city-boy," and Mags had utterly forbidden him from fighting, so until now, he hadn't been able to establish his place in the servant-boy pecking order.

Now, however, there was no doubt that he was on the tip-top. He'd even been offered presents to gladden a boy's heart if he'd just "tell us'n 'bout tha' business where tha' 'Erald broket 'is arm agin," and since Mags had not forbidden him from taking presents, he gleefully accepted. Now he had a fine collection of slings, practice cabochons made by the Gemcutter 'prentices, bone fishhooks, chipped flint arrowheads, glass rings, fancy scarves and kerchiefs, and other similar trinkets. He was going home with an entire box full of the sort of things that children cherish.

Mags let Coot do the boasting for him. He, in the meantime, was modest, would only tell Kirball (and Herald) stories when coaxed to, and refused all attempts at giving him anything more than a drink or a tasty treat with "I cain't, Lor' Jorthun wouldn' approve." This established *his* persona as someone who was very trustworthy.

A second match had been played here at Attlebury, much to the satisfaction and delight of the entire town. This one had been won by Mags' side, but it had been hard-fought all the way to the end, and both sides had been treated to a celebratory feast by the Gemcutters and Assessors Guild. Just as an aside, Mags was actually coming to appreciate the finer points of being a Kirball *rider.* And the finer points of bonding with ordinary horses.

All this was bearing some interesting fruit. But for now, he needed to return his attention to what Lady Keira and Lord Jorthun were saying.

". . . I don't think there's any doubt that they are seriously courting me now, my lord," Keira was saying, as she fanned herself with one hand and sipped sweetened tea that had been cooled in the well. "I don't think they'd have warmed to us nearly fast enough for the lads to come calling if it hadn't been for Mags."

"If it had been autumn, you could certainly have accomplished the same thing by riding out to the hounds or to hawk," Jorthun pointed out. He had divested himself of his tunic and was taking advantage of the fact that they were in his private rooms by being arrayed only in his shirt and breeches. Mags could not help but notice that Lord Jorthun still had a physique that would put many men younger than he in the shade. *Then again, practicin' sword an' knife-work with your Weapsonsmaster three candlemarks a day, not t'mention the ridin' and huntin' an' hawkin' will surely keep a feller fit.*

"I could, if I were equipped to do such things," Keira replied, with a shrug that implied more helplessness than indifference. "Alas, my parents were unable to supply more than a single horse, and that was my father's warhorse and unsuited to hunting, and no one was likely to loan the little daughter of an impoverished knight one of their hawks. And of course, when I went to the care of my *kindly* relations, they had other plans for me that did not involve anything like recreation."

"We'll have to remedy that, later," Jorthun told her. "But *not* knowing these things might have worked just as well."

"Except that it isn't autumn, no one is going to be able to do any hunting until moons from now," she countered. "Given the circumstances, it is almost miraculous that we have exactly the combination of talents that we do."

"I could not have planned this better had I known exactly what we would require," his lordship agreed, with a smile and a wink for Mags.

"Mags has broken down every possible social barrier between us and our suspects," Keira pointed out. "I have most of the miners' second or third sons coming around, several of their eldest sons, and all of their sisters. If there is any sort of funny business going on, and the offspring are aware of it, I'll have it out of them."

"Has anyone offered you presents he can't really afford?" Jorthun wanted to know.

Keira pursed her lips. "Now that is a very difficult question to answer. Under normal circumstances I would say *yes,* but we are dealing with the case of the confectioners' son here."

"Which means?" Lord Jorthun was puzzled.

Mags was astonished. For once, Lord Jorthun didn't have every bit of information, however obscure, at his fingertips!

Mags answered before Keira could. "Ye got th' sons of men what owns gem mines givin' milady pretty things, it's kinda like the sweetmeat seller given *his* sweetheart candy. T' anyone else, that'd be special. T' them, it's jest what comes outer the ground."

"Ah, your point is taken, Keira." Jorthun steepled his fingers together. "Still, in the little tokens that have been given you, have there been any that stood out?"

"Tiercel," she said decidedly. "He's been *extremely* generous with some rather interesting little tokens. Do you want me to cultivate him in particular?"

But Jorthun frowned a little. "I am loathe to think that a family that treats their workers so well is involved in chicanery."

The hum of conversation below stopped. Mags checked to see if something was amiss, but it was only that the Cook had brought round fresh bread and butter for everyone. Coot's audience was too busy stuffing their faces to talk.

"Well," Mags put in, returning his attention to the others. "If they *was* up t'somethin', best way t'keep their people shut 'bout it is t'treat 'em good, so tellin' on 'em is gonna feel like betrayin' 'em."

"Good observation." Jorthun sighed a little. "Well, then, the best way to find out anything is to accept an invitation there again."

"I expect I can manage that." Keira nodded. "Probably by the end of the afternoon."

They went on to talk of commonplaces, and Mags returned his attention to Coot, to make sure the boy wasn't getting himself, and them, into anything compromising. But he was troubled. He liked Tiercel; from the little he had seen of Tiercel's father, he liked the older man. He, far more than Lord Jorthun, was well aware how *extremely* well Lord Mendeth treated his workers. He did not want to discover that the man was up to no good. He didn't want to bring justice, in this case, should there be treachery involved. For surely such actions—deliberately sending off valuable stones, avoiding taxes on them, to purchase arms for a rebellion in another country—were treacherous, if not precisely treasonable. And for what reason would he be *doing* such a thing? Profit? Was he somehow getting untaxed income out of this?

:He could be,: Dallen observed, sounding as if he felt just as troubled about this as Mags was. *:It would be easy enough to hide any amount of money; the man has a mine, after all, and it would be child's play to conceal a fortune in one of the played-out shafts.:*

Mags ground his teeth a little. *:All right but what if money ain't the thing? What if it's somethin' else?:*

:I can all too easily think of what the "something else" might be, Mags. Tiercel's father has six sons and not all of them can inherit the mine. The other mine owners are in a similar case. What is the first thing that a conquering monarch does when he ascends the throne?:

Mags was at a loss for that one. *:Dunno. Collegium history didn' treat with that.:*

:He generally impoverishes his enemies and rewards his followers, usually with land and titles. I would imagine that any of the young men in this town would be very happy to discover that their father's shrewd backing of the rebellious cousin had resulted in titles and property being awarded to them.:

Mags blinked at that. Yes, he could see that. As he could readily see how convenient it would be for a father to ship off a restless and sometimes troublesome son to the south, there to sink or swim.

:I can all too easily think of a number of other things to be gained here. Trade concessions. Access to things they do not now have access to—or outright gifts of mining grants. We've always heard that the hill-country between Valdemar and Menmellith and Rethwellan is all but useless, but what if it isn't? What if there's something valuable under those hills? That could be what these mine-owners want.:

Mags didn't want to hear this, but he knew that he had to, and consider it in his dealings with them.

:This ain't makin' me happy, horse,: he growled mentally.

:It's not making me happy either,: Dallen agreed. *:But I think you have full reason to do more than a little snooping in surface thoughts now. I think that you need to dig deeper.:*

:Aye, dammitall. Specially since I don't want to.:

Lady Keira was as good as her promise. Before the afternoon was over, she had teased an invitation out of Tiercel for an afternoon, followed by dinner, with his family. "No more ridiculous tours of the mine and works this time," he said firmly. "We have quite nice gardens that my mother is very proud of, and would love to show off to you."

Keira laughed, and accepted. And since it was all four of them going, Harras readied the carriage, and they went in that, rather than by horseback. This meant that they could stay until after dark, and the lanterns on the carriage would give the horses enough light to get them home.

Which, of course, gave Mags a place to put gear he might possibly need for his "snooping." Chief of which was a suit of all-black clothing, which covered him from head to toe. *Not* the sort of thing that was easy to conceal in a saddlebag. Not to mention that it would have been a bit foolish to try and ride horseback after dark. Horses broke legs that way—unless there was a full moon to see by. But tonight was nearly moon-dark, which was exactly how Mags wanted it. If he couldn't get anything by merely asking some gently leading questions, there was something else he could do. Once he left Coot to tell tales in the kitchen and claimed he was going for a walk, he could don his black clothing and do some snooping.

This time, since they were not making any effort at speed, the ride was actually comfortable. *Mebbe we can take our time goin' home,* he thought, without any real hope that it would happen . . . but then again, going home there would be no more need for this masquerade, and he could ride Dallen.

But for now, the carriage was pulling up to the Rolmer Great House, and it was time to play his part.

———————

The village had been given a couple of wild boar to roast, and enough beer to satisfy everyone, which was, on the whole, quite a *lot* of beer. Several barrels, in fact. Wild boar were the only animals that were fair game even in the spring; fierce and highly dangerous, they were more pests than game, bred outrageously, and had almost no enemies except humans. Even bears and wolves would think twice before tackling a wild boar. So earlier, in the early morning, in fact, in anticipation of this visit, the Rolmers had formed a strong boar-hunting party and had bagged three boar, a sow, and all the sow's piglets. This might have seemed unfair, but it was more unfair to leave the piglets to starve. There was suckling pig enough for the dinner guests, the house staff got the sow, and the village got the boars, one of which looked to be nearly the size of a small pony. All the adult animals had been roasting since they were brought in, and the smell of succulent pork drifted over the village.

The mood in the village was festive, and enough beer was circulating to make everyone loose-tongued. Mags asked his leading questions . . . and got nowhere. Frustrating. Intensely frustrating. But he didn't show his frustration, he simply bided his time until darkness fell, put on his black suit, and did what he did best—slipping around and listening in places he was not supposed to be.

But he learned nothing. Or rather, nothing having to do with the situation at hand. He did learn rather too much about who was trysting with whom. And *much* too much about whose wives were where they shouldn't be. He quickly learned that people have trysts in the most *uncomfortable* of places. . . .

He was lingering outside the window to a study he assumed belonged to the elder Rolmer, thinking about slipping inside and seeing if there were any ledgers or record books he could examine. He was about to do just that, when the door opened, and Master Rolmer entered, followed by Lord Jorthun.

Quickly he ducked back below the windowsill. He considered leaving, but then it occurred to him that Lord Jorthun was about to ask some leading questions himself, and if things somehow got out of hand—if Master Rolmer realized where the line of questioning was going, for instance—he might be needed to create a distraction. So he stayed.

"We'll let the young people frolic," Rolmer was saying. "I don't know about you, but after that boar hunt, my bruises are a little too tender for dancing."

"I can't claim the boar hunt, but I can certainly claim years," said Jorthun. "More of them than I care to admit to." He chuckled. He sounded relaxed, exactly as a highborn gentleman of his ilk *should* sound after a good dinner and good wine.

Mags made himself comfortable—after years of making himself comfortable on rooftops, it was easy to do so huddled up against the side of a building on nice soft grass on a lovely spring evening. He made himself exactly the right sort of irregular, not man-like shape that could be a shadow, although with next to no moon, it was unlikely that anyone would spot him. It was too early for many insects—which made things even easier.

Master Rolmer sounded very relaxed, and just a little tipsy. That edge where one says injudicious things . . . and Mags had a good idea that Lord Jorthun had been the one to get him there. It would have been hard to refuse such a high-ranking guest, one who at the same time was very democratic in his ways, when said guest urged "another toast" on his host. There were any number of ways in which you could appear to be drinking the same amount as the other fellow, yet not get tipsy. Some of them even allowed you to actually drink that much.

"I have a lovely little bottle of spirits of wine here that will be just the thing to finish off the evening with," Master Rolmer said, and then there came the sound of a bottle being uncorked, and the clink of glass against glass as he poured.

Mags breathed slowly and easily, eyes half closed, all of his attention on the sounds and the surface thoughts. Surface thoughts of Master Rolmer, at least, who was thinking of nothing more than how gracious his guest was, and how completely without the airs that many of the highborn put on around him.

"Now this is a real treasure," said Jorthun, after some silence that Mags knew from Jorthun's surface thoughts was appreciative. In fact, Lord Jorthun was a little surprised that Master Rolmer had a bottle of something this good in his possession. It was causing him to raise his estimation of Tiercel's father a little higher, and Lord Jorthun already thought highly of the man. "It makes me wonder what other treasures you have hidden here."

"Oh well, as to that—" Master Rolmer laughed. "I'd be happy to show you, milord. Not everything that comes out of our mines leaves this property." *Aye. He's a bit tipsy, all right.* "You know that we don't have to declare what comes out of the mine until it goes to the Assessors and Gemcutters, correct?"

"You don't?" Of course Jorthun knew this very well by now. But he was going to lead Rolmer gently down the path he chose without Rolmer ever realizing he was being led.

"Oh no, it wouldn't be fair to the mine-owners! After all, rocks are not like crops, not intrinsically valuable in themselves, only in how other people regard them. And the Crown is nothing if not fair! No, they are just pretty rocks until they go to market. So until then, if we like, we are permitted to store as much as we want against times when the mine is not doing too well. We have a tradition that we only store the really spectacular stones. Would you like to see?"

Mags sensed Jorthun's interest—and of course, neither Mags nor Jorthun had known until now that mine owners typically *did* store uncut gems against hard times. "I would indeed," Jorthun replied. "I didn't get the little tour of your sorting rooms that Keira did."

I wonder why these windows don't have bars on 'em? Mags thought—because he would have thought that if the valuable stones were stored *here,* this would have been the best protected room in the house. . . .

Which would give away the fact that there's somethin' here to protect, he realized in the next moment. His thought was confirmed when Jorthun said, with admiration, "Now that is a truly cunning design, Rolmer! I don't suppose the creator is still alive?"

Mags was shocked. He had not heard the sound of *anything* moving in there. All he could guess at this point was that Rolmer had done something to reveal a hidden vault door. Opening it was evidently so routine for Rolmer that he hadn't even thought about it. Surface thoughts only gave a vague hint of a cupboard-sized area, hidden between the walls.

"Now, don't be expecting a robber's cave. We don't keep masses of gems in here, we only keep the really unusual specimens," Rolmer cautioned. "Mostly the eyepoppingly large ones, but there are a few with some flaws that make them interesting curiosities, and people often pay more for the interesting ones than they do for the big ones."

There still was no sound of anything opening. But Jorthun bit off an exclamation. Jorthun was incredibly controlled when it came to not leaking things, but the impression that Mags got was of dazzling crystals, fist-sized and bigger, that had been carefully cleaned but otherwise left untouched. Jorthun's thoughts were full of beautiful colors and flashes of light.

"This . . . is amazing," he said, finally.

"We've been extraordinarily lucky, actually," Rolmer said modestly. "We've never had to touch the vault, as we have never had a time when the mines weren't producing at least adequately. Well, we almost never had to touch the vault. My grandfather sent some nice bits as our contribution to the war in Vanyel's time, since we didn't have any trained fighters. And we did contribute some stones recently to General Thallan's needs."

What the hell? Every hair on Mags' head stood up. He was pretty sure that Lord Jorthun was feeling the same, but the man's voice remained absolutely calm. "Asked you to help too, did he?"

"Well, it certainly isn't the Guard's fault that the harvests were so poor last year in the south, and it seems harsh to cut their allotments just because the expected taxes didn't come in. It was very clever of him to ask for donations to cover the loss. I've got more than enough in that vault to keep this household going until we found something new to profit from even if the mines failed tomorrow. Which they won't. I could certainly spare a dozen this size."

:*Jorthun!*: Mags thought tightly, thrusting his words into

Jorthun's mind. *:Get him talkin' 'bout this Thallan character! I need a face!:*

"That is extraordinarily generous of you, Rolmer," said Jorthun. "My contribution was in fodder and meat-on-the-hoof from my Home Farm. Did the General seem at all anxious to you? I think he was a bit upset that I didn't dip into some hidden vault of my own and present him with silver bars." Jorthun laughed. "He should have known better than to come to a man whose fortune is in his farms. Still I did contribute a very pretty packet-worth."

Well, now, if ever, was the time it was ethical to use his Gift to read the thoughts of someone else. Mags concentrated as hard as he could, slipping into Rolmer's head and waiting to see an image, a memory of this General Thallan—because he didn't recognize the name. At all.

:Nor do I,: said Dallen.

The memory swam into view and started to ebb away, slipping out of Rolmer's slightly wine-addled thoughts. *Dammit!* Mags thought, struggling to follow it. It was like trying to catch a fish with your bare hands.

"He presented me with a stack of official papers about as thick as my thumb," prompted Jorthun. The memory suddenly solidified and Mags snatched for it.

Rolmer laughed. "Oh, aye, he did me, too, and I was so nervous at dealing with the man that I nearly dropped them all." In Rolmer's mind's eye, the memory scrolled forward; the stack of very official-looking documents, with all the appropriate seals dangling from them by ribbons. Mags memorized them all . . . but the seals looked authentic. Especially the one from the Seneschal and the Lord Treasurer, explaining the dearth of tax revenue and the need to economize. Then the memory moved to the General's face as he caught the documents that Rolmer had inadvertently fumbled. The General was frowning; his demeanor was that of a stern, impatient man who was not

in the least used to having to come to people he considered
beneath him for favors. And he looked like a man with a temper, a man who knew how to use those weapons he was wearing. Small wonder Master Rolmer had been nervous.

It wasn't anyone Mags knew, and he could tell from Dallen's reaction the Companion didn't know this man either. He
felt every muscle in his body go tense with the need to *find*
this man, and shake the truth out of him! This . . . pillaging of
Rolmer's treasures had certainly not been at the behest of the
King, nor the Lord Martial, nor anyone commanding the Guard
known to Mags. So who was he? And where had he gotten all
those official-looking papers?

The one thing that Mags *was* sure of was this: this was the
man who'd bought all those weapons and smuggled them to
the Menmellith rebels. He was no closer to knowing why, but
at least he knew who, now.

He didn't dare move, not yet. There might be something
more to learn. How in the names of all the gods was Jorthun
remaining so calm?

"Now this stone . . . I kept because it was such a curiosity.
It's just common rutilated quartz, but have you ever seen the
filaments line up like *that* before?"

"By the gods, it looks like a golden star, or a sun-in-glory
or something," said Jorthun. "Am I right in guessing something this unusual, you could ask what you cared to and
someone would pay it?"

"Quite right," replied Rolmer, as Mags felt as if he was on
fire with the need to get out of there, get on Dallen, and head
back to Haven. "Absolutely correct. Those golden threads ar-
en't anything valuable, not gold at all—not even something
like fool's gold. But you'd swear they were threads of pure
gold, and formed up in that star shape like that, well, I could
probably ask as much or more for it than any other stone here.
And get what I asked, too."

Jorthun actually laughed easily. "Well, that is the trick of it. You can *ask* all you like, it's the getting that's the hard part."

"Now look here—" Rolmer continued. "Look at this citrine. Absolutely flawless and as big as your fist. You could do a full set of completely matching stones out of this one, and you can't do that too often, let me tell you."

The two men continued to natter about stones as Mags slowly inched his way out from under the window, then slipped more quietly than any cat around to the side of the Great House, where the deepest shadows were. *:Dallen! How quick kin ye get here?:*

But the Companion surprised him with his answer. *:Not yet, Mags. There is no good reason yet to rush back, and then cause questions about where you are. We don't know that this "General Thallan" hasn't left a spy or two planted in Attlebury, and if you vanish with no explanation, any competent spy will smell a rat. Confer with Lord Jorthun on the way back to the inn. We need him to manufacture a reason for you to be sent back to Haven. He and Keira certainly should not leave the area—Master Rolmer might remember what he has revealed tonight, and the gods only know what he'd make of all of you dashing off. He might assume you all are thieves sent here to get him to reveal the secrets of his vault. He would almost certainly alert the local authorities and if he doesn't have a spy in the town, this "General" almost certainly has one in the local Guard. We must go carefully in this. Get your livery back on, and go back to the festivities.:*

Dallen was right of course. But it took every bit of control Mags had to go back to the carriage, change his clothing in its sheltering darkness, and rejoin the staff in the kitchen. By this time the remains of the feast had returned to the kitchen, and Mags was urged to help himself to suckling pig, roast onions and apples, and the remains of the fancy sweet that had been served to the family and their guests. "What don't get et be goin' inter a fancy pork pie fer th' fambly," said the Cook, who already had what he needed laid out to make the treat the next day. "Wishet they'd hunt pig in spring oftener."

"That'd be pressin' luck, Cook," one of the house servants pointed out, as Mags nibbled on pork and bread, and reminded himself that Dallen was right, that nothing would be gained by letting his anxiety get the better of him. "Got lucky this 'unt. Them pigs was wallerin' an' still stuck i' mud. Iffen they'd'a been up an on their trotters, 'twould'a been a differen' end t'tale."

:Dallen, do you think you can possibly reach Rolan and tell him what we discovered?: Mags asked, suddenly thinking of a way he *could* accomplish something right now.

:I can certainly try. At this distance, what I can tell him will be bare bones, however.:

:Bare bones'll do,: Mags replied. *:I druther ye could send 'im th' face too, but bare bones'll do.:*

Dallen's "presence" in his mind withdrew a little, by which Mags knew that the Companion was concentrating with all his might on reaching the King's Own's Companion. But at least now *something* was being done, and that was a comfort. He was able to settle and pretend that everything was normal, and even regale the kitchen staff with a Kirball story.

Coot, meanwhile, being utterly oblivious of everything that had just happened, was joyously stuffing his face full of what must have been the best food he had ever eaten in his life. He was eating suckling pig as if he was never going to get to eat it again in his life—which was very probably true—and the Cook was aiding him in his endeavor to eat himself into a state of comatose bliss. Every time he finished a piece and was licking his fingers clean of the rich fat, the Cook slipped another bit onto his plate.

Of course, the Cook was doing that with everyone in the kitchen to an extent, but evidently he did not like Coot's perpetually skinny state and was determined to do what he could to put some meat on the boy's bones.

Finally just as Coot reached satiation, Dallen spoke up again. *:I was just able to reach Rolan and give him the name and what we had discovered. He confirms that there was no such sanctioned outreach, asking for voluntary donations on behalf of a mysteriously underfunded Guard. He also confirms that he does not personally know of a General Thallan.:*

Mags sipped at his mug of beer. *:Now that I think on it, th' man'd be a damned fool t'use 'is real name. But from ev' thin' I saw in Rolmer's head, he's some kinda leader an' fightin' man. So why's 'e doin' this? Is it even possible 'e's with the Menmellith rebels, an' 'e's managed t'get enough clever bits t'gether t'pass as a Guard General?:*

:Anything is possible. I don't know how he'd get those seals, though . . . :

Mags mulled that one over, and had a thought. *:Iffen ye could get the seals off somethin' else, a clever lad could fasten 'em to new stuff.:*

:Or a clever lad could make molds out of the seals and make a new stamp to make all the seals he liked out of it,: Dallen mused. *:They wouldn't fool anyone who knew what the seals looked like or what tampering looked like, but they'd fool someone like Master Rolmer who wouldn't be allowed to look at them for very long in any case. I'd bet this "Thallan" deliberately made him nervous so he wouldn't do more than quickly read all the documents he was given.:*

:If that,: Mags agreed. He would have said more, but he caught sight of Harras waving to him from the doorway. He reached out and shook Coot's shoulder gently, as the latter contemplated the remains of a sugared pastry swan, as if he was trying to figure out if he could force a few more crumbs into himself.

"Time t'go lad. Milord an' milady need us." Coot looked up;

Harras, satisfied that they were both moving, left, presumably to return to the carriage.

Coot moved with reluctance, and who could blame him, given he had just had the best meal of his entire life? But Mags could not get to the carriage fast enough.

There was a lot that was going to have to be decided on the way back to the inn. Much as he would have preferred to, he could not follow his instincts alone.

Makes me wish I'd done this solo. But if he had, would he ever have gotten this far, this fast? *Probably not.*

But next time . . . and there would be a next time . . .

Dammit. I'll do what Jorthun advises.

15

"**D**allen was right, Mags. We cannot abandon our personas and go dashing back home," Lord Jorthun said, as the carriage took them back through the darkness. Harras was making good speed, considering the only light was from the two lanterns on the front of the carriage, but Mags was impatient for them to be back at the inn. "There is almost certainly a spy somewhere in Attlebury; I cannot think how this pseudo-General would have known who to approach with his proposition otherwise. If we debunk suddenly, without a messenger turning up, that spy will certainly think this is suspicious, and who did we *just* visit? One of General Thallan's victims."

Mags sighed. "At least we know Master Rolmer ain't in on it," he said. "That's one blessin' in all this." They all swayed back and forth with the rocking of the carriage, but at least this road was smoother than the ones they'd taken getting to Attlebury.

"True enough, and I would have felt very badly for the entire family if he had been," Jorthun replied. "Very badly indeed. As it is, he seems to be an ordinarily shrewd man who was defrauded by someone with a very plausible tale indeed. Now, let us concoct what we can as a good excuse for Mags, at least, to leave."

"Yer stayin' then?" Mags asked.

"I think we must." Jorthun coughed slightly. "The problem with concocting a good excuse for all of us to leave, when up until now we've only shown great enthusiasm for *staying,* is that we'd have to involve a lot more people in our secret. Even bringing in other Heralds is not a good idea, given that the King asked us to keep the current crisis among ourselves."

Dammit, he's right. Mags had thought of contacting whatever Herald was closest and asking him or her to send a messenger that they could pretend bore an urgent message calling Jorthun and Keira home. But to do that, he'd have to reveal that they were here on a private task for the King at the very least. *Or I could ride Dallen a couple of towns away an' hire a messenger an'—that's gettin' too complicated. Too much t'go wrong.*

"There is likely more to learn here. It will have to be learned the hard way, of course, careful observation and questioning, but I think we stand a good chance of accomplishing things if we remain." Lord Jorthun shifted his regard to Coot. "Coot, we shall have to rely on you, solely, as our information corridor to the servants and common people. Can you do that?"

Coot scratched his head. "Reckon I can try it. That wuz part'a m'job fer Harkon; listenin' an' tellin' 'im whut I heerd. I'm purdy good at rememberin' things."

"Good." Lord Jorthun nodded in the darkness of the carriage; Mags had excellent night vision, but even he could just barely make out the shapes of his companions. "Keira is already making do with one of the female servants as her handmaid; do you think you can make shift to be my valet?"

"I bin watchin' Mags, reckon I kin." Coot laughed a little. "You ain't th' most demandin'a masters, milord."

Jorthun answered that with a laugh of his own. "Probably not. There have been times when *I* was playing the valet, after all. I actually can make shift for myself, but there is an image to be maintained here. So, now all we need is the excuse to send Mags off. What shall it be?"

"It'd have'ta be somethin' that weren't terrible urgent, or ye'd have sent me afore this," Mags mused. "But it'd have'ta be somethin' that cain't wait till ye go home."

"And something that was urgent enough to warrant taking the Kirball champion away from his game," Keira pointed out. "We more or less promised him to the Kirball team, and we have established ourselves as considerate masters. So whatever this is to be, it must be something that cannot wait."

"Not an illness on the part of either of us," Jorthun thought aloud. "A Healer would certainly be called from the House of Healing right here in Attlebury, and we would never deceive him."

"Nor running out of ready money; Master Rolmer would just invite us to stay with him until an ordinary messenger went back to Haven and returned with what we needed," Keira pointed out.

Jorthun tapped his foot on the carriage floor. "This is a pretty little puzzle indeed."

"What 'bout somethin' ye figgered ye'd do, when ye got back, only ye've stayed longer than ye reckoned to, on account of ye've been havin' such a good time?" Mags offered. He didn't know enough about the lives of the wealthy to hazard a guess what that might be, but maybe Jorthun could take that as a direction to go in.

It appeared Jorthun did. "Just the thing! I expected to be back home in time to handle all the matters regarding my lands that my Chief Secretary cannot. I'm sending you to tell him as much and send him on to me. When you get to Haven, tell the King that, and ask Dia to send me Walther and Petras. And see if you can find someone that can be spared that used to play Rider position on the Kirball teams—*not* yours—tell him as little as you can, swear him to secrecy and send him back here with them. That way all our obligations are covered, and Keira and I can see if there is anything more here we can learn."

"I'll start t'night," Mags said immediately. "Ye can say ye sent me off first thing in th'mornin' in early dawn, afore anyone in th' inn was awake. Dallen kin be t'th' inn afore you could blink."

"Not a good idea. Dallen might be seen. Even if he was not we'd have to explain what, exactly, you rode off on, since all our horses would be accounted for. You can set off tonight, but I'll give you the riding horse I bought for myself. Leave it somewhere along the way, far enough that it won't wander back here." Jorthun waited to see if Mags was going to object.

But Mags shook his head; it was a good thing Lord Jorthun was better at picking up all the little loose ends of a plan and weaving them back into the fabric than he was. He would just have gone on Dallen, leaving people to ask questions that should not be asked.

Mags really didn't want to be burdened by a horse that wouldn't be able to move nearly as fast as Dallen, but there didn't seem any choice if they were going to avoid arousing any suspicions. It wasn't as if he would set off *walking,* after all, not when it was a week by carriage, and the errand was purportedly urgent enough that it couldn't wait for Lord Jorthun himself to return home.

So once they arrived at the inn, Jorthun made a play of "discovering" what the date was, and being exasperated with himself for losing track of time. There was a good bit of palaver with the innkeeper as to what was to be done, with Jorthun hinting that he was reluctant to leave now "because of my daughter," with the hint that this had to do with all the mine owners' sons flocking around. The innkeeper offered several options, including the loan of one of the inn horses, but all of these options required waiting until morning because Jorthun would not "risk another man's horse on the road at night." Finally, and after much lecturing of Mags about "taking care" and "not breaking a leg" it was decided Mags would take the newly purchased riding horse and Lord Jorthun would buy another. Since the *last* horse had been bought from the innkeeper's brother-in-law, that made the innkeeper very happy indeed—happy enough that his suspicions evaporated like snow in the spring.

And after all the play-acting was finally done, Mags found himself in the saddle of Jorthun's horse, and off on the road. The innkeeper was shaking his head over the folly of riding at night—but his surface thoughts told Mags *it's his lordship's horse and his lordship's man, an' if he wants to trust both of 'em in the dark, then it ain't my place to tell him different.*

And there was the very deep satisfaction of knowing he'd be getting his share of the new horse Jorthun would buy, and that another of the inn servants would be on permanent duty to his lordship to replace Mags . . . something that would put even more coin in the innkeeper's pocket.

So off Mags went, the horse moving at a reluctant fast walk, and he doing his best to soothe the poor thing. He didn't blame the horse in the least. The poor thing was picking up its feet unnaturally high, to avoid tripping over things it couldn't see. He tried to soothe it, but he couldn't overcome the poor thing's natural instinct not to move at night.

Both of them were nervous and sweating when they reached the Waystation where Dallen was waiting for him. The horse seemed pathetically happy to see "another of its kind" even though Dallen wasn't anything of the sort, and even happier to see the rudimentary stable. Too bad the horse was not going to get a chance to settle down in it! "I wish I dared leave this nag 'ere," he told Dallen as he dismounted and began removing the horse's saddle to put on the Companion. "But the stupid brute'll eat all th' hay an' grain at once, and founder an' likely die."

:Very likely,: Dallen agreed. *:Well, we won't be able to make much speed, but I can keep him calmer and keep him from breaking a leg on the way, and at dawn we can turn him loose and I'll meddle with him so he won't be able to find his way back home.:*

"And some'un'll git hisself a nice horse. That'll do." He transferred saddle-blanket and saddle to Dallen's back, but left the bridle and reins on the horse. He could put tack on Dallen in full dark like this, easily, when he needed to, and the horse was close enough to Dallen's size that it wouldn't matter for a few days. But he didn't need a bridle or reins to ride Dallen, and he'd need the reins on the horse to lead the beast.

Or rather, for Dallen to lead the beast; Mags tied the reins to the back of the saddle, mounted up, and they were off.

Just at dawn, before the sun was up but the sky was a nice pale, pearly gray, Mags turned the horse loose within sight of a farm that Dallen assured him took good care of their animals. Just as Mags took the bridle off the horse, a pony whinnied in the distance, and the weary beast pricked up his ears and snorted. A second whinny and a slap on his rump convinced him that wherever that pony was, *he* wanted to be there too, and off across the fields he trotted. The hedges that bounded the fields were nothing he couldn't easily jump, and he was so eager to find a stable and food and water that he lofted over them like a butterfly.

Mags didn't bother to wait to see that he got there. He was back in the saddle again in a trice, and they were off like a shot, this time at Dallen's best ground-eating long-distance lope.

The innkeeper had packed a saddlebag full of food, so Mags didn't even have to stop at inns. And he didn't. They stopped for water, for some mouthfuls of grass for Dallen and mouthfuls of pocket pie or bread and cheese that he didn't even taste for Mags, and then they were off again.

The journey that had taken nearly a week by coach was over in two nights and a day. It was grueling, but a Companion's pace was so smooth that Mags could literally sleep in the saddle, and a Companion's endurance was supernatural. Oh Dallen would *pay* for stretching his resources like this; he'd sleep for days, and eat like a fool pony with all the grain in the world in front of him, but that endurance was there, all the time, to be drawn on when the need was great enough. So Mags rode, and drowsed when the sun went down, snapping awake at intervals to make sure Dallen was still up to the pace, stopping twice so they could both drink at a stream or a village well.

They stumbled in through the gates of the Palace at dawn on the morning of the second day. Already alerted by Amily, who had been kept up-to-date by Rolan, stablehands ran out to lead Dallen to food and his stall and get him out of the increasingly uncomfortable saddle.

As for Mags, there were people waiting for him, too. Once he was out of the saddle, Amily and Prince Sedric led Mags off to the rooms he shared with Amily, where the artist who had worked with Bear in the process of rebreaking and re-Healing Amily's leg was waiting for him, rubbing sleep out of her eyes. With the very last of his energy, Mags first set the image he had gotten of "General Thallan" into her mind, then hovered over the page with her, correcting her as she drew. When she was finished to both of their satisfaction, Sedric carried the drawing off to his father, she went with him to make more copies, and Mags literally fell into bed and slept until nightfall.

———————

Mags came awake all at once, feeling very much as if he could sleep more, but it was hunger that had awakened him, and his stomach said forcefully and out loud that he had not eaten in too long. "I've food and lots of it," came Amily's voice out of the dark, and welcome it was, too. "How are you feeling?"

"Like I could'a slept th' clock 'round. Ye git Lord Jorthun's men off?" he asked. "An' thenkee, 'cause yer a wonder. I don' think I coulda stayed awake t'see to it m'self."

She stood up, silhouetted against the light of a small fire in the fireplace, and picked up a tray that had been on a table beside her. She brought it to him, and he sat up straight and began eating without any apology for poor manners. "Yes, Jorthun's men are away with his orders as to what parts they are to play. They went on horseback, and one of them joked that it was about time His Lordship supplied him with a better wardrobe and Attlebury would be as good a place as any to get it. They did not go alone, for yesterday when you fell asleep and Lord Jorthun's men were packing their gear, I realized that I already knew exactly who you needed for your Kirball replacement—you actually know him, Mags, he's father's man, Larek, one of the grooms in the King's stable."

Mags snapped his fingers. "Aye, he's perfect, but I didn' know 'e was a Kirball player!"

"While you were gone, when you'd been kidnapped, he joined the North team. He's very good. I just told him that this was on father's business, which it is, and that he was to tell Lord Jorthun or Keira, and no one else, that he works for father, and do what Lord Jorthun tells him to do." She sounded very pleased, as well she should be. He put down his food for a moment and took her chin in his hand and kissed her thoroughly. He already knew why Nikolas had an informant in the stables; you needed one for the same reason you needed informants among the servants and the pages if you could get them. A stablehand knew when people took horses out of the stable, and when they got back, and if he was astute and trained by Nikolas, he would probably be able to make a good guess about where the horse went by what he found in its hooves. Having one of Nikolas's men helping Jorthun was the best possible solution there could have been. He would obey without needing to know just what "the business" was about, and he would keep his curiosity in check for the duration.

"An' 'ere I was worryin' 'bout 'ow ye'd manage, an' ye managed better nor I could'a," he said warmly. "I should'a knowed better."

"We are still very far from having anything that Aurebic can take to the Regency Council," she warned him. "And the evidence you have is very flimsy stuff indeed. No matter how highly regarded Heralds are here, and how certain we are of what Mindspeech can do, I do not think that the delegation from Menmellith would accept what you allegedly pulled out of someone's head. But at least now we have a direction, and there's already a copy of the portrait on its way to father."

"An' the delayin' tactics?" he wanted to know.

"Better than we could have dreamed. Last we knew, the party from Menmellith come to fetch the Ambassador back was caught in a torrential, two-day downpour. *They* couldn't move from the inn where they took shelter, and when the storm cleared, the road was practically impassable, with several bridges washed out." Amily shook her head as if she couldn't believe the miracle. Mags scarcely believed it himself. "The King has decided that when they finally arrive, if there still isn't enough evidence in our possession to satisfy them, he's going to override anything they might say by pretending he thinks they are here for our wedding. *They* won't be able to tell him no, and that will buy more time for father to see what he can find."

"So th' weddin's back on then?" Strange, how calm he felt about it, as if this was just some new festival or other, something in which there was a minor part for them to play, but which was centered around something else entirely.

Well . . . it is. It isn't about us, it's about delaying tactics. The more we delay, the better off we are. Maybe if we delay long enough it will be so late in the growing season that even that idiot who started all this in the first place will think twice about trampling crops and starving people.

:*Dream on,*: Dallen said, cynically.

:*Maybe the Regency Council will decide they had really rather not fight a battle on two fronts?*:

:*Maybe,*: Dallen agreed. :*Assuming anyone on the Regency Council gives two hoots about the common folk. Or is a decent military strategist. Which is doubtful.*:

:*Aren't you just full of optimism today!*:

"Dia has it all in hand. She can mount it on a couple days' notice, and we'll have at least a week's notice before they arrive." She kissed him. "And of course, if it has to be postponed again, *we* don't care." Her soft laughter made him smile. "Though it is a most amazing gown. It's going to become my Formal Whites. I have the feeling you will like yours just as much."

He had to smile at that. Of all the things he was likely to actually use. . . .

"As if I'm likely t'need Formal Whites," he scoffed. "Th' on'y time I'm likely t'be at Court's disguised as a servant. Or, jest mebbe, as our ol' frien' Magnus. An' *he* ain't likely t'be wearin' Whites!"

She smiled mysteriously, as if she knew a secret she wasn't telling him. "Well, you'll like them all the same. They'll make you look like the amazing, handsome fellow you are, and not the ruffian Harkon or the ne'er-do-well Magnus." She held her hand against the side of his face, and he turned it and kissed her palm.

Then yawned tremendously.

And flushed with embarrassment. Here Amily was telling him all manner of romantical things, and he *yawned* at her. "Dammit, love, I didn' mean t'do that!" he blurted, and yawned again.

She laughed, reminding him of yet another reason why he adored her. "You've just ridden nonstop for almost two days," she told him fondly. "I've just stuffed you with the first food you've had since the sun went down yesterday. *Of course* you want to go back to sleep. Do."

He didn't wait for another invitation; he just laid himself back down again and rolled over on his side. The last thing he remembered before he fell asleep was Amily slipping into bed behind him and curling up against his back.

———

And that was the last good rest he had.

The Menmellithians, so the Heralds shadowing them reported, were *unbelievably* determined to get to the Capitol. Where the bridges were out, they hired boats to take them and their horses across, even going to the extent of blindfolding the beasts and making them lie down in vessels barely big enough to hold them and a rider, and being rowed across, one at a time. Where the roads were blocked, they either detoured around, or rolled up their sleeves and joined the road-clearers, without regard for rank or position. They were on the way, and since as yet there was no response at all from Nikolas, King Kyril had launched his last defense, the wedding.

Making good use of the idea that had served her well before, Dia was setting it in a giant tent in the case of inclement weather, or on the Palace grounds in the case of good weather. She had ruthlessly dragooned help from every source that could be flattered, bribed or browbeaten into giving it. And she had timed it all so exquisitely that the little festival being held the day before the wedding proper would be starting just as the Menmellithians arrived at the gate. No matter what they believed, they would see a Valdemar that was in no way preparing for a war. And no matter what they wanted to do, *they* could not make a declaration of war. They were not empowered to do that—and in any land but Valdemar, they'd have probably lost their lives if they had. Their only function was to get Aurebic and bring him home, so the Regency Council could declare war without having their Ambassador become a hostage.

If they actually *could* make a declaration of war, now that Amily had talked the Rethwellan Ambassador, and thus the government of Rethwellan, quite out of cooperating with them. Of course, they wouldn't know that. They had left Menmellith long before the Ambassador of Rethwellan arrived home.

Mags was so proud of her for pulling that feat off that he hadn't bothered restraining himself when she'd told him about it. He'd picked her up and twirled her around until they both were dizzy.

At the worst, she'd bought them more time, and they wouldn't have to fight on two fronts. At the best . . . the Regency Council might rethink their plan, and give the Heralds more time to actually *find* whoever was behind this.

Of course, staging this wedding on such short notice meant that everyone recruited by Dia for this pageant—and it *was* going to be a pageant, rivaled only by Sedric and Lydia's wedding—was working nonstop, from morning till night on it. And meanwhile the business of Valdemar could not come to a screeching halt, so Amily and Mags were beginning to feel as if they each needed to be three people at once.

The gathering of information on everything *other* than

their current crisis was nothing that could be put off. First, there was no telling when some crumb someone dropped would lead them straight to "General Thallan." And second, information, Mags had learned, was like bread. It was of very little use when it had begun to grow stale, and when it grew mold, no one wanted it at all.

He had made the rounds of his planted pages and had gathered nothing of any great use, so now he was Harkon again—the Harkon of the streets. And already today he'd gotten hints of a possible alliance between two gangs of thieves that would have unpleasant consequences if it went through, the identity and location of a fellow who was selling a dangerous intoxicating herbal concoction at prices that made it cheaper than beer, the identity of a very wealthy merchant who actually had a home up on the Hill who had made an exceedingly poor choice of mistresses, and the final piece of information that told him exactly who the new spy for Hardorn was.

Now, the latter was actually not much of a worry for him at the moment. Valdemar had been in a peaceful concord with Hardorn for a very long time indeed. Centuries. Nevertheless, every country generally kept informants in every other country bordering it, for the simplest of reasons; you couldn't always trust your allies to tell you the truth. But it was a very, *very* good idea to know who those informants were. The last one had left just before Nikolas had nearly died, and Amily became King's Own. Nikolas had not had the strength then, and later the time, to find out who the new one was. He'd left that up to Mags.

Today, one of the local lads who came by the shop to peddle what he'd learned had told Mags that a man who sent packets of letters concealed inside bars of soap to Hardorn was named Ethan Dalliger, and he had a shop on Gooseneck Lane.

So Mags was going to pay him a little visit and make sure

he was what that clever lad Provo thought he was. In the guise of Harkon, of course, who was himself a seller of information.

His directions took him into the aforementioned Gooseneck Lane, a quiet little side street in a middling part of town. It was not bad, certainly nothing like the slum where the pawn shop was, but it was not the sort of place where someone like, say, Tiercel Rolmer would feel at home. These were mostly small shops with living quarters above them; plastered walls white-washed rather than painted, but in excellent repair. Most of the upper stories boasted flowerboxes at the windows, but most of those flowerboxes were full of thrifty herbs, not flow-ers. These were small merchants, making a small living. Good craftsmen, but not brilliant, getting by. No one here was in want, but no one here had much in the way of luxuries either. The fellow he had come to see was a seller of soap, candles, and oils. As he opened the door to the shop, he noticed some-thing immediately; the only scent was of beeswax and the native, clean scent of plain soap. No floral or woody, spicy or green scents. And no colors, either. It was clear that these goods were utilitarian, candles ranging from plain tallow-dips to simple beeswax pillars, soap from the harsh grade used to clean floors and clothing to a finer grade used for bathing. All of it was neatly arranged around the shop; the cheaper goods were in barrels around the walls—tallow-dips in bundles of five and ten, cheap cleaning soap in large blocks so that chunks could be carved off and weighed. The more expensive candles were arrayed on shelves divided up into square parti-tions, with candles or bars of soap stacked inside.

The man behind the counter looked up expectantly as Mags entered. Mags spoke first, as "Harkon" would, with a tone of assurance. Harkon, after all, was a bold fellow, and felt that his time was valuable. In this case, he wasn't going to beat around the bush very much. "Little bird tells me thet ye does buyin' along'a sellin'."

The shop had very good glass windows, and the light flooded the room. This actually put the chandler at a disadvantage. He could not see Mags' face, but Mags could see his, very clearly. The man allowed an expression of puzzlement to creep over his face, but his surface thoughts told Mags that he wasn't puzzled at all; he just wanted to wait until he knew if what Mags knew was worth having or not before showing his cards. "I am a craftsman. I buy such things as I need for my craft—" He spread his hands to indicate his wares. "Wax, rendered fat, lye. I do buy ash as well, but you don't strike me as an ash-seller."

"I meant somethin' less substantial," Mags said, leaning back against the doorjamb with his arms crossed. The last thing he was going to do was give up the advantage of having his face in shadow. "Like, f'r instance . . . I were t'know somethin' 'bout a lady lives up on Hill, say? Like, I were t'know thet she goes t'see a gemmun who ain't her husband ever' three days or so at th' Rose'n'Crown?"

Ethan's gaze sharpened. "A lady, you say? Who lives up on the Hill? Gentry?"

"Or a man. Say, a man what's been playin' a bit fast'n'loose wi' the trut', an wi' 'is partner's siller, down over t' Tailor's Court, iffen yer taste is more t'ever'day doin's. I mebbe don' look like much, but I got ears all over." Mags touched his index finger to his ears and crossed his arms again. "All over. I heerd ye was most innerested in what goes on up the Hill. I don' get a lotta thet, but I gets some."

"And you would be . . . ?" the chandler said cautiously.

"Harkon. M'Nuncle's Willy th' Weasel. We got a pawn shop." He paused expectantly.

The man's eyes showed his sudden recognition. Probably because his predecessor had done quite a bit of business with Willy the Weasel, and without a doubt, had informed the one who was to take his place. "Ah yes! Yes, of course. I am glad to make your acquaintance, Harkon. I presume your example of the lady in question was merely a hypothetical example, rather than something you wish to sell me at this moment?"

"Aye, although 'twas good four moons ago, 'tis stale now." Mags allowed one corner of his mouth to quirk up. "That there's the problem wi' bread an' doin's. Don't git to 'em quick, they goes stale, an nobody wants 'em."

Ethan nodded. "Quite so. I assume you will be the corridor through which your uncle's insubstantial merchandise flows?"

Mags shrugged. "Useta was, Nuncle did the peddlin' hisself, but these days he don't get out much. Gettin' old, likes t'sit in shop or stay home. 'Less ye feel like comin' ter us, reckon I'll come ter ye."

The man smiled thinly. "And I suppose that will cost me a little extra? Well worth it. Never let it be said I do not pay full value for what is offered me." Mags stiffened a little as his hand moved under the counter, but when it came up, it had a few silver pieces in it. "Since you have saved me the trouble of seeking *you* out, allow me to offer you a little token of gratitude, in anticipation of further business."

Mags unfolded his arms and approached the man, taking the money and swiftly slipping it into a hidden pocket. "Thenkee kindly." He allowed himself a thin smile. "I'm mortal glad when a feller is reasonable t'work wit'." He touched two fingers to his temple. "Iffen I has Hill-doin's, I'll come ter ye. Ye need ter talk ter me, ye go to Rising Sun tavern over in Tinker district. Ye tell any on them lads as is runners yer wants ter see me. No charge iffen it ain't thet ye needs ter see me right then. Penny fer the lad iffen ye do. Iffen it be *thet* needful, penny, an' ye goes in fer a drink. I'll be there afore ye finish it. But I don' reckon thet's likely t'happen, 'lessen ye needs somethin' . . . fixed quick. An' ye strike me as the kinda feller thet kin fix 'is own."

It was a bit strange, talking to someone about matters

so . . . dirty . . . in a shop that sold the means for making dirty things clean.

The man nodded. "An admirable system. I assume the boys are yours?"

"Aye." Mags nodded. "They runs fer me all over 'Aven. An they keeps their liddle ears open. It's fair 'mazin' whut people'll say 'round a wee lad, thet they'd never let drop 'round a man."

"That, good sir, is a truth that I will keep in the forefront of my thoughts from now on." The man bowed a little to him.

"An' I'll be on me way. Pleasure doin' business wi' ye," Mags gave him a little salute with two fingers, and let himself out, altogether pleased with how smoothly that had gone.

But that ended his tasks down here. Time to go back up the Hill and be a Herald again.

Right now he was rather weary of this version of Harkon. Peddling compromising information to foreign agents made him feel a bit dirty. It would be good to get back to being Mags.

They were all meeting in the sitting room of Mags and Amily's suite of rooms at Healer's Collegium. It was the quietest, most comfortable, least obtrusive, and most secure place they could meet, without causing anyone to wonder if something was going on. For one thing, their suite held one of the few sitting rooms that would hold six without everyone sitting elbow-to-elbow, and for another, Heralds came into Healer's Collegium all the time, spent a lot of time in there, and emerged with whatever had been wrong with them taken care of—or whatever business they had with patients there disposed of. There would be nothing suspicious about Prince Sedric, Herald Yvan (the Seneschal's Herald,) and Herald Gerd (the Lord Martial's Herald) dropping into Healer's Collegium in the course of the day, and once they were inside Healer's, there was no way of knowing where, exactly, they were heading. Mags and Amily *lived* there, of course, and Lady Dia could come in through the exterior door openly, since she was the one orchestrating the wedding and presumably would be consulting with them. Or ordering them about!

Gerd and Yvan were as alike as two brothers, both very dark of hair and eye, and both about thirty years of age. Both even had similar square faces, and heavy eyebrows.

Amily had kept all the lanterns in the otherwise dark sitting room out, and it was a nice enough spring day that no fire was needed. Anyone peering in through the greenhouse would see nothing in the darkened room beyond the door left open for air. No one would need to get anything *from* the greenhouse that was not already growing in the herb garden, and all the dried stock had long since been transferred to a new stillroom so Mags and Amily were not disturbed by someone hunting for something. This was as private as they could get.

They sat in a circle, white uniforms and Lady Dia's pale gown making them look like ghosts in the darkened room. There was only one window, and Amily had drawn the heavy curtains over it. And, of course, there were five Heralds here, three of whom had powerful enough Mindspeech that they would likely pick up anyone lurking about just by the presence of their surface thoughts.

"Have you heard anything from Nikolas?" asked Gerd, once they had all settled into their seats.

Amily nodded. "I already told the King. This morning we got a message relayed up that he had uncovered something very peculiar at the third armory he checked. The Armorer started to send him away, as the others had, telling him that every weapon they had made had gone to the Guard. But then he called Father back. He said that something was bothering him. That his Armory had filled a second, unexpected order for the Guard a few months ago. He was told at the time that there had been a flood and the weapons stored at a particular post were unsalvageable. And the officer who had brought the order had all the right paperwork, with all the right seals and signatures. But instead of paying in Crown Scrip . . . he paid in silver and gold."

Gerd nodded tensely. "That sounds like what Mags read from that mine-owner, now, doesn't it? A fellow saying all the right things, with all the right paperwork. A fellow that looked proper for what he was supposed to be. Everything normal. Except, this time, for how it was being paid for."

"Father said he looked into the Armorer's thoughts with the man's permission, but the fellow who made the order, paid, and took the weapons away didn't look anything like the drawing we sent him, and the Armorer didn't recognize the man in our drawing. So . . . this might be the second piece of the puzzle, but we're not much closer to solving it," Amily told them with a sigh. "Father's gone silent again, and Rolan says he's too far to reach, even for him."

They all sat in silence for a while, as they thought through this. "Signatures really are not that difficult to forge unless the person you are trying to fool is someone who gets a great deal of correspondence from the people in question," Yvan pointed out. "It's the seals that trouble me. It would have to be someone very highly placed to have access to similar documents in order to copy the seal, or steal the seal itself."

But Gerd had other ideas. "Not necessarily highly placed," Gerd pointed out. "Any clerk in the right place—or for that matter, in the right archives—could get his hands on the seals. Archives would be best; no one ever checks to see if seals are intact when they're looking things up; they are far too focused on what is *in* the documents, not on the verifying seals."

Sedric's eyes lit up as he thought of something. "Besides, those things fall off over time all the time," said Sedric. "When I was researching old Guard requisition reports a couple years ago, half of them had lost their seals. They'd all fallen into the bottom of the records box, and I certainly didn't take the time to make sure that they were all there and matched the documents. It just never occurred to me. You could probably snitch all the seals you needed from archive boxes and reattach them to another document. Father's seal hasn't changed in twenty-five years, and neither have any of the other officials."

"So . . . we don't have the time at the moment to go checking up on every clerk that has access to the Guard archives!" Yvan protested. "The Guard doesn't send their copies here to store until they run out of room at the local outposts!"

Glum silence, which Mags finally interrupted. "I'm thinkin' Nikolas has got, or is lookin' fer an artist of his own t'make up a picture of the feller that paid in money," Mags put in. "That's what I'd do."

That seemed to lighten the atmosphere a trifle. "That's what Jorthun would do," Dia agreed. "He'll most likely look among the Healers. There's always someone in a House of Healing that draws, and it will be easier for him to communicate the face to someone who has Empathy or a touch of Mindspeech himself."

Silence fell again. Mags could tell that Gerd and Yvan were feeling the same frustration at not being able to *do* anything, while at the same time, the time was inexorably slipping away. . . .

"This has me very troubled," Gerd said, finally breaking the silence. "And I need to voice it. The man had proper Guard paperwork. I presume he was wearing a Guard uniform, and I think the Armorer would have noticed if he turned up to take the weapons away in common carts. All this implies he *must* be associated with the Guard. Taken together with this 'General Thallan,' who also had all the needful paperwork to gull at least one mine-owner out of some very valuable gems, I am beginning to suspect a conspiracy *in* the Guard. . . ."

Mags' heart sank. That *was* a possibility, although he could not at the moment think what an entire Guardpost could be offered that would make it worth starting a war with Menmellith—

Except they prolly didn't know it would. Prolly didn't figger anyone would notice where the goods came from. An' if they didn't figger that, how's it hurt Valdemar so far's they know? Nawt. Some big sparklies that just sat in a room that didn't cost no one nothin' t' give away, a couple fellers get t'feel big 'cause they helped out the Kingdom. Nobody's hurt. Ev'body wins . . .

"It could be something as simple as the fact that a handful of conspirators have relatives with or sympathy for the Menmellith rebels," Sedric pointed out, although he sounded uncertain. "It doesn't have to be that an entire Guard post is involved. . . ."

"But it would simplify things for those conspirators if one was." Yvan said solemnly. "Amily, I hope your father is being very careful indeed. All that is needed is for the wrong person to see that drawing—or drawings—and he would be in very grave danger."

"This is scarcely the first time that Nikolas has been in very grave danger," Dia replied, sounding much more calm and sure than Mags was feeling. "And from what I know of him, he has already concocted a volume of possible explanations for this, including a conspiracy of not just one, but several Guard posts, *none* of which will indicate to him that he should do anything other than keep himself out of sight as much as possible, investigate via his Gifts without taking the chance of detection as much as possible, and take every precaution."

"My father has often told me, *Just because you are seeing enemies everywhere, it doesn't follow that they aren't there,*" Amily said evenly. "He may no longer have Rolan with him, but his Companion now is every bit father's match in caution and cunning. In fact, I dare say she's better at cunning and caution than Rolan is."

"Well, what kin *we* do if this's some kinda Guard conspiracy?" Mags wanted to know, feeling even more helpless than before. Because if it *was* a conspiracy within the Guard, then it wasn't just Nikolas who might be in danger. "This's right outa anything Nikolas ever taught me."

Gerd and Yvan exchanged a look, and very probably, thoughts. "We have one priority. Make sure the Menmellith Ambassador is safe," said Yvan, his voice betraying his anxiety. "We don't know what this 'conspiracy' has as an ultimate goal, but if it actually *is* to involve Valdemar in Menmellith's quarrel, the fastest way to accomplish that would be to kill the Ambassador in such a way that blame falls squarely on the Crown."

Gerd snorted. "Merely having him murdered would do that, without needing to have any indication that we did it. The Regency Council could declare that we did it, or colluded in it, and nothing we could say or do would make any difference to what they believed down there."

"Then we need someone checking his food, and we need a guard on him that cannot be bribed or lured away," Yvan stated, slapping his knee for emphasis.

"Dogs," said Dia, before anyone else could speak.

"I beg your pardon?" Yvan sounded as if he thought she had gone mad.

"Dogs, I said," she repeated. "I breed and train dogs, all sorts of dogs. Not just my little muff-dogs, but dogs for searching for lost children or escaped prisoners, dogs for protection, dogs for just about every purpose except hunting. Dogs have a very keen sense of smell. I've trained some of my hounds to detect poison. And I have guard dogs that will *only* obey their handlers. Dogs can't be bribed, and mine are so well trained that they can't be lured away."

"Aurebic is very fond of dogs," Sedric put in, before anyone could raise any objections. "I think he'd prefer them to human guards."

"It's settled then," Dia said firmly. "I'll bring one of my poison-hounds and a set of guard dogs and their handlers. If you think we've discussed as much as we can, I'll have them here within the candlemark." Her teeth shone faintly in the darkness as she smiled. "I'll have it put about that they are all gifts from me to my dear friend Aurebic. It won't even be a lie. He can even take them with him when he leaves, if he likes; I'll make sure the handlers teach the dogs that he is a handler, too."

"Lady Dia, that is brilliant." Sedric stood up. "I think anything more would be discussing this to death when we need to act."

Yvan and Gerd also stood up in unison. Yvan spoke for both of them. "We agree, Highness. There is very little we here can do to aid Nikolas, and there is quite a bit we can do along with Lady Dia to make sure Ambassador Aurebic is safe. Further discussion in the absence of firm information is going to waste time better spent elsewhere."

"Thank you, Lady Dia," Sedric said warmly. "You never fail to come up with original solutions to our problems."

She smiled again, and stood up with Sedric's assistance. "Perhaps it is because I have come to trust my canine friends more than most people," she replied lightly. "Amily, if you'll go tell Aurebic what's coming, and help him prepare his suite for his new friends, I'll get the pups. Oh, and when we are all done, I am going to want you two for wedding fittings of a most athletic kind."

"Uh—excuse me?" Mags stammered, not at all sure what she meant.

"My dear Mags, you don't really think I planned to truss you up like a flower arbor do you?" This time she laughed. "I've been working with Amily and my seamstress to make sure that not only will you both outshine Sedric and Lydia . . . you'll be able to outfight them in your wedding outfits, should it come to that."

"Dear gods," Sedric muttered. "Let's just hope it doesn't."

It seemed that someone was trying to split Mags' head in two with a blunt chisel at his left temple. Someone must have already tried to split it at the back, because there was a dull ache there as well. He cracked open an eye, and immediately regretted it, because the light sent another stabbing pain in through his eye-socket. He didn't even have time to register anything except that it *was* light and it was *far* too bright before he had to close his eyes again.

But that wasn't the most disturbing part. The disturbing part was that he didn't know where he was. He had no idea how he had ended up here. In fact, right now he was having a hard time even thinking.

And the last thing he could remember was. . . .

It was hard to remember anything, his head hurt so badly. But there was a sense of urgency in remembering, because . . . because . . . because if he'd been hurt, he *should* be at Healer's Collegium, and he certainly was not there.

So . . . work it through.

We had that meetin'. Then me'n Amily got lunch. She had t'go do Lesser Court. I had t'go check wi' Tuck an' m'lads. Late afternoon, Dallen sez Amily wants t'meet me at Lady Dia's an' we put on the weddin' kit, an' Lady Dia sent us off t'the garden t'spar with Lord Jorthun's Weaponsmaster in th' kit. . . .

It was slowly coming, as he thought through step by step of their day. Sparring in what—outwardly at least—appeared to be highly formal and impractical garments had been hilarious. Especially when Amily pulled on two tabs on her skirt that kirtled it up above her knees. The poor Weaponsmaster had been taken completely by surprise by that, and hadn't known where to look. Amily had scored three times on him before he recovered. They'd found out just how *practical* the gorgeous garments were, even though they were having to be very careful about spoiling them.

But the nearer in time he got to *now,* the harder it was to think. Which . . . was beginning to feel sickeningly familiar. This wasn't an injury . . . or perhaps it was more accurate to say, this wasn't *merely* an injury.

Not again. . . .

He could. . . .vaguely . . . remember the Weaponsmaster leaving, and he and Amily setting off on a walk around the manor's surprisingly extensive grounds. And that was where the memories ended, and the pain wouldn't let him get any further. Which would match with a head injury. When you got hit in the head, you often got memories shaken right out of you.

I need Dallen!

But when he tried to Mindspeak to Dallen . . . the strange, soft wall he hit inside his head was also sickeningly familiar. Oh yes, he had hit this particular wall once before, and it had nothing to do with someone trying to crack his skull for him.

Which meant he probably wasn't anywhere he recognized, and very probably *not* among friends.

Goddamnit. Amily an' me'll haveta change our names t' Mags and Amily Victim. Or mebbe Mags an' Amily Hostage. I'm'a gettin' right sick'a this. How come ever'thin' has t'start wi' "an' let's crack Mags over th' head an' carry 'im off"?

He rolled over on his side without opening his eyes, and heard a *clank,* and felt something heavy around his left ankle.

Well, that was confirmation he would rather not have had.

"Oo! An' let's chain 'im up! 'e loves thet!" Lord Jorthun had told him that humor was a good way to keep fear in check. Might as well try it.

When he cautiously cracked open his right eye, and waited patiently for the pain to ebb and his blurred vision to clear, he finally saw that he was in a tiny stone cell with a door made of stout iron bars. There was a single lantern placed outside it. There were no windows, and there was a manacle and chain around his left ankle, attached to the floor some distance away.

Although it was difficult to tell, he thought there was probably enough chain that he could get to every part of the cell itself. *'Ow nice of 'em. Make me feel right at 'ome.*

All right. This ain't m'first Kirball game. He closed his eyes, waited for the pain to ebb a little more, then prodded, forcefully, at that "soft wall" between himself and Dallen. This time, he knew from experience that whatever drug he had been given—and he was sure he had been dosed with *something*—it was interfering with Mindspeech, and it *would* wear off. Every time he "poked," it felt as if he got a little closer to piercing that wall, or that the wall itself got a little thinner.

He wasn't feeling quite the same symptoms he had with the drug that the Sleepgivers had forced down his throat, so there was that. *Thank the gods for small favors. At least it ain't them.* But Bear had told him that many drugs had the side effect of dulling or blocking Mindspeech, and most Healers knew all the ones that did that that were known in Valdemar. They had to, after all; they never knew when they might have to treat a Herald. Most of the time, you *didn't* want to block Mindspeech, so you needed to make sure the drugs you were giving him wouldn't do that. But if the Herald in question was hallucinating and broadcasting, you most emphatically *did.* No one wanted to share in your fever-dreams, not even those closest to you.

With his eyes still closed, he carefully moved his right arm and hand upward and backward until he could feel the back of his head. There was definitely a tender spot there. No, more than tender. A lot more than tender. *Damnit!* Someone had definitely bashed his skull for him, and maybe had *cracked* his skull. That would account for the headache. Bastards. *Why didn' they just come up to us an' ask politely? Whatever 'appened t' the genelmunly art'a trickin' some'un inter a trap?*

He brought his hand down and felt around himself. Canvas, padded canvas in fact, and beyond that, stone. Clean stone. No grit, no slime, no dirt. *Well, whoever did this wasn't all bad. . . .* He seemed to be lying on a crude mattress of the poorer sort, canvas stuffed with straw. Which was a damn sight better than stone.

And from the smell—which was just clean, cold stone, with not even a hint of rat urine—he wouldn't have any nasty visitors.

First things first.

So he lay quietly and kept probing at that "barrier," as he felt more and more awake (and, alas, more and more miserable with the pain). And finally, after a span of time he could not measure, he heard something, as if in the back of his thoughts. Faint and far off, and horribly anxious, Dallen was calling his name, over and over.

:Here,: he called back. *:Here.:* Over, and over, and over himself, until finally, he heard, stronger, and clearer, a joyful response.

:Mags! Where are you?:

:Dunno. Looks like a dungeon.: He cracked his eyes open again; the light didn't hurt so much now, and he got a good look around before he closed them again. *:Don' look like anyone's used it fer a while. Clean. Dry. No rats. No bugs. Whoever "they" are, they left me on a mattress an' didn' change m'clothes. Took all m'weapons, though. E'en m'wrist knives an' the trick sheaths. How long I been out?:*

:All yesterday evening, all night, and most of today. So they can't have taken you too far. But I can't tell where you are, other than "not too far to Mindspeak with.":

Pity, that. But unlike Farsight, Mindspeech didn't really come with a sense of what direction it was in. *:Well, start movin'. Ye'll know when I get fainter that yer movin' away. That'll be a start.:*

:Don't try to teach your grandmother how to boil an egg, brat,: Dallen said testily.

:I'll gladly trade places wi' ye, horse,: Mags replied. *:Ye kin have m'cracked pate, too.:*

:Is Amily with you?: Dallen replied.

:Not in this cell.: He opened his eyes again, but all he could see were the stone walls of the cell, and the door made of iron bars, with the lantern right outside the door, sending light into the cell. *:Not that I kin see.:* He refused to panic. They'd been together. Dallen—and presumably Rolan—did not know where she was. It was logical to assume that she was somewhere nearby and had been given the same drug he had been. *:Rolan cain't reach 'er? Lemme try.:*

:Wait. . . .:

He waited. To be honest . . . he had a feeling that if Amily had been badly injured, or worse, he would know. So he did as he was told, and waited. If he breathed very carefully, and just . . . accepted the pain . . . it wasn't quite as bad.

:Rolan has her. She's been hit on the head and drugged, like you.: Relief washed over him in a wave.

:All right. Let me know when Rolan can actually, like, talk to 'er.: She'd been treated as he had been. She was probably right *here* somewhere. There was a reason why they had been taken, rather than just murdered, and that implied whoever this was had a reason to keep them alive.

Once again he opened his eyes, and this time took a better and more thorough look around the cell, by moving his head very carefully. There was a pitcher and a cup in one corner, actually quite near him, and within relatively easy reach. Moving slowly so as not to jar his head, he got himself up, supported on one arm and elbow, and reached for it. There was cold, clear water in the pitcher; all his borrowed Sleepgiver memories told him how to detect the vast majority of drugs by taste, except when they were covered up by heavy spices, and so far as he could tell there was nothing in the water. He ignored the cup, and drank it straight from the vessel. But slowly. Very slowly. He knew now he had been a long time without water, and there were consequences to gulping it all down at once.

:She's in the same sort of cell you are.: Dallen sounded relieved. *:I think you must be together.:*

"Amily?" Mags called out, and not softly, either. There was no point in keeping their captors from knowing he was awake, after all. And if they knew, they might send someone to deal with him, and he'd get a chance to find out what was going on.

"Mags!" Amily called back immediately, and the relief in her voice made his eyes sting a lot, and his throat close up for a minute.

"I thin' yer in the cell right next t'me," he told her. "As-

sumin' m'head ain't clean addled from gettin' coshed. I'm gettin' right tired'a this. We gotta stop gettin' kidnapped."

"I agree with you completely," she replied. "Is there water
in your cell?"

"Aye." He knew better than to caution her about drinking
carefully; as Dallen had said, *don't try to teach your grandmother how to boil an egg.* "We might's well keep talkin'.
Sooner or later, some'un'll 'ear us, an' mebbe we'll find out
what this's all about."

*:Mags. Amily says there are lockpicks hidden in the waist-
band of your trousers, several very strong, flexible sinews you
can use to strangle someone that you can pick out from underneath the silver embroidery on the front, a knife in your left
boot sole, a short pry-bar in your right boot sole, the hem of
your tunic is padded with a long, extremely strong cord that
should bear the weight of both of you, and your belt has four
curved pieces of metal and a wire that can be bound together
into a grappling hook between the outer leather and the lining
leather. She also has more useful things about her person.:*

It was a good thing that there was no one there to see Mags
at that moment, because his jaw just dropped with astonishment. *:How in the name of—:*

*:She and Lady Dia worked with Tuck while you were gone.
She says that they were all concerned that there were times
when the two of you had run off without any weapons at all,
or ones that could be taken from you. She had intended to
surprise you with the information later.:*

*:Well, she surprised me all right. Tell Rolan to tell 'er she's
a bloody genius. An' I hope that ain't literal.:*

"Anythin' else in yer cell?" he called, not wanting to make
too much time pass between bits of conversation just in case
someone was listening. Whoever had them might or might not
know how Gifts, particularly Mindspeech, worked. He probably did not know what Mags' and Amily's Gifts were as that

was *not* common knowledge. Really the only people likely to know what your particular Gifts were, were those you had told yourself, or your immediate teachers.

Better not assume too much. Assume he figgers we kin talk to each other an' Dallen an' Rolan. If he don' know that, bonus.

"Just a hole in the floor." Her tone was dry. "Nice of them. Well, at least it isn't a bucket."

"There's that, I s'pose that keeps 'em from havin' t'clean th' cells out," he said, and then heard footsteps approaching, echoing through the stone hallway. Hallways? There were a lot of echoes. This must be a big place, with a lot of cells.

Amily must have heard them as well, for she fell silent. Mags went back to his mattress and sat there, cross-legged.

The footsteps were slow and deliberate. From the sound of them, the walker was a man. The sound suggested weight, so he was either overweight or heavily muscled. And from the way he was walking, Mags guessed that he was using his slow approach to deliberately induce apprehension or anxiety in his prisoners.

Mags had plenty of that, and he bet that Amily did, too. Still, he couldn't, shouldn't betray that. To be greeted with neither might throw their captor off a bit.

So Mags composed himself, controlled his expression, and simply listened as the steps drew nearer. *Don't show anythin'. Make 'im do all th' work. Make 'im have all th' slips.*

Finally the footsteps stopped. The walker was just out of sight, beside the door.

Do I talk first, or let him? There were advantages to both. But the man was staying silent, and out of sight, and appeared to have the patience to wait him out. Whereas Mags was dealing with a pounding head, and not a lot of energy.

Finally he decided. "Ye already know I'm awake. I'm kinda curious t'see m'host."

A chuckle drifted in through the door. "Well. What if I'm not anxious for you to see me?"

"Then go 'way an' lemme go back t'sleep, an' ye walked a long way fer nothin'," he replied.

"Hmm. A point. And how is your head?"

"No worse'n I got playin' Kirball," he said truthfully. "Ye should try it sometime. I'd like ter see ye on th'field. Learn a lot 'bout a feller in Kirball. They do say th' true nature of some'un comes out i' th' game."

"Do tell," the speaker replied, dryly. "I suppose you would say that." And then he stepped in front of the door.

Of course with the light from the lantern behind him, there was nothing at all to be seen of his face. But Mags didn't need to see his face; the man was instantly recognizable given the memories he had from Master Rolmer, and from the general silhouette, he knew that this was the mysterious "General Thallan." Which was something of an unpleasant shock, since he had assumed that "General Thallan" was somewhere in the south, not so near to Haven.

But all the time the man had been standing there, Mags had kept tight control over his expression, so he was certain he showed no more than a calm interest. "So, I don' suppose ye got somethin' fer m'headache? Or at least somethin' t'eat?"

The man at the door regarded him without moving. Impossible to read his expression, of course, since his face was hidden by the shadows, but Mags could *easily* read his surface thoughts, and it wasn't that hard to get even deeper. He was annoyed that Mags was calm. He was even more annoyed that Mags wasn't groveling, or begging. He had expected both. Evidently he did not know Heralds very well.

:Dallen, tell Rolan to tell Amily t'be a ice-girl wi'this lad. Annoys 'im no end.:

"I'm rather surprised you are thinking of your stomach at a moment like this," the man said, with just a hint of testiness in his voice. "I thought you were supposed to be terribly clever. Are you so dull you haven't considered the repercussions of the fact that you are in my custody?"

Mags shrugged. "Wut else am I gonna think of? Ye got me locked up in 'ere, I ain't goin' nowhere, an ye ain't 'xactly supplied me wi' Bards an' dancin' girls. Besides, been a long time since I et."

That annoyed the man even further. This was a good play. Get him irritated enough and he might just spill something. "You might like to know that now that you two are missing, that play-pageant of a wedding has been called off. There is no reason for Ambassador Aurebic to remain a moment longer. As soon as the delegation from Menmellith arrives, he will be constrained to leave by them, and as soon as they are past the border, the Regency Council will declare war on Valdemar. Valdemar will be forced to hold the border at least. And meanwhile I have supplied the rebels with another lot of arms. The true King, Astanifandal, is heavily in my debt at this point. And he is well aware that by the time he takes his throne back from that child, much of the cropland will be ruined, and he will require still more aid. He will be willing to pay quite a price to get that aid."

Did he actually know *we were doing all that?* Mags thought, startled, and suddenly feeling the chill of fear. He probed deeper, and what he found did not reassure him. No, Thallan had not been told this by an insider to the plot. He had *deduced it* from their actions. That was what had brought him up here, away from his men. He knew he needed to stop the wedding in order for his plan to continue working. He really was that clever. That made him horribly dangerous.

"Ye think?" Mags responded coolly. "Well, I reckon there's people who got 'nother say in that, most 'specially th' Heralds." *Don't give anything away. Let him be th' one doin' the talkin'. Don't let him guess that Amily's already taken Rethwellan outa the picture.*

"And if there are no Heralds in all of Valdemar who are able to oppose all this?" The man's voice took on tones of menace. "If the Heralds are paralyzed and unable to act, including the King and the Prince? You forget, *boy,* all you white-clad do-gooders have hostages to fortune, and even your lives, in the form of very large, easily targeted Companions. And we know where every one of them that matters is. Eliminate the Companions, and you eliminate the Heralds. Eliminate the Heralds, and the King will grasp at anything in the way of a lifeline that is offered."

Mags went cold. Then in the next moment, *:I heard!:* Dallen exclaimed. *:Rolan is shouting it now to all the others.:*

And in the moment after that, *:We are going into hiding, Chosen. In half a candlemark, neither we, nor many of our Heralds, will be able to be found.:*

:Don't you get caught!: he urged.

"Reckon ye must'a learned that particular lesson from th' lad wut tried t'burn down Companion's stable," he drawled. "Should'a figgered ye couldn' come up wi' an original plot t'save yer soul."

The man spluttered with anger for a moment, but then got control over himself. "It doesn't matter. What *does* matter is that even if the Regency Council elects not to attack Valdemar, I have another plan. I have enough men willing to cross the border in support of the rebels to help them win the day, good, loyal Guardsmen who know what an opportunity for our Kingdom this is. The result will be the same. Valdemar will be drawn into war, the rebels will be supported, King Astanifandal will have his crown and he will know that to keep it, he will have to petition Valdemar to become a client-state. You're a fool, boy. You think you are serving Valdemar! *I* am the one serving Valdemar here! I am making it possible for Valdemar to annex Menmellith! I am making it possible for you little white law-givers to bring peace and prosperity to a lot of bar-

barians! I am assuring Valdemar's future by giving us a flanking border on Karse, so Karse cannot slip their agents into Valdemar through Menmellith ever again! *I* am the patriot here, you puling little infant, with your ridiculous games and your misplaced pride! *Me!* I will make Valdemar great, while all you can do is bat a ball around a field!"

His voice rose with every word until he was shouting. And he finally realized he was shouting as he came to the end of his speech, and stood there, clutching the bars of the door, and panting with rage.

:That's . . . a very cunning plan. And he can pull it off. All he needs is for the King and Prince to be getting no information from the Border, and he can do that if the Heralds are out of play. By the time the King discovers what has happened, it will be too late. Or if he is truly maniacal, all he needs is to have as many of the Companions as he can killed, and that will throw such confusion into the country he can do as he pleases for quite some time. Even merely threatening *us has done exactly what he wanted. Now we're in hiding. Now our Heralds are out of play. Now the King has to come up with a counter plan, and meanwhile he does as he pleases.:* Dallen seemed stunned, and Mags wasn't feeling much better.

I gotta keep 'im off-balance. I gotta make 'im rethink ever'thin'. I gotta make 'im think we got somethin' right now as can stop 'im an' make 'im waste 'is time tryin' t'figger out wut it is.

"Fer a great patriot, ye sure do seem pretty set on doin' shit thet risks th' whole damn country," Mags replied coldly. "Fer a great patriot, ye sure don' seem all that innerested in followin' laws. I reckon ye figger laws don' apply t'ye. Happens there's been other lads as thought th'same. Happens they all end up th' same place." He shrugged again. "Think wut ye want, *big man.* Jest make sure some'un brings me an' Amily sommat t'eat."

For a moment, as the bars of the door rattled as the man shook with rage, Mags thought he might just come in there and beat Mags to a pulp. But instead, he tore himself away, and his angry footsteps pounded off into the distance and faded away.

"Well . . . now he's angry," Amily said carefully. And then she shut up. Mags had an idea that she was trying to talk to him mind-to-mind, and he reached out to her and listened, very carefully, to her thoughts.

Now we know his plan, she was thinking, over and over.

:Yes we do,: he replied, placing his words into her mind. He sensed that she had heard him.

And now the Companions are safe.

:Yes, they are.: But this wasn't something that would hold for very long. Valdemar could not be without its Heralds. For them to just vanish would eventually cause a panic. And meanwhile. . . . "General Thallan" would be carrying out his alternate plan. Or plans. No good strategist ever relied on just one plan; there was no telling if the man was *good* or not, but it would be folly to assume he wasn't. After all, he'd gotten away with illegally smuggling arms to the Menmellith rebels all this time. There was no reason to think that the discovery and subsequent reaction of the Menmellith Regency Council hadn't also been in his plan.

All right, so he hadn't directly eliminated the Heralds or the Companions, and now that the Companions were all going into hiding, he was not going to be able to blackmail the King into doing what he wanted by threatening the Companions but . . .

He still held all the high cards at the moment. He had Amily and Mags. He might believe that he still might be able to get something out of the King by threatening his hostages, once he realized the Companions were no longer in play. And he surely knew that the Companions could not vanish for very long.

:Now that I made 'im mad, I think mebbe 'e's gonna leave us be,: Mags explained carefully, even though placing each word in Amily's mind made his own head ache with the effort. *:That'll mebbe give us a chance t'get outa 'ere. I'll look fer guards an' all down 'ere that might be close.:*

There was a long pause, and he "watched" as she thought quickly and hard, her mind whirling a bit too fast for him to read. Then came the concrete thoughts again. *I will try and find a rat or a cat or something that can show me the way out of this area. There must be something living that prowls the halls.*

:Brilliant,: he thought warmly, then went about his own task. Bracing his back against the wall, he calmed his anxieties and opened his mind to everything immediately around him.

It was excruciatingly hard. His head throbbed with pain, and his neck muscles cramped. He had to fight the urge to lie down and sleep. He had to fight off the last effects of the drug. But it was no harder than it had been to fight against the Sleepgiver potion and remain himself.

One by one, he identified those guards that he had known must be there. There were not as many of them as he had thought. But there were still too many to overcome easily. He and Amily were the only prisoners down here, so he and Amily were the only people the guards needed to pay any attention to.

When you added it all up . . . their odds for escape were not very good.

His spirits sank right down to the bottom of his toes. And that moment was when he heard footsteps again. Two sets of footsteps.

This . . . cain't be good. . . .

He recognized the heavy, angry footsteps. Thallan was back.

And with him—

A timid face looked in at the door. It was the Healer that had been responsible for so much grief and pain to Bear back when they were both Trainees, who had been sent into virtual exile on the Border for his role in providing information to what Mags now knew were Sleepgiver assassins assigned to destroy Valdemar.

Healer Cuburn.

Mags felt his heart doing double-time. Cuburn was no friend. If it hadn't been for Mags, he never would have been caught.

"This Healer has something for your headache, boy," Thallan said, in an oily tone of voice that told Mags that what Cuburn had was nothing like that. "He's a good Healer, even if he *did* irritate everyone so much at his last posting that they couldn't be rid of him fast enough." He laughed. "Our good luck. He learned manners quickly enough with us."

Thallan unlocked the cell, and gave Cuburn a little shove when he didn't move. The Healer had a bottle in his hands. Thallan's surface thoughts told Mags everything he had been dreading. Without a doubt, it contained one or more of those potions that dulled or blocked Mindspeech.

The Healer stumbled into the room, his eyes on Mags. He looked terrified. Did he think Mags was going to attack him? And what was in that potion? Was it whatever he'd been given while he was unconscious? How long would it take to wear off? Cuburn was very, very good at holding barriers against having his thoughts read, but then, Healers generally were. They had to keep up Empathic barriers so the pain and turmoil of their patient didn't overwhelm them, and Empathic barriers acted very nicely as thought-barriers, too.

What to do? There was absolutely no way that he could avoid drinking whatever that was. If he refused, Thallan would call guards, hold him down, and pour it down him. If he knocked it out of Cuburn's hands, Thallan would only order the Healer to make more. There would be no chance in this bare cell for him to use the sort of sleight of hand Lord Jorthun had taught him, and appear to drink the stuff but actually pour it away . . . not wearing white clothing, he couldn't.

:*Dallen, I—:*

:*I know. You can weather this. We've been through worse and come out the other side. Whatever it is, it will wear off. You can make it wear off faster by working at it. If all we have is half a candlemark between doses, we'll work with that. I'll find you, Mags, I swear I will!.:*

And Thallan clearly intended to keep them alive, so the situation for him and Amily was not that dire. . . .

But Thallan could do a *lot* of damage, and it could take decades to make it all right again, if it ever could be . . . black despair flooded up over him, and in that moment, if the bottle had held poison, he would gladly have drunk it. He'd tried to do everything right, and yet he'd been out-maneuvered and now there was nothing he could do to stop the avalanche.

Cuburn leaned over him and handed him the bottle. "This will fix your headache right up," the man said. There was something in the *way* he said it that made Mags look up into his face, sharply.

Cuburn had his back to Thallan. *Just drink it,* the Healer thought, so strongly it was practically a shout in Mags' mind. *Then pretend to sleep. It's all I can do. I'm sorry. I'm sorry for everything. I'm so very sorry I can't do more. You must stop this fiend. He'll destroy this land for the sake of his own pride. He's a madman. I wish I had never seen him.*

Mags did not show his surprise. He took the bottle from Cuburn with a little sneer. "Ye might'a brought me summat t'eat. Potions go down poor on'a empty stomach."

"Just drink the damned stuff, boy," Thallan snarled. Mags started to down it and nearly choked on the bitter, burning taste, as Cuburn scuttled back out the door, and then out of sight. His Sleepgiver memories automatically cataloged some of what he tasted. Raw alcohol, but not enough to make him drunk. A lot of bitter willow. Some yellowflower. Bristlehead, lanceleaf, and corris-root. Nothing poisonous, and nothing that would render him unconscious . . . but would any of it wipe out his Mindspeech? He just didn't know; he wasn't like Bear, with the knowledge of thousands of herbs and their interactions at his fingertips.

Thallan locked the cell again, and loomed behind the bars of the door. He could not have been said to stand, since he was deliberately being as menacing as possible. Mags just put his back to the wall, glared back and waited for his sense of Dallen to fade away. The fear in him ran deep and cold as a mountain river at flood. Not so much fear for himself, as for everything else.

But the only thing that began to fade was his headache.

It didn't actually go away, not entirely, but . . . whatever Cuburn had given him was taking the edge off. His Mindspeech was just as sharp as ever, maybe more, since it wasn't troubled by headache pain.

And taking that as his cue that he should probably begin pretending to pass out, Mags began nodding . . . and jerking his head up to glare at Thallan . . . and nodding . . . he had seen enough people who'd drunk themselves into a stupor that he knew what it should look like.

Finally he let his chin sink to his chest, then slowly toppled over sideways. Thallan uttered a satisfied chuckle and Mags heard his footsteps retreating.

:Scummy bastard. Not you, Dallen.:

:You could call me anything you liked, I am so grateful to still be able to hear you.: Dallen heaved a long, mental sigh.

:We're still right where we was,: Mags objected. :Amily an' me are still stuck in 'ere, this crazy lunatic kin do wut he pleases an—:

:I'm working on that. Right now, please talk to Amily, she thinks you're dead or headblind or worse.:

He turned his attention to Amily; he quickly discovered she was not anxious, she was furious. The things she wanted to do to Thallan would have shocked him, had he not been sharing the same sentiments.

:*When ye git done fixin' t' take 'is skin off an' boil 'im alive, kin ye tell me iffen ye found a cat'r somethin'?:*

Relief nearly made her incoherent for a moment. *Not yet. I'm working on it.*

With some of his pain gone, he could think—it did gall him to feel even the least little bit of gratitude to that snake, Cuburn, but he had to admit the Healer had done him not one, but two enormous favors.

:*Dallen . . . is there any way we kin cut Thallan off from 'is men? I mean, he ain't given th' word t'attack yet. Whatever Guard Post 'e managed t'take over, has t'be on the Border, an' somehow 'e'ed haveta reach 'em with a message. We're still pretty much where we were afore, right? An' if 'e don't git back an' take over whatever Guard Post 'e managed t' gull, ain't nobody gonna step up an' do it, right?:*

:*That might work, Mags. That just might work. All we need to do is figure out where you are. And by extension, where he is. There are only a limited number of ways he could send a message . . . but my feeling is he would want to command in person.:* There was silence for a long while. Mags used it to rest and let Cuburn's potion do its work on his splitting head. And think.

As long as we're 'ere, we kin be used as hostages. So we still need t'get out. There's gotta be a way.

There's just got to.

Amily was disassembling her wedding finery, quietly, so as not to arouse any attention. She already had triggered the hidden latch on the soles of both boots that let the soles swivel at the toe and release the thin daggers hidden in each. She'd pulled the bones out of her corset that turned into a tiny bow and half-sized arrows, and gotten the sinew-bowstring from beneath the embroidery on her bodice. She'd removed the really nasty little weapon from the hem of her tunic, that was a chain with weights on each end. That one could kill a man with one blow if she struck him in the temple, and at the moment she was visualizing doing just that to their captor. Thallan hadn't really paid any attention to her so far; he had stopped just long enough at the door to her cell to sneer. She had just stared back at him, stone-faced. She would let him read into that whatever he chose.

Probably that I'm too terrified to move. Someone like that would be sure that a woman in a pretty dress was useless, helpless, and petrified.

Her head hurt, but whoever had hit her had been very good at knocking people out; it had been just a little tap, that had left a bit of a bump, and a bit of a sore place. She thought, from the taste in her mouth, that she must have been given some sort of drug, but now it was completely worn off.

She wished she knew how to pick locks. *I'd hide out of sight until he came back, then get him as soon as he stepped into the cell to look for me.* The thought of *thwacking* him in the temple with that lead weight was infinitely satisfying.

The sight of that toad, Cuburn, scuttling past had made her gorge rise. Now more than ever she regretted the fact that the King hadn't locked him up in a gaol in Haven and thrown away the key. Or locked him up in the gaol for the worst sort of prisoners and made him act as their Healer. Or . . . well she could think of a lot of fates she'd like to consign him to right now.

Then again . . . he hadn't done what he'd been told to do. He hadn't drugged Mags. She wasn't feeling charitable enough to give him the benefit of the doubt however. She didn't think any sort of altruism had inspired *that* gesture. It was more likely that he was hoping that when Mags and Amily were rescued, or got themselves out, he'd get clemency. *I guess he discovered someone he's completely terrified by. Good. I hope Thallan gives him nightmares. I hope Thallan keeps him chained to a dog kennel.*

Once she had her weapons out, and either hidden on her person or under her skirts, she closed her eyes and began searching once more for animals. A cat would be best. Maybe she could induce it down into the dungeon with a suggestion there were mice down here. She had discovered that, although she could not command animals to do anything, she could make them think there was something they wanted where she wanted them to be. She had also discovered that, within limits, there were things she could suggest they might want to do.

She found the pigeons before she found a cat.

At first, she didn't know what she had found; just a mass of sleeping birds; not sparrows, not chickens, not crows—nothing she'd ever had much to do with. Then some of them woke up a little and cooed in their sleep, and she realized with a start what they must be. Not just a lot of pigeons roosting in a roof, but *messenger* birds, in their closed-up dovecot. Well, that answered the question of how Thallan was communicating with the rest of his men so far away on the border.

Hmm. I wonder. . . . There just might be something she could do with this.

She sent her mind roaming farther, and as she had hoped, she found owls. Eagle-owls, specifically, which nested *very* early in the year, and now had a clutch of two youngsters to feed. They were looking for prey. The easier the better, as the fledglings were learning how to hunt at this stage.

I'm sorry, pigeons. . . .

The female was hunting already, lofting silently along, and Amily flew with her. Now she was very glad she had been memorizing maps for as long as she had. As the owl flew over a village, and then a town, she recognized by the configuration of the latter, and especially by an outsized and very imposing temple to the goddess Hestapha of the Hearth in the very center of town. This place had been mentioned quite a lot in the Heraldic Chronicles of this part of Valdemar. Women came to this temple from all around, when their men were going off to war; Hestapha was reputed to bring them home to their own hearths again in time of battle. One of the Chroniclers had noted wryly that there was no guarantee on the part of the priests what sort of shape the men would be in when they returned, but enough grateful spouses, sisters, and daughters had made thank-gifts over the centuries that this temple was quite splendid indeed.

The village was Swallownest. The town was Hestaford.

And there was a mostly unused Guard garrison-post just above the town, about two leagues away. Not *abandoned;* this post was a relic of the old days, when even the capitol of Haven could be menaced by bandit-lords, warlords, and other hostile sorts. The post was kept in good repair, just in case it might be needed for some other purpose—to house people rescued in the event of a disaster, or the Guards sent to rescue them, or both. It took very little to maintain a set of buildings in good repair, especially if they were made of stone, with slate roofs, as these were. From time to time, especially in war-times, the garrison was put to use as a recruiting and training station for the Guard.

And that answered the question of where she and Mags must be. Thallan must have taken over the fortress. There would have been no one there to question or oppose him, and it was within striking distance of Haven.

She suggested to the owl that there was tasty prey at that normally empty garrison. Having found starlings and wild pi-geons there in the past, the owl hooted a summons to her family, and bent her wings in that direction.

It was very, very odd to experience this flight through an owl's senses. Everything was black and white, of course, the owl could see an *enormous* amount, and her eyes were as keen as any falcon's. But better still was her hearing. She ac-tually heard the pigeons cooing in their sleep before Amily spotted, through her eyes, the dovecote that had been put up in the observation tower. *They must have put it there so the pigeons would get a good start flying, and to protect them from weasels.* If Amily hadn't alerted the owl to its presence, though, likely enough the owl would never have known it was there, either, until Thallan and his men were gone.

That cooing certainly got the owl's attention.

She had never seen a dovecote before, however, and as her mate and two owlets landed on the rail behind her, she prowled the little structure, staring intently at it, the pigeons inside utterly oblivious to what was about to happen.

Because as the pigeons shifted on their perches, made soft little noises, and slept on, Amily pointed out the place where the thatch covering the top of the dovecote was thin, and put an image in the owl's mind of how using her powerful talons to tear it apart at that point would bring a rich reward.

A few moments later, there was carnage.

A couple of the pigeons escaped the adult owls slaughtering the rest in the dovecote by flying out in a panic, but it was *dark,* and they landed almost immediately, becoming easy prey even for the unpracticed youngsters. The owls ate their fill of the best parts, then each seized a bird and lofted away, carrying it back to be cached near the nest for another meal later. They left behind nothing but blood, headless birds, and feathers.

Not one pigeon escaped.

And, of course, besides cutting off Thallan's means of fast communication, now Amily knew exactly where they were jailed.

:And now so do I,: said Rolan, triumphantly.

:We know where you are,: Dallen said, interrupting Mags' search to identify every man within the walls of this place. He left off what he was doing and lay down for a little on the mattress; the straw inside crackled and gave off a clean scent of dried grass. His head might not have been hurting as much, but it had been a very long time since he last ate, and he was feeling a bit nauseous and a little weak. He had to get through that. He couldn't afford weakness.

:Well, th' bad news is, they're locked up tight's ticks in 'ere, they're all right cozy, they're bein' careful, an' this place was made fer a siege. Thallan pretty much has 'em set up as

if they was *in a siege. Ain't crackin' this place soon.:* Mags had drifted through minds waking and sleeping, and learned that although the garrison was small, it was of handpicked, battle-hardened men who knew exactly how best to defend what was essentially a fortress. Unless someone needed to enter or leave with a cart, the main entrance was kept shut, barred, and the portcullis down. There was a hidden postern-door around the back of the fortifications that the men used in case only one or two needed to get in and out. They had not revealed themselves to the people of the town; they'd brought in their own provisions, and they had brought a *lot.* This had not been an impulsive move on Thallan's part. He had planned to be here, right now, probably because he had correctly deduced that getting Menmellith to declare war on Valdemar was the weakest part of his plan. These were probably not all of the men he had brought North with him, either. He probably had the great portion of them scattered around Haven, each with a particular set of Companions to target. They would fit right in. No one ever looked twice at a member of the Guard in and around the Palace, nor in and around Haven.

Mags had located Cuburn, but the Healer had his shields up again, and there was no getting inside without alerting him to the fact that someone was trying to read his thoughts. He thought about forcing his way in . . . but it was unlikely he'd learn anything of use. The Healer was cowed and rattled, a very different man than the one that had bullied Bear and informed on Bear to Bear's father. He'd spill whatever information he *had,* if Mags got hold of him and pressed him, but it was highly unlikely that Thallan had told him very much.

He'd also located Thallan, who was asleep. He'd taken the best room in the garrison, but it was fairly sparsely furnished. Whatever was motivating this man, it wasn't greed, nor a desire for the luxury that came with rank. *Could* it be that he was driven by patriotism, as he claimed?

:If so,: Dallen said dryly, *:It's not the sort of patriotism that you and I would recognize as such, at least not for this land. He thinks he is the only arbiter of what is right for Valdemar. He thinks the King is weak because he is merciful; he thinks the Heralds are unnecessary at best, and an impediment to getting things done at the worst. He's perfectly prepared to bring fire and the sword to innocent people in order to bring about the sort of changes he wants to see here.:*

Mags regarded the man's dreams, which were, oddly, *not* full of the sort of martial imagery he had expected. No first-person view of battle, although there was battle raging in this dream. It was all at one remove, as if Thallan viewed it from above. As if it were all a military sand-table, where counters were moved to represent, not individual troops, but groups of them on the battlefield. As if troops were not people at all, but things, toys he could use and discard.

:I don' think he's ever been in a real fight,: Mags said, slowly.

:I don't think so either. I think he's sent men to fight, but never fought himself.:

If anything, that made Mags even sicker. This was one of those despicable men who didn't even regard his own men as human and important. They were just counters in a grand game, to be used up and dispensed with as it pleased him. *:You think he plans t'make hisself King?:*

Dallen's reply surprised him. *:No. I think if his wildest wish came to pass and Kyril was murdered or deposed, he'd pick some amiable, empty-headed highborn in the line of succession and set him up as a puppet. But I think what he intends to do, practically speaking, is that same thing in Menmellith. He's going to win the pretender's throne for him, then call in the debt and become the power behind the throne. He might well advise the new King to make Menmellith a client-state of Valdemar, but I doubt he'd ever let Heralds across the border. I think that is what this is all about; putting himself in real* *charge of an entire country, behind a figurehead that can be used to deflect all blame.:*

That made an ugly sort of sense.

Dallen had more information, this part of it somewhat better. *:Amily has just eliminated the likeliest means of his sending a message. She's arranged for some owls to remove all of his messenger pigeons. That leaves only sending a human as a messenger, or gathering up his men and just making a charge for the Border or for Haven. He'd be an idiot to march on Haven; he has to know that by now Haven's been warned.:*

All right then. Mags had plans of his own. *:I don' want Heralds within bow-shot of 'ere. I'm pretty certain-sure this bastard's tol' 'is men t'shoot th' Companions first. I don' think that was an idle threat, I think 'e don' give a crap about Heralds or Companions. It ain't worth the risk.:*

Dallen went silent. Mags sensed he was arguing—with Rolan, perhaps or maybe many Companions at once.

:I ain't backin' down on this,: Mags warned. *:I ain't gonna be the one respons'ble fer a buncha dead Companions an' a buncha Heralds broken. It ain't gonna happen. I got better idears. Hear me?:*

Dallen did not reply.

Mags waited, *feeling* something in the air, something like a storm, only this was a very personal storm. There was the sense of tension, building, building, building . . .

Then the tension broke. Dallen responded in almost the same moment. *:All right, we will follow your lead.:*

Mags did not smile; the situation was too grave for that. But there it was; the acknowledgement from Dallen . . . and likely, Rolan . . . that he knew what he was doing. *Really* knew what he was doing. This was the moment when he had been accepted as Dallen's full partner, Dallen's equal.

I jest hope I act'lly do know what I'm doin' . . .

:Right then. 'Ere's the basic plan . . . :

Amily clung to the bars of the door of her cell, her knuckles going white with tension, and her ears straining for the faintest of footfalls. Not Mags . . . she was fairly sure she was not going to hear Mags coming. But just in case something happened, and one of the guards decided to take an unexpected stroll. She hated this place. The cell was cold, the air was slightly damp, and everything smelled of stone. And there were almost no sounds. A hint of a cough far in the distance, a single drip of water somewhere, nowhere nearby, but nothing else, not even the squeak of a mouse. It made her feel a little frantic, this silence. It was horrid.

She peered down one way, and then the other, her cheeks pressed tightly against the cold iron bars. The corridor outside the cell went on for about five lengths in either direction before ending in a T-junction. The walls, the floor, and the ceiling were all made of the same smooth, brown stone. Light from the lantern on the wall opposite her door reached all the way to the T-junctions, and there was light from another source gleaming off the walls down there. She wasn't sure how far away Mags was, or which direction he would be coming from. She still hadn't been able to coax the garrison's only cat down here to find out what the place looked like. The cat already knew there was nothing she wanted, no prey to be found in the area of the cells, and she was disinclined to leave the kitchen.

It was almost dawn. That, she knew from the cat, the horses drowsing in their stalls, and the birds on the roof. Some crows had already discovered the poor pigeons, and were having a feast in the guard-tower, but as yet no one had noticed the slaughter, for no one had gone up to feed and water them. They couldn't be released, of course; if they were, they'd just return to their home-cote, so probably tending them was the last of the morning chores.

The current guards were tired and sleepy, and the new ones, she knew from Mags, were not due to take their watch until after breakfast. They had at least a full candlemark before the next watch woke, got their meal, and came down to relieve the night-watch.

Their hope was to get out via the postern door before the morning watch woke. That was the hope . . . because there was a heavy force of Guard troops on the way under the command of Sedric; they had been riding, not marching, most of the night, carried double behind Heralds on Companions, who would leave them just out of weapon-range of the garrison-fort. Rolan had told her all of this while Mags had been setting his own plans, disassembling *his* outfit, and getting out of his fetters. Once there, now that Thallan had no way of sending messages, they'd lay siege to it. The patient sort of siege, where the goal was to starve the opponents out. All the Valdemarans had to do was stay out of weapons' range, and this would be as bloodless a conflict as possible.

Meanwhile, back in Haven, at least according to Rolan, the King was explaining to the Menmellith delegation just what exactly was going on, and what he was doing about it. Of course, the Menmellith delegation might not accept that they had their miscreant and the King intended to bring him to justice. That was the chance they were going to have to take.

Amily happened to be looking in the right direction as Mags ran silently into her hallway. Her heart leapt to see him; he looked dreadful, his eyes had a sort of bruised look to them, his hair was a fright, and his face was greenish. He dropped and slid to her door on his knees, lock-picks in his hands, and as she waited, wishing there was something she could be doing to help him, he deftly picked the lock and the door swung open. It was like magic, and she longed with all her heart to hug him and hold him—but instead, after he picked the lock on her ankle manacle as well, she ran to the end of the corridor and made sure there was no one coming while he put his tools away and got out his knife.

Another few moments, and they were easing their way along the wall together, backs to the wall, hands lightly gliding along it on either side; she could not help here, either, as he was using his Mindspeech to determine where the next guard was. She tried not to shiver. It seemed unnaturally cold. She just watched the hand he held behind his back, and when he shook it once and clenched it, she stopped, her little chain-weapon in her hand. They had decided that would be the better of her weapons to use, if she had to attack anyone. She also had a sling, but no bullets or stones for it. Those they hoped to get once they got out of the gaol. The sling, which would keep her out of reach of someone who would certainly be bigger, taller, and heavier than she was, was the weapon she should use even in preference to her tiny, but powerful, bow. The Guards would certainly be armored, but probably not helmeted. A stone would knock them out. An eye-shot with an arrow would probably be fatal.

Mags inched forward along the wall until he came to another T-junction. She remained where she was, weapon ready to use. He paused. She felt all her muscles clench up, and her heart start to pound as she held her breath.

Then he whipped around the corner, and she quickly advanced to where he had been, staying out of sight. He would only call out if he needed her. There was a brief scuffling of feet, and a grunt, and then. . . .

A faint whistle.

She whisked around the corner to find him bending over an unconscious man in a blue Guard uniform, using his own equipment and clothing to tie him up and gag him. Working together, he at the head, and she at the feet, they took him back to the nearest cell, laid him down out of sight, and shut and locked the door. The Guard had had a sword and a knife;

she took the knife, Mags took the sword. He was horribly heavy, but she wasn't going to complain.

They repeated this three times in complete silence; she took the second one's sword this time, while he took the knife. The third, they merely took the weapons away and left them in another cell. She was beginning to feel hopeful. There was only one more guard to go. . . .

And then an alarm bell sounded frantically through the empty halls, echoing and reverberating everywhere.

Mags swore. "All right. That's done it. Dunno what they found, but now we run for it."

She nodded, and followed on his heels as he dashed down the last corridor and around the corner and right into the startled guard. Mags hit the man in a running tackle and brought him down. The Guard wasn't ready for it, and hadn't prepared to fall. His head it the stone floor with a sickening *crack*.

"Bloody hell," Mags cursed, got up, and left the man lying. From the blood starting to pool sluggishly under his head, his skull had been pulped. He wouldn't be getting up again.

From the strange way he was breathing, Amily realized with a sinking heart that he might not survive.

She felt her gorge rise at the thought, but swallowed it down. *I don't want to murder one of our own!* her thoughts wailed in the back of her mind. But it was too late to do anything about it now. Mags headed down the corridor, leaving him lying, and she followed.

Her stomach was in knots and her hands were shaking. It was one thing to have killed those Sleepgivers . . . the Sleepgivers had been trying to kill *them,* after all, and anyway, they weren't even Valdemaran. But these were members of the Guard. Their own people. She'd been cuddled and scolded, picked up and carried about, guided and protected by the Guard all her life. That familiar blue uniform had always meant safety. Someone you could always count on, or run to.

And now . . . now they might have murdered one of them. Someone who could have been a friend.

Please don't let him die, she prayed helplessly to whoever would listen. *Please don't let him die.* Thallan was one thing, but these poor men . . . all they had done wrong was to allow themselves to be persuaded by a madman.

Mags was running as fast as he could, and all she could do was follow him. Only he knew the way out—

And then he suddenly stopped dead and caught her with an outstretched arm, just outside a wooden door. "Armory," he said, wrenching the door open.

There was a stone room beyond the door, about the size of one of the cells with a single lit lantern at the right side of the door. There were weapon-racks on the walls, some of them empty, some of them full. There was a small table and four little stools around it, with a game-board of some game Amily didn't recognize carved into the top of it.

But there was nothing much there they could use. Lots of pikes, swords and daggers similar to the ones they already had. No bows, which would have been the most useful. Amily did find a double handful of stone counters, half dark and half light, for the game that had been carved into the table-top. She pocketed them; they'd be useful for her sling at least.

Back to the hall they went, but this time Mags held out his arm and she waited with him, holding her breath, while they both listened intently, and he presumably used his Gift. "They found th' dead birds, but they got no notion 'twas owls," he said, with a snort. "They think some'un got in an' killed 'em t'keep from sendin' messages. They got that half right anyways. We *might* git away wi' this . . ."

Amily had switched from the chain to her sling, and she, rather than Mags, was the first to see a Guardsman coming around the corner ahead of them. Before Mags could react, her stone was in the air; it hit the side of the man's head and he dropped. They both ran up to him, and found to their shared relief that he, at least, had merely been knocked unconscious. Mags trussed him up and left him while she retrieved her precious stone; they had no time to spare now to tuck him out of the way.

Just beyond him was a staircase; Mags headed for it as Amily followed on his heels. There were two flights of stairs, with light at the top—a different sort of light from the yellow gleam the lanterns had put out. This was cold and gray and dim. Morning?

The stairs were no place to be caught; they rushed up the treads as fast as they could, then stopped on the landing at the top. Amily's heart beat so hard it was making her shake a little, and for a moment she felt faint. She felt a cough coming, too, and swallowed it down.

The landing led to another corridor. Stone again, everything was stone . . . *of course it's stone. They have to be terribly careful of fire here. Or had to, back when this place held off besiegers and sheltered all the farmfolk nearby. One pot of flaming oil exploding in the courtyard of a wooden fort, and the entire place would turn into a death-trap.* This corridor, however, had slit windows all along one side, slits that presumably archers could fire through, if an enemy got as far as the courtyard. The cold, gray light of morning shone in through them. Slit windows without glass, of course. You wouldn't want glass in something you were supposed to shoot through.

Mags dropped to his hands and knees, below the height of the windows, and she copied him. Those windows overlooked the central court, as she had thought. More than one alarm bell was ringing now, and without a doubt the courtyard was full of men searching for a presumed intruder. The only reason they hadn't looked *here* yet was probably because no one had thought to check the gaol.

They crawled as fast as they could to the end of the corridor, then got up and pressed themselves into the shelter of the shadows. Mags closed his eyes, the better to use his Gift. Amily waited tensely, stone in her sling, trying to see without being seen. Outside past the windows, there was the sound of running feet, but no shouting. That was not a good sign, actually. It meant these men were highly disciplined, and were running a search they must have practiced enough that they needed no directions.

Mags opened his eyes and gestured; it was now too dangerous to speak. Even a whisper might be heard. She followed him with her heart in her throat and every muscle knotted with tension. There *still* was not much of a scent in the air; nothing to tell her that anything but ghosts populated this place.

And now she alternated her prayers between, *please let that man live,* and *please, let us get out of here.* If they could get out, then the small army of the Guard that was coming could settle down to a nice, bloodless siege. Eventually the Guard in *here* would come to their senses, and turn over Thallan, surely. But even if they didn't, they could be starved into submission. No one would have to die.

She added a third prayer. Because Guard fighting against Guard was the worst nightmare she could think of, short of the impossible one of Herald fighting Herald. *Please. Please, make it so that no one has to die . . .*

———————

Mags knelt in front of the postern door, every bit of his concentration bent on the delicate manipulation of his lockpicks. This was not a sort of lock he had ever encountered before. The locks on their manacles had been simple; the locks on the doors of their cells had been very old, and had taken no time at all. This one was new . . . and complicated. As his teacher had told him; he had to have eyes and ears in his fingertips. He was concentrating so very hard on what he was doing that he didn't realize they were in trouble until he heard Amily gasp.

And then he heard the very last thing he wanted to hear.

"Stand up slowly, boy," said Thallan, with cold cruelty in his voice. "Or I am afraid your girl will have her pretty white dress badly stained with blood."

Mags stood up and turned, as he had been directed. Thallan had Amily's neck in the crook of his arm with her back to him, and a knife pressed up against her side. His heart started to pound with fear—but then he noticed something odd. *Amily* didn't look at all frightened.

Amily looked furious.

"Now, I want you to be a good little boy, and put those weapons of yours on the floor," Thallan continued. "Then we'll march back to the prison and put you where you belong." His face was contorted with a sneer. But Mags was not paying any attention to *him*. He was listening to Amily's thoughts.

I am going to count to three, Mags. Nod if you hear me.

He nodded, and hunched his shoulders a little, as if Thallan had cowed him. Thallan's sneer turned into a nasty grin.

When I get to three, charge.

He hunched his shoulders a little more, and fumbled for his sword, clumsily, as if he was so frightened he couldn't properly control his hands.

One. Two.

"Hurry it *up*, boy!" Thallan snapped, pushing the knife-point harder against Amily's side.

Three!

He launched himself at the two of them, at the same time that Amily grabbed the wrist of the arm holding her neck, somehow turned in Thallan's grasp and ducked *under* Thallan's armpit, taking the wrist and arm with her. Her leg made a wide sweep at Thallan's as she got behind him. A moment later, Thallan was crashing to the floor, with Mags landing atop him. Mags got the knife away from the man as Thallan screamed in pain—not from the fall, but from Amily twisting the arm she still had firmly by the wrist, with her foot on his buttocks.

"My corset is lined with very fine chainmail," she said, panting and twisting. "He really chose the wrong person to threaten today."

Thallan's screams had reached an impressively high note. "We need to get him trussed up before someone comes looking to see who's screaming," Mags said, divesting Thallan of the rest of his weapons. Amily relented a little and eased up on her twisting, so Thallan could get to his feet, actually sobbing with the pain she'd put him through. Mags secured his hands behind his back quickly, using some of the sinew he'd pulled out of the embroidery on his tunic. He tied them rather more tightly than was strictly necessary . . . and used another piece of sinew to tie his thumbs together as well, a trick Nikolas had taught him. *Good luck gettin' outa that, 'less some'un cuts 'im loose.*

By this point, Thallan had stopped sobbing, gotten a few breaths into him, and looked as if he was about to start shouting. Perhaps he was going to shout for help, but from the look of his furiously flushed face, Mags had an inkling that *help* was the last thing on his mind.

"Shut up," Amily snapped, as he took in a long, deep breath, and opened his mouth. And before he could do anything, she stuffed a piece cut from her undershift into his mouth then handed Mags another strip so that he could bind the wad of fabric in place. This didn't stop Thallan from *trying* to shout, but his muffled grunts and moans didn't carry very far.

"Now what?" Amily asked. "Do we get the door open and

drag him with us?" She eyed the furious "General." "That could turn out to be quite a task. He's going to be everything *but* cooperative."

Mags grabbed Thallan's tightly bound hands and shook them until the man's shouts turned to whines of pain. "No," he said. "No. Now we *end* this."

They marched into the courtyard, with Thallan slightly ahead of them. Each of them had one of his elbows. Both of them had their swords out, lodged against his ribs, and Thallan was most decidedly not wearing a chainmail-lined corset. In fact, he wasn't wearing any armor at all, which rather cemented in Mags' mind the notion that he had never actually been in combat, since the first thing that a combat-seasoned veteran does when hearing an alarm bell is to throw on his armor, or at least the upper part of it.

The alarm bells stopped as they stepped out into the courtyard, and an ominous silence fell. They walked a few more steps into the middle of the courtyard, and stopped. There were Guards all around, in their familiar blue uniforms, in the courtyard, on the walls, two at the main gate. Some stood there, looking stunned. Some looked puzzled, others angry. The angry ones had their weapons in their hands after a moment, and there was more than one archer with an arrow nocked to his bow, pointing at them.

Bloody hell. Hope this works.

And then Amily stepped forward, leaving Mags to control Thallan. "For the sake of the gods, look at yourselves!" she snapped. "Look at us! We are *Heralds of Valdemar.* You are the *Guardsmen* of Valdemar! And here you are, pointing weapons at *us,* perfectly prepared to kill us, and why? All because of this sick and depraved man's *lies.*"

Silence as she let that sink in.

"We are Heralds of Valdemar. You know you have always depended on us to speak the truth. Here is the truth. You have been manipulated from the beginning. This so-called 'General' Thallan is no 'General' at all. He's nothing but a scheming highborn with a lot of theoretical knowledge who has been impersonating a high officer of the Guard in order to gain control of you. There *is* no 'General Thallan' in the Guard, and there never has been. He's a complete fraud. And now look at you! He's managed to twist you around until some of you, at least, were preparing to murder *Companions* in cold blood!"

Most of the Guards that Mags could see were giving each other startled looks . . . but a couple were trying to back out of sight, as quietly as possible.

"There!" he said, pointing to the ones in question. "And there, and there! They know! Stop 'em an' question 'em!"

The men nearest the three trying to flee seized them by the elbows. They wilted.

It's working. . . .

"And do you know what this fraud, this liar, this scheming spider has brought you to?" Amily demanded, as some of the Guardsmen leapt for the ones trying to escape. "Guards ready to fight and kill Heralds! Guards ready to fight and kill *Guards!* Your own brothers! Is *that* what you want? Do you want to kill men you fought beside, trained with? Because in a candlemark or two, no more, that is *exactly* what you will be facing! Prince Sedric is on the way with a force of *loyal* Guards ready to put you to a siege and starve you out! And the only way you will get past them is to try and kill them. Men you know. Your brothers."

The weapons began to droop with the hands that held them; the archers that Mags could see were letting the bowstrings go slack and lowering their bows.

"It's time for sanity again," Amily said, now speaking in a

calmer tone of voice. "It's time to let go of this madness. I don't know what this man told you to convince you that he knew the one true way for Valdemar, but what your mother taught you at her knee should have warned you that anything he said was as false as a demon's promise. You know this above all. *There is no one true way.* This is how we live in peace with each other. This is how we live in peace with those outside our borders who do not seek to impose their ways on us. And this is the only way we can continue to live in peace. I should not have to tell you this. You already knew it. You somehow forgot it. Now is the time to remember, and live it again."

Silence fell then, broken only by the sound of men slipping swords back into sheathes, and arrows back into quivers. Mags glanced at Thallan. He had gone from red to white, nearly as white as the strip of cloth binding his mouth.

"Now, open the gate and the portcullis," Amily said, calmly. "And we will all walk out together to surrender this piece of manipulative trash to the King's Justice, where his own words out of his own mouth will condemn him." She now took the time to look slowly around her, at the men in the courtyard, on the walls, meeting each set of eyes in turn. "You can come with me, and plead your cases. Or you can run, and never wear the Blue again, and try and find a new home somewhere far from Valdemar, but you will always know that you deserted your true kin for the sake of a proud man's lies." She paused again, then repeated, "Open the gate, please."

This time, the gate swung open, and the portcullis was raised, the winch and chain creaking in the continued silence.

Dallen and Rolan were waiting outside the gate, glowing and splendid in the rising sun. Mags and Amily prodded their captive toward the Companions, and slowly, by ones and twos, the Guards joined them, empty-handed, filing out of the gate in complete silence, and leaving the fortress behind them empty of everything but shadows.

EPILOGUE

The sun shone down on the flower canopy overhead, and the air was so thick with the scent of blooms that it could intoxicate. Mags held Amily's hands in his, and smiled at her, as the flower scent wreathed around them.

"People of Valdemar," proclaimed the High Priest of—some temple Mags had never heard of. But that didn't matter, because the High Priest was Father Gellet, who Mags had met many times at Master Soren's house, and liked immensely. Like Mags, Father Gellet had come up in the world considerably since that first meeting so many years ago, and was resplendent in gold robes with an embroidered band around the neck.

"People of Valdemar," High Priest Gellet proclaimed again, holding his hands over their heads. *"Now rejoice with me, for Mags of the Heralds of Valdemar, and Amily, King's Own Herald, are now man and wife."*

There was a tremendous cheer from a crowd that would

have overwhelmed Mags, not that long ago, and made him blush until his skin burned. There were . . . a lot of people here. The garden where Lydia had celebrated after wedding Prince Sedric was so crowded that the gardeners had been forced to erect hasty barriers of ribbons and garlands around some of the flower-beds.

Mags took that cheer as the signal to kiss Amily, which only made the crowd cheer harder.

There were plenty of friends in that crowd—but plenty of strangers, too. As the King had hoped, delegations had been sent from Menmellith, Rethwellan, Hardorn, and even representatives of some of the larger cities of Valdemar itself. The King had been busy from dawn to dusk with meetings— meetings that had included Nikolas rather than Amily, since Lady Dia had been keeping both Mags and Amily quite busy, and the King had decreed that *both* of them deserved a bit of a respite from "work" for a while.

The first of those meetings had occurred with the representatives of Menmellith, including Aurebic, where the King had turned over Thallan, now bound securely in chains. With him had come a transcript of the many very interesting things he'd had to say when under Truth Spell.

The Menmellithians—all but Aurebic—had been shocked at this development. Shocked speechless, in fact, which gave the King an opportunity to give them a piece of his mind. "You *could* have found all this out for yourselves, if you'd put some effort to it, instead of jumping to conclusions," he said sternly. "Take him away. Do what you will with him. Although his crimes against Valdemar are many, the only punishment for them is exile. His crimes against Menmellith are far graver, and we deliver him to you for your justice."

So half the delegation had carried Thallan off. The other half had stayed with Aurebic.

As Mags and Amily finished their leisurely kiss and turned

to face the crowd, Mags smiled particularly at the friends he saw there. Lady Dia and Lord Jorthun, of course, and Keira. And . . . Tiercel Rolmer, who kept glancing hopefully at Keira.

There were two "special sections" set aside for those who were particular friends of the bride and groom. Coot, scrubbed until he looked polished, sat beside Bear and Lena, resplendent in Healer Green and Bardic Scarlet in one section, along with Nikolas, Jakyr, Lita, and those other friends among the Heralds, Guards, and other folk that Mags had made since he had been Chosen. The Royal Family of the King and Queen, Prince Sedric and Princess Lydia occupied the other. They were shaded by more bowers of fragrant flowers, just like the platform on which Mags, Amily, and Gellet stood.

Tuck and Linden, Aunty Minda, and all of Mags' little band of sharp-eared informants were even now having a festival of their own, courtesy of the Crown, in the yard of the laundry. Mags would have liked to have them all up here, but as Amily had gently pointed out, they would have mostly been uncomfortable in such surroundings, Tuck would have been terrified, and all things considered, they were probably having a much better time than ever they could up on the Hill.

As for Mags, he waved to the crowd, and Amily took her cue from him and did the same. Then they descended in their (mended) wedding finery to join their friends. Meanwhile, everyone *else* who was here because it was an Occasion, and needed to be Seen and See People, did what they had intended to do from the beginning: go find other Important People, gossip, and play politics. But right now, now that they were done being the showpieces for the King's pageant, they could be just Mags and Amily surrounded by the people they loved, and who loved them.

Which was just fine with Mags.

Tomorrow would come soon enough.